BETRAYED

Meredith's shock was eclipsed by a blinding fury. She tucked her handbag under her arm and stormed toward the Do-Drop-Inn.

Perched comfortably on a barstool, Seth sent the first bourbon down the hatch with an effortless flick of the wrist. He offered a smile to his neighbors and was about to buy them drinks when his eyes lifted to the bar's gold-filigreed mirror. Seth stared uncertainly at the hazy figure of his wife like a man who had never totally trusted his hold on reality.

"Sugar, what a surprise."

"You son of a bitch—"

"Now hold on a minute, honey."

"Where's my horse?"

"What horse is that?" was all he could come up with, and a timid smile.

Seth knew instantly the lie had been a tactical error. The indignation and injury that passed over Meredith's face alarmed him. He watched, dismayed, as she thrust her hand in her purse.

A silver derringer appeared, the one Meredith always carried when alone at night. . . .

Texas Bred

MICHAEL FRENCH

BANTAM BOOKS
TORONTO · NEW YORK · LONDON · SYDNEY · AUCKLAND

For Preston and Nancy

TEXAS BRED

A Bantam Book / January 1987

ISBN 0-553-26164-9

Published simultaneously in the United States and Canada

Bantam Books are published by Bantam Books, Inc. Its trademark, consisting of the words "Bantam Books" and the portrayal of a rooster, is Registered in U.S. Patent and Trademark Office and in other countries. Marca Registrada. Bantam Books, Inc., 666 Fifth Avenue, New York, New York 10103.

PRINTED IN THE UNITED STATES OF AMERICA

KR   0 9 8 7 6 5 4 3 2 1

"You can cuss my wife and kick my dog, but don't badmouth my horse."
—ANONYMOUS

"It's a short walk from the hallelujah to the hoot. . . ."
—VLADIMIR NABOKOV

"It were not best that we should all think alike; it is difference of opinion that makes horse races."
—MARK TWAIN

PROLOGUE

THE TWO MEN PICKED UP A COUPLE OF SIX-PACKS AT THE 7-Eleven before it closed and then drove down an unlit county road that was straight as a rail. They drove slowly, glancing at their watches and the full, luminous moon, and impatiently spinning the radio dial. Neither liked country music. Behind their pickup an empty horse trailer jigged and groaned as if it might come unhitched, but nobody looked back, trusting that because the trailer had never come loose before, it wouldn't now. The flat, shimmering stretches of Oklahoma ranch country were foreign to them. Under the truck's flickering dome light the man in the passenger seat, who was thin, with tousled hair, and rheumy eyes, squinted at a crude, hand-drawn map. "Jesus," he mumbled in frustration, and tossed it to the burly driver.

Four miles down the road the pickup braked in front of a pasture fence with a lopsided gate. The map was checked again. After downing several beers for courage or perspective, the two men took the pasture road until they reached the designated barn. There would be no night watchman, the anonymous caller had promised. A week ago he had mailed them the map and the cash—more money this time than last. The horse tonight was a large sorrel yearling in the second stall on the right.

The driver killed his headlights and waited a moment in the cab, just to be sure about the watchman. "You're drinking too much," he muttered to his companion.

"I don't like doing this."

"It's easy money."

"I don't like the guy who gives us the money. I don't trust him. One of these days he'll turn us in."

"You don't know that. You don't know him."

"He's a jockey. That's the word I hear. From Texas. Sell his grandmother if he had one."

"You don't know him." The driver ended the conversation by stepping out of the pickup and fumbling for a halter inside the horse trailer. The other man switched on a flashlight.

Once in the barn, they approached the second stall on the right, but it was empty. In the third stall the flashlight traveled up the legs and torso of a sorrel colt and focused on a blaze face. Spooked, the colt lurched to the back of his pen.

"Shit," the skinny man whispered, more nervous than the horse.

"He was supposed to be in the second stall," the driver added, clearly worried. They glanced across the corridor to another bank of stalls. A filly, also a shiny sorrel, stood in the second. "Maybe the guy meant the left side of the barn," the driver said. He had no idea which was correct and was angry about the confusion.

"He said *colt*," the other man murmured slowly.

"You sure?"

The barn stirred with restless horses. "Jesus, I knew you'd ask me that."

The driver, still annoyed, finally slipped the halter around the colt. Carefully maneuvering him out of the stall, the two men wrapped burlap around his hooves so there'd be no tracks, then led him without any difficulty into their trailer.

Back on the road they finished the beer, relieved that this part of their job was over. They glanced back at the trailer. It wasn't going anywhere. New Orleans was still a long haul, but they had done it before, and even if that Texas jockey really was an asshole who might turn them in, both admitted that for the money they would gladly take the risk again.

After a while a pair of headlights appeared in the rear-view mirror and followed the pickup like a luminous shadow. The driver watched uneasily, wondering where the car had come from. The vehicles were drifting along, one behind the other for a long mile when suddenly blue and red flashing lights exploded in the pickup's mirror. "Goddammit," the driver said. His mouth turned dry as he felt for the revolver under the seat. He would use it if he had to. Only he knew it wasn't true. He didn't have the guts to shoot a cop. They were up shit creek without a paddle.

He started to pull over when the police car abruptly swerved around them, jumped ahead, and was swallowed by the night.

I
Semi-Famous

ONE

A CONVOY OF MERCEDES SEDANS AND FORD PICKUPS streamed up the long snakelike drive to a massive-walled adobe hacienda overlooking an endless green valley. The three-thousand acre horse-breeding operation known as the 5555 Ranch, a good hour's drive north from Dallas, was usually honeycombed with broodmares and their owners, hoping for the right stud to produce spectacular progeny. Tonight under a radiant fall moon, the ranch boasted a more elegant look. Caterers scurried around in Indian buckskins and feathered headdresses to offer guests buffalo steak skewered on arrows. Barbecue pits gave off the sweet aroma of ribs, venison, and lamb. On a platform garlanded with hundreds of freshly cut roses, Willie Nelson lifted his wobbly, heartfelt voice in a paean to the deep Texas sky. There were horses for guests to ride; an Olympic-size swimming pool to cool off in; a slickly polished outdoor dance floor to get cozy on. Enough booze was on hand, with a nod to Jack Daniels and Wild Turkey, to float a navy. And hanging from nearby towering oaks, pinatas filled with horse-shaped chocolates waited to be struck down by the first drunk cowboy.

There were parties and there were *parties*, Calvin Garrison thought as he waded through the photographers from *Ultra*, the *Dallas Morning News*, and the *Sherman Democrat*, and entered the more-expensive-than-God bash which was already jammed cheek by jowl. Adobe homes

7

were rare in this part of Texas, and Meredith Kingsley had given hers an elegance that Calvin never tired of admiring. The stark white walls had the sheen of hand-troweled plaster. *Vigas* of rough-hewn pine and *latillas* of spruce and aspen decked every ceiling. Early Navajo weavings in brilliant vegetable dyes, and carved mesquite Mexican furniture decorated the rooms.

Calvin, Dallas County state senator, glided through the rooms with a sweet young thing on his arm. Lifting a bourbon and branch water from a caterer's tray, he began to work the party. Thrice voted Texas's most eligible bachelor by sundry debutante societies, and a lawyer by training, Calvin had mastered the skill of pumping flesh years ago but found it difficult to always come up with snappy repartee. Tonight, however, he had no difficulty turning on the charm.

For the cowboy jet set with its mix of blue jeans and Cartier jewels, bolo ties and Hermes pocketbooks, this was no idle gathering. The Kingsley party was the kickoff for one of the richest horse races in the world, the All-American Quarter Horse Futurity, held every Labor Day at Ruidoso Downs in neighboring New Mexico. Its $2.5 million purse was greater than the Kentucky Derby, the Preakness Stakes, and Belmont Stakes combined, and the horses running in it weren't even thoroughbreds. They were quarter horses—the offspring of the cutting, or cow pony horse, and the thoroughbred—built for speed more than distance. They ran on a straightaway track, usually for only a quarter mile, hence their name. For that humble feat, as Calvin and everyone at the party knew well, the winner ran away with a cool million.

Among tonight's one thousand guests Calvin knew at least half by first name, and he had the social grace and angular good looks to be recognized by most of the others. Though in his mid-forties, his thick black hair had not begun to recede. His jaw was strong and aggressive, he owned the voice of a choir tenor, and his hooded eyes radiated intelligence and concern. He was, in fact, a deeper, more patient thinker than most politicians. Where his colleagues in Austin saw black or white, Calvin looked for the gray, and if he didn't consciously look, he seemed to stumble on it anyway.

What made Calvin an especially welcome guest tonight was his senatorial outspokeness in favor of horse racing. Because of a sense of honor he'd been taught by his father, and Calvin's own impatience for bullshit, he didn't duck unpopular issues—and Texas, despite the will of its masses who considered themselves the greatest gamblers in the world, was officially against legalized gambling. Thanks to a strong and vocal contingent of Bible-thumping Baptists, and the self-interest of race-track owners in Louisiana, Oklahoma, and New Mexico, pari-mutuel wagering had been strenuously lobbied against for decades in the Lone Star state. Calvin thought the opposition was narrow-minded in refusing to consider the obvious economic benefits of racing. In gratitude for his efforts on their behalf, the horsey set, which grew tired of running *their* horses in *somebody else's* state, contributed mightily to his campaign coffers. With this year's senate race less than three months away and tissue-thin close, Calvin was going to need every penny.

Pistol shots suddenly peppered the air. A woman dressed as Annie Oakley, wearing a sequined mask, had commandeered the outdoor dance floor, her six-shooters raised in the air. Calvin and his date and the rest of the guests streamed out of the house. When they had all gathered outside, Meredith Kingsley removed her mask. On her cue, a dozen caterers-cum-Indians pulling on heavy ropes led a giant wooden horse two stories tall out of a nearby barn, thundering toward the dance floor, *AAAA* emblazoned in gold leaf on the horse's flanks. Then a trap door in the belly flopped open, and out rolled a gangway and another wooden horse; a second gangway emerged from that to release a third and final horse. The reinvention of the legend of Troy, Meredith Kingsley style, produced raucous cheering.

"As all of you know," Meredith began when the crowd finally quieted, "none of my horses has ever won the All-American Futurity. This is about to change. My humble filly, Four Aces, is the fastest quarter horse God ever made.

The 5555 Ranch has never raised a finer animal. If she had wings, she'd be an airplane. But should there be any doubters here, I'm willing and able to match, dollar for dollar, any fool who wants to bet against her. If Four Aces wins, all money goes to charity. If I lose the race—and I damn well better not—those who bet against me get the whole pissing pot." Meredith fired off a final round. "All right—any takers?"

The gauntlet having been thrown down, Calvin understood, someone was duty bound to pick it up. But this was hardly the Oklahoma land rush. Most guests, even drunk, were hesitant to openly challenge Meredith for fear of offending their hostess. Meredith could be as prickly as a cactus. Her feistiness came as a surprise to those who didn't know her, because Meredith looked almost cherubic. Her features were soft and delicate, her reddish-brown curly hair recalled Little Orphan Annie, and she had a pleasant, enthusiastic voice.

Light, staccato clapping suddenly rippled through the crowd as three figures edged toward Meredith and her wooden effigies of Four Aces. Slowly the clapping built to a crescendo. Courage begetting courage, Calvin thought. A little drama tonight wouldn't go unappreciated by the members of an audience accustomed to fierce ego clashes and constant one-upmanship in their daily lives.

Calvin knew the first gentleman well. Austin Mirabeau, a Dallas real estate developer who'd been bitten by the racing bug a decade before, had his own breeding ranch on the other side of Dallas. His horse, King's Ransom, was also entered in the All-American, and many track pundits thought the muscular colt could take it all. As he did for Meredith, Calvin had miles of respect for Austin.

With the help of several hungry banks, the developer had gobbled up a healthy chunk of downtown Dallas years ago, before prices had exploded upward, and he'd been building his empire ever since. He looked almost cowboyish with his lean, leathery face deeply textured by the sun, and a high, broad forehead. His eyes were coffee-colored, and he sported a slightly roguish graying mustache. Austin was a proud man, often defensive, with his share of quirks and eccentricities. But he had a basically good heart, felt things deeply, and seemed as devoted to his family as to his horses and real estate. As Austin took the stage, his wife Fern sat quietly in the crowd nursing their five-month-old baby, both oblivious to the raucous party.

"Meredith, honey, y'all know I respect you and your horse-breeding ranch to bits," he began, "and I'm right glad to be at your party this evening. *But* . . ." With mock flourish he pulled out his checkbook, and with a thousand pair of eyes witnessing it, wrote a check for $50,000. He strolled over and gave Meredith a peck on the cheek along with his check. "*But* I'm here to tell y'all my horse is going to leave Four Aces in the dust!" Great whoops of surprise and glee erupted at his words.

The second challenger was a stranger to Calvin, until he gave his name as Billy Sullivan. Calvin studied the young man, no more than thirty, with tousled blond hair and movie-star good looks. His father, Henry Sullivan, had been as much a Texas legend as Katie Kingsley, Meredith's mother. Henry had risen from roustabout in the oil patch to form his own petroleum company, becoming an overnight millionaire when he sold out to Standard Oil. Then he taught himself polo, and became one of the United States' first ten-goal players. Now his son Billy, with a stunning woman at his side, smiled affably to the crowd, enjoying the limelight. His wager was modest by the cowboy jet-setter's standards—only five thousand dollars—but then Billy was not quite one of them. Like his father, he played professional polo, steering clear of quarter horses except as an admirer.

The last gentleman was a stranger to everyone there. Meredith introduced the Arab in the Saville Row suit and Gucci loafers as Zallaq Al-Khalifa. She tripped twice on the pronunciation, but the guest wasn't bothered. He looked as if nothing could bother him—as if he'd belong anywhere in the world. With a salt and pepper beard and a seamless face, he was unusually handsome. There was something so cosmopolitan about him that for a moment made Calvin wonder if it was the Texans who were out of place tonight. In perfect English Zallaq spoke about his passionate interest in quarter horses—particularly in embryonic transfers and test-tube breeding. The crowd seemed to know as much about that as roasting marshmallows on the moon. Then Zallaq wrote out a check for $100,000. "You have a fine horse," he told Meredith, "but I play the odds, and this year's field is too strong." The cheers were deafening, and Meredith nodded gracefully at the Arab's challenge.

As impressive as Zallaq's wager was, Calvin thought, the real betting on the All-American wouldn't begin until Labor Day. Over a quarter million dollars would pass through the track's betting windows for the tenth race, and it was anyone's guess how much via bookies—all to see who would be the world's fastest horse.

"Come on, time to leave," Calvin whispered to his date. He strolled over to give Meredith a friendly hug, and wished her well for the race. Then he asked about Seth.

Meredith's fourth husband was one of Calvin's oldest and closest friends—the two had roomed together at law school—and while Calvin had thrown his hat into the political ring years ago, Seth had stuck comfortably to law and earned a reputation as one of the state's top criminal attorneys. He'd defended Houston society matrons accused of shooting their rich and cheating husbands, defended bribe-soliciting highway commissioners, smooth-talking embezzlers, attorneys who bilked helpless widows, even a gang of militant Mexicans who'd openly plotted to assassinate the mayor of San Antonio and retake the Alamo. He was an unusual man, quiet and ruminative, and clearly subservient to Meredith—the secret, in Calvin's opinion, why their marriage had survived. Like a typical Texas wife, Meredith let her husband think *he* was making the decisions for them, but it was really Meredith in control.

"Haven't seen Seth in a while," Meredith told Calvin. "He's not exactly a social creature, you know."

"Never was," Calvin allowed.

"You have to leave so soon? Fun's just starting."

"I'm a little like Seth—all work, no play," he said, and gave Meredith a good-night kiss.

Suspecting that Seth might be somewhere in the house, Calvin made a brief search on his way out. The party was starting to turn rowdy. Guests were falling or being pushed into the pool, the pinatas were coming down, and one fool had climbed atop Meredith's wooden effigy of Four Aces as if riding into the sunset. Calvin excused himself from his date for a moment and checked the library, the master bedroom suite, even called down to the basement. Peeking in a guest bedroom, he found a Dallas Cowboy cheerleader, bare bottom glistening in the air, spread-eagled over the side of the bed. She was adorned only in cowboy boots and hat, and her wrists were tied with a lariat to the upper bedposts.

"Honey . . . honey . . . honey . . ." she repeated in a building frenzy.

Calvin looked to see who she was talking to. The man, his back to the door, was kneeling as he fastened the girl's ankles to the lower posts. Calvin had seen a lot of strange things, but a naked Arab in spurs pushed its way to the top of his list. If you were as rich as Zallaq, he thought wryly, your imagination was your only restraint.

Calvin ducked out before he was spotted, and meandered back outside to rejoin his date. By the pool he noticed a young man staring at him, but Calvin avoided eye contact and said a final good-bye to some close friends. As they drove away from the ranch, his date remarked lightly that he seemed nervous. Calvin said nothing. The skein of thread holding his life together was very close to unraveling, and not for the first time. The matter was one of great delicacy, not to say urgency, and the state senator made a mental note to call Seth first thing in the morning.

TWO

ON THE BRIGHT, BRASSY LABOR DAY MORNING, THE PRI-
vate jets touched down one after another at Ruidoso's muni-
cipal airport. Framed by the rugged Sacramento Mountains
and dotted with fragrant pines, the tiny, southwest New
Mexico city, swollen to ten times its official population, was
still filling up with tall, strapping cowboys wearing $2000
lizard skin boots, gold Rolex watches, Halston blazers, and
the inevitable Stetsons that had trademarked their families
for six and seven generations. In his own Learjet 35, Austin
Mirabeau and his wife descended in the pale champagne
sky to 8000 feet, waiting for landing instructions from the
control tower. In the plane's rear seats were a nursemaid
and the baby. Austin was growing itchy. The race of races
started in only a few hours, and he wanted time to settle in
and talk to friends. It was also his habit to take a leisurely
stroll around the paddock with his horse, in order to give
King's Ransom a personal pre-race pep talk. Austin was a
firm believer that horses emoted just as human beings did,
could understand love, enthusiasm, anger, and jealousy,
and psyching them up for a race was not an exercise in
futility. King's Ransom and his trainer had been in Ruidoso
for several weeks to allow the horse to get acclimated to the
mountain altitude. As a yearling the colt had been a
bleeder, the trifacial veins in his nose rupturing when he
ran too hard—or the air was too thin to breathe—which in

14

turn impaired his breathing and slowed his speed. Despite the horse's adjustment period, Ruidoso's 7000-foot altitude made Austin a little nervous. He crossed his fingers now as the control tower finally radioed a clearing on the runway.

"Hold on, honey," he said to Fern in the co-pilot seat, and once he made certain the baby and nurse were fastened in, Austin pushed the throttle to what he referred to as the kamikaze position. At a good forty-five degree angle, the jet glided toward earth like a runaway meteorite, slowing only a few thousand feet from the runway. The touchdown was butter smooth.

Horses were fun, but could be a pain in the butt; planes were just fun. And not just for the speed or the sensation of floating in air. When Austin had ordered his plane six months ago, he didn't shortchange himself on the trimmings. The Learjet was custom fitted with quadraphonic stereo—Dolby sound—two Sony televisions, a bar with an armadillo-skin counter, a built-in fish tank that Austin had stocked with Tangs and Rock Beauties, and a microwave that chimed out "The Yellow Rose of Texas" when the timer went off. Some friends found the furnishings gaudy, or just ridiculous, but Austin had never been one to apologize for his taste. He didn't mind when Fern relied on those guys with tight pants to decorate one of their homes, but the plane was *his* castle and kingdom, and no decorator was coming near it.

As Austin and his family ducked into a waiting limo and were whisked to the track, the horse breeder's thoughts focused on the race. He had come today not just to be entertained but to win. At her ranch party, Meredith Kingsley had strutted and crowed all night long about Four Aces. While her filly had run the fastest time this year, a 21.45 at Los Alamitos in Southern California, the horse had won only a couple of races. With the chips on the table, Four Aces had come in second to King's Ransom in the Kansas and Rainbow Futurities, the quarter horse world's equivalent to the first two legs of the Triple Crown. Defensive, Meredith had huffed afterward that the races had been so *close*, and if not for a poor start out of the gate Four Aces would have won both. Austin had only smiled politely, but inside he'd been laughing in triumph. *Close* only counted in dancing, horseshoes, and atom bombs.

Today, for the All-American, he was confident that Four Aces would lose again. The morning tip sheet had King's Ransom as the bookies' pick; Austin was sure that the tote board would reflect a similar feeling from the track bettors. More importantly, Austin's *gut* told him his horse would win, that 1984 was his year. And high time too. For five races in five years he had brought his top two-year-olds to Ruidoso—geldings, fillies, and colts—and five times he had been denied. With each loss the degree of agony seemed to magnify, and by now had become almost physical, like a deep, searing pain in the chest. He was tired of the pain. He wanted satisfaction.

Austin was a rich man, and the $1 million purse did not matter; winning mattered—oh, did it matter. And kicking dust on Four Aces' sweet little head counted almost as much. Austin, who knew the value of public relations, was always careful to appear as Meredith's good and caring friend, as he had at the party, but his real feelings were different. In his opinion the woman had the balls of a Texas Longhorn and the mouth of a truck driver, and he trusted Meredith about as much as he would a twelve-foot rattler. With damn good reason. Austin didn't like to think of himself as vindictive, but he could never forget what Meredith had done to him long ago. One day soon she was going to get her comeuppance.

"Hon, you look a little nervous," Fern said gently to her husband as the limo edged through the sea of cars to drop everybody at the entrance of the $1000-a-seat Jockey Club.

The truth was that Austin appeared relatively calm; *she* was as skittish as a weanling. A slim-hipped, cheerful blonde who went about life as normally as anyone could who was married to a man who owned $500 million of Dallas real estate, Fern loved horses, hated races. What she really hated was competition, but competition was what drove her husband, and long ago she'd acquiesced to his world of real estate deals, board meetings, high finance, and above all, to his quest for victory in the All-American Futurity. The more times Austin was denied, the stronger was his obsession for victory. She had never known a prouder or more ambitious man, or anyone who believed so much in himself, which was why she had married him.

Seventeen years ago Austin Mirabeau had had only $130 in a savings account, and a battered '61 Chevy. Fern had tried to shelter their five children from the driving nature of their father, but his ambition inevitably rubbed off, especially on her oldest boy, no matter how she tried to soften it with warm hugs and good-night kisses. Fern suddenly felt a pang of regret that her children weren't with her now. But she knew they were better off at home with a responsible housekeeper than at this madhouse of a race track.

"Christ on a side car," Austin remarked as they climbed the steps to the Jockey Club. "I dearly love my plane, but I hate traveling to other race tracks. One of these days we're going to have pari-mutuel wagering in Texas. Just as soon as Calvin Garrison gets reelected and tells those other jack-asses in the senate how to vote. We're gonna have a race bigger than the All-American not far from our doorstep." He grinned. "Even if we have to kick the Baptists out of Texas to do it!"

Inside the Jockey Club, as frilly, miniskirted waitresses slipped back and forth with bourbons-and-Seven and Shrimp Louis salads, the jammed room with an open view of the track was unnaturally quiet. There was too much nervousness for any bragging or grandiose predictions. Everyone knew that racing quarter horses was one of the biggest crap shoots known to man. In the twenty-two seconds it took a horse to sprint a quarter mile, anything could happen. Not surprisingly, the wives huddled together to talk about their children, the hottest restaurants in Dallas, charity fund-raisers—anything but the race. Austin shook a few hands, read the tout sheets, and felt a rush of pleasure that the handicappers favored his horse. Then he walked over to Meredith Kingsley and Seth Cartwright.

"Afternoon." Austin beamed, reaching over to pump Seth's hand. "Wonderful day, isn't it? Last Labor Day it rained cats and dogs."

"I feel fortunate," Meredith volunteered. "Four Aces loves a dry, fast track."

"Some filly you've got. She's a world-beater, all right," Austin said, not believing a word of it. "Seth, how've you been?"

He might consider Meredith lower than a rattlesnake's belly, but Austin genuinely liked Seth. He was a cracker-jack lawyer and a gentleman. Austin just didn't understand why he'd married Meredith.

"Been fine, Austin, thank you. Sorry I missed you at the party. I wasn't feeling too well. Understand you made some bet!"

"Sure did," Austin echoed. And he couldn't wait to collect from Meredith. He shook Seth's hand again and gave Meredith a polished smile. "Y'all take care now."

As the first race was announced, Austin pulled a thick wad of bills from his jeans for Fern to bet. That was for luck—always let the little woman do your betting. To please the great goddess of fortune, Austin had also passed out to friends duckbill caps inscribed with KING'S RANSOM—SIXTH TIME'S THE CHARM, carried a railroad watch handed down by his great-grandfather, and donned the same gold-tipped, hand-crafted Dixon boots he had worn when his horse had won the Kansas and the Rainbow.

When the tenth race was only half an hour away, Austin wandered outside. The crowd of short-sleeved bettors spilled out of the bleachers and hugged the rail for a better view. Some had brought folding chairs to stand on, others just angled their necks up and stood on their toes to see. The air smelled of beer. Flashing his pass to a guard, Austin ambled through an underground passage to the paddock area.

"You're beautiful," he said as he held the reins of King's Ransom, pushing his nose up to the horse's. The trainer and jockey stood to one side as Austin inspected the muscular roan colt with the blaze face and chocolate eyes. His conformation was truly astounding. Austin had looked over many a horse in his time, but none had the balance of King's Ransom. The steep angle of his shoulders and hindquarters allowed the horse a maximum stride. The long neck let him reach up easily for air. His fetlocks were large and sturdy, absorbing the shock from the pounding on the track. And he owned as muscular a chest as Man o' War. Austin slipped both arms around his colt. "I love you, you know that, and I know today you're going to run your heart out for me, like you always do. You're one of a kind. You're the most beautiful horse the world's ever seen. I love you."

As Austin led the handsome colt around the paddock area and continued his pep talk, David Sanders, the twenty-two-year-old jockey who had mounted King's Ransom for eight consecutive victories, watched his employer. The jockey was unusually strong for someone only five feet six inches tall, and had wide shoulders and large hands that could control the reins on any horse. His innocent blue eyes made him look eighteen at most, but his manner was mature. And he loved horses every bit as much as his boss did. As David listened to Mr. Mirabeau whisper sweet nothings in King's Ransom's ear, he thought it was a man talking to a beautiful woman, an expensive woman with fine taste. Mr. Mirabeau even bought his horses little trinkets when he won—and sometimes not so little. For King's Ransom he had commissioned a Texas artist to create a three-foot high bronze of his favorite horse blazing toward a finish line. A lot of people thought Mr. Mirabeau was obsessed, but David wasn't so sure that his horses didn't understand the owner's passion and gratitude.

The jockey had certainly never known anyone with Mr. Mirabeau's horse sense. A lot of smart people could judge a horse's conformation, knew what good lines were, or could trace a bloodline, especially with a computer. But it took a special talent, an intuition, to read a horse's mind and heart—and those were the intangibles that won races; those were the differences between a good horse and a great one. King's Ransom, Mr. Mirabeau had told David, had the mind and heart of a true warrior. To fight, to win, was everything. David had mounted the colt enough times to become a believer, and he was grateful, in a sport where success was hard to come by, to have the chance to ride King's Ransom. His status as a jockey had risen considerably this year, and for weeks now his hopes had pointed to this race.

"Just be sure you're ready at the gate," Austin reminded David as he returned with the horse. For a moment they turned to watch the start of the All-American pre-race ceremonies. Raucous cheers rose from the crowd. A breeze raised a fine layer of dust from the track and swept it toward the paddock. "And let the horse set his own pace. When he's ready to make a charge, he will. He knows he's going to win, just don't give him any reason to think he won't."

"I'll do my best, Mr. Mirabeau." David tried to ignore the bubble of nervousness in his gut that inevitably rose before every race.

"One more thing—don't let Four Aces too close. She'll be coming out of the next hole, and we know she tends to lug out. I don't want any lugging out today." Austin restrained himself from saying anything less charitable about his rival's horse.

"Yes, sir."

Austin patted his jockey affectionately on the shoulder and strode back to the bleachers, trying to relax. All that could be done had been done. For a moment he allowed himself to dream. Austin had kingly plans for King's Ransom. While winning was the most important thing to him, the reward for winning couldn't exactly be overlooked, which was to say money, and not just the purse. The purse, in fact, was only the iceberg's tip. After his colt won the All-American he could be syndicated overnight—buyers would be waiting in line with the hope of breeding their prize broodmares with the world's fastest horse—and each of the forty shares of ownership could fetch up to $300,000. That meant $12 million for Austin. But if he waited until after *next* year, when King's Ransom would be a three-year-old and competed in the top derbies, the colt could be worth $500,000 a share, maybe more. Hadn't the famous Dash for Cash fetched $1 million for one share? Such were the sugar plums that danced in a horse breeder's head.

As he always did before crucial races, Austin left Fern up in the Jockey Club to watch from their box while he fought for a place near the finish line, rubbing shoulders with the beer-swilling proletariat. For a moment he glanced at the older man next to him, pale and a little shriveled, yet somehow elegant in his Goodwill suit, a flower in his lapel. He looked at Austin as if he knew him, even offering a sympathetic smile, yet Austin was hard pressed to identify the gentleman. The horse breeder focused back on the tote board as it flashed still another set of numbers, reflecting the continuing change of bettors' hunches. Four Aces had held steady at 1:2, but King's Ransom had dropped from 3:5 to 2:5, which meant a two-dollar wager would return $2.80 for a win.

The level of excitement had also climbed. TV crews scurried around readying their cameras and sound equipment as if for the Second Coming. As the ten horses were led from the paddock toward the starting gate, the announcer proclaimed the great and glorious traditions of the All-American Futurity, pre-race awards were presented with the self-congratulation more typical of the Academy Awards, and the horses and jockeys were introduced. Then a quiet descended over the crowd with the suddenness of a winter norther. Austin liked to think he had ice water in his veins, but at the moment he couldn't remember his middle name.

The horses, some as nervous as their owners, were enticed by handlers into their respective gates. Twenty-two goddamn seconds, Austin thought. The time it took to brush his teeth.

With a blink of an eye the horses sprinted out like bullets. To the uninitiated they resembled a darkish blur, punctuated by the color of the jockeys' silks, but Austin kept his eye unflinchingly on a single horse. King's Ransom broke cleanly, edged to the front of the pack, and with the long, confident strides that were his hallmark, surged into a lead. He was a finely honed machine, a marriage of muscle and finesse, Austin marveled, and he did not know how to lose.

High in the irons, David Sanders could barely feel the fiery engine below him. So sure and smooth were King's Ransom's strides that the young jockey had the sensation of being carried on air. But his senses were not unaware of the dangers around him. The pounding hooves and husky, desperate breathing closed toward him like a pursuing assailant. Without warning, David felt a lurch below him. It was almost imperceptible, but it was readable to a jockey: the horse had shortened his stride. Something was wrong, he thought. The race was only half over and King's Ransom was laboring. Mr. Mirabeau had always told him to let his favorite horse dictate the pace, but David could feel Four Aces closing. He slashed his riding crop down and leaned forward. "Come on, baby," he whispered. King's Ransom swung his head out, as if for air. Then its back sagged and swayed. Oh, shit, what the hell was going on? David thought. He suddenly realized he was no longer in control of the horse, or the race. Helpless, he held on and prayed.

Austin, at the finish line, struggled to push his head above the crowd. What he saw on the track opened a pit in his stomach. King's Ransom was losing speed. Four Aces was only half a length back. He watched as David slashed his whip down a second, third, and fourth time. Suddenly Austin's colt, now a good head behind Four Aces, wobbled to one side as if a hand had come along to give a furtive and decisive push. Without warning the colt's front legs collapsed. Austin stood there, stunned. The muscular torso plunged into the dirt. David was pitched off only inches from the hooves of pursuing horses. A silence dropped over the track and hung there. Even when the race finished, there was no cheering.

As a frantic Austin broke through a phalanx of track attendants and grooms, he saw that his jockey was all right. Then he dropped on his knees by his horse. A vet wasn't needed to tell him that both front legs were hopelessly shattered. King's Ransom was trembling, barely conscious, sweaty to the touch.

In a volcanic rage Austin screamed at everyone to move away. He dropped his head in tears on the neck of King's Ransom. Goddammit, he thought bitterly. Four Aces had bumped his horse, he knew it. Four Aces and Meredith Kingsley had killed the love of his life, the fount of his dreams.

With all the fury of a man who had been denied one time too many, he swore to Almighty God he would take revenge.

THREE

THE TOPLESS JEEP PITCHED UP LIKE A BRONCO ON THE
bumpy road, levitated up a final hill where a wooden sign
proclaimed 5555 RANCH—NO TRESPASSING, and rolled to a
stop on a plateau of fenced grazing pasture. Meredith, her
husband, and trainer caught their breaths almost collectively as they surveyed the lush panorama that was the
ranch. It almost seemed too green to be real, like a velvet
painting sold in a discount shop. Around them were paddocks, barns, foaling pens, indoor training arenas, storage
sheds, a man-made lake, fenced pastures of gamma and buffalo grasses, and a cluster of mare motels where, for thirty
dollars a night during the January to June breeding season,
eager owners brought their mares while waiting for stud
service. The preciousness of good horse sperm, Meredith
knew, was as indisputable as the roundness of the earth.
What could fill a twelve-ounce Dixie cup might be worth as
much as a small jet or the salary of the president of IBM.

Breeding, for Meredith, was also a matter of personal
interest. In the quarter horse world natural breeding, always dangerous with one horse climbing on top of another,
was being replaced by artificial methods. Most common
was the use of a phantom mare, a horse-size model into
which a horny stallion was only too pleased to ejaculate.
Meredith often stood in the stud room as a spectator admiring the sexual energies, not to mention equipment, of stallions. She was no pervert, but she could understand

Catherine the Great's admiration. Unlike the human species, male horses always knew how to go about their business.

Meredith's eyes lifted again to her kingdom of endless rolling pasture. She had her mother to thank for the real estate. Meredith liked to call Katie Kingsley the first feminist of Texas. She had played poker, chewed tobacco, roped horses, and during the Depression served as postmistress in a tiny panhandle town called Lambert. It was mostly cattle country, where the men spent days gathering dust in their throats and nights washing it out. But the county was dry, the nearest booze eighty miles to the east. It was a long haul just for Jack Daniels, and Katie, knowing an opportunity when she saw it, plunked down her life savings of a couple hundred dollars and purchased thirty acres of desolate land. She got herself an attorney, and with the help of a loosely worded statute of Texas law incorporated herself as Kingsley County. Since there were no Baptists to oppose her, Texas's newest county wrote its first and only law: anyone could purchase and consume liquor till he passed out on the street. In the next twelve months Katie purveyed more booze to more thirsty cowboys than angels had wings.

Then good turned to bad, as Katie told her daughter. Jealous businessmen from the next county burned her saloon to the ground. Katie's insurance had lapsed, and new bank loans were scarce. She sulked for a while, drank too much, lost what money she'd saved, and played a lot of poker. In a midnight game in the middle of a January snow, a sour-faced cattleman stared down Katie and threw his deed for 3000 acres of grazing land into the pot. With a cocky smile he showed off his full boat. Katie smiled back. She was holding four fives. She had no idea where Sherman was, but quickly renamed the property after her winning hand.

A year later she married a man named Cleo Fortune. He fathered one child with Katie before going off to war. After Rommel blew his tank sky-high in the deserts of North Africa, Katie never remarried. She raised Meredith to be independent, and taught her ranching as they slowly transformed the grazing land into grassy pasture. Later they bought a few quarter horses, won a couple of races, and bought some more. When Katie died in 1970 from a fall off a horse, the ranch was appraised at $3 million. Meredith promptly took over the reins. It hadn't always been easy. But four husbands later she was still going strong.

"Come on, darling," a voice called. Meredith looked out from the Jeep to find Seth reaching out to her. She took his hand and eased herself to the ground. On a high from Four Aces' victory two weeks ago, she'd indulged in a steady binge of friends' parties through half of east Texas.

"I surely love to party," Meredith remarked to Seth, "but my head feels like the goddamn Grand Canyon." She took a breath and pulled herself together. As usual she sported what she called her Dale Evans look—ankle-length blue-jean skirt, frilly blouse, and silver pendant earrings to complement her concho belt. Ralph Lauren had labeled the same style Southwest, but Meredith had never given a horse's hair about fashion.

"What do you think, hon?" Seth said as he and Meredith studied the pack of fillies behind the pasture fence. A gentle, thoughtful man whose bulky frame towered to the sky, with his squinty eyes and large ears, Seth was admittedly no Paul Newman, but Meredith had given up choosing men on looks long ago. Seth was honest, reliable, sincere—salt of the earth.

"I think we've got some winners here," Meredith answered, focusing on one filly in particular. She jumped on the fence and whistled melodiously. "C'mere, Five Deuces," she called to a copper-colored yearling. "Come here, baby!"

Pride flickered in Meredith's eyes as she studied the filly's lines. Bred on the 5555 Ranch, Five Deuces boasted the same sire and dam as Four Aces; each had won over $500,000 in stakes races, and Meredith expected the same for the progeny. Obviously Four Aces was already far ahead, and she held out just as much hope for Five Deuces. The big filly already broken in, had easily won a yearling race last week, despite being lazy and a poor starter. Meredith was convinced that under the care of her trainer, Abel Hanson, any horse's bad habits could be erased.

"Why don't we put her in one more race this year?" Meredith suggested, watching the trainer stroke the filly's neck.

Slow moving and deliberate, Abel carried a paunch on his mid-size frame, and his faded jeans matched his weathered face. "I don't know, m'am," he replied. "It might be pushing things—"

"Why? She's big and strong. Fifteen hands easily."

"I honestly wouldn't race her again this year," Abel allowed in his soft Oklahoma drawl. "Her bones are still fragile. Come January, she'll be a lot more mature."

Meredith almost always took the opinion of her trainer. Abel was a man of few words—from cowboy stock, he probably didn't breathe more than a couple dozen sentences all day—but when he did speak, it counted. He was the most important man on her ranch, even more than the vet in charge of Meredith's breeding program, and Abel was paid accordingly: a $100,000 salary, plus five percent of all her horses' winnings.

While futurity races, which were for two-year-olds only, offered some substantial purses, it was the derbies, the races for three-year-olds, that had Meredith thinking. If Four Aces won six or seven of the major derbies, she could earn as much next year as she had this. Whatever sliver of that pie Abel took home, thought Meredith, she was all for it. Not only was Abel a good and loyal friend whom she could count on in fair and foul weather alike, but he had a helluva difficult job. It was the trainer who determined how soon a horse should begin working out—or "legging it up"—the duration and type of training, the feeding program, what races to enter, what jockey to use, and a strategy for winning. In short, he took the praise or blame for whatever happened. Every autumn Abel also helped Meredith cull her foals and yearlings, deciding which to keep for racing and which to sell at auction or to private parties.

Some years none of her yearlings looked promising, so Meredith would take her bankroll to the All-American Select Quarter Horse Yearling Sale at Ruidoso the week before the Labor Day race. But with Five Deuces in her stable, there was no need to look for outside help. The filly was blessed with intelligence, grace, and speed. On January first, when all horses officially had their birthdays, Five Deuces would become a two-year-old, and eligible to the 1985 All-American.

"You think she can win come September?" Meredith asked Abel. "Like I tell my friends, I'm not just interested in starting a winning tradition. I want to to build a dynasty."

"Leave it to me," said Abel. "It's important not to push, that's all. Look what happened to King's Ransom."

The mention of Austin Mirabeau's horse brought a shake of the head from Meredith. With a mixture of dismay and irritation she had first read of Austin's charge in the *Dallas Morning News* sports pages that Four Aces had bumped his horse. Austin's trainer had made a similar accusation just after the race—in the heat of passion, Meredith felt—asking track stewards to cite Meredith's jockey for fouling King's Ransom. True, the whole field had been bunched around the 220-yard mark, and there was the usual jostling, but after studying the race film the stewards couldn't see any fouls. Meredith thought that would be the end of it. But after reading the story, she had called Austin and demanded a retraction.

"What kind of friend are you?" she'd asked, bewildered.

"Your horse fouled," Austin shot right back. "She didn't deserve to win the race. You can keep my $50,000 because I don't welsh on bets, but I want you to know your horse didn't win fairly. And I'm not retracting anything."

"You better," Meredith said firmly.

"Your horse fouled and you know it. I'll never forget it."

"This is ridiculous," Meredith said. "I'm sorry for what happened to King's Ransom, honestly. But it wasn't my fault. The race is history now. There's no reason for you to be vindictive. You have to think ahead to next year."

"Don't tell me what to think about," Austin said with uncharacteristic anger, and hung up.

Meredith couldn't believe it. Austin had never even apologized. She could understand his being upset that his horse had been put down and that he might have felt the need for a scapegoat, but why her? They were friends. It just wasn't like Austin. Meredith felt badly, but had no choice but to have her attorney file a nuisance libel suit, hoping it would make Austin back down. When all this craziness was over, she wanted them to be friends again.

The real reason King's Ransom had fallen on the track, Meredith was convinced, was that the colt had tried too hard to win. There was a racing bromide—"only good horses get hurt"—and Austin's colt was a competitor, one of the best. But his overzealousness, and a schedule of eight races in four months, was too much for a two-year-old. The problem had started earlier in the year, when King's Ransom broke his maiden—won his first race—only to come up limping. As Abel had indicated, that was a signal that his bone structure hadn't fully matured, which wasn't terribly uncommon with two-year-olds. The horse was also a "bleeder," as everyone in track circles knew, and not getting enough oxygen in his lungs also weakened him. Austin's trainer had gotten the horse healthy again, but only superficially. In Meredith's judgment, King's Ransom was tired and overworked and should have been scratched from the All-American. She thought Austin had the right to shoot his trainer for not knowing any better.

Meredith patted Five Deuces affectionately and looked over at Abel. "Okay," she agreed, "we won't start racing her again until after January, but get one of the grooms to bring her down to the stables. We can at least tie her on a walker and start getting the laziness out of her."

As Meredith turned to the Jeep she saw the flicker of anxiety on Seth's face. "Don't worry," she said. "This little baby will make us a ton of money, just like Four Aces. First at the track, and then with her foals, if we breed her right."

Seth nodded absently, as if hardly assured. Meredith didn't mind the skepticism—it was always fun proving her husband wrong. As financial overseer of the ranch, it was Seth's role to fret over every dollar expended, while it was Meredith's to worry only about horses. She also genuinely liked spending money. She wasn't one of those rich Texas bitches who couldn't open a charge account somewhere without telling her friends how guilty she felt. Meredith never felt guilt at all. She could spend money with the best of them—on parties, cars, fur coats, vacations. And especially on horses. Plunking down a quarter million for an untested yearling hardly fazed her.

Sometimes she wondered why Seth worried at all. Thanks to the Sport of Kings tax law, the 5555 Ranch always made a tidy profit. Seth had patiently explained the basics to her. A horse was a depreciable asset, just like any of the buildings, fences, or capital equipment on the ranch. Meredith knew that a horse breeder with a good tax lawyer, or savvy husband, could shelter virtually all of a ranch's income with the blessing of the IRS. In Meredith's case that meant, from track purses and stud fees, an easy $10 million a year, and often more.

As the three passengers got back in the Jeep, Meredith couldn't help talking about her victory again. "That was some race, wasn't it?" she said. "Four Aces just turned on her afterburners when it counted. Like a little lady, she pushed her nose across the finish line. Only won by six inches. The difference between a million dollars and $343,500—between instant stardom and an also-ran." With a mischievous smile Meredith nudged an elbow into her husband's ribs. "Six inches, sweetie," she said. "That's just about the size of your pecker."

The pale sky lit up a fiery red in celebration of another balmy Texas night. Lying that he had an upset stomach, Seth Cartwright gracefully excused himself from dining with Meredith, then waited for the cover of darkness to move toward his electric-blue Cadillac Eldorado, a forty-fifth birthday present from his wife. Meredith had been disappointed they couldn't at least talk. She was having a communication problem with her daughter Alexis again, she said, but no matter what advice Seth offered, he doubted it would improve the mother-daughter relationship.

Alexis had just left for her junior year at Bennington, an elite East Coast institution that Meredith distrusted as much as she did a vegetarian at a Texas barbecue. Her only child's intellectual proclivities grated on her nerves. "Why can't my daughter be more like me or my mother?" Meredith often demanded of Seth, as if there were some magical explanation of the gene pool. "I'm not asking too much, am I? Why can't Alexis rope horses instead of playing the French horn? Just tell me, what is so compelling about medieval architecture that says my daughter can't like horse breeding too?" Whenever Alexis' name came up in conversation, Seth usually tried to appease Meredith's anxieties and let the subject die. He didn't like to dabble in his wife's previous marriages, though he did care for Alexis. She was a nice girl, a little quiet and reserved, but smart as a whip.

Compounding the problem, Seth knew, was that Meredith, while a conscientious mother, was not the most intuitive or natural. When Seth had made his obligatory social round of the All-American party, before escaping to the guest cottage with a good novel, he had caught Meredith looking at Fern Mirabeau as she'd contentedly nursed her baby, as if wondering why motherhood came so easily to some but not to her.

Seth paused near the stables where his Cadillac was parked as two grooms finished mucking out the stalls, tossing the offal into a concrete-lined compost pit that would later be used to fertilize the pastures. Unobserved, he slipped behind the steering wheel and flicked the ignition key. The car came to life with a smooth, soothing purr. His stomach began to burn again, but he took a calming breath and drove into the night.

Seth was not accustomed to lies or skullduggery, yet the urgency of tonight pushed him to new heights of improvisation. He felt like a thief sneaking off in the night, and worried that Meredith might grow suspicious if she found him missing, which would lead to questions he didn't want to answer. A lot was at stake, maybe even his marriage. *That* possibility made him genuinely uneasy. He was in love with Meredith.

She possessed the spark and spirit that his own dull, sober life had forever lacked. That had been what convinced him several years ago to leave the ranks of bachelorhood. In turn Meredith, after three disastrous marriages to egomaniacs and prima donnas, found in Seth a gentle and unpretentious soul who was no threat to her. He was respected in his profession, and went about his work with a quiet, becoming dignity that was a steadying influence on their marriage. Meredith still cavorted in public and was prone to stick her foot in her mouth, but Seth was tolerant, just as he was of her digs about his looks and sexuality.

The truth was, part of Seth liked being in the spotlight that followed Meredith. Just as he got a vicarious thrill in representing wild divorcees who shot their ex's for being one day late on an alimony payment, so too did he enjoy Meredith's reputation for color. He recalled the Cattle Baron's Ball—one of Dallas' major charity events—when the governor, with much fanfare, introduced the guest of the evening, Xao Chen Dao, Minister of Trade of the Peoples' Republic of China. The minister was ready to order tons of prime Lone Star beef for his populous country. Meredith, unimpressed, if not insulted, had cupped her hands around her mouth and shouted, *"Get the goddamn communist out of here!"* To the governor's further chagrin, the supporting applause built to a crescendo. Seth couldn't help enjoying the spectacle.

Even before Four Aces' victory in the All-American, *Ultra*, the Houston-published celebrity magazine, had run a four-page spread on Meredith as "Texas Woman of the Year." She might not have been a household name in Peoria or even New York City, but in east Texas she was famous. The bottom line was that Meredith administered her own kingdom in the Lone Star state, and Seth was pleased to have a very major role in it.

Yet as his Cadillac negotiated a gravelly back road into Sherman, Seth wasn't so sure about his role. He felt nervous and vulnerable. An inkling of trouble had come earlier in the week with a call from his long-time friend, Calvin. The senator's voice had the quaver of a man looking down the muzzle of a gun.

"We got ourselves a little headache," Calvin had said after the obligatory exchange of pleasantries, "and a couple of aspirin aren't going to chase it. We have to talk."

Seth, in confusion, fell silent. As a legislator, Calvin was reputed to have the skin of an armadillo, as fearless as

Roger Staubach in the pocket. "Talk about what?" Seth finally inquired, disliking mystery on general principle.

"Listen," said Calvin uneasily, "just meet me Friday night at seven. There's a bar called Henry the Ninth."

The city of Sherman, 70,000 strong and birthplace of Dwight David Eisenhower, boasted many watering holes for politicians, but the bar mentioned was part of a fleabag hotel on the city's outskirts. Calvin didn't explain the cloak of secrecy. But Seth, no dummy, had only to sit in his library for a moment to guess the problem.

Seth lost his way twice before discovering the seedy rendezvous. He stared down the lightless hallway until his eyes adjusted, then meandered uncomfortably toward a distant table. Calvin, slouched in a chair, looked tired and distracted. Glancing up as Seth approached, bags showed under his eyes.

"Have a seat," Calvin said in a voice that matched his looks. "Need a drink?"

"I've already had one, but I think I'm going to want another."

"Right you are," Calvin said, and sat back in silence.

Seth had never seen his friend quite so down. Good times had been so plentiful over the years, it was hard to accept there could be any problem now. With a twinge of nostalgia Seth remembered their fishing trips to the Pecos River in northern New Mexico, quail hunting near Big Bend. Good fun, good company. He finished one bourbon and ordered another, hesitant to introduce the subject that both knew had to be brought up. The problem seemed unfair, after all these years.

"Seth, I've got some people leaning on me," Calvin finally spoke up. "Leaning hard too. It's eight weeks before the election and they're threatening to blow the whistle on us. I guess the sins of our past have caught up with us."

A hole opened in Seth's stomach. The feeling of helplessness was like a paralysis, and he hated it. There were some fortunate people, he had observed, who could cope with anything. They had natural, organic personalities, blossoming confidently like plants in a greenhouse, while others—like himself—were self-manufactured, nail by plank by brick, and had never learned to deal effectively with crises.

Seth could pretend to know what he was doing, but in truth he was usually at a loss. As a child growing up in a middle class home in Corpus Christi, he had been oversensitive about his looks, did not make friends easily, and had deep, abiding fears about being swept aside and forgotten by his peers. It was all he could do just to survive. If his bicycle chain broke or he misplaced his wallet, he would almost collapse. In school he found refuge in books and solitary fantasies of someday, somehow, being looked up to by society.

When his father's shoe business fell into bankruptcy, Seth put himself through UT at Austin, and later Rice Law School. There he met and roomed with Calvin. Seth admired and liked his new roommate. He was one of the first real friends Seth had. Sensitive and thoughtful, Calvin wasn't the academic elitist or cutthroat that most students were. The two were just a couple of quiet, hard-working kids who had their sights set on the future.

"Who's doing this leaning?" Seth finally asked, screwing up a courage he wasn't sure was there.

"It's me they want to hurt," Calvin explained, "but you'll be dragged through the mud with me. I don't know how they found out. Point is, they've got us skinned six ways to Sunday."

"But who?"

"I can't tell you that."

A line of sweat began to bead on Seth's brow. The nightmare was coming true, just as he'd been afraid. If word got out, he could anticipate Meredith's reaction. A divorce would come instantly. This wasn't the sort of transgression she could tolerate. Seth didn't favor the idea of public embarrassment either, having seen enough of his clients fall from grace, then held up to ridicule when their private lives became public. There was no vicarious pleasure from *that*. The sins of our innocence, Calvin should have called it.

Seth remembered quite clearly. On a bleak winter night he and Calvin had first answered one another's loneliness, a simple and humane act by two young men who felt shut out from the rest of the world. What was so wrong or unnatural about turning to one another for affection? Neither one had thought of describing himself as a homosexual, though they had repeated the act several times. The practice stopped after law school, replaced by a strong and platonic friendship. And Seth had never slept with a man again. But history was history. No doubt now it was about to be resurrected in the name of moral righteousness. If that dealt a mortal blow to an earnest and hard-working politician like Calvin, no electorate would shed tears. In California or New York, a politician might survive the charges of being queer. But in Texas to be gay was tantamount to renouncing your mother, spitting on the flag, and kicking your dog. Folks just didn't accept it.

"You have to trust me, Seth. These are bad people. I've opposed them politically, and now they want to hurt me. And frankly . . ." He glanced up. The handsome face twitched in resolve. ". . . I can't let that happen. It just isn't fair to me."

Seth had always disliked politics, and now he was reminded why. It was a business for chickenshit jackals. "How are you going to stop them?"

"I can't. All I can do is give in to them. These people want something, Seth. In fact, they want something that you have."

"Now wait a damn minute—"

"Just hold on. I don't cotton to blackmailers any more than you do. But under these circumstances—"

"What the hell is it?" Seth said cautiously.

"A horse. They want a horse."

"What?"

"A yearling."

"What yearling?"

The senator looked his friend in the eye. "The yearling Meredith wants to race in next year's All-American."

Seth rolled his eyes. A feeling of cold astonishment washed over him. "You mean Five Deuces?"

"It's what they want, Seth."

"Well, those sombitches can't have her! She's ours!

She's gonna win the whole goddamn shooting match! Meredith wants a racing dynasty. . . ."

Calvin sighed at his friend's thick-headedness. "I don't think we have a choice."

"Those *sombitches*!"

"It was suggested to me that Five Deuces can be stolen—"

"*What?*"

"The interested parties will do all the work. We'll have nothing to do with it."

"Jesus," Seth fumed. His large face squinched in anger.

"Take it easy." Calvin studied his friend, sympathizing. He was not exactly pleased himself with the idea of committing a felony, as this conspiracy surely was, but neither was he willing to have his career destroyed. He saw no choice but to surrender the horse. The end justified the means. Calvin loved politics, and knew he served his constituents well and wanted to continue to serve them. In the process he and Seth were being put through the wringer. But adversity was a test of character, wasn't it? That's what his father had always preached. The old man was in a nursing home in Dallas now, physically enfeebled but sound of mind, a man of stark and unyielding principles. Calvin didn't relish the idea of his father finding out about any of this. One wasn't supposed to build character by submitting to blackmail.

"A theft?" Seth mumbled. "We're just adding to our troubles."

"Believe me," Calvin said, "I've been thinking about this for a long time. There're a lot of pros and cons, but the bottom line has to be survival."

"If Meredith ever finds out—"

"She won't, I promise. We'll be extremely careful."

Seth pushed his hands to his face. "God Almighty, I just can't go along with this."

"It's not the end of the world, Seth," Calvin said, trying to placate him. "If we cooperate this one time, I've been promised the subject will be dead and buried."

"Bull!" he exploded. "And why do they want a top quarter horse anyway? They can't race her. Once she's missing, everyone will be looking for Five Deuces. She's got her registration number tattooed on the inside of her lip. . . ." He was so out of breath from anger, he wheezed out the last words.

"Horse racing is a high stakes business," Calvin reminded his old friend gently. "There's a lot of risk, but a lot of money, too."

"Calvin, you better tell me—who the hell are these folks?"

"You don't want to know."

"Why not?"

"Seth, I'm sorry," Calvin replied, looking pained as he rose to leave. "I'm honest to God sorry." He went to shake his friend's hand, but Seth glanced away.

"Call me tomorrow about what you want to do," Calvin said, and slipped into the cover of night.

FOUR

As the Palm Beach sun glinted off the helmeted riders, the eight ponies, nostrils flaring and coats shiny with sweat, charged at breakneck speed down the 300-yard-long field of immaculately trimmed grass. To the delight of the Pimm-drinking spectators lazing on the sidelines, the Argentine and American teams wielded their mallets with surgical precision, trying to break the scoring deadlocks as the fifth chukker ticked away.

The polo was not yet high goal at the eleven lush acres that comprised the Palm Beach Polo and Country Club, located on the old farmland of Wellington, but the players galloping urgently up and down today were hardly weekend aficionados. The cream of polo society was practicing in earnest. In three months their professional season would begin, starting at Palm Beach and moving to Buenos Aires, Santa Barbara, Paris, London, and finally Palm Springs and San Antonio. The men traveled like nomads, but nomads in style, and they took their livelihood very seriously. As local wags boasted, there was no more challenging game known to mankind than polo. You had to ride like a Comanche, think like a chess player, and have a swing like Jack Nicklaus—all while the opposition was trying to break your kneecaps.

Billy Sullivan gracefully cut his horse in front of two Argentines without committing a foul, stole the ball with a crisp backhand from the left side of his pony, and galloped toward the opponent's goal with the ball sailing in front of him. He loved to surprise the Argentines, who arguably played the best polo in the world. The country's national pastime, it was introduced by an aristocratic immigrant Irish family named Cavanaugh in the mid-nineteenth century, taught to the gauchos, and was now played by almost anyone with access to a horse. The Argentines and the British boasted at the moment the only ten-handicap goalers on the international circuit, which meant they played with the gods. But Billy, rated five goals by the United States Polo Association, knew he almost belonged in their class. Recently he had led an American team to victory for the Danbury Cup, and before that, in France and England, he'd outsmarted, outhustled, and outplayed everyone. Now he was giving it to the four Latin hotshots.

A whistle suddenly shrilled to end the chukker only seconds before Billy, outracing the Argentines at a good thirty-five miles per hour, whacked the hard plastic ball cleanly through the red and white goalposts. He heard the sighs of disappointment from the crowd, but was hardly upset himself. There was still one chukker left, seven and a half minutes to make the winning goal. As a groom saddled a fresh horse on the sidelines, Billy smiled, confident that he would score it.

"Hey, Señor Gallegos," he called good-naturedly to

the lanky, severe-looking Argentine standing beside him, one of two nine-goalers on the other team. Friends for several years, both men were breathing hard, exhausted, but Billy, at twenty-seven, ten years younger than Ricardo Gallegos, was more fit. He had the tall, blond good looks of a film star, an angular chiseled face, broad shoulders, slim waist. His athletic abilities had won him recognition at Yale in wrestling and ice hockey, and he could shoot a small-bore rifle with Olympic-level skill. But horses were his first and lasting passion. "I have a proposition," Billy said, looking his friend in the eye. "Something that might make the last chukker more interesting."

Gallegos managed an indulging smile. "You want to bet something, don't you?" he said in almost perfect English. There was nothing like an Oxford education, Billy thought, to cultivate a foreign tongue. "You Americans are always betting."

"I like your horse over there," Billy said, letting his eyes swim to the young colt tied nearby. The animal had nearly perfect lines. "How old is he?" Billy asked, though he already knew.

"El Cid is a yearling. And you can't have him, my friend, under any circumstances. The colt was born and registered in the United States, but I've trained him on the pampas. Now he's back in the States for good. He's a quarter horse. Next year he'll race in California and New Mexico. Already he runs like . . ." The Argentine made his hand into a missile and shot it into the sky.

"Really?" said Billy, acting surprised, then turned to one of his grooms. On cue the young man led a darkly handsome stallion from the country club stables. Gallegos studied the animal carefully. The well-orchestrated act of showmanship was Billy Sullivan's style. Always anticipate, his father had taught him; know what cards the other man's holding, then make your bet.

Billy's father, Henry Sullivan, had led a remarkable life. He'd grown up a cowpuncher's son in the hill country of south Texas, and taught himself polo after watching a demonstration match in Dallas in 1927. In the next five years he became, next to the legendary Tommy Hitchcock, Jr., the second best player in the United States, rated a full ten goals. He also enjoyed a gift for making money as easily as he did friends. After amassing a small oil fortune in Texas and Oklahoma, he moved to New York and produced Broadway plays, and finally to Hollywood, where he bankrolled motion pictures. And the list of his accomplishments didn't end there, as his father's friends continually reminded Billy.

Henry Sullivan had been dead for five years, and still Billy lingered under his shadow which, incredibly, seemed to lengthen with time rather than retreat. Billy had mixed emotions. He had loved and respected the man—not just for what he accomplished, but as a caring father—yet there was an implicit standard of judgment imposed on him, and though it was never said, Billy felt he had not measured up. He was not the success his father was or wanted Billy to be. In professional polo Billy was near but not at the top, and outside of polo's cozy world he was absolutely nothing: a bright, polished, good-looking young man who was popular and got along with almost everyone, particularly women, but who had a nagging sense of not belonging, of secretly floundering, of wanting to find a niche. At Meredith Kingsley's party he stepped onto the dance floor to offer a bet not because he was drunk or flamboyant, but because he had a need to be noticed and recognized. Yet he knew that more people at the party remembered his father than would remember him.

"That stallion was the sire of Firestorm and Lady Luck," Billy explained, "both of whom made it to the Kentucky Derby. He's only nine, so he can stand at stud for another ten or eleven years."

Gallegos nodded in admiration as he stroked the horse's neck. "And you'd like to sell him?"

"Do you want him?"

"I might," said the Argentine carefully.

"He's yours if your team wins today. If we win, I get El Cid."

"Fool," Gallegos said after a moment, and shook Billy's hand.

The two men mounted their horses and rejoined their

teammates on the field of combat. An outside observer of the hasty wager would have sided with the Argentine, agreeing that Billy Sullivan was a victim of poor judgment, risking a stallion that commanded $30,000 for a single stud fee for an untried colt, no matter how good El Cid *looked*. But Billy knew what he was doing. The bet had been thought out carefully. Maybe he was a fool for loving to gamble, but the fact was, Billy had ambitious plans for El Cid.

Ever since Meredith Kingsley's party, the prospect of racing a horse in the All-American Futurity had intrigued him. Gallegos didn't have to tell him that his yearling would make a splendid quarter horse; Billy had already put out feelers to the Argentine's grooms. Everyone instinctively felt the horse could be a winner. What Billy knew about racing he could carve on a pin head, but if he owned a great animal, how much did he have to know? What really mattered was the purse for the Labor Day race—$2.5 million—and that the winner took home almost half of it.

Billy liked the numbers. He liked them more than anyone could imagine.

With the start of the final chukker a new ball was tossed into play and immediately hammered by a zealous Gallegos to a teammate, who lofted it toward the goal and watched it sail wide. Then it was Billy's team, passing adroitly, that thundered up the field, their ponies cutting right and left with the nimbleness of a dancer. It was the first rule of polo that a horse didn't know how to *think*, it only *remembered*, so Billy had patiently schooled each of his ten top ponies until they could execute strategic maneuvers in their sleep. Suddenly he pulled his horse to the right, startling the Argentine beside him, held back a moment, then sprinted ahead of the pack. When he was in the clear, a teammate passed him the ball, and with a clean, steady swing Billy rammed in the go-ahead point. For five more minutes the Argentines labored, but even with the opportunity of a thirty-yard penalty shot, which Billy blocked, they came up empty-handed.

"Too bad," Billy consoled Gallegos as their horses trotted off the field together. Gallegos said nothing, silently fetching El Cid and handing the reins to Billy. In any other business or sport bets were welshed on as often as they were honored, but in polo's small world a man's word still counted. The sport and the people it attracted were proper, if nothing else. Billy mixed easily in almost any crowd, but the wealth and formality of polo's elite amazed even him sometimes.

As Gallegos rode off quietly, Billy knew better than to feel sorry for the Argentine. There would be other horses for him to breed and raise, and no matter what setbacks he suffered, Gallegos had countless ways to assuage any sorrow. Most Argentine players were from wealthy families, scions of old land patriarchs whose plantations made millions. The polo-playing sons were a privileged lot who were dispatched to private schools abroad, pampered with luxuries, flattered by an adoring public. And with the advent of corporate tournament sponsors like Gucci, Piaget, and Cadillac, which needed top players to lure crowds, the Argentines were also paid salaries that ranged up to $500,000 a year plus expenses—as if they needed it. Lower-goal players like Billy commanded $100,000. To an outsider the salary might sound high for what looked like idle play, Billy knew, but an outsider had no concept that the game was as physically dangerous as football, nor of the monstrous expenses required in keeping up to twenty ponies in your stable, paying grooms and feed bills, buying new equipment, finding housing in each city you played. And Billy, who looked for every edge to improve his game and handicap rating, continually shopped for faster, more expensive ponies.

He instructed his grooms to cool out the six horses he'd used for the match, then walked toward the stands. He did not avert his eyes from the bevy of young women who flocked around the players. Every sport had its groupies, but the polo set, like the game's top players, attracted a very high class—daughters of society families; bored, pretty wives of traveling executives; wealthy divorceés and widows who simply loved polo. There was also a contingent of teeny-boppers that Billy shied away from, wary of the law and fickle young girls, but who were much admired by the Argentines. As Billy signed his autograph for a cute blonde with china-blue eyes, underneath he wrote the address of his condo, and then, "after ten tonight." He slipped the paper in the girl's hand without a word.

The phone shrilled again. In the darkness Billy rose reluctantly, admiring the pert breasts of his companion as she dozed beside him. He wondered if he should answer. He could guess the caller—the same man who'd been trying him for the last several days. Even tonight at the Colony— where Billy had treated his teammates to dinner, as custom required of the winning team captain—the maître d' had brought a phone over to the table. Billy had politely declined to take it, charged the $500 meal to his account, and departed as if nothing were wrong. He had returned to his condo on Australian Way to find China-Blue Eyes waiting in the lobby. After a nightcap of Courvoisier they had made love, after which Billy had endured the usual questions.

"Are you married?" she had asked him.

"No."

Then, teasingly, "Do you like me?"

"Yes."

"But you like polo better?" She laughed nervously.

Billy only smiled. He was silk smooth with women.

"Do you think I could ever play polo?" she asked.

"You're left-handed," he observed. "Southpaws are barred by the USPA. That's because of the risk of a head-on collision when two players charge a ball from opposite directions."

"Okay," she murmured, but she really didn't understand. And then they had made love again.

Billy decided to take the call. "Hi, Sam, how are you?" he said in a chipper voice before the caller could identify himself. The moody silence told Billy he'd guessed correctly.

"Why the hell have you been avoiding me?" Sam Cohen yelled into the receiver. "For Chrissake, I'm your friend."

Not exactly a friend, Billy thought. On the same team maybe, but he and his accountant had lately been at each other's throats. "More doom and gloom?" Billy said.

"Things are bad, Billy."

"You've already told me."

"And they're only going to get worse, unless you start changing your ways. When are you going to start believing me?"

"What's that supposed to mean?"

"I'll put it to you bluntly, Billy. Either you stop spending so much goddamn money or you'll have to buy yourself a printing press."

"Very funny." Billy liked Sam, who'd been his father's accountant and a family friend for twenty years, but the man was growing cantankerous and self-righteous in his old age, inclined to look over Billy's shoulder like a stern uncle. Billy didn't have the guts to tell him about his wager at Meredith's party. Another $5,000 down the toilet. "How do you expect me to stop spending, Sam? I've told you how expensive polo is."

"Young man," said Sam, taking a breath to calm himself, "your father, God rest his soul, left you a million dollars and change when he died. That was five short years ago. You've gone through nine tenths of your inheritance. I have bills on my desk right now—charges from London, Paris, and Buenos Aires—that will wipe out almost nine tenths of the rest. If either of your parents were alive they'd be turning purple. Now listen to me—"

"I need one more year," Billy broke in.

"What?"

"Time. One more year, and then I'll be comfortable. I promise you, Sam."

"You want me to stall your creditors for a *year*? Shit on a shingle, Billy, this isn't Pluto! This is earth! Thirty day net billings—remember?" He calmed himself again, his curiosity piqued. "And what in the hell is going to happen in a year?"

"I'm going to win $1 million."

"Oh, yeah? How?"

"With a quarter horse named El Cid." As usual, Billy's voice shined with confidence.

"How much?"

Billy repeated the figure.

"Sure. And Hitler is alive and well in South America," replied Sam, hanging up in disgust.

Billy smiled to himself. O ye of little faith, he thought, returning to bed. He didn't see any reason for wringing his hands. Give him the full year; with a good trainer and jockey, he'd transform the yearling into a winner.

No sooner had Billy settled back with China-Blue Eyes than the phone shrilled again. Grumbling, Billy stretched for the phone. "Sam, enough is enough," he barked into the receiver.

But the voice on the other end was not Billy's accountant. It sounded old and feeble, and was made even more tenuous by the long distance connection. Billy sat at attention, retrieved a pencil from a nearby drawer, and took careful notes.

FIVE

ON AN OVERCAST MID-SEPTEMBER MORNING BUCK HART rolled his Porsche 911 Carrera out of the driveway of his exclusive Malibu Colony home and purred toward the security gate that was the community's only entrance. He glanced over to Adam Jeffrey. The five-and-a-half-year-old's chubby cheeks puffed out with an ominous war cry as action figures Major Bludd and King Cobra prepared to do battle on his lap. Buck tousled his son's fine blond hair, but failed to distract him from the business of war. The boy played with an intensity and single-mindedness that Buck almost envied, so content was he and so indifferent to the rest of the world. The kid would turn out all right, Buck knew. He regretted having to drop Adam Jeffrey at a day care center every morning, but single parentdom carried built-in limitations, and Buck countered his guilt by rationalizing that it wasn't the quantity of time spent with one's child but the quality.

"Will you paint a picture for Daddy today?" asked Buck.

"Whooooshhhh . . ." Major Bludd landed on Buck's shoulder.

"Paint me the ocean again," Buck said. "I love the way you do oceans."

"With a lot of blue?"

"And greens."

"Oboyoboyoboy." He grinned happily.

"And tonight we'll go out for dinner. Your choice."

"Long John Silver's?"

"You got it, pal."

"Whoooooossshhhhh . . . Turn up the radio, please," said Major Bludd.

The large blue eyes twinkled with charm. Buck thought again that Adam Jeffrey had the looks and presence to be in the movies, though he knew better than to encourage the idea. As Bruce Springsteen's voice filled the Porsche, sea gulls soared overhead in an ever-changing mosaic. The roar of the Pacific and the ubiquitous southern California sun drowned the senses. Just another shitty day in paradise, thought Buck with a moody laugh, and steered his car up to the security gate. Potential intruders, mostly young girls holding mementos to autograph, clustered on the other side. They were kept under watchful eyes by three guards, part of the team responsible for one of the strictest security systems ever designed. Burt Reynolds, Goldie Hawn, Martin Sheen, and Alan Alda did not plunk down millions for a homestead to have their privacy easily violated.

Buck flashed a smile to one of the guards, then flipped up his dark glasses in front of the celebrity worshipers. Buck owned traditional Hollywood good looks—jet-black hair, lazy doe-brown eyes, a strong nose—with a way of setting his jaw that said, nicely, "don't mess with me, pal." He kept his figure slim with daily visits to a spa and his face youthful with a rigorous mix of vitamins and herbs. Yet as he stared at the group of young ladies, no one rushed an auto-graph pad toward his window.

The story of his life, Buck thought with rekindled frus-tration. He thrust the Porsche into second and headed onto the highway. There was no worse fate in Hollywood than to be a star in eclipse. Today was supposed to change his fortunes, but Buck was skeptical. His agent, Sidney Pomerantz, a cigar-smoking glad-hander who'd been camped in Hollywood since he was seventeen—when he stood on Sunset Boulevard and hawked maps to stars' homes—had arranged an interview with *Image* magazine at Buck's Malibu home this morning. Everything had been set—Buck was going to keep Adam Jeffrey home so he could be in the photographs too—when the *Image* reporter had called with dizzy breathlessness to say she was running late. Would Buck mind meeting her at the Griffith Park Equestrian Center where she was wrapping up a *more im-portant* story? Her name was Rachel Lang—Buck had met her last year at a Warren Beatty cocktail party—and in the category of striking *and* intelligent women, Buck would place her near the top. That made it all the harder to dislike her for putting him down.

The *Image* article would be a nostalgic look at the orig-inal cast of *Citizen Army*, a sort of what-are-they-doing-now thing. The sixties antecedent to *The A-Team*, *Citizen Army* had endured seven years in prime time and enjoyed re-run status with a die-hard core of devoted fans, including an overseas contingent that stretched as far as Hong Kong. A few of the faithful still wrote to Buck, saying how much they loved his role as a strong/silent John Wayne type who meted out justice. In his glory days there had been other TV shows for Buck, and many roles he turned down. Critics compared him to Robert Wagner and David Janssen for projecting a small-screen intimacy that viewers found believable.

Buck's star had continued in its ascendancy until the early seventies, when Sidney convinced him that he should make the jump from TV to the movies. The lure of more money, greater celebrity, and artistic freedom were irresist-

ible to Buck. But the first film had a trashy screenplay—
Sidney urged his client to grab it anyway, promising that
good acting overcame anything—and it was yanked from
theaters after two morbid weeks. The second, a Western
called *Sunset Ride*, did even worse. The third was never
completed because the director got into a pissing match
over artistic control with the producers, who finally pulled
the plug in revenge. Buck, tail firmly between his legs,
knocked again on television producers' doors, only to learn
he wasn't wanted anymore. Behind their polite smiles,
Buck sensed, everybody was laughing at him. They wanted
to teach him a lesson for his pretense to big-screen stardom.
Sidney, repentant himself, did his best for Buck. In the last
ten years there'd been guest shots here and there, sometimes a variety-show appearance, but no offers came for a
series of his own. Though Buck owned his Malibu home
clear, having bought it when he was flush with cash, his
income from re-runs was only adequate, while expenses
seemed to creep ahead every day. A new series, he told
Sidney almost every time they met, would help nicely, and
more importantly, allow him to regain his place in the sun.

The Porsche turned off Sunset Boulevard onto Doheny
and glided toward the First Step Day Care Center. In a new
brick Colonial building, the preschool was staffed with experienced teachers and had plenty of educational materials,
but for $5,000 for his son's kindergarten year, Buck didn't
expect anything less. He scooped up Adam Jeffrey's lunch
box from the back seat and took his son's hand as they
marched toward the building. Adam Jeffrey was embarrassed by kisses in front of the other children, so Buck, as
always, gave him a parting embrace at the door.

"Knock 'em dead, A.J.," Buck said affectionately.

"I love you, Daddy."

"Love you too, son."

The way Adam Jeffrey waved good-bye before slipping
inside reminded Buck of the boy's mother, a thought that
gave him a jolt of discomfort despite the three tranquil years
since the divorce. When Buck had married Ava Wine in
1971, she was a young actress of limited talent but shatter-
ing beauty, a fresh-faced, deep-voiced blonde who could

charm a snake in its sleep. She easily charmed Buck, at the time on top of the heap with his success in *Citizen Army*. Ava promptly abandoned her career to settle in the comfort that came with a husband's success. As a fashionable young couple they made the rounds of the Hollywood parties. Gossip, which energized the town's central nervous system like a little white pill, quickly wrapped its arms around Buck and Ava. What made them not just Hollywood's darlings, but *interesting* darlings, was Buck's predilection for giving away money. He had met Warren Beatty at a party, listened to the actor espouse his left-wing causes, and when Buck was asked if he'd donate something for Cesar Chavez and the migrant grape pickers in California, he saw no reason to say no. He had lots of spare cash, commonly referred to in his circles as "fuck-you money," and there was something about being on top that filled Buck with stirrings of guilt. Why should he be living so well, he asked Ava, when a lot of people were suffering? He had a moral obligation to help, didn't he?

The first time Ava didn't put up resistance, but when Buck continued his philanthropy, she dug in her heels. "You're like a hyperkinetic kid on a sugar binge," she said. "You practically begged Jane Fonda to take you with her to Hanoi! When are we going to start spending money on *ourselves*? We could buy a nicer home, a new car, and how about my clothes?"

Ava, with a flat-pitched voice that could break a brick at fifty yards, grew less charming and more demanding. Buck didn't enjoy the tirades, and almost out of spite, continued with his largesse. They agreed on a divorce in the summer of 1976, though by then Buck was floundering with his movies and had curtailed his spending. Two years later they reconciled, remarried, and Ava became pregnant with Adam Jeffrey in celebration. But Buck's inability to rebound in the industry fueled more fights—Ava claimed his left-wing causes had gotten him blacklisted—and a second divorce became inevitable. The custody fight over Adam Jeffrey was finally resolved when Ava, in a Jaguar XKE driven by a nineteen-year-old punk rocker, collided with a Mack truck on the Golden State Freeway. Adam Jeffrey, only two, was told his mother had gone to live with the angels. Buck thought otherwise.

It was a quarter to ten when Buck pulled into the parking lot of the $15 million Griffith Park Equestrian Center, careful to straddle two spaces to better preserve his Porsche. The recently completed seventy-four acre complex stood directly across from the Park and was a living testimony to the equine pleasures of jumping, riding, polo, and show competition. It was a shrine to the horse lovers of Southern California, which boasted more horse ranches per capita than any area in the world. Buck himself wasn't exactly a stranger to the four-legged creatures. Growing up as Henry Hartzell on his grandparents' ranch in Idaho, he had roped calves on a local rodeo circuit, entered and won several cross-country races, and broken in a fair number of ornery stallions. In his first TV drama he'd played a down-and-out cowboy, one of the few roles he'd genuinely felt comfortable in.

Buck strolled past the 4000-seat indoor equidome where polo was played and found the stables Rachel Lang had designated as a rendezvous. Several young ladies in rust-colored jodhpurs, navy jackets, and paddock boots clustered around a jumping arena. They were prim and proper enough to be on a fox hunt, and Buck offered his most affable smile. The return stares were blank, even distrustful. With a stoic breath Buck marched into the tack room adjoining the stables.

He found the *Image* reporter looking very comfortable, wearing snug jeans and a flannel shirt, perched on a bale of hay, peering over her glasses as her pencil raced across her notepad. The man she was interviewing, a handsome Arab gentleman who might have been on the cover of *GQ*, was talking in perfect English about his horses. Buck waved to make sure Rachel knew he was there, then sat back to wait his turn. In her late twenties, Rachel was tall, slim, graceful, and athletic-looking. Her face was definitely feminine, with its well-proportioned features and peaches-and-cream complexion, and the fine blond hair that fell almost to her shoulders reminded Buck of Adam Jeffrey's. The sparkle in her eye made her appear too sensual to call wholesome, yet there was something so intense and businesslike about her that it put her beauty at a distance. As at the earlier cocktail party, Buck found her intriguing.

He stood at a respectful distance, trying to be polite and patient, but close enough to pick up the conversation. Buck had learned the art of eavesdropping long ago, a necessary skill at Hollywood parties when a producer on the other side of the room was telling someone he was looking for an actor. The Arab, as Buck digested the facts, was from Bahrain, an archipelago off the eastern coast of Saudi Arabia, in the Persian Gulf. It was an oasis of enlightenment compared to other Arab countries. Men could drink, women didn't wear veils, movies and television were plentiful and uncensored; there was even a horse track for betting. Zallaq Al-Khalifa's claim to fame consisted of being the brother of the emir of Bahrain. Zallaq was also, not coincidentally, president of the national petroleum company. More germane in *Image*'s eyes, he had just donated $2 million to the Griffith Park Equestrian Center because he loved the United States, and above all loved horses, particularly fast ones. That was an Arab's prerogative, Zallaq told Rachel Lang with pride, because most race horses could trace their bloodlines to Arabia. The definition of a thoroughbred, after all, was a horse whose ancestry was linked to one of three founding sires imported into England from North Africa and the Near East: the Byerly Turk, the Godolphin Arabian, and the Darley Arabian. In all cases descent was through one of those three horses' sons: Eclipse, foaled in 1764, the year of the Great Eclipse of the sun, was great-great-grandson of the Darley Arabian; Matchem, foaled in 1748, a grandson of the Godolphin Arabian; and Herod, foaled in 1758, the great-great-grandson of the Byerly Turk.

Zallaq then spoke of some top quarter horses he'd recently purchased and now planned to race in the United States. Buck gathered that the man was enamored of speed. For someone who earned $20 million in a slow week, there wasn't much Zallaq couldn't automatically possess, but the world's fastest horse was one of them. Which was probably why he was so determined to own it, Buck thought. The quest was as much scientific as romantic. Why was it, Zallaq asked Rachel, that while human athletes were continually improving their running speeds, horses today could run no faster than their ancestors fifty or one hundred years ago? In 1954 Roger Bannister was a hero for shattering the four-minute mile; today any serious miler could do better. But the fastest quarter mile ever run by a horse happened in Mexico City in 1945—20.80 seconds—by a colt named Big Racket. No horse since had come close to breaking that record. With advances in genetic engineering, Zallaq asked, why shouldn't a breeder be able to improve a horse's speed? Then the Arab admitted that in fact he had formed his own bioengineering company to pursue just such a goal.

When the interview concluded, the Arab gallantly gave Rachel a departing kiss. Buck found himself envying Zallaq's smoothness with women, not to mention his position of privilege and wealth in the world. As Buck shook Rachel's hand and said hello, he knew the Arab would be a tough act to follow. Still, as Rachel began her questions, Buck kept his feelings of inadequacy at bay.

Had he been able to keep in touch with the other actors from *Citizen Army*? "I've tried to, Ms. Lang, but we've all drifted in different directions." Did he miss the series? "Not really. It was fun and a challenge at the time, but an actor outgrows his roles." Did he regret trying to jump from television to the movies? "Acting is taking risks. That's the name of the profession." The questions continued for another fifteen minutes. It wasn't a bad interview, Buck decided, but he was annoyed there'd been no photographer to snap his picture. Restless, he glanced at Rachel as she closed her notepad, suddenly recalling some gossip about the reporter that picked up his spirits.

"Ms. Lang, would you like to join me for a drink?" Buck asked chivalrously.

"No, thank you. I've got a deadline to meet." The honey-sweet voice was polite but firm.

"Hey, come on," coaxed Buck. "You've never seen my place. We can take a walk on the beach, have a drink, talk—"

"It's very sweet of you to ask," Rachel interrupted, "but I can't."

Buck, undaunted, and banking on the direct approach, circled an arm around Rachel's shoulder. "I understand," he said, "that it's your signature to *really* get to know the stars that you interview."

Rachel pulled off her glasses. She looked pained and embarrassed for a moment, but made a quick recovery. "It was nice chatting with you, Mr. Hart," she said, extending her hand. "Good luck with your projects."

She managed a tight smile before closing her briefcase and hurrying off. Buck felt stupid and clumsy for what he'd done. Rachel Lang probably thought he was a total jerk. When you were down, you were really down, Buck decided. A familiar self-pity washed over him as he meandered out of the complex toward the parking lot.

From out of nowhere a voice stopped him. "Buck Hart?"

He turned and saw it was the Arab, Zallaq. Shaking his head in curiosity as the man approached, Buck ignored him, fumbling for the keys to his Porsche. But Zallaq wouldn't go away, calling Buck's name again. The actor managed a faint, indifferent smile. What did one of the world's richest men want with him anyway? "You are Buck Hart, aren't you?" Zallaq persisted. "Buck Hart, the television star? I'm sorry I didn't recognize you earlier—"

"What?" said Buck.

"I'm a great fan of yours, Mr. Hart. In my country your shows are very popular."

Buck slowly pumped the Arab's hand. Then the squeeze grew warmer and more grateful. This, thought Buck, could be the start of a beautiful friendship.

"This is a great honor for me," said Zallaq.

"It's always a pleasure to talk to my fans," Buck answered adroitly. Really, it was a joke—Zallaq treating *him* like a god?

"Are you working on a new show now?" the Arab inquired.

"Actually, I'm in-between shootings." Far in-between, he thought.

"Then you're not busy right now. Not this moment?"

"Actually—"

"Would you do me the honor of having lunch with us? I have a date with some employees of my bioengineering company."

"Well—"

"Please. We'd all be flattered."

The Arab would be treating, Buck knew, so why not? It felt good, oh so good, to be recognized again. With another handshake, Buck graciously accepted.

The lunch, at the Bistro Gardens in Beverly Hills, turned out to be anything but a normal business meeting. The party included two biologists, a veterinarian, a horse breeder, Zallaq and Buck. The maître d' sat them in the restaurant's garden room, where each table had an umbrella and fresh flowers and the waiters were as aloof as the clientele. Except for a few standard Hollywood anecdotes and a story about his horse days in Idaho, which everyone found entertaining, Buck kept silent. The discussion focused on experiments in horse embryonic transplants, increasing sperm motility, and advances in artificial insemination. The Jockey Club, the official organization that registered thoroughbreds in the United States, forbade reproduction that wasn't natural. But with quarter horses, which were registered by the Quarter Horse Association out of Amarillo, Texas, artificial breeding, within limits, was permitted. That, said Zallaq, was one reason he was so infatuated with quarter horses.

Between rounds of drinks the research chief of Zallaq's bioengineering company explained to Buck how they had taken the romance out of horse breeding and with the help of the computer made it into big business. Until the advent of digital technology breeders had to match sires and dams by consulting pedigree information yearbooks and examining race results in the *Daily Racing Form*. But now, by loading a computer with concentrated information on some 400,000 quarter horsess, Zallaq had evolved what he called a Standard Starts Index that allowed him to compare racing records of horses across generations and thereby predict which gene pools might produce the fastest horses. He also rated each horse alive today by a system called "dosages," where a number was assigned to characteristics such as a horse's sprinting ability, stamina, longevity at the track; on a statistical basis he could then calculate which horse had the best shot at winning.

Armed with that information, the scientist continued, Zallaq had spent the past few years acquiring sires and dams with the highest dosage ratings and the most superior gene pools. He was determined, with the latest advances in breeding techniques, to make a super-horse from these bloodlines. In fact, the research chief confided after a nod from Zallaq, they had already "created" just such an animal. The horse was something akin to a test-tube baby. A fertilized egg had been surgically removed from the uterus of a pregnant broodmare named Mountain Wind, which had topped Zallaq's dosage scale. The sire, Prince of the Desert, had equally impeccable qualifications. The broodmare's egg was fertilized and then injected with special hormones, and replanted in the uterus. Eleven months later, the average gestation period for a horse, a very special foal was born. A yearling now, the colt named Desert Wind was faster than any creature God had naturally made, Zallaq said. In a 300-yard race for yearlings at Blue Ribbon Downs in Oklahoma, Desert Wind had won by seven lengths in a strong field. Buck was impressed. A seven-length victory in an eight furlong race was eminently respectable, but to win by that margin over 300 yards was unheard of.

"What are you going to do with your horse?" Buck inquired.

"When he's two in January," said Zallaq, "we're going to race him seriously. He's got the strength, speed, and stamina of a stallion. We think he can win the All-American Futurity. The publicity from that victory would be of incalculable advantage to our business. Have you heard of the 5555 Ranch? Someone named Meredith Kingsley?"

"No," Buck answered to both questions.

"I was at her party several weeks ago. It was Meredith Kingsley's horse who won this year's All-American. She's confident she can win again next year. I want to prove her wrong."

"If what you say about Desert Wind is true," Buck interjected, "I don't see how any horse could beat him."

"We don't either, but we want to take one race at a time."

"Best of luck," Buck said cordially.

Zallaq's face filled with a smile. "Excuse me for being presumptuous, but I was wondering if you'd like to help us."

Buck squinted back with amiable curiosity.

"For some time I've been thinking of ways to publicize my horse and bioengineering company. Desert Wind isn't your normal quarter horse. He's a miracle. So far we've kept his breeding a secret, but starting January we want a public relations campaign. We want to establish a breeding operation that will transform ranches everywhere, and make our company a small fortune. Frankly, we intend to revolutionize horse breeding and racing. No one has ever done that, not the way we intend to."

"That sound promising," Buck observed, "but just how would I fit in?"

"It may sound unscientific to have a Hollywood celebrity in our campaign, but we don't mind being splashy. Celebrities endorse and publicize everything else, and we want you to help us with our horse."

"You want me?" said an astonished Buck. Sidney Pomerantz would swallow his cigar.

"Of course. You know horses, don't you? And you are a celebrity."

Buck drew a contemplative breath. The offer was generous and flattering. But something didn't feel right. He couldn't see himself being at Zallaq's beck and call, or running around the country preaching the glories of Desert Wind while missing out on opportunities on the home front. "I would really love to help you gentlemen out," Buck said kindly, "but I don't think I'm going to have the time."

"Are you sure?" said a disappointed Zallaq.

"Yeah, I'm sorry. You'll have no trouble finding somebody else."

Buck excused himself. He was convinced his decision had been the right one. No doubt Sidney would agree. But halfway to the spa for his afternoon workout, Buck was given to second thoughts. Maybe publicizing a horse could help his career. Other Hollywood personalities were associated with race horses—Jack Klugman, Mike Nichols, Sam Shepard. It hadn't hurt them, had it? Race horses added a dimension of glamour and class to their lives; the public tended to see them in a new perspective. Buck needed *something* to pull him out of his tailspin. Maybe, just maybe . . .

Late that afternoon, after picking up A.J. at his day care center and indulging him with a double scoop of Häagen-Dazs, Buck put in a call to Zallaq.

II
Players

SIX

RACHEL LANG, ONE STEP BEHIND THE *IMAGE* PHOTOG-
rapher, fought for a place next to the filigreed wrought-iron
gate entrance to the Dallas cemetery known as Restland. As
the retinue of ebony-colored limos approached the gate,
headlights blazing in the cool fall morning, a swell of humanity held back by a dozen security guards began to shout
angrily and ball their fists in Christian outrage. Other spectators, the sort who flocked to Evel Knievel death jumps or
a coroner's inquest of grisly murders, looked on with mischievous delight. Still others that Rachel had interviewed
thought of the burial this morning as a flashy and grotesque
public relations stunt scripted by a Hollywood studio. As
the lead limo passed through the gates, the *Image* photographer raised his Nikon F3 and aimed the 180 mm tele-
photo lens at Austin Mirabeau.

"Did you get him?" Rachel asked her companion, a
lanky, bearded black man in a red beret. The other limos
slowed momentarily to edge past the spectators, then
jerked forward one at a time like an impossibly long cen-
tipede.

"I think so. You know," he said, changing rolls of film,
"I've been on a lot of assignments, but this gets the prize—
burying a horse in a human cemetery."

"Maybe it has something to do with Texans," Rachel
suggested. "Next time it'll be E.T. they want to bury."

Summoning her considerable charms, Rachel once

again approached the security guard at the gate. Despite brushing her tongue over her teeth and batting her large gray-blue eyes, she was stonily refused admission. Funeral services were meant to be a very private affair, the guard with unruly, spiked hair lectured her—especially this one. Rachel surrendered and walked back to her photographer.

In a way, she understood. The funeral was certainly a *sensitive* affair. The interment of King's Ransom had been a hot item in the Dallas media for a week, ever since Mirabeau's attorneys had successfully fought off the Texas attorney general's efforts to block the burial. Citing an obscure Texas statute that forbade animals to be interred or cremated in a human burial park, the attorney general's office had gone to court to argue that God Himself would be offended at the sacrilege. But the Mirabeau attorneys had told the judge that the animal in question was no ordinary horse, and that if not tragically struck down in his prime, he would have become perhaps the greatest quarter horse in history. How could the court deny their client his choice of a burial site, which happened to be next to Austin Mirabeau's family plot?

Despite the man's professed sorrow, it was Rachel's suspicion that Austin Mirabeau was simply grandstanding, making a public display of his grief. All she had to do to prove it was get an interview. Telling her photographer to wait, Rachel sneaked through the crowd and hurried toward a service entrance down the road, but not before paying twenty dollars for a bouquet of yellow roses at a road-stand florist. If she wasn't resourceful enough to find a way in, Rachel told herself, she should turn in her press card. Mr. Mirabeau had twice refused her an interview in his downtown Dallas office. This was her last, best hope.

Personally, she wished to God that Frank Beardsley had never sent her to Texas, but the *Image* editor had lately become horse-blind. First there'd been a story about Robert Redford personally leading a roundup of wild mustangs in the canyons of Nevada, then Jack Klugman's love affair with his thoroughbreds, and finally that Arab in Los Angeles, Zallaq, with his search for the world's fastest horse. Now it was a crazy Texan with an outsize ego who'd been overheard to swear revenge for the death of his beloved King's Ransom; high drama, Lone Star chapter.

Rachel might have mustered more enthusiasm for her story, but after four years with *Image* she knew that even the most profound dramas and conflicts she wrote about were ultimately chopped by editors into digestible tidbits for a readership more interested in photos than text. Rachel longed to sink her teeth into something with substance, at least scratch the surface not with a fingernail file but a crowbar. When she'd graduated from journalism school at Northwestern six years ago, she'd come to Manhattan bent on instant stardom as ace reporter. *Newsweek*, *Time*, or *The New York Times* would do nicely, she'd thought. Despite her considerable skills and glowing references, she had zilch experience and humbly accepted a copyediting job at McGraw-Hill. Eventually she became editor of a trade journal. The work was as exciting as doing her income taxes.

When a colleague mentioned an opening at *Image*, Rachel jumped at the chance. Selected over twenty other candidates, she basked in the warm smile of Lady Fortune. Her parents and friends were thrilled, and at first so was Rachel. The pay wasn't exactly great, but she jetted here and there to interview celebrities who'd overcome their alcoholism or survived radical mastectomies, was privy to behind-the-scenes gossip about theater and film productions, wrote profile pieces about a Nazi hunter in South America and the discovery of a 200,000-year-old man in Africa. She soon was everyone's darling. And why not? Pretty, bright, and eager to write down as gospel everything she was told, she didn't really comprehend how much she was being manipulated. Invited to chic restaurants, Beverly Hills "snow" parties where cocaine was as common as the swimming pools, on private jets that whisked her to secluded Mexican beaches, Rachel was only too happy to make herself available. After the pressures and drudgery of the trade journals, this was heaven. Invitations to bedrooms were dispensed as easily as a handshake, and Rachel found herself succumbing too often. It was all beyond her wildest fantasies, making love with the rich and famous on yachts, in planes, once in a French château. If she'd been in the blackmail business, she might have retired a millionaire.

But after a couple of wild, fun years the novelty had worn thin. She'd grown colder and more detached from the people she interviewed. It was bad enough that almost every celebrity tried to make her, but then the goddamn magazine scrambled all her facts around anyway. There was also the problem of dealing with men like Buck Hart. There was no shortage of Bucks in this world, down-and-out dreamers who'd lost their place in the sun and now wanted desperately to reclaim it. She should know; she'd slept with a few of them.

In more contemplative moments she couldn't help wondering if her problem with men wasn't *her* fault. She was intelligent and physically attractive, so maybe she wasn't being serious. But she didn't just have casual affairs for the thrill of being liberated; in her heart of hearts she really *was* looking for Mr. Right. The fantasy persisted that around the next street corner she'd bump into the perfect physical, emotional, and moral specimen who would become Her Husband, and Her Life would finally begin.

The problem was, she just hadn't found the right street corner, and time was running out. At twenty-nine she was closing in on the rocky shoals of her fourth decade. Most of her friends were wondering if it was time to have kids. Rachel just wanted a man to love. But if you weren't married by thirty, she'd been warned by her mother since grade school, you might as well apply to the federal government for a disaster loan.

After a five minute walk, her bouquet of yellow roses in hand, Rachel approached the service entrance to Restland. She smoothed the wrinkles from her black dress and flashed a smile to the overweight young man whose uniform pinched his neck. "Excuse me, sir," she murmured sweetly. "Ah've been tryin' to visit ma father's grave, but there's such a commotion at the main gate—"

"I know all about it," the young man answered, genuinely concerned.

"Ah was hopin' ah could git in this way." Rachel wondered if her half-ass Texas accent was fooling anybody.

"Right this way, m'am," the guard answered solicitously. He started to escort her up the footpath that led to the grassy knolls of Restland.

"That's quite all right," Rachel said, "Ah can find my own way."

Left alone, she hurried toward the distant rows of parked limousines, finally glimpsing the stately mausoleum that had been erected as King's Ransom's final home. The horse had been buried several days ago, locked behind heavy bronze doors and fluted limestone columns, with a pair of lions' heads at the entrance that surveyed half of Dallas. The crowd gathered today were the official mourners: the trainer, jockey, and grooms, who to the man loved the horse like a son (so the sympathetic Dallas media had reported); the elite of the Texas horse breeding crowd; and the oil, gas, and real estate magnates, who for reasons of tax shelters or a sheer romance with horses, owned syndicated shares in Mirabeau Ranch's stud horses, and whose absence today would have been impolitic.

Rachel squeezed into the back row of mourners while a clergyman read from the Book of Psalms. He was followed by a flowery-voiced soprano who gave new meaning to Mendelssohn's *Hymn of Praise*. As the crowd dispersed, Rachel watched well-wishers flock around Mr. Mirabeau and his wife. Approaching him now, she knew, would be an obvious tactical error. Instead she circled around the phalanx of limos until she reached the one in front. Mirabeau's chauffeur was gone. Taking a breath, Rachel climbed in. This was the part of journalism she both loved and hated: loved because of the challenge of confronting a reluctant subject; hated because of the unpredictability of the outcome. Nothing felt very certain today. Rachel was sure she'd been in stranger places for an interview, but nothing came to mind.

The car door swung open abruptly and Austin Mirabeau stared in.

Calmly, Rachel introduced herself. She had tried for an

interview at Mr. Mirabeau's office, she explained, but with
no luck. Austin's dark, brooding eyes registered confusion,
then disbelief, and finally fury.

"I'm not talking to reporters, Miss. Not in a period of
grieving. Now I'd be right pleased if you left my car."

"Just one or two questions, Mr. Mirabeau."

"No, m'am. No questions, no answers."

"Did Meredith Kingsley attend the service today?"

"I'm asking you nicely, Miss. If you need a ride, I can
put you in another limo."

"Our readers would like to know if it's true you threatened Meredith Kingsley's life?"

"That's bullshit!"

Austin's face paled in shock.

"Her property?"

Angry silence.

"We have several sources," Rachel continued, trying to
stay cool. This man acted as if he were ready to do something. She'd always had a sense of survival, knowing with
finesse or the right words she could pull through any situation, but at the moment her heart had caught in her throat.
"A bartender at The Palm heard you saying to a friend—"

The notepad suddenly flew from Rachel's hand. A
burly arm reached over from behind and wrapped around
her shoulders. She was too startled and frightened to look
back. Austin said nothing as his associate pulled Rachel like
a piece of luggage from the Cadillac and calmly deposited
her on the curbside of Restland. Most of the other limos had
already vanished, but the few stragglers who saw Rachel did
nothing to help. You goddamn bunch of clannish Texans,
she thought, outraged as she picked herself up. At least in
Hollywood she was treated like a lady.

Rachel had only a few seconds to examine herself for
bodily damage when the beeper in her handbag went off.
When she finally got to a phone and called her editor, she
was still furious and told Frank Beardsley so.

"Well, you've still alive, aren't you?" he said cheerfully.
Frank was such an optimist, she thought. The Russians
could drop a bomb on the capital and he would be doing
cartwheels about the news story.

"I thought you were supposed to get mugged in New York, not in a cemetery," Rachel answered. "I deserve hazardous duty pay." And she meant it. Her salary as a reporter was embarrassing. She lived practically hand to mouth. If it weren't for her expense account, she'd be applying for food stamps.

"I've got something to cheer you up," Frank said. "A great story."

"Not about horses again—"

"Of course it's about horses. Horses are what's happening in this country right now. Horses are what people like to read about. And I'm designating you horse-reporter-at-large."

"Terrific."

"Do I detect a note of cynicism?"

"What's the story?" Rachel said in resignation.

"A stringer just phoned this in from a city called Sherman. I checked a map, it's an hour or so from Dallas. I want you up there, pronto."

"What's in Sherman?"

"Ties in beautifully with Austin Mirabeau. You said he threatened the owner of that other horse, Four Aces—"

"So?" The tender spot behind Rachel's eyes was starting to throb. All she wanted was a glass of water and twenty aspirin.

"So the very same Meredith Kingsley just called the police, and probably the Texas Rangers, the FBI, the CIA, and maybe the president. The woman is really freaking out. Someone kidnapped one of her horses. A very special one too."

"More fun and games."

"Could be a great story," Frank prodded her. "This Austin Mirabeau character must have a lot of balls."

"Tell me about it," Rachel said, and with a why-me-God sigh, motioned to her photographer to hand her the road map.

SEVEN

THE PAN AM 747 FROM MIAMI SWOOPED OUT OF THE SKY, its shadow lengthening on the blue Atlantic, and touched down on a distant runway at Ezeiza. With a sigh of amazement Billy Sullivan studied the monstrous, sprawling Buenos Aires airport, conceived by Perón at the height of his power as the largest, grandest airport in the world. But even today it was badly underutilized. The sprawling monument to folly demanded two hours of patience before Billy could clear customs and pile his luggage into a rattletrap taxi. From the heavily trafficked highway he spied the vagrant plumes of smoke rising from the villas miseria on the city's outskirts. The sprawl of shantytowns seemed unstoppable, growing more populous each time Billy visited. When he finally entered Buenos Aires proper, he rolled down his window to enjoy the capital's fine October spring. Despite its poverty and inconveniences, he loved this city, the Paris of South America. The cosmopolitan mix of people and architecture, and an historical richness, helped it transcend its temporal problems. For a moment Billy focused on the polo he would play in the next few days, and on seeing Aymara and her father, Señor Olguin. Part pleasure, part business, he thought, but it was the business part that was his real reason for coming south.

The taxi ferried him past the famous obelisk in the Plaza de la Republica and dropped him at the hotel opposite Plaza San Martín. The spacious, meticulously cared for square was named after the famous general, El Libertador himself, patron saint of Argentina. Almost every city in the country, Billy knew, boasted a street or plaza or building for the man who had defied the wishes of Spain and declared independence for his country; Buenos Aires had a good dozen.

Billy signaled to a bellhop to take his bags. The young man eyed him back, sizing him up as a tipper. The Plaza Hotel was too touristy for Billy's taste—too many Americans and Germans who inevitably called the city "Bway-ness Airs" and went around asking to have their photos taken with a real live gaucho—but the accommodations were relatively cheap. When he'd first come here to play polo, he had always stayed at the Sheraton, maybe the finest and most expensive hotel in Argentina, and he missed now the comforts and status that the best always conferred. At least, he thought, his polo wouldn't cost him anything this trip. In the past he'd purchased enough top-flight ponies, paying up to $25,000 each, to warrant favored treatment from ranchers and players intent on selling him still more. His hosts always wined and dined him and scheduled tournaments for Billy to play in. Everyone still thought he was rich from his father's estate, an illusion that carried too many advantages for Billy to dispel.

When he'd showered and changed, he called for another taxi. As agreed when Olguin had phoned him two weeks ago in Palm Beach, Billy was to meet the courtly old gentleman promptly at four at his gallery. The art dealer could be fussy and demanding, especially when it came to time, and Billy, as if he saw his own father in the old man, didn't want to disappoint him. As the taxi weaved through the crowded streets, he studied the automatic-weapon-toting soldiers who seemed ubiquitous, even more than on his last trip. Argentina had a nervous, unsettled quality to its life. Government repression, rampant inflation, poverty, and political scandal combined to give off the scent of trouble, a powder keg about to explode. But these were only facts of life to Buenos Aires natives, called *porteños*, who went about their lives as if nothing could be done about their problems. Or maybe, as Olguin liked to tell Billy, they were waiting for another Juan Perón and Eva to rise from the working class with a new brand of justicialismo.

Billy reached Calle Florida, with its curious but attractive mix of boutiques, art galleries, cafés, and high rises, and entered Señor Olguin's musty Galería Santa Fe. Faded and scarred Colonial-period oils haphazardly lined the walls, and on tables were wooden icons and religious statuary of dubious quality. José Olguin's was hardly a prestige gallery among the art cognoscenti, Billy knew, but the old man managed to draw a number of patrons, and his collection easily fooled and impressed tourists. His really valuable oils, with their deep patinas and famous signatures, were never sold in the gallery.

From behind a tattered curtain an elfish figure suddenly appeared with a face of deep crags and a bemused, intelligent smile. The eyes, always skeptical, were magnified by thick lenses and pored over Billy now as if the art dealer hadn't seen the young man in a decade. Olguin embraced him and bade Billy sit at a dusty corner table.

"It's so good to see you, Billy Sullivan," he said in decent English, as he clasped his hands around the young man's with approval. "It's been so long."

"I was here two months ago," Billy reminded him gently.

"It might as well have been two years. Inflation is up twenty-two percent, my clients aren't buying, I've got bills, and you know my daughter. . . ."

Billy smiled patiently, already familiar with the litany of complaints. The proud, fussy man threw his hands up, looking disgusted and helpless, a cue that it was time to discuss business, particularly with the shop empty at the moment. Billy silently followed the art dealer to a back room, where a half-dozen polo mallets had already been dismantled and put back together. To make his ruse more effective, Olguin used the top mallet on the market, Casa Villamil, which was made locally. Deep holes almost an inch in diameter had diligently been drilled into the nine-inch-long heads, which were fashioned either of sycamore or ash, the latter being the heavier wood and preferred by players who wanted heft, while sycamore offered greater quickness and finesse. But these mallets were not meant for any match. Billy picked up and examined one carefully. No one would have guessed that a tightly rolled canvas was inside the hollowed-out head. A wood plug, sanded down and varnished, covered the hole almost seamlessly.

Olguin did his work well, Billy thought. He had already made five trips from Argentina back to Miami with the doctored mallets, and never once had he been suspected of carrying contraband. Being an international polo star was a perfect cover. And Miami customs agents were so intent on ferreting out drugs, their trained dogs sniffing innocuously at his mallets, that Billy had to smile. Once he got past customs, he sold the valuable oils of saints and martyrs to a middleman in Palm Beach, who paid handsomely for the historical works that the Argentine government forbade anyone to sell or buy, let alone "export" as Olguin did. But the art dealer had no compunction about breaking the law. He needed the money as much as Billy did, and the Argentines had always justified committing small crimes in the name of survival. Olguin didn't even strenuously hide his caper. Friends knew he was up to something, as did some of the polo players Billy hung around. What people didn't know was the amount of money involved. The five trips had grossed over $140,000 with Billy keeping a fourth for being the courier.

Initially he'd had reservations about helping Olguin, but it wasn't exactly drugs he was smuggling, just harmless old paintings. Once he made his first run, he even liked being a courier—the sense of danger was a high, not unlike playing polo—but lately, with his debts escalating, the missions had taken on a more urgent, less dramatic nature.

As the two walked back into the gallery, Billy told Olguin when he would be leaving—he had two tournaments to play in, that was all—and a time was arranged for him to pick up the mallets on his way to the airport. Business out of the way, the old man fixed them both hot tea and they sat at the table again. As always, Olguin began to reminisce about the old days, when he'd been one of his country's top polo players, and how he'd first met Billy's father in an exhibition match at Hurlingham. The British polo club, with its manicured grass, elegant Tudor buildings, and stodgy, old-boy traditions, was as impressive as any club in Mother England. Even when the Falkland Islands crisis reared its head and Argentina had turned decidedly anti-British, the traditions of Hurlingham had gone on unrepentant and undisturbed. Olguin finally got around to asking Billy about his life. It was then that Billy mentioned the quarter horse he'd won from Gallegos, and his plan to race him in the All-American Futurity next year.

"What do you know about horse racing?" Olguin said skeptically.

Once again Billy felt as if his father were interrogating him, and that he had to justify every step he took in life. "I know about horses, believe me," he answered confidently. "And I know El Cid has great potential. I plan to get a good trainer, pay the nomination fees for the All-American, and the horse will take care of the rest." He could see that Olguin regarded the answer as naive and simplistic, and maybe it was. But Billy was determined to accomplish something in his nomadic, unfulfilled life, and was annoyed with the old man's lack of faith. Didn't he believe Billy could make it happen? Didn't desire and motivation count for anything?

"So how's your polo?" Olguin got around to asking in the lingering silence.

"Fine," said Billy. "I'm playing better than ever. Tomorrow I've got a match at Palermo Park with your best players, including Gallegos. I'd like to beat him again," Billy added.

"And so you will!" the art dealer toasted cheerily, changing his tone as he raised his teacup.

The conversation drifted back to the fierce polo Olguin had once played with Billy's father, but after a while the old man fell into a troubled silence, and he peered at his watch. He was expecting Aymara, Billy knew from their earlier phone conversation, and as usual she was late. The independent young lady kept her own schedule, flouting her father's values, and there was nothing he could do about it. In a way, Billy considered, it was Olguin's own fault. After his wife had died nearly a decade ago, he had come to worship his daughter for the beauty and spirit she had gotten from her mother. Even her name—from the Indians in the Bolivian mountains—summoned the image of someone special. So he had spoiled Aymara shamelessly—the best schools, the most expensive clothes, the highest social circles he could enter. She worked as a fashion designer for a couturier in the city, but she'd told everyone confidently that she had plans to start her own line of clothes. Over this precocious daughter old Olguin hovered and fawned, critical of most of the men she dated, determined that his Aymara, now twenty-three, would marry only the best. Someone to indulge and pamper her, Billy thought, as her father had done, as she was used to. Aymara was the old man's redemption, his reason for living—but also the reason for his debts.

The bells by the front door suddenly chimed, and both men's glances flew to the stunning young woman. The sun filtered through Aymara's lace dress as she rushed over to give Billy a warm hug, which he happily reciprocated. She retreated to her father, letting her arms drape playfully over his shoulders. Aymara looked more beautiful than ever, Billy thought. Tall and slender, she had high cheekbones and large eyes with a mischievous luster. Her complexion was flawless, her mouth thin and sensual. And her skin was light enough to betray only the smallest amount of Spanish blood. Her mother had been a United States citizen who, having fallen in love with Olguin, had promptly moved to Buenos Aires and changed her citizenship. Aymara's manner was so sophisticated, her English impeccable, that she could have been from any number of places.

"Welcome to Buenos Aires," Aymara said, leaving her father a moment to sit beside Billy.

"I was expecting you to meet me at the airport," he teased. He let his eyes parade over her again.

"How thoughtless of me. I was with a friend," she teased back.

"You mean I'm not as important as a friend? What am I?"

"I haven't decided," she said, still smiling.

"I take you out every time I'm here, don't I?"

"And I love your company," she said.

"How about tonight? Are you with your friend again, or can I take you to dinner?"

Aymara shook her head. Her smile dissolved and petulance crept into her voice. "I wish you'd told me earlier. Maybe we can get together tomorrow night."

Billy said nothing. There weren't many women who refused him like that, but Aymara liked to play little games—the more men pursuing her, the better—and Billy, despite being wiser, went along. The truth was he found Aymara totally intriguing. She knew it too, which only made her keep playing with him. In unguarded moments Billy imagined marrying her. Once, he'd even told her. Why not, he had thought, Aymara was beautiful and poised and talented. She was spoiled, true, but with time she'd mature. And they'd make a good couple, handsome and happy together.

Billy had gone to great lengths to hide the idea from Olguin. Aymara, of course, wanted him to be more open, but Billy knew good diplomacy. In the eye of the fussy art dealer, he was hardly worthy, neither rich nor famous enough to marry her. All that could change, Billy knew, if El Cid won at Ruidoso.

Billy rose from the table and said good-bye, promising to pick up Aymara tomorrow night after his match. At the door she was suddenly at his side. She circled her arms around him, in front of her father, as if to show Billy that she wasn't afraid to declare her emotions. Billy let her kiss him, but he couldn't help noticing Olguin's disapproving eyes.

Just as well that Aymara hadn't accepted his offer for dinner that night, Billy thought as he walked to his hotel, because he would have taken her out again tomorrow anyway. One evening would be expensive enough. Aymara always wanted to eat at the finest restaurant, hear the latest band, dance until morning. There was no one he knew quite like her, sheltered by her father, yet assertive and independent in her own right. She thought she had the world by the tail, and a woman like that wasn't easy to handle.

Six years ago Billy had fallen in love with a French girl with a similar temperament. Simone was very charming, a pretty blonde with classic European features, and very sure of herself. Her family owned a struggling bakery in Tours, a bourgeois city in the Loire Valley. To Simone and her family a polo star in their midst had the color and feel of a dream. Billy had a dream too. Tired of the polo circuit at the time, of too many long nights and faceless women, he wanted to marry this striking, headstrong girl and settle down. His father objected almost instantly. Simone wasn't quite right for him, he suggested quietly, but in a way that indicated total disapproval. Angry, Billy married her anyway. He didn't care if his father refused to attend the wedding. Billy saw the marriage as a triumph of his independence. But then things began to go wrong. Simone and he fought over everything—when to have children, about a house Billy wanted to purchase, spending Sunday afternoons with Simone's parents. Billy's friends sensed long-term disaster, and so did Simone's. Because Billy wasn't Catholic, the family was able, mercifully, to have the marriage annulled.

For three months Billy wandered around Europe in an uncharacteristic depression. He didn't want to see his father again, to have him say that he had been right about the marriage and Billy wrong. In Monte Carlo he ran up a gambling debt, then tried to run from it. Later he found his father had paid off the markers, which only made him furious. He gave up polo altogether, as if to cut any last family ties, and opened a small restaurant on the Left Bank. For a while he did fine, but his cooks kept quitting and he struggled to maintain a steady clientele. Finally an early morning fire and gas explosion put a sure end to the endeavor. The insurance coverage was inadequate. There were debts again. He waited, resigned, for his father to come to the rescue once more. Instead, after getting drunk at a Montmartre bistro one afternoon, he received a cable from Sam Cohen.

FATHER SUFFERED HEART ATTACK YESTERDAY P.M. SPENT UP AND DOWN NIGHT IN HOSPITAL. DIED THIS MORNING 10:15 NEW YORK TIME. FUNERAL ARRANGEMENTS PENDING. FLY HOME IMMEDIATELY.

The guilt had washed over Billy as he bought a plane ticket for the States—and since then, it had never left him. Even in death, he marveled, his father had maintained his grip.

At the Plaza Hotel Billy nursed a beer in a downstairs lounge and declined, out of fatigue, a dinner invitation from a local horse breeder. In his room he ordered a sandwich and another beer and dozed off. When he woke, the sky was dark and someone was pounding on his door.

"Who's there!" he shouted, but there was only more pounding. He opened the door reluctantly. Five uniformed soldiers and a young, angular-faced major blocked the threshold, their rifles breasted.

"*Identificatión! Cédula personal!*" the major demanded.

Billy retreated into his room for his jacket. The major's dark eyes swam over his passport photo, up to his face, and back to the passport again. He didn't seem happy, even though everything was in order. Billy lingered by the door to see if the soldiers approached the next room, but they only vanished down the stairs.

In the end he went back to bed. What the hell was going on? Soldiers acting like storm troopers, and in a tourist hotel? As much as he loved Buenos Aires, this might be his last visit for a while, he thought. He needed the money from Olguin, and he was infatuated with Aymara, but instinct warned him to stay away from a place so volatile. It was hours before he surrendered to a tenuous sleep and dreamed he was already back in Florida.

Billy saddled his horse for the first chukker, trying to ignore the raucous cheering. The Palermo Park stadium, a large, grassy setting in the heart of Buenos Aires—not unlike Central Park in New York—was still filling up with colorful humanity. Like in the fútbol games sometimes played here, the chanting of the crowd was at crescendo pitch. Spectators were not altogether friendly to non-Argentines, Billy knew from experience. In the States and England, matches were more formal, less passionate, but here the crowd added a dimension to the combat. Today's match was twenty-six goals, meaning that the combined handicaps of the players on each team had to equal that number. Billy's side included two Britons and a Frenchman, all of whom he respected as players. The Argentines boasted Gallegos and two other high-goalers, plus the seventeen-year-old son of a wealthy Cordova industrialist who was rated at three goals. The boy was clearly a ringer, probably playing several goals above his handicap—Gallegos's revenge, Billy thought, for his defeat in Palm Beach.

Billy handed his gelding back to a groom and examined the other horses put at his disposal. He'd ridden each and every one this morning, deciding in what order to use them. The geldings, colts, and mares were all fresh and strong, each good for a strenuous chukker, but he wanted the more experienced horses early on, hoping to build up a lead. He watched as the two referees saddled up, tossing the three-and-a-half-inch ball back and forth as they waited for the Argentines to appear. The crowd waited too, but with considerably less patience.

Restless, Billy slipped down a passageway to the locker room and poked his head in. He stood uncertainly as he recognized the little formality. The four Argentines, laughing, sat in a loose circle on the floor, a polo mallet in their midst. Gallegos's arm swung out and playfully spun the mallet like a dial on a game board. When the long end pointed to the smiling, innocent-faced seventeen-year-old, the boy picked up a mirror laced with several lines of white powder and indulged himself. Billy had seen the little game often enough. The cocaine heightened senses and quickened reflexes, or so the rationalization went, but Billy knew the real reason was the sense of omnipotence that came from the drug. The mighty always wanted to be mightier. Billy was amazed how much more arrogant and petulant the Argentines were on their home turf than on the road. Gallegos suddenly flicked him a cold, quizzical glance, as if to ask what Billy was doing there.

"Time to play," Billy said.

"All in good time, my friend," answered Gallegos. He let out a mock scream when the mallet end found somebody else. The room filled with laughter again.

"We're already late," Billy added.

"What's the hurry?" another player asked.

"The stadium's full. The match was supposed to start at one."

"Well, this is our country and we'll start when we want. Why don't you go practice some more? You'll need it. You Americans always need it."

Billy turned and left for the field. He didn't care about being ostracized from their tight little fraternity, but the Argentines' put-down of his ability, their untempered arrogance—that was too much. His anger overwhelmed him. He would show them today who was best, along with any corporate sponsors who thought the great year Billy was having was a fluke. He would show the whole world.

Fifteen minutes later the horses came out flying. Mallets slashed down and the ball shot back and forth in a white blur. The roar in the stadium never subsided. Billy played with an intensity and sure-handedness that surprised everyone. Most of his life he'd spent in second gear, waiting for something to happen, to ignite him, but at the moment he was a man on fire. He scored the first goal for his team, watched the Argentines counter, and promptly scored a second. By midway the match was tied at seven. Gallegos seemed to be tiring, Billy saw, but the man was so skilled on a horse that he could compensate for the sins of a soft life. Billy's response was to try even harder. He rushed breakneck at the ball and stole it from the Argentines repeatedly, and ran circles around the seventeen-year-old wunderkind. With one chukker left and the crowd in a frenzy, Billy changed to his final horse.

"You're not going to win, you know," a voice taunted from behind. Billy stole one glance at Gallegos and went back to saddling his mare. "I'd bet on it," the Argentine added.

The words sounded a familiar chord to Billy, and he wanted to laugh. "Bet what?" he answered, his back still turned.

"I want El Cid back."

"Sorry," Billy said, pleased to have the upper hand for once.

"If my team wins, I get my yearling back. Your team, I'll buy you the best polo pony in South America."

"Forget it."

"You aren't so brave away from home, Billy."

"Brave enough to beat you on your home court."

"*Two* top polo ponies," he said, upping the ante.

"You're stoned."

"*Three.*"

A referee blew his whistle to resume play. When Billy focused on Gallegos, he looked impossibly cocky, king of the polo world, invincible and not to be denied. A voice admonished Billy "no"—his father's voice, he thought for a second—but he suddenly found the wager irresistible. The two shook hands coolly. Billy didn't care about winning a couple more ponies, or four or five, he just was certain that he could beat his rival. That El Cid and his plans for salvaging his future were now in jeopardy hardly troubled him. The great Gallegos, his Latin blood at a rolling boil, his pride on the line before tens of thousands of his fans—the king was ready to be dethroned.

Billy stroked his pony on the neck, waited for the referee to toss the ball into play, and brought his mallet down with a vengeance. He missed by a good inch, his mare rushing past the ball. From the corner of his eye he watched as Gallagos capitalized on the mistake and spiked the ball in the other direction. The Argentine darted past the Frenchman and scored effortlessly. Like the egomaniac he was, Gallegos's arms rose in triumph and the crowd thundered its approval. Embarrassed by his mistake, Billy flew at the ball again. This time he passed it to one of the Britons, who flicked it back, then another pass and another before the Briton sailed the ball through the goal. A volley of boos greeted the third tie of the match.

When play resumed, Gallegos rode ferociously toward the ball, his clean drives speeding it ahead of the opposing horsemen as they tried to intercept. Finally Billy closed in on him from behind. They rode neck and neck for a moment, and then Billy, focusing on the ball in the still grass, elevated his arm and angled the mallet down. It froze in midair. A pain flared in his side. His breath left him. Reflexively he pulled back on his reins. The quick jab from Gallegos's elbow had gone unnoticed by the referee. He watched, dismayed, as Gallegos pulled ahead and with a final easy swing speared the ball toward the goal.

Incredibly, it skittered just wide. The jeers from the crowd poured down. Gallegos seemed stunned too. Billy couldn't believe his good luck. When the ball was dropped back in play, there was less than a minute in the match. The Frenchman swooped down and passed the ball to a Briton, who flicked it to Billy. There was no one in his way. He charged ahead, daring to hope as he drove to the Argentines' goal. He had a clear shot. For a second he was jittery, wondering if he'd suffer the same fate as Gallegos. But his mallet came down confidently, hammering the elusive white ball straight between the goal posts.

His teammates rushed over and slapped him joyfully on the shoulder. The Argentines, still dazed, clustered together moodily, as if in defense from the boos which were still building. Gallegos looked particularly humiliated.

"When do I get my ponies?" Billy said as he rode over. He couldn't help gloating—this was one sweet victory.

"What horses?" said Barrantes.

"The bet—"

"What horses? What bet?" he repeated insolently. His hands shook with anger.

Billy only smiled. He was more surprised than anything. No one ever welshed on a bet in polo. This was a sport of gentlemen. Billy partly blamed the cocaine. Without a word he handed his exhausted horse to a groom and walked away.

That night, riding in a taxi to pick up Aymara, he felt like celebrating. Never had a polo match left him feeling so good. He was still shocked about Gallegos's behavior, but he would do fine without a few more horse mouths to feed. More important, he still owned El Cid, his dream of money and success still alive. The bet had been foolish, he acknowledged now, and he'd been lucky to have come out on top. But Billy knew that despite his considerable ups and downs, he'd always been a little lucky in life. Whenever he got in a scrape, somehow he always got out—like in the match, when Gallegos's chip shot had sailed just wide of the goal. Luck was nothing to count on, of course, but some people seemed to have it and others didn't.

The taxi hurtled through the streets, jockeying for position at the signal lights with the city's certifiably mad drivers, and finally dropped Billy at Olguin's house in Buenos Aires's prestigious old quarter. The art dealer had purchased his home years ago, in better financial times. Olguin opened the door and gave Billy an embrace that the Argentines reserved for old and trusted friends. Despite the scene with Aymara at his gallery yesterday, the art dealer didn't consider Billy a serious suitor, merely a cherished friend of the family who happened to make a convenient and handsome escort. When Aymara appeared, dazzling in a silver lamé gown, she kissed her father good night and put her arm through Billy's.

Olguin's house was only a few blocks from the restaurant El Repecho, which arguably offered the city's top cuisine, certainly its most expensive. Aymara wouldn't be disappointed, thought Billy. As they strolled down the crowded sidewalk flanked by Spanish Colonial houses, he told her of his polo match and scoring the winning goal. If Aymara felt any joy for him, her face didn't show it. Instead she talked about her own day. Her company's fall line was already at the retailers. Half the creations were her own, but she wasn't getting credit! It was wrong and she was furious over the slight. Billy tried to sympathize.

As they approached the restaurant, Aymara suddenly took Billy aside. "Let's not go here," she said.

"But I made reservations. It's a lovely restaurant."

"I don't like it."

Billy was dismayed. "Why not?"

"I just don't. Who's hungry anyway?"

I am, Billy thought, but he could see Aymara's moodiness would win out.

"What do you want to do?" Billy finally asked.

Aymara drew closer and kissed him. The scent of her perfume, her warm body, worked their charm. "I love you," she whispered. "Do you love me?"

He was startled again by the mood change. "Yes," he said. He meant it too.

"Can we go dancing tonight? La Boca?"

"No more changes of mind?"

"I'm sorry about the restaurant. I just want to be close to you."

Billy flagged a taxi. La Boca, formerly a slum neighborhood, had been renovated into a trendy and lavish night spot. Billy had taken Aymara there several times. The clubs were plentiful and colorful, but Aymara's favorite was an upstairs hideaway that drew few jet setters or tourists. The band played only slow music. A quiet bar sat to one side of the gray marble dance floor, the lighting subdued. As they danced, Aymara clung to Billy in a way she never had before, more possessive and dependent than even when they made love. Maybe she was giving up her little games, he dared to hope. He began to relax. He wanted the night, which had begun so uncertainly, to go on forever.

"I'm in love with you," she suddenly whispered.

He kissed her tenderly.

"I always miss you when you're away," she said.

"You never told me."

"I'm telling you now. Do you miss me?"

"Of course."

"Do you ever dream about me when you're asleep?"

He smiled, trying to remember.

"I dream about you," she said.

"What happens?"

"We make love."

"Is it better than in reality?"

She stroked his hair. "No."

"I want to make love tonight," he said.

"Billy . . ." She pulled back, hooking her arms around his neck. "Billy, I want to marry you."

His face reddened. Passion was one thing, but marriage? He'd mentioned it to her once, granted, but because of her father, not with any seriousness. It was almost too much tonight—everything was coming at once. Did Aymara, in her mood swings, swear allegiance to other men too?

"I'm flattered," Billy said carefully.

"I want to marry you. And I don't mean in the future," she clarified, as if reading his mind. "I'm talking about now. I need you, Billy."

He looked at her uneasily. Even if her sincerity and passion were real, Aymara was asking the impossible. How could he support her in the style she wanted? She needed time to mature, and probably so did he.

"Marrying you would be wonderful," he said, careful again, "but I don't know if I'm ready just yet."

"Is there somebody else?" she asked.

He smiled. "Maybe. Your father—"

"What does he have to do with us?" she snapped. "Who cares what he thinks or wants? This is *my* life. . . ."

"He's very concerned about you, that's all."

"You're afraid of my father—that's the truth. I don't know why, but you are. You're a coward."

"There's also such a thing as practicality."

"Practical? I'm in love with you! And if you're in love with me— What kind of man are you?"

"Aymara, you have to understand something—"

"Don't lecture me."

He watched the storm gathering in her face. She was like a little girl denied her favorite toy.

"You don't want me!" she suddenly announced for the whole world. Tears started to flow.

Billy was immobilized. His polish and sophistication deserted him.

"I told you that I needed you. . . ." Aymara's trembling voice seemed ready to explode. She suddenly turned and fled. Billy gave chase, but twice he was blocked on the dance floor. In the street all he could do was watch, helpless, as the taillights of a taxi led into the darkness. He started to follow, but gave up. Aymara was too upset and angry to appease tonight.

In his hotel room Billy ordered a half liter of scotch but still couldn't sleep. He half expected the storm troopers to pay him another visit, but the silence that came instead was no less troubling. He began to realize how much of a bust this trip had been. Nothing was going smoothly. Murphy's

Law rode triumphantly over his normal lucky streak. There
was little point in staying on for an extra day to play polo, he
thought, or to see Aymara, who needed a good week to
calm down. After a restless night he called Pan Am and
changed his flight. Then he phoned Olguin and told him
he'd stop at the gallery in two hours for the mallets. When
he asked to speak to Aymara, the old man said she wasn't
in, and Billy didn't push. A final call was made to Gallegos.
A sultry female voice answered, and Billy simply left a message apologizing that he couldn't play today.

At Ezeiza he waited impatiently in the Pan Am lounge
for his flight to arrive from Miami. He ordered a beer at the
bar, thinking how relieved he'd be to fly to the States, and
put Aymara and Olguin out of his mind to focus on El Cid.
Billy had the horse stabled in Florida under the care of a
reliable groom. Once he sold Olguin's oils, he'd find a good
trainer and see how fast the promising colt could really run.
The All-American was a good ten months away, but if he was
serious about entering, that wasn't much time. He ordered
another beer, picked up a Dallas newspaper at the international kiosk and found an inside article on Austin Mirabeau.
Billy remembered the real estate developer from Meredith's party, a confident, ambitious man whose horse, unfortunately, had collapsed in the All-American. Burial
services were scheduled for this morning, the paper reported. Mirabeau was still upset over his colt's premature
death, and vowed to return to Ruidoso next year with a winner. Well, let him try, Billy thought, but he just wasn't
going to find anyone as fast as El Cid.

The announcement of Billy's flight came over the loud-
speaker. He gathered his bag and polo mallets and edged
toward customs. As he hoisted the bundle of mallets onto
the shiny counter, the Argentine agent peered over his
glasses at Billy.

"*Pasaporte, por favor.*"

"I already showed my passport."

"*Pasaporte,*" he said with less patience.

Annoyed, Billy produced the document. Then, with
quiet disbelief, he watched as another agent, a scowling,

officious man, walked up to untie the brown wrapping that protected the mallets.

"I'm a polo player. I travel to and from Argentina all the time," Billy spoke up. "Those are my mallets."

The agent scooped up one and methodically twisted off the head. With a screwdriver he pried open the wooden plug that Olguin had carefully implanted. Slowly, a rolled-up canvas was teased out. Billy's stomach turned soft.

"What is this, sir?" the agent inquired in English.

"I have no idea," Billy said smoothly.

"You have no idea? These are your mallets."

"I have no idea," he repeated.

The agent shook his head, more in pity than in disbelief. "Come with me, Mr. Sullivan."

"I have a plane to catch."

For the first time the man smiled. "I don't think so."

Billy thought of running, but there was no escape. Maybe he could talk to a higher-up in customs, bribe the man if necessary. Several agents closed in around him. One held out handcuffs. Jesus, thought Billy, suddenly scared. He was angry too. He'd been set up, that was the only explanation. He remembered Gallegos's humiliated, haughty face.

"I want to call a lawyer," Billy said as the cold handcuffs were wrapped around his wrists.

One agent delivered a rude shove as Billy was led down a hallway, out of sight of the terminal passengers. In a small, windowless room he was forced to strip and was searched for drugs. A small, sallow man opened Billy's wallet and took out his money.

"You bastard," Billy said, wanting to take a swing.

"Señor?"

"Give it back," Billy demanded, but another man struck him hard across the face, and he dropped to the floor.

EIGHT

"YOU'D THINK IT WAS THE LINDBERGH KIDNAPPING ALL over again," Rachel said to her photographer as she surveyed the flurry of activity. A plume of dust followed them up the drive to the sprawling 5555 Ranch hacienda. They parked behind a dozen police cars, some with their lights flashing. Reporters were scurrying around like mice looking frantically for the cheese, the frustration of unanswered questions etched in their faces. The police huddled in clusters of threes and fours, except for a few plainclothesmen who still roamed the grounds for evidence. Undaunted, Rachel shook the tiredness out of her legs from the drive up from Dallas and marched up to a willowy, unshaven man with bright blue eyes. He tipped his hat as she approached. A sheriff's badge was pinned lopsided on his lapel.

"M'am?" he drawled.

"Could you tell me something about the horse theft?" She produced a spiral pad and waited.

"Not much to say."

"A horse *was* stolen, wasn't it?"

"'Pears so."

"Well, could you give me some facts? I'm a reporter."

The sheriff parked a toothpick in his mouth and looked up at the hazy sky.

"When did it happen?" she prodded. "Any witnesses? Leads? What's Mrs. Kingsley have to say?"

"We're still investigatin'," the human wall responded

with a polite but distant tip of his hat. Rachel knew she was stranded.

Near a paddock she found a *Dallas Morning News* reporter, fresh out of journalism school, who was charitable or just naive enough to share what he'd learned. A promising yearling named Five Deuces had been abducted sometime last night. There were no telltale hoofprints. Strands of burlap sacking were found near the stables, and there were fresh tire tracks from a horse trailer in the north pasture. Meredith Kingsley and her husband, Seth Cartwright, were asleep at the time. The night watchman also apparently had been snoozing. Nobody was talking much. Apparently there were no leads, no notion of a motive. No ransom note or call either.

Rachel thanked the young man and headed toward the stables where Five Deuces had been kept. She wondered again about Austin Mirabeau. Maybe the man had made open and undisguised threats against Meredith, but would a prominent real estate developer really resort to horse rustling? This wasn't exactly the wild frontier anymore. The man just had been mouthing off—Texans seemed to be either incurably garrulous or devoutly laconic—but if so, who was behind the theft? It wasn't a reporter's role to solve crimes, Rachel realized, but to uncover facts, even from uncooperative principals. Besides, Frank Beardsley would read her the riot act if she came up empty-handed. Horse-crazy Frank thought this story could be the biggest thing since Francis the Talking Mule.

At the barn Rachel was turned back by the police. She couldn't even see the stall where the poor horse had slept. She asked where to find the negligent night watchman, but it turned out he'd been fired by Meredith that morning. Rachel retreated to the house and peeked in a kitchen window. What did a desperate reporter have to lose? Meredith or Seth was probably inside. She slipped in the back door, feeling much the same as when sneaking into Mirabeau's limo—like a guilty trespasser. It was a thin, thin line between being a diligent reporter and invading someone's privacy, but after a day of cataclysmic frustration, she was determined to get a story from somebody.

She moved freely through the mammoth rooms, handsomely decorated with Indian blankets and old Winchester rifles. The place felt deserted, deathly quiet. The master bedroom was the size of her entire West Side apartment. She roamed around, lost, when she noticed the bathroom door ajar. A shadow cut toward the vanity where goldplated horses served as faucets. The pale, overweight man, tall and hardly handsome, raised a safety razor to his cheek with an unsteady hand. Seth, she deduced. He was in jeans and a cowboy shirt he was attempting to button with his free hand. He nicked his chin twice before the phone rang repeatedly and he moved into the bedroom. Rachel dropped behind the bed.

"Calvin, I want to talk too, but not now. How can you be calling me now anyway?" Seth said in a preoccupied way. "For the love of Jesus, Meredith's still on the warpath, you know." And with a quaver in his voice to match his hand, he hung up. The poor man was upset about his horse, Rachel figured, wondering who Calvin might be. Seth finished shaving, but not without stealing several glances through the window at the police outside. Then he trailed into another part of the house. When she felt safe, Rachel delicately opened drawers and peered into closets. She wasn't sure what she was looking for, just something about Seth or Meredith.

Someone stirred behind her. She grabbed a breath and turned around slowly. The double-barreled shotgun was aimed at chest level, and the cold eye peering down the sight at Rachel was unflinchingly hostile. Reflexively, Rachel raised her hands in the air. Maybe this was the Wild West after all.

"You must be Meredith," Rachel managed, her heart racing.

"Who are you?"

"My name's Rachel Lang. I was sort of looking for your horse."

"In my bedroom?"

"You have to start somewhere." Rachel smiled brilliantly, but the shotgun wasn't lowered. She quickly gave her full credentials and offered to call Frank Beardsley if

Meredith wanted confirmation. She also apologized for being in the house. Meredith the statue didn't seem to hear. "Look, lady," Rachel finally said in exasperation, "I'm a reporter who's just trying to do her job. I want to get your story, just who you are and who could possibly want your horse. It's been a long, tough day, believe me. And if you don't put that stupid gun away, I'm going to have a heart attack."

The tirade must have been convincing. Meredith's head finally peeked above the shotgun and her face relaxed a degree. "You want a drink?" she suddenly asked.

"What?"

"You look like you could use one. I know I damn sure could."

In the country kitchen Meredith poured two four-finger glasses of straight Wild Turkey. Down the hatch, thought Rachel. All in the line of duty. Her face puckered and her throat burned, but she asked for a second. Actually, the medicine wasn't so bad, but she saw it didn't help Meredith. The woman was totally disconsolate, as if it had been her child who'd been kidnapped.

"Any idea at all who might take Five Deuces?" asked Rachel. "I spoke with Austin Mirabeau this morning. Granted the man is upset, but I still don't think he's the one—"

"Probably not," Meredith conceded.

"Then who? And why?"

"There's lots of jealousy among rival horse breeders, a lot more than there is of honor. Some aren't above poisoning another man's horse. And if that had happened to Five Deuces, it would make more sense than what did. Why steal a horse? A ransom is ridiculous because Five Deuces isn't *that* valuable. Maybe to me she is, because of sentiment and because I think she can win the next All-American, but she's an unproven commodity. And if someone stole her to race in another state, that's even more incredible. Every quarter horse, just as soon as it's registered, is given a breeder's certificate that's kept on file with the American Quarter Horse Association. The certificate includes a photo of the horse, lists all identifying scars and markings, names its sire and dam, and includes its registration number. The same thing for thoroughbreds registered with the Jockey Club. No track stewards will allow a horse to race without that breeder's certificate and the registration number tattooed inside the horse's lip. Someone might try to forge a certificate, but stewards always cross check with the AQHA, and besides, every track in the country will soon know that Five Deuces was stolen and what her registration number is. The thief hasn't got a chance."

"It may all seem crazy and illogical to you," Rachel said, "but it has to make sense to somebody."

"All I know is the sorry S.O.B. is going to be twice as sorry when I catch him," Meredith swore as she glanced out to the stables. "Horse rustlers are the lowest of the low, one notch below insurance salesmen and two below politicians. In my mother's day if you shot a horse thief in the act, no one was going to shed tears. It was justifiable homicide. And when I find out who this joker is, and if one hair on Five Deuces' mane is out of place . . ."

Her voice trembled. Rachel knew right then she didn't want to be in the thief's shoes.

"I'm offering a reward of $100,000," Meredith promised solemnly, "for any information leading to an arrest . . . and if Five Deuces is returned in good health. Cash on the barrel head. You can put that in your magazine."

Rachel wrote it all down. Frank would love it. Right out of the Old West. "Anything else?"

"Whoever took my horse is making a lot of trouble for himself. The idiot put the wrong bridle on her. Five Deuces can be one temperamental little lady without the right bridle. It's rare for a horse to be so attached to her equipment, it's damn eccentric actually, but that's the way she is. . . ."

Rachel kept the pen moving across the page. Unprompted, Meredith digressed to tales about her ex-husbands, the ups and downs of her breeding operation, and even about her crazy daughter Alexis, whose blind indifference to the horse world drove her mother up the wall. Meredith had spun a half-dozen stories before she stopped and looked at Rachel. "What about you?" she asked.

"Me?"

"Is your life as crazy as mine?"

"I don't think so," Rachel said automatically, but when she thought about it, she wasn't so sure.

"Are you married?" Meredith pressed.

Rachel shook her head and poured herself another bourbon.

"A girl as pretty as you? Are you like Alexis? She can't get her head out of a book long enough to look at a man."

"I've been close to getting married," Rachel admitted, thinking back. "There were three Mr. Almosts."

"Tell me."

"Well . . ." The memories weren't exactly her fondest, but Meredith was ready to listen. "The first guy I got really serious about," Rachel said, "was a Beverly Hills plastic surgeon. He was one of the first people I interviewed for *Image.* He did cosmetic surgery on a lot of movie stars. We hit it off right away. He was bright, handsome, articulate. I adored him. The problem was, he was very married to his profession. He talked continually about breast and buttocks 'reconstruction,' as if it were highway work he did for a living. Then, slowly, he began to criticize *my* looks. 'A small tuck would be nice here,' he would say after we made love, running his hand over my thigh. At first I laughed, but the little digs kept coming. 'You could be so beautiful,' he would say, 'if you just did something about your eyes.' I made endless trips to the mirror. One morning I woke realizing that the doctor was a hopeless perfectionist, and that everything in his life, from his Ferrari to his girlfriend, had to measure up. I left on my own before being jettisoned."

Meredith laughed. "I thought *I* had a rotten time with men."

Rachel giggled. "Wait till you hear about my brilliant artist. His paintings hung in top museums and private collections throughout the country. On our first date he immediately put me on a pedestal. I mean, you talk about worship—this guy was fixing me breakfast in bed, sending fresh-cut flowers to my office, scribbling poetry on restaurant napkins. I have to admit it felt great. But pretty soon the periods of worship alternated with his bouts of self-doubt and anxiety. Why didn't more museums in Europe like his work? Was he losing his touch? Did people just like him for his fame and not for himself? Sometimes he would literally drop to the floor and weep, begging me for help. The more I consoled him, the more self-indulgent he was. The morning he asked *me* to fix *him* breakfast in bed was when I had to say good-bye."

"And number three?" asked Meredith, absorbed in another woman's troubles.

"It was horrible."

"What happened?"

Rachel sighed. "A year ago I met a Chicago attorney on a plane flight from Kennedy. We had several dates, and I just fell in love. The man was sweet-natured, hard working, and tolerant of my wild schedule. He was also crazy about me. He said he wanted to get married. He took me to the small town where he grew up. I was introduced to his mother, his high school principal, his old football buddies. I waded through his yearbooks and petted his dog. After all I'd been through with the Mr. Slicks of the world, I needed this homespun stuff. I was promised that whatever I wanted—to keep working or have babies or become a woman of leisure—was all right with him. A summer wedding was set. I told all my friends. My mother, who thought I'd never make it to the altar, was overjoyed. A week before the wedding I found my dream man in bed with his Jamaican housekeeper. I burst into tears and flew back to New York. That night I found a note in my purse from some anonymous soul telling me my fiancé was a cad and a liar. He'd been married before, was behind in alimony payments, and had been engaged to another woman while chasing after me."

"Jesus Christ," Meredith interjected, "was it true?"

"Every bit of it."

"I think I would have hung the bastard."

"Not me. I just took a vow of celibacy. It was no stigma to live the rest of your life unmarried, I figured, just as long as you had a strong career. So I put my heart into journalism. I keep hoping I'll find a major story to put my name in lights."

An impatient rap on the kitchen window from her photographer brought Rachel back to reality. As she said good-bye to Meredith, she thanked her for being so friendly and understanding. She was starting to like Texas a little more than she had this morning, and in particular she liked Meredith. The woman might be eccentric, and she'd had her ups and downs, but she had a strong will and an ability to persevere. She shaped events rather than let herself be shaped by them. For a moment Rachel was envious. Why couldn't she be the captain of her destiny like that?

That night, in a Dallas hotel room, Rachel called Frank at his home. She could imagine him in his silk PJ's, poring over galleys or brainstorming for new story ideas. He was a modern-day Walter Mitty, his fantasies sparked by *Image's* eavesdropping on the lives of the famous. Everybody was a voyeur, Frank liked to say.

"How was your day? No more muggings, I hope?" Frank said in his relaxed, home-is-where-the-hearth-is voice.

"No, but I did get a shotgun pointed at me."

"I love it!"

"You love it? What if it had been pointed at you, Frank?"

"Rachel, for Chrissake, you're in Texas. What did you learn?"

"Not much about the horse theft. The police aren't talking, basically because they don't know anything. But I did get an interview with Meredith Kingsley."

"Terrific! You're my best reporter, did I ever tell you that? And forget the theft, it's the human side that our readers are interested in. We've done some research on this Kingsley woman. One tough cookie, right?"

"There's a little more to her than that. I wouldn't mind doing a story on her."

"Give me five hundred words. Let's get something on Austin Mirabeau too."

"Besides burying his horse?" Rachel tried to sound indifferent. A paragraph or two on the PR stunt at Restland would be plenty. If she didn't run into Austin again until the twenty-first century, it would be too soon. "I don't think he had anything to do with the horsenapping."

"Who cares? Stress the rivalry between him and Meredith. Aren't both aiming for a showdown in next year's All-American?"

"I suppose so, if Meredith gets her horse back."

"Rachel, show some enthusiasm, will you? Write this story like you're involved. Pretend you're one of the players—"

"But I'm not," she said. She didn't *want* to be involved in any more of her stories—four years of being exploited had taught her the virtue of independence—but she remembered she was talking to Mr. Mitty himself, who couldn't be involved enough. "I'm just a spectator, Frank. That's all I'm supposed to be. Remember the ideal of the objective journalist?"

"Is that a joke or something? Objectivity is fine if you're writing obits, but our readers want living, breathing plasma—they want to identify with the movers and shakers. And so should the writer. Now get a good night's sleep and call me after you interview Mirabeau."

"What am I supposed to ask him?"

"About horses," Frank said blithely, and clicked off.

Rachel turned on the bathwater and opened a pint of vodka from the hostess bar. She was still high from her drink fest with Meredith, but now she wanted to get totally smashed. She'd had it with hotels, the lonely one-night pit stops that left her tired and depressed. It was hard not to feel exploited. Frank Beardsley had been good to her, letting her write free-lance using her own byline, and giving her the plum *Image* assignments, or what he *thought* were the real jewels, but right now he was at home by a roaring fire while Rachel was stuck in the hinterlands.

Face it, Rachel, she thought, maybe you're just burned out.

When she'd finished with her bath she stretched out stark naked on the queen-size bed and studied the view of city lights. She'd used to catch her Beverly Hills plastic surgeon doing the same, lying on his bed in the glory of his birthday suit, just gazing at his body. It was his pastime, like collecting stamps. But Rachel knew she didn't have that confidence, even with a few belts of vodka. After a while the booze, which she'd hoped would make the solitude more bearable, only made it painful. Human beings just weren't meant to live alone, she concluded with lucid certainty, and drifted off to a troubled sleep.

Austin Mirabeau sat uneasily behind his desk in his penthouse office. The suite was soft and sumptuous, with a large teal-blue kilim on the floor, expensive lithographs of the modern masters, and an expanse of glass that commanded a panoramic view of Dallas and Austin's considerable real estate holdings. Fern and her decorator, over Austin's strenuous protests, had furnished the office with the aim of not offending New York and Los Angeles clients with the downhome Texas geegaws that Austin was so fond of collecting. A shiny brass cuspidor was finally allowed in, but only because Austin refused to give up chewing tobacco.

At the moment he was oblivious to everything but the glossy four-color sales catalog in front of him, having taken but one bite of the shrimp and lobster salad his secretary had brought in for lunch. A dozen more catalogs with dogeared pages littered the floor. He had studied them all diligently—the history, pedigree, dam and sire race records of a hundred top yearlings—but he'd yet to find one he could be sure was a winner. How the hell did he expect to take the 1985 All-American? Austin had already attended a halfdozen yearling auctions in the last three months, from the Super Select at Ruidoso to the Pacific Coast Quarter Horse Sale, only to come up empty-handed. A horse would look just dandy to Austin in a catalog, but seeing him in the flesh, judging the conformation, was inevitably disappointing.

And time was running out. The deadline for paying the first of the nomination fees for the All-American was normally at the start of a horse's yearling year. Coming in later was allowed, but then fees were hiked considerably. Austin had already entered seven horses he'd bred on his own ranch, though none inspired that feeling of confidence he'd had with King's Ransom. In payments staggered well into next year, hence the idea of futurity, each horse would cost a total of $3,250 to nominate. Last year there'd been over

1500 nominations, but many horse owners dropped out
after making their first payment, and another 500 scratched
before the elimination heats. Nomination fees, which comprised the $2.5 million purse, were never refunded.

gambler's sport, Austin thought again, remembering
with a twitch the fate of King's Ransom. He'd been the
greatest sprinter Austin had ever seen, let alone raced, and
the scars from that tragedy wouldn't heal quickly. There was
a pain that went beyond pride, that spoke of a great in-
justice that infuriated and troubled him. Austin knew he
was not a complex man or great thinker—ambition, pure
and simple, was the engine that drove him—but lately he'd
brooded about the unexpected twists and turns of life, the
meanness of fate. He prayed that one misfortune of this
magnitude was all the Good Lord would visit on him in this
life. Besides the emotional loss, Austin estimated that the
horse's death had cost him millions in potential race money
and stud fees. The blow had been severe and humbling, and
a lesser man might have been driven from the sport altogether.

Austin still blamed Four Aces for bumping his horse
and throwing off his colt's rhythm. That was what had ultimately caused the fall, he knew. Track films didn't always
show cause and effect. But after yesterday's theft of Five
Deuces, Austin had elected to keep his mouth zipped. For
one thing the police had already questioned him, and while
innocent, it *sounded* self-incriminating to badmouth his
rival. Second, his attorneys told him to quiet down because
they wanted Meredith to drop her libel suit. Austin had
already phoned Meredith this morning to say he was sorry
to hear of the horsenapping. Thieves were cowards, and
Austin deplored cowardice. He also wanted Five Deuces
returned safe and sound for the next All-American—so he
could trounce Meredith once and for all.

The phone buzzed. Austin brought his head reluctantly out of the catalog. His secretary told him once again
that Rachel Lang from *Image* was still in the reception area
and growing visibly impatient. Austin gave the young lady
credit for persistence, but he'd be damned if he'd give an
interview. It would only mean an invasion of his privacy and

an attempt to link him to the pompous, self-serving sons of bitches that magazines like *Image* loved to showcase.

Also, he just didn't like anyone or anything out of New York, which, inexplicably to Austin, considered itself the center of the universe. He hadn't had too much commerce with reporters, but New York bankers strutted into his offices every month like clockwork, thinking they were the smartest sons of bitches since Einstein and ready to take advantage of a dumb hick cracker Texan and college dropout like Austin. They would tell him why he should sell some of his prime real estate, spouting off about sale/leasebacks or leveraged buyouts or ground leases, as if they really didn't think that Austin understood and *they* were smoother than whale shit in an ice floe.

But Austin understood everything. In college he might not have ever received his degree, but that didn't mean he wasn't bright. Alone among Dallas developers he'd gambled heavily when he bought up much of the city's neglected West End, the "warehouse district," six years ago, the heart of which was the infamous book depository from which John Kennedy had received Lee Harvey Oswald's bullet. Until the mid-twenties the West End had been elegant and fashionable, but with the decline of the railroads, the area's fortunes quickly ebbed. The Kennedy assassination only gave it a new black eye. But Austin had seen opportunity in the stigmatized wasteland, and with an infusion of renovation dollars and a burgeoning Dallas economy, the area today was once again elegant and pricey. It had helped make Austin a very wealthy man. No banker from Chase Manhattan or Citicorp had possessed that foresight.

"Tell Rachel Lang that I can't see her," Austin told his secretary.

"I've already tried that, Mr. Mirabeau. She refuses to leave."

"No shit, " he said. The corners of his mouth inched up suddenly.

"What should I do?"

"Why don't you get Jimmy up here."

"Jimmy?"

"Like we always do, sweetheart," Austin said.

In the reception area Rachel rose from her chair, twisting a magazine in her hands with the thought it might be someone's neck. Her frustration capacity was peaking. There was no way Mirabeau was *not* going to see her today, even if she had to camp the night on his doorstep. Tenacity was one of her strong points. She watched, puzzled, as an elderly black man in a maintenance uniform took the chair beside her. He smiled warmly at Rachel. After a moment the receptionist told the man that Mr. Mirabeau would see him now.

Rachel, incredulous, turned to the young woman with dimples and streaked blond hair. "You said your boss was busy."

"This was a previous appointment, Ms. Lang."

"The man's a janitor."

"Actually, he's one of Mr. Mirabeau's closest advisors."

"Really?" Rachel bristled. "And I'm president of General Motors." Despite the secretary's fluttering arms Rachel stormed into the Mirabeau suite.

The handsome office surprised her—she'd expected something more garish—and then she focused on the man who had made her existence acutely painful in an amazingly short period. Austin only gazed back coolly, as if she were interrupting something important.

"You'll have to excuse me for barging in," Rachel said, "but I've been waiting since early morning—"

Austin wagged his head with even more impatience. "Jimmy," he said to his janitor, "I have to apologize for the interruption. This young lady is a reporter. She wants to ask some questions. What do you think?"

"I don't know, Mr. Mirabeau, suh. What kinda reporter?"

"She writes for *Image*."

"Dat's a bad magazine, Mr. Mirabeau. I wouldn't talk to no reporter from *Image*."

"Now wait a minute—" Rachel said in dismay.

"Whatever Jimmy recommends is good enough for me, Ms. Lang," Austin explained, lounging back in his swivel chair. "Just yesterday we had some banker in from Chase Manhattan wanting to buy one of my office buildings on Preston Road. So I turned to Jimmy. What did you tell me, Jimmy?"

"I said, suh, not to sell da building fer a penny less than six million!"

"Right," said Austin, remembering. "So I turned back to Mr. Chase Manhattan and I said, 'six million it is.' You know what, Ms. Lang? The son of a bitch bought the building."

Very funny, thought Rachel. She had a choice of screaming, walking out, or hanging tough. "Now look," she said, "enough is enough. All I want is five minutes. I'm not going to ask about any threats you might or might not have made, just about your interest in horse racing, particularly next year's All-American."

"Do tell."

"Would you please cooperate?"

"Hell, no. You already desecrated the memory of my poor horse, now what the hell am I supposed to think you're going to do to me?"

"Why don't you give me a chance, and you'll find out."

Austin's door suddenly pushed open and for a moment the sparring was halted. The intruder offered an apology and started to retreat, but Austin motioned him back in. Rachel couldn't help staring at the tall, striking man with the strong jaw and understanding eyes. He had a calm, quiet presence that balanced Austin's hard edge. The janitor took the opportunity to slip out the door.

"Miss Lang," Austin announced, "I think it's best you leave now."

"You haven't given me my interview," she said. Austin sat up like a menacing bear. Rachel remembered how she'd been bodily removed from the funeral limo. Wisdom dictated a gracious surrender before history was repeated, but she had too much professional pride. Austin, as if contemplating his next move, pushed a pinch of tobacco in his mouth.

"Name's Calvin Garrison," the good-looking stranger

said in a low-key way, and his hand extended to Rachel's. "As far as I'm concerned, you can stay. What I have to say to Austin is hardly top secret."

"Hell, no, Calvin, this little reporter and me just finished our business."

"I'm a state senator up for re-election," Calvin replied with good humor, "and any time I can get next to a reporter, I try to be as civil as I can."

"Christ on a popsickle stick, Calvin—"

"It's fine by me. I'm just here to talk election politics. Then maybe I'll ask this persistent young woman to have a drink with me."

That'll be the day, thought Rachel. It was all déjà vu. Another good-looking guy making a pass. But she smiled pleasantly and pulled out her notepad.

The two men talked about the upcoming session of the state legislature, which ran every other year from January to June, and the chance of the solons finally allowing individual counties to pass referendums for pari-mutuel wagering. Horse racing itself wasn't prohibited in Texas, just betting on it. Overcoming this myopia wasn't easy, Calvin told Rachel. In previous legislative sessions the pro-gambling forces had simply been outnumbered, though the vote was getting closer all the time. After all, thirty-three states allowed some kind of horse track betting—thoroughbred, harness, or quarter horses—so why shouldn't Texas? One of the obstacles to enlightenment was the Texas Anti-Crime Commission—wolves in sheep's clothing, said Calvin. A state agency born in the thirties to fight bootleggers and organized crime, the commission today was a panel of chest-thumping, self-righteous hypocrites, some of whom had a vested interest in keeping betting out of Texas.

"What do you mean?" Rachel interrupted. It sounded like good background.

"He means," Austin picked up, "that the head commissioner, one Thom Warfield, is slimier than lizard eggs. The man owns a big chunk of Aztec Park race track in New Mexico, just across the border. That's where half the horses raised and bred in Texas end up running. That's where our money disappears to. No wonder he doesn't want pari-mutuel tracks in Texas. The smoke screen is crime, but horse tracks don't bring crime, they bring jobs, recreation, and money. Money—that's the real and only issue—Thom Warfield's or Texas's. I'll tell you eyeball to eyeball that Warfield is a giant sleazeball. He's been involved in one shady deal after another, but in public he sounds so sincere and righteous that nobody minds. The Baptists should be aiming their arrows at him instead of Calvin and me."

An agitated Austin puckered his mouth and unceremoniously launched a stream of brown juice into the spittoon. Then he pulled out a checkbook and made a donation to his favorite senator's campaign. "Let's get 'em, Cal," he said, leading the charge.

Rachel began to see a different side to Austin, someone who stood up for what he believed in. Maybe he wasn't such an ogre after all. He even volunteered information about his breeding ranch and plans to race next Labor Day. She thanked him and moved out the door, unsure what to say to Calvin Garrison. But in the elevator he did all the talking. He liked her magazine and read it regularly, he volunteered, and he knew Rachel from her byline.

"Really?" she said, flattered.

"You're semi-famous."

"Not really. I'm just another of the world's struggling, underpaid writers."

"Don't put yourself down. I think you're good. And writing is a talent. Not many people do it well, including my speech writer."

"You wouldn't just be buttering me up for a free plug in my next story."

"I can't deny it. I told you I was a politician."

She smiled. "What if I said I won't mention you?"

"I'd say I still wanted to buy you a drink. It's after five, isn't it?"

Rachel was tempted, but she was tired from her frustrating day, and she didn't see what she had in common with a Texas politician. "I'd love to join you," she lied, "but I've got some facts to check with an editor."

"Then let's make it a business meeting. I'll give you more dope on Thom Warfield. And one drink only."

"Just business?" She cocked her head skeptically. "Tell me one thing, Mr. Garrison, are you married?"

"It's Calvin. And the answer's no. Never been."

"That's hard to believe."

"It's all true. I never had the time to find the right woman. I wouldn't make a good husband anyway. What politician does?"

Calvin took her to a colorful bar called Confetti on Greenville Street, which reminded Rachel of SoHo or parts of the Village, and then to dinner at Calluaud's, a three-star French restaurant that he said was Dallas's latest find. The one-drink promise quickly got lost along with the revelations about Thom Warfield. Rachel didn't object. She was tired of work anyway, and Calvin's combination of persistence and charm was an easy winner. He was obviously a good politician and well liked, because wherever they went he seemed to know people. When Rachel was introduced to his friends and supporters at the chic restaurant, she felt flattered, even important. A reporter's solitary life suddenly seemed like slavery. There was nothing wrong with good booze and good food. By the end of the evening, staring at her dessert, she was embarrassingly drunk and told Calvin so.

"And here I thought you were so innocent," she said, propping her chin on her hand. "Look what you've done to me."

"I'm sorry," he said, and she thought he meant it. "I'll take you back to your hotel."

"What if I don't want to go to my hotel?"

"Well, there's a jazz club I know, or if you like dancing—"

She gathered her courage. "What I'd like most is a nightcap in your apartment," she ventured. A small interior voice protested, but Rachel couldn't help herself. She knew she was her own worst enemy when it came to men. And she liked this guy in particular.

"I guess I'm not behaving," Rachel said, trying to sober up as Calvin just looked at her.

"I think you're behaving just fine."

"Tell me, do you have high standards?" she asked.

"Probably too high."

"And do I measure up?"

"Just fine," he promised. "Behind that my-profession-is-my-life attitude of yours, I think you're pretty warm and sympathetic."

Rachel said nothing. She wished he'd called her a conniving, scheming, self-interested bitch—then she'd know he wasn't using her. But in her fundamentally insecure state, Rachel melted inside. She loved Calvin's speech. A man who saw right to her essence and liked her. Granted, she was always more charitable when drunk, but there was something about Calvin that was reassuring, and he was nice to be around.

They drove to a steel-and-glass high rise in the fashionable Turtle Creek section of Dallas, not far from Highland Park. Rachel expected to find a disheveled bachelor's pad, but the place was immaculate and tastefully furnished—modern leather couches, Warhol lithographs on the wall, designer rugs and light fixtures. Clothes were hung on hangers, papers stacked neatly on a desk, pillows placed symmetrically on the bed. No doubt his socks all matched too, Rachel thought. She suspected the hand of an efficient housekeeper, but Calvin denied it. You have to have order in your life, he said quietly; if you didn't, the world would swallow you whole. Rachel toasted her nightcap to that.

Undressed and under the sheets, she held a body that was as perfect and in harmony as the man himself. She'd expected to be nervous as Calvin glided a hand over her bottom, but everything felt natural. As a lover she gave him high marks—confident, aggressive, yet patient too. The love-making went on forever. Afterward she teased him that he was too vigorous for a man his age. He promptly made love to her again. When Rachel finally slept, it was deep and trouble free.

She was wakened in the morning by a low, adamant voice. Someone was talking, but not to her. Still half asleep, she heard a name that was familiar yet too slippery to hold on to. Her eyes fluttered open. Calvin was at his desk, the phone cradled on his shoulder.

"Now look, Seth, you just take it easy. Everything's going to be fine. Have faith . . ."

Seth. Even in her groggy state, Rachel refused to believe in coincidence. When hiding in the Kingsley bedroom she'd heard Seth Cartwright speaking to someone named Calvin. It had to be a small world among horse breeders and their state legislators. She tried to pick up the thread of conversation, but Calvin suddenly glanced back to the bed. Rachel smiled innocently, but he seemed to know that wheels were turning in her head.

"Morning," he said, hanging up the phone.

"Hi."

"Sorry to tell you this, but I've got a meeting downtown in thirty minutes."

"No time for breakfast?"

"No." The tone was polite but firm.

"Okay," she said reluctantly. She wanted to thank him for the wonderful evening, but his voice put them at a distance. It was enough to put the future on ice too, Rachel thought, hurt and disappointed. Calvin was now leery of her, and she hadn't really done anything except overhear a piece of a phone conversation.

As Calvin slipped into the shower she put her feelings aside and let her reporter's curiosity take over. There was the imprint of a name on the writing pad by the phone on Calvin's desk. It had been penciled on the previous page and the marks pressed through. Rachel took a pencil and lightly shaded over the letters. The name jumped out at her—the same one she'd heard when just waking up, and then forgot.

She peered more closely at the bottom of the page. There was a second name. She worked the pencil again: *Five Deuces.*

Jesus, she thought, ripping off the page. As she was dressing, Rachel began to wonder. What had she stumbled into? All this was only circumstantial, but her instincts were aroused. Frank had warned her to stay clear of the crime aspect of the story, to concentrate on personalities. But that was impossible—how could she not think about the horse-napping? She was burned out on conventional stories and personalities. Here was real excitement. Maybe the great story she was waiting to sink her teeth into had been dropped in her lap.

There were just some things an editor couldn't appreciate, Rachel thought as she ducked out of Calvin's apartment, and the name Thom Warfield was one of them.

NINE

UP BEFORE DAWN, DAVID SANDERS FELT HIS LEGS GROWing as tired as the yearling's he was exercising. The late morning sun was still low in the cloudless sky, gently bathing the 1200 lush acres of paddocks, stables, mare motels, and rolling grass pastures that was the mosaic of Mirabeau Ranch. On the outskirts of Frisco, about an hour's drive from Dallas, the ranch was modest compared to Meredith Kingsley's, but the young jockey knew it was run with an efficiency and dedication that counted for more than size or opulence. The fact was that here everyone worked his butt off. For three straight hours David had been legging up several of Austin's colts that had been nominated for the All-American, alternately loping and breezing them around the soft dirt track, but knowing full well that the horses lacked the desire and depth through the chest of a King's Ransom. The blaze-face colt he mounted now probably wouldn't survive the first elimination heat.

There were some eight million horses in the United States, of whom maybe 300,000 were registered thoroughbreds and 100,000 registered quarter horses; only a mere hundred were proven winners at the race track.

Breeding and training a champion was as dicey and difficult as breaking into Fort Knox—and just as lucrative. But the cost of failure was aggravating. Every year tens of millions were spent to match the right stallion with the right mare; and tens of millions went right down the proverbial toilet. Mr. Mirabeau had a knowledgeable trainer and vet to supervise his breeding program, David conceded, but his last crop of foals had been nothing to write home about.

The 112-pound jockey forked his fine sandy hair from his eyes and began to walk the handsome colt around the track to cool him out. In the stables David threw on a blanket, then kneeled as he lathered the horse's ankles with a solution of rubbing alcohol and vinegar which would tighten its bones and tendons. He wrapped each leg for extra support, and the front legs particularly well because they carried about seventy-five percent of the horse's weight. Then he stood up cautiously. Like a brush fire the fingers of pain swept through his back. Damn, was he hurting! He'd been riding professionally for only three years, but already he'd taken a half-dozen falls, the worst being off King's Ransom in the All-American.

That had been a black day for everyone, particularly Mr. Mirabeau. David honestly thought King's Ransom hadn't been bumped by Four Aces, that the colt had somehow just stumbled, but he understood Mr. Mirabeau's frustration and pain. David's pain had been real too. It was two weeks after the accident before he could ride again. Except for prescribing painkillers, doctors couldn't help. Pain was an occupational hazard. Probably half the 1800 registered jocks in the country rode hurt at least some of time, he'd been told. Many had pins in their legs or steel plates in their backs or partial prostheses in their knees. Ask any of them and they'd tell you that riding a horse was every bit as dangerous as playing nose guard or racing Formula One cars. Last year two jockeys had been killed while riding, and another was now a paraplegic. The great Ron Turcotte, who'd taken a spill at the height of his career, would forever be in a wheel chair. But you could never think about the dangers of the sport, David knew, or you wouldn't get on a horse again.

Whenever David called his parents in Chicago and mentioned his back or his seven-day work weeks, there was little sympathy. They still wondered why he'd skipped college to hang around seedy race tracks and foul-smelling barns. They just didn't understand his enduring love for horses. He'd been riding since he was eight years old. Summers in high school were spent as a groom at Arlington Park and later as a jockey's valet. He was always hustling mounts to exercise, mucking out stalls, hanging around jocks. Finally he got a chance to ride on a probationary basis and won three of his four races. Emboldened, he applied to the Jockey Guild to become an apprentice, won some more races and a riding contract with a Chicago trainer, and within a year he'd become fully certified.

In his brief but peripatetic career he'd mounted both thoroughbreds and quarter horses in five states. Riding styles and the invisible aids, or cues, that a jock gave a horse were substantially different between thoroughbreds and quarter horses, and David's agent had warned him that sooner or later he'd have to choose between them, but right now he managed to do both well and didn't understand the rush to decide. Eighteen months ago, though, he'd met Mr. Mirabeau at a quarter horse auction outside of Chicago and the smooth-talking Texan had convinced him to come south. He had never regretted the move. Mr. Mirabeau had taught him a hell of a lot about horses, and David had never objected to hard work.

Hard work and a lot of anxiety, he reminded himself. Few outside the horse world knew what a jockey went through. Life meant more than a casual Sunday mount at the track. Most jocks were under contract to work six and seven day weeks, helping trainers and exercising the mounts they'd be riding at the track for money. The pay was ten percent of the purse—no base salary—so if you didn't ride well, you starved. Sometimes jocks were hired on a per diem basis, making a couple hundred dollars for an afternoon of riding plus their ten percent if they finished in the top three, but David found it preferable to be under contract with one trainer or owner. It made for a better relationship and more understanding. And a jock needed moral support. Life could be lonely for someone who worried constantly about keeping his weight down, avoiding slumps much like a hitter in baseball, spending hours if not days in the rain and mud, and just trying to stay healthy. Not least of a jock's suffering was the schizophrenia of winning one day, cheered by the crowd, then losing the next and tiptoeing in disgrace through the discarded Coke cups and hot-dog buns on the way home.

But as in any sport, if you could survive the drudgery, the rewards for greatness and success were tantalizing. A Cordero or Pincay made millions, was seen on television, and had the respect of his peers and the public. There were trips to Europe, important people to meet. It was David's not-so-humble dream to join the elite of racing. For someone who'd been raised in a working-class family and still hadn't been to New York City, it was a dream that sometimes seemed ridiculous even to him. But David knew he was an excellent athlete, and very determined. His record on 364 mounts was ninety-one wins, thirty places, thirty-four shows. It was damn respectable, considering some of the mules he'd had to ride, and a springboard, he hoped, for landing a winter contract from a Dallas breeder named Robert Huss. Because a winter schedule wouldn't affect his quarter horse races, Mr. Mirabeau had already given him permission to approach the thoroughbred breeder.

Mr. Huss was even wealthier than his current employer, more formal and stiff too. From a family of old money, he'd been racing thoroughbreds in Florida and California for two decades. David had spoken to the man by phone, candidly admitting his desire for national exposure, but Mr. Huss told him he didn't need any new jockeys. David wasn't discouraged. He would keep trying, and one day he'd make things happen for himself.

"Hey, David!" an amused voice called out. "Get out here."

He finished wrapping the horse's legs and wandered outside to find his friend Sal wearing a smug grin. The thirty-year-old jockey threw David a wink and gestured toward a rider on a bay gelding galloping hell-bent around the track.

"Who's that?" asked David.

Sal Forester's flat, sallow face quickly turned judgmental. "Her names's Trixie McKinney. She's an apprentice jockey. She wants a per diem job with Austin, so he asked me to give him a report."

"I like the way she rides," David volunteered after checking out her form.

Sal was hardly jubilant. "Are you serious? A woman jock?"

David knew how much Mr. Mirabeau respected Sal's opinions. Born and raised in Texas, he'd been around horses all his life, and when he wasn't substituting for an injured David at the track, he helped oversee the ranch. David got along with Sal—David liked to think he got along with everyone—but there was a self-righteousness, almost an arrogance about the older jock that was hard to take sometimes.

"I am serious," David answered. "She's handling that gelding well."

"But what happens if she gets on a frisky colt? This girl's nineteen years old and a mighty ninety-three pounds."

"We're only talking about a quarter mile. A woman can handle that distance as well as a man. It's not like going six or eight furlongs and needing the stamina."

It was the same with most jockeys, David thought—they just didn't like competing against women. It was hard enough on a man to be physically slight and short. For many that translated to a built-in inferiority complex. One compensated by marrying tall, bosomy women, or driving a sports car or flashing a big diamond ring. But on the track a jock's only defense was to put women down, or patronize them, or preferably keep them out of the sport altogether. David was different. He didn't feel threatened or see why women couldn't ride alongside men. The criterion wasn't sex, but ability, and for the moment he was impressed with the way Trixie McKinney handled her mount.

"I'm telling Austin no way," Sal said.

"You've only seen her ride once."

"Hey, whose side are you on?"

"I'm not on anybody's side."

"Doesn't sound like it."

"It's all beside the point. Why don't you give her a chance?"

"Because I'm too busy, Mr. Bleeding Heart. Tell you what, since you like the girl so much, you give her the bad news."

Sal clasped him on the shoulder, chuckled, and disappeared into the stables. David didn't relish the task, but he approached the girl anyway. He was sympathetic not just because he thought she wasn't getting a fair shake, but because he was going through something similar with Mr. Huss.

"Hi," David called as the girl dismounted. He introduced himself and took the gelding's reins. Trixie McKinney wiped some dirt from her eye and smiled back. For a moment David studied her. She was cute, he thought— shiny, thick black hair; a cherubic face with intense eyes; a soft olive complexion.

"How did I do?" she asked. She seemed eager to please.

"I thought you rode well."

"But the other man, Sal . . ."

David hesitated. "Sal's a stick in the mud, I guess. You have to prove things to him."

"You mean he didn't like what he saw?"

"He wants you to come back and try again," David lied.

A tear welled up in Trixie's eye, but she quickly brushed it away. "That's okay," she said in a businesslike voice.

"I'm really sorry."

"You don't have to be. Everyone's got an opinion. I'll get a contract somewhere."

"If you like quarter horses, I know some trainers I could recommend. Here," he said, scribbling out his address and phone number, "look me up."

"I'll be fine," she insisted. She took David's note anyway, and with a brave smile turned and headed toward her car. He thought she was about to cry again. A feeling of protectiveness inevitably came over him when he encountered a girl who was upset or in trouble. He wanted to run after Trixie and assure her that everything would work out, that sometimes it took time. He also wanted to know where she lived, and did she have a boyfriend, and would she be free later this week. It felt like light-years since he'd had a date. Being a jockey was precariously close to taking a vow of celibacy. But Trixie was already gone. Resigned to the missed opportunity, David led the gelding back into the stables.

When he'd finished cooling out the horse, he approached another yearling to leg up, only to freeze awkwardly at the stall. Clenching his teeth, he waited for the pain to recede. It felt like a knife was stuck in his back. Slowly, the muscles relaxed and he could stand again, but he wondered when the pain would strike again.

When he was sure Sal wasn't around, David slipped into an empty stall. His hand sliced through some straw to a paper sack. Opening the first vial, he dry-swallowed the capsule of codeine. The he popped a Black Beauty from a second container. All he needed was for self-righteous Sal to waltz in and catch him with amphetamines. Then it would be good-bye to riding for Mirabeau Ranch. When it came to his employees, Mr. Mirabeau was a stickler for clean living. And Sal, who particularly walked the straight and narrow, was Mr. Mirabeau's watchdog.

In some ways David resented the tight ship. It was common knowledge that jockeys drifted easily to drugs and pills. The solitary life, the pain from accidents, the anxiety before races—you were pushed into it. But as long as your head was clear during a race and you didn't become addicted, what was the harm? A lot of athletes took drugs. And though illegal in most states, horses were often shot up with Phenylbutazone, or "bute," so they could run without pain. Why shouldn't it be the same for jockeys?

A shadow cut across tha path leading to the stall David was in. He practically sat on the paper sack. Give me a break, he prayed. When he focused on the intruder, he let out a breath of relief. "What the hell are you doing here?" David asked good-naturedly.

The older, cheerful-faced gentleman was dressed in a

vintage Salvation Army double-breasted suit, and his shirt collar was at least two sizes too big. David speculated that the red velvet bow tie was a discard from someone's prom. The wizened face hadn't enjoyed the benefit of a shave in a good week. David rose with an effort, waiting for the pills to work their magic, and shook Sparky Maligan's hand.

"I came to pay my respects, and say I'm sorry for what happened in the All-American," Sparky announced in a clear baritone voice. "I was sitting on the rail when your horse fell. Poor Mr. Mirabeau. Boy, I hate to see that happen to a horse or its owner. I thought you were a goner too, sonny. But you didn't even need a stretcher!"

"A cat's got nine lives," David said proudly.

"You okay?"

"I'll survive. What's a little pain to a jock, right? What really hurt was not winning the race. Horses like King's Ransom don't come around every day. It was my chance for fame and fortune—"

"You'll get another," Sparky assured him.

And David knew it was true. He was in this business for the long haul. "Did you bet on the All-American?"

"Of course I bet—I bet on you, sonny! You're one great young jockey. Five hundred big ones. Whoosh—right down the kitchen sink!"

They laughed together. It was nice to see Sparky again, thought David. He was always cheerful and bubbly, even when down on his luck. David really didn't know much about the man. They'd met while David was working as a jockey's valet at Arlington Park. But Sparky's face was as familiar at race tracks and paddocks and breeding ranches as any horse owner's. Widowed and living on Social Security, he had spent the last seven or eight years crisscrossing the country on Greyhound buses, sleeping at cheap motels, and stopping at every city that boasted a track. From Belmont to Santa Anita, from Churchill Downs to Oaklawn Park, he unfailingly made his trips to the betting window. Racing seasons were sufficiently staggered to keep him busy year-round. He knew as much about horses as anyone, and he used that knowledge to sharpen his handicapping skills. A tout sheet was always sticking out of a pocket. Most of the time he made enough to survive, but his dream, as Sparky put it, "of getting as rich as the Rockefellers," was a tease, David thought. You can beat the race, but you can't beat the races, went the saying. Only David would never tell Sparky that. The man lived on hope.

"Sonny, I was wondering if you could help me out a little," Sparky said a little sheepishly.

David had already anticipated. From his wallet he dug out a couple twenties. He'd done it before, and he'd do it again. He couldn't even remember how much Sparky's tab was.

"Sonny, I don't need this much—"

"It's okay," David said.

"You know I'll pay you back one of these days. Real soon, I hope."

David smiled, told Sparky where he'd be riding next, and said good-bye. In the tack room, checking on equipment, David's back stiffened again. He couldn't believe it— he'd just taken some codeine. Maybe his back was getting worse, not better. How the hell was he supposed to work, let alone sleep well, if he didn't get relief? How was he supposed to take that ride to fame and fortune? Retrieving his cache of pills, he swallowed another upper. He told himself he didn't need the pill but it was there, and his pain was something else today. Tomorrow things would be better.

TEN

IT WASN'T EXACTLY YOUR TYPICAL TEXAS SOCIAL, FERN Mirabeau thought, and it especially wasn't a Meredith Kingsley party. Fern pushed her arm through Austin's and entered the antebellum brick Colonial with the feeling that she was as out of place here as a horse on skis.

Brooks Meadow, just outside Lexington, was one of Kentucky's oldest and most famous thoroughbred breeding farms. Its roots were traced to the early nineteenth century, when horse races were considerably longer and on hilly terrain, but the breeding farm had always produced winners. The main residence, with its elaborate winding staircase and velvet drapes, was something out of *Gone With the Wind*. Oils of family patriarchs hung on the walls alongside equally elegant portraits of their horses, who had won the Derby or the Preakness or the Belmont Stakes. The black-tie guests looked as stodgy as their judgmental forebears.

Tonight's party and auction of thoroughbred yearlings was of no interest to Austin, but he had to come, he told Fern, because of urgent business with one of the guests. Austin wouldn't elaborate on the mystery—it would bring bad luck, he insisted. So an invitation had been wangled, and two hours ago they had said good-bye to the kids and promised to be back around midnight in their Learjet.

Part of Fern wished it was already time to leave. In a designer dress of black-dotted marquisette with feather shoulder puffs, purchased last week at Neiman-Marcus, Fern knew that she would have been at ease at the snobbiest Dallas fund-raiser. But here, mingling with Southern women in their traditional silk gowns, she felt swift, sharp glances of disapproval, as if she were dressed much too playfully. Austin was even more conspicuous. His Dixon lizard skin boots contrasted starkly with his tux, which in turn had a stranglehold on his neck. But nothing ever embarrassed Austin. Sometimes she thought that he just liked being different, if not ornery.

He suddenly stopped a waiter, picked up a mint julep in a silver goblet, sniffed it, and put it back. "Tom, you rascal," he said, "bring me a straight bourbon and some home-baked ribs!"

Fern watched her husband disappear into the crowd to search for his friend. Left alone, she felt lost and uneasy in the labyrinthine mansion. She wondered about her insecurity. Was it just from being in a foreign setting, or were there deeper reasons? She and Austin were as rich or richer than almost anyone here. They owned a jet, a yacht, four homes in four states, a healthy chunk of downtown Dallas, and their horses were collectively worth, if you counted breeding shares, $25 million. Yet she felt looked down upon. Maybe that was because she was used to looking down on herself, she thought. There were times in her life when Fern felt she didn't deserve all her luxury and status. She'd grown up the only child of a widowed oil wildcatter who had made and lost a million dollars four times and finally died poor. Moving vans had ceremoniously put them in then hastily pulled them out of east Texas mansions too many times for Fern to remember places and dates. She had had wardrobes lavished on her, then gone without a new dress for three years; had rich friends and poor; been to tony private schools, and public ones where some teachers had never graduated from college. The ups and downs had left her with the sense that nothing good lasted forever, and therefore it was unwise to trust her own happiness. Maybe that was why she had never quite acquired the social confidence that wealth usually begot. Her father certainly had never found it. He never even knew how to spend money graciously. With his first oil fortune, because he'd never owned a car, he promptly bought nine of them; boots, twenty-five pair; paintings, crude imitations of the European masters.

But that's the way a lot of Texans were. They wanted the biggest and best and most expensive things they could get their hands on, as if quantity and price tag made up for past deprivations. Before the vast discoveries in the famous east Texas oil fields in the early thirties, Fern knew, much of the state had been almost as poor and desolate as Mexico. There was cowboy hospitality and a natural friendliness, but people had no real social conventions, no standards of taste, no traditions to shape them. With the oil came money, however, and people suddenly had the freedom to shape themselves. Dallas and Fort Worth, once little more than cattle towns, overnight aspired to be sophisticated metropolises. A small but ambitious haberdasher named Herbert Marcus, with the help of his sister Carrie Neiman, started Texas's first real department store and taught the wealthy locals how to dress. Up from faceless poverty, Texans flaunted their possessions—clothes, horses, homes, art—as if to mask their feelings of inferiority; and if the world still looked down they just flaunted them some more.

Fern knew that Austin was a little that way. He had always loved horses, but he really got into the breeding and racing game because he thought it was expected of him. Being a success in real estate just wasn't enough. He always had something else to prove. If he ever won the All-American, and she was sure one day he would, Austin would find another gauntlet to pick up.

Fern strayed toward a handsome oil portrait in one of the sitting rooms. Several women were nearby, talking, but none made an effort to say hello. Uncomfortable, Fern gazed at the painting of the young, lean-faced man with a rifle across his lap.

"Who is he?" Fern finally asked, trying to break the ice.

"Why dear," one said, hiding a smile, "you must not be from around here."

"No," said Fern.

"That's Robert E. Lee as a young man."

"Oh," she acknowledged.

"Where are you from?" the woman asked.

"Dallas."

"Then no wonder you don't know. The last person from Texas who was here swore to me that it was a portrait of Sam Houston."

The polite smiles didn't fool anyone. Fern knew they were laughing at her. She said nothing, and turned away. Her father would have answered the insult with one in kind, but Fern liked to think she had learned graciousness and tolerance in her generation. Still, the slight hurt, and all she wanted now was to get back to Texas.

Austin watched, amused, as guests began to spill out of the mansion and move toward the mammoth gold and blue striped tent, erected to help rich fools part with their money. Life-size ice sculptures of horses guarded the entrance, and a lavish buffet table had been set up for the prospective buyers, along with a fountain of champagne. Nearby was the cemetery for Brooks Meadow's illustrious thoroughbreds, each grave marked by a hand-chiseled stone tablet, and beyond, a vista of grazing pastures of famous bluegrass, supposedly ideal for horses because it contained natural deposits of lime.

Everything around Lexington was supposed to be horse heaven. The water was purer, the days sunnier, the air finer—so the locals claimed. As shrines went, Churchill Downs was worshiped and revered as much as the White House, and the Run for the Roses was next in importance only to the Second Coming. But to Austin it was all a matter of bragging rights. Sure, thoroughbreds had been racing longer and in more places than quarter horses, but Austin could honestly see the day, with the right media coverage and the legalization of betting in Texas, when quarter horses would be as glamorous as thoroughbreds.

History needed to be corrected, that was all. In the Colonial days wealthy farmers and landowners imported English thoroughbreds, called bloods or breds then, for the pleasure of racing. But whereas most Southerners belonged to the Church of England, which was not opposed to races and betting, in the north a stern Puritan heritage frowned on wagering. The consequences were that racing and breeding thrived in the south, particularly in Virginia and Kentucky, where the weather and terrain seemed more suitable, while in the north horses were used for pulling buggies and hauling carts in road work. The latter were the forebears of the standardbreds, which became trotters and pacers, still the predominant racing form in the north today. Both parts of the country ignored the West, Austin knew. There the horses were descended from those of the Spanish explorers and the Indians' Chicasaw horses. With the help of an imported English thoroughbred named Janus, selective breeding helped improve the conformation of the Western horse, but basically it had always had a more compact, heavily muscled front quarters than a thoroughbred, enabling it to run short distances at a greater speed.

If quarter horses were ever going to challenge the supremacy of thoroughbreds, Austin knew it wouldn't be easy. The South was a clever and stubborn enemy. It had certainly succeeded in stealing the thoroughbred crown from England. At the turn of the eighteenth century, when the British were importing the three foundation sires from Arabia to cross with their own mares, England was the racing capital of the world. Royalty staged the first races among themselves, placing gentlemanly wagers and earning their little pastime its moniker of Sport of Kings. One Lord Derby started his own annual race at Epsom, and thus lent his name to history. Yet as early as 1730, right out from under the royal British nose, southern Colonists bought and shipped over the first English thoroughbred, Bulle Rock—whose sire was the Darley Arabian and his dam a daughter of Byerly Turk—to stand stud. In the next fifty years plantation owners used guile and money to import over 200 top stallions and mares, which became the foundation of thoroughbred breeding in the States. By the middle of the nineteenth century the quality of American horses was equal to the British.

Once racing caught on, there were more and more raids on European breeders to meet American bettors' demands for faster horses. Whenever a top horse was for sale in the world, a Southern breeding farm seemed to snatch it up. The British stallion Bahram, who won the 1935 Derby, the St. Leger, and the Two Thousand Guineas—the Triple Crown in English racing—was one of the more spectacular acquisitions. Horse empires were soon established in Virginia and Kentucky, and kingly fortunes along with them.

What the South worked so mightily to acquire, Austin knew, it did not give away frivolously. At various points in history the British, French, Italians, and Germans had attempted to buy America's quality stallions and mares to bring across the Atlantic and reestablish European racing supremacy. But the Southern breeder inevitably kept the best stock for himself. Even shares in the really great horses were rarely offered. Southern clannishness demanded that the best be kept in the family, so all that outsiders got was the second kiss of the pig. They paid dearly for it too.

In the seventies, Austin recalled, wealthy sheiks flush with petrodollars had descended on farms like Brooks Meadow with suitcases of cash, demanding to buy the top horses. All they succeeded in doing was paying top dollar for ordinary horseflesh. More recently a cartel of European businessmen was trying again. Austin had seen a few there tonight. Back in July, for the Keeneland Selected Yearling Sale, they had come in droves, representing powerful British and Continental syndicates. Sixty-five million dollars had been dropped on a mere twelve horses. Most of the Europeans were legitimate businessmen, but a few were considered less scrupulous, some even with mob ties. Austin loved it—the Boy Scouts of Italy were involved. The Europeans wanted the racing crown back in the worst way.

A trumpet blared from the arena floor, as if a fox hunt were being staged. When the crowd quieted, the first yearlings were brought out and trotted around for inspection. Austin knew that tonight's sales wouldn't match the Keeneland auction, but buyers here would still drop a couple million, every cent of it on unproven commodities. Austin smirked as he studied the horses. They looked like they'd been to beauty parlors. Grooms had stuck ginger salve up their asses so their tails pointed out, their hooves had been polished, and Lemon Pledge was smeared on their coats to make them shiny—all to fetch a few more dollars for Brooks Meadow.

"Hey, Austin!" a gravelly voice called.

An older, heavyset man with a weathered face and unruly spikes of gray hair motioned him outside. If not for his tux, Austin thought, Stanley Marcowski would have been taken for a decrepit stable hand.

"Where the hell you been, Stanley?" Austin said.

"My horse trailer had a flat."

"I've been suffering through this whole night waiting for you. They're about to start singing Dixie in there."

"Austin, you're going to fall in love. This horse is gorgeous—"

"As the good Lord knows, you've got more shit in you than a constipated buffalo. Just lead the way."

In his eleventh-hour search for a top yearling, Austin

had resorted to calling bloodlines agents across the country, hoping one of the horse brokers could save his ass for the All-American. Stanley had been a sports writer for *The Pittsburgh Press* for three decades when he decided to quit writing about horses and start buying and selling them. He knew virtually everyone in the horse world, and entree came easily. When Austin had spoken to him two days ago from Dallas, Stanley had waxed eloquent on a yearling colt bred in Louisiana. Since he had to be at Brooks Meadow for the auction, and he was bringing the yearling along for another possible buyer to check, why didn't Austin meet him there?

The two men slipped through the darkness to a road above the house, far enough away for no one to spot them. Bringing a quarter horse anywhere near Lexington was bad taste in the least, Austin knew, and possibly insurrection. Thoroughbreds and quarter horses were as likely a mix as Kentuckians and Texans. That wasn't to say there weren't some thoroughbred breeders in the Lone Star state—Assault, the 1946 Triple Crown winner, had come from the famous King Ranch—and not a few Texas businessmen had invested in Kentucky breeding farms. But on balance you were talking oil and water. Austin didn't much care whom he offended, but agents like Stanley, who worked both sides of the street, had to be circumspect.

Stanley retrieved a flashlight from the cab and then struggled with the trailer gate. He stopped to give Austin his most polished smile. "This horse is the genuine article. To see is to believe. Both sire and dam won a half-dozen quality stakes races—in Oklahoma, Nebraska, Louisiana. The horse was foaled back in February 1983, so come this January, as an official two-year-old, she'll be about as mature as any of her competition."

"*What?*"

"I said come January—"

"You said *she*. A filly. You told me *colt* on the phone."

"That poor little devil came up lame, Austin. So I picked up Miss Muffet for you instead. Same sire, actually."

"Miss Muffet? Jesus, what kind of name is that? What kind of horse is this?" Austin demanded, his mood changing. "Stanley, if you've led me on a wild goose chase—"

"You won't be sorry you came," Stanley insisted. "I don't have to apologize. I don't have to blow trumpets either. This little filly will speak for herself."

Austin stood back as the gate swung open and Stanley carefully backed out the horse. Austin was skeptical before even setting an eye on the animal. He just didn't trust fillies on principle. When they went into heat, they were easily distracted. And generally they were more temperamental than colts—couldn't keep their minds on a race. In a quarter-mile run concentration counted for a lot.

"Isn't she a beaut?" said Stanley as the horse stood quietly by the trailer. The flashlight swept over her.

"Oh, shit, Stanley!" Austin moaned. He wanted to strangle the horse broker. He couldn't believe what he was looking at. Was this a horse or a prisoner of war? "What the hell is that around her eyes? And her ears!"

"Miss Muffet is a very sensitive horse," Stanley explained quietly. "She doesn't sleep well unless she wears a blindfold. And the earmuffs are to keep out noise, natuarally."

"Naturally," Austin deadpanned. He watched as Stanley gingerly removed the satin blindfold. The earmuffs were left on. Miss Muffet gazed warily at Austin.

"Gawd Almighty," Austin exclaimed, "does she wear that blindfold when she races too?" He was tempted to give up and head back to the auction.

"She does wear blinkers when she races," Stanley confessed. "But that's not so uncommon. A lot of horses are distracted by a race crowd. I grant you, the earmuffs are on the rare side—"

"She wears those woolly things in a race?" Austin said with incredulity.

Stanley only nodded.

"Blinkers and earmuffs. And her name's Miss Muffet." Austin let the filly sniff his hand, horses trusting their sense of smell more than sight, and patted her on the neck. "How the hell did she get a name like that?"

"The owner submitted a couple names to the AQHA and got turned down. So he let his daughter give it a crack.

She's four. You know, 'Little Miss Muffet sat on a tuffet . . .'"

"Terrific." Austin knew the frustration of naming a horse. It couldn't have more than three words or a total of sixteen letters, including punctuation; couldn't be named after a living person, unless they gave permission; couldn't be a name used in the last fifteen years. But Miss Muffet?

"Has she raced much?" Austin asked.

"Twice at Delta Downs. A place and a show. Her owners swear she would have won both times, but she was a little slow out of the gate. They're only selling her because they're cutting back on their quarter horse stock."

If this wasn't buying a pig in a poke, Austin didn't know what was. But as he looked more closely at the filly, he couldn't help being impressed. Her conformation, even under a distorted flashlight beam, looked impressive. She was handsome too. Three white stockings, white star on her forehead, a long connecting stripe down her nose. "You know," Austin spoke up, "as much as I dislike comparisons to thoroughbreds, this horse has pretty much got the same markings as Secretariat."

"Now you're talking," Stanley beamed. "And don't forget what Penny Tweedy said when she first saw Secretariat as a colt."

"Yeah. She said *wow*. I don't know what I'm saying, except that Miss Muffet isn't your typical horse. How much?"

"Austin, she's a steal."

The filly suddenly approached Austin and pressed her nose against his. "Look at that," marveled Stanley, "didn't I promise love at first sight?"

"How much, Stanley?"

"Twenty thousand."

Austin gently grabbed the halter and led the horse to the privacy of an old cottonwood. He looked the filly right in the eye. "Miss Muffet, I'm thinking seriously of putting my hard-earned cash on the line for you. I'll give you a nice home, plenty to eat, good company, and a cushy retirement. But you've got to run your tail off for me. You look like you could be great—if you're not lazy and you've got a winner's heart. I sure hope you do. . . ."

With an agreeing whinny, Miss Muffet nuzzled her face against Austin's.

"I'm hardly a desperate man," Austin lied to Stanley as he brought the horse back, "so I'll offer $15,000. Not a red cent more." Buying and selling horseflesh was not unlike dealing in real estate, and Austin relished the little rituals. "But I want to see Miss Muffet's papers first, and I want to speak to her vet. If that's acceptable to the sellers, you can deliver her to my ranch within the week."

"I'll do my best," promised Stanley.

The two shook hands, and Austin trailed back to the auction to find Fern. His thoughts wouldn't leave Miss Muffet. Despite her eccentricities and his initial reservations, he had instinctively liked the horse, and Austin trusted his instincts. Two races under her belt wasn't much, but at least the filly was familiar with a race track. If he turned her over to his trainer and David within a week, there would be time enough to prepare for the All-American.

Two hours later, buckled in the pilot's seat of his Learjet, Austin streaked down the runway of the Lexington airport and shot into the cloudless sky. He suddenly felt terrific, and smiled at Fern.

"How'd you like the party?" he asked.

"Not much. I don't think I have anything in common with those people."

"Who does? I'm sorry I left you high and dry, honey." He leaned over and kissed her. "I'll make it up, promise. But as my daddy used to say, *bidness* is *bidness*."

"Did it turn out all right?"

Austin smiled again. "I think we just bought ourselves a horse to run at Ruidoso. Her name's Miss Muffet."

"A filly?" said Fern, as skeptical as Austin had been.

"You won't believe this horse when you see her. But I've got a feeling in the old gut—I think she can take the whole shooting match come September."

"Really?" Fern was pleased by Austin's mood. She

hadn't seen him this hopeful in months. "That would be wonderful."

"Yesiree," he said, flipping on the tape deck. Willie Nelson's voice flooded through the cabin. "Seventh time's the charm."

ELEVEN

"FRANK, CAN'T YOU SHOW SOME MERCY?" RACHEL shouted into the hotel lobby phone. A pair of grandmother types took notice of the subway-decibel voice and gave Rachel a glance. "I don't want to fly to Florida. I don't want to interview a dolphin trainer who just defected from the Soviet Union. I've had it up to my eyeballs with that kind of—"

Frank offered his patented sigh of martyrdom, as if it weren't enough that he had to cope with the usual office headaches, now he had a rebellious reporter. "Rachel, a couple days ago you couldn't wait to get out of Dallas. Now you practically want to move there."

"I told you why. I've got some leads on this horsenapping."

"You just said the police don't know anything."

"But I do. I've gotten to know a couple of the principals." She thought to tell him about her night in Calvin's apartment, then decided to keep her little escapade private. Details might not convince Frank anyway. Once the man made up his mind he turned into stone.

"You're not a detective, Rachel. Maybe in your other life you were, but in the here and now you're employed by

Image. When something breaks on the horse story, you can fly back to Dallas. Until then be a good trooper, will you?"

Rachel did something then she had never done before. She hung up on her editor. She'd had enough of desperate movie stars, obsessed Nazi hunters, and dolphin trainers who couldn't speak English. The really sad thing, she decided as she headed toward the nearest public library branch, was that she'd gotten used to being the good trooper. It gave her the perfect excuse when her life turned into a dead end. Hey, it wasn't her fault—she was just following orders. Well, no more, Rachel thought. She was her own boss now, and she'd take responsibility for the consequences. She wanted this horse story, and with or without Frank's permission she was going to break it open.

In the library she pored over old magazines and newspapers to find the thread that was Thom Warfield's colorful life. He'd grown up the only child of a mostly-unemployed carpenter in a poor Amarillo suburb. Smart, personable and hell-bent, young Thom had dropped out of high school to smuggle in wetbacks for cattle ranch labor in the panhandle. He'd also been picked up fencing stolen Porsche and Mercedes parts to a reconstruction gang in Missouri. A friend described him as someone who liked to test limits. The freewheeling entrepreneur had been arrested several times on a variety of charges but never convicted. Judges inevitably felt sorry for the bright, charming young man who said he'd had to leave school to support his poor parents. He had just gotten sidetracked, he explained, and hung out with the wrong people.

The words were more prophetic than Warfield realized. In the summer of 1963 he picked a fight in a Juarez bar and for his efforts received nine knife wounds in the chest. Six months later, surviving several major surgery and cliff-hangers with death, he walked out of an El Paso hospital a changed man. Born-again Christians had a new member in their ranks. Thom Warfield promised to mend his ways. Finishing high school, he went on to college and law school, then promptly started his own corporate law firm in Dallas. He was the shining example of reformation and initiative that Rotary and Lions clubs loved to toast, and they welcomed Thom with open arms. The man could do no wrong.

Warfield, Henson, and Iason soon doubled and tripled its client load, in the process making its founding partner a well-to-do man. Money begat money. Thom Warfield invested wisely in oil and gas tax shelters and bought a partnership interest in Aztec Park race track. The latter was philosophically possible because while Thom was a churchgoing man, he was not a Baptist. He began hitting the chicken-and-green-pea Rotarian lunch circuit, became president of the Jaycees, and in 1976 threw his hat into the ring for a seat in the state house of representatives. He lost by a narrow margin but was later appointed by the governor to the Texas Anti-Crime Commission for a six year term. In 1983 he was reappointed, over the protests of pro-betting lobbyists who complained that his owning a race track was a conflict of interest.

Well, on the evidence the man was extremely well liked, Rachel thought, and to some he was a hero. He spoke out for law and order. He had a beautiful family. His teenage past was behind him. Or was it? Despite his image of integrity, there were hints of improprieties. That's what Austin had said too, Rachel remembered. One story alleged Warfield had had inside information that the city of San Antonio wanted to annex land for industrial zoning, and the enterprising lawyer quickly bought vast tracts of nearby real estate then resold it to the city for an undisclosed profit. Another story had him involved in a scandal at Aztec Park, allegedly paying jockeys to hold back on their mounts while a Warfield proxy bet heavily on other horses. A suspended jockey testified that the track owner had personally approached him, but no grand jury was convinced. It was hard for Rachel to swallow too. The stunt was totally stupid. But maybe, she thought, there was still a naive, reckless side to Thom Warfield. She'd always been skeptical of sudden character conversions, especially coupled with religion.

After lunch Rachel changed twenty dollars into a purseful of change and parked herself by a pay phone. The young man answering at the American Quarter Horse Association in Amarillo had never heard of *Image* magazine, which Rachel somehow found refreshing, but he was intrigued about talking to a reporter.

"What happens when a horse like Five Deuces is reported stolen?" Rachel asked.

"Among other things, we notify every track in the country."

"You mean in case someone tries to change her papers. But wouldn't that be obvious? There're safeguards—"

"It almost never works," the young man agreed, "though God knows people keep trying. And if it does work, it isn't for long."

"No one has any leads on Five Deuces?"

"Not that we know of. We've alerted police in every state."

"I see. Thank you," she said. She started to hang up but lingered a moment. "There haven't been any other race horses missing, have there?"

"As a matter of fact, there have."

Rachel's ears perked up. "Could you be more specific?"

"None got the publicity of Five Deuces, but we've had thirteen reported disappearances in the last six months. Four in Louisiana, two in Texas, three in Nebraska, and four in Oklahoma. That's a lot. All good stock too. Usually you can attribute some to runaways and local theft, but those kind are recovered in a week or two."

"Then what do you attribute these to?"

"If I knew that, m'am," he said politely, "I'd be a hero."

"Is there anything else you can tell me about the thefts?"

"One thing, they're all yearlings. And most owners had plans to race them next year."

"Really?" said Rachel, making notes. "What do you think all those horses are worth?"

"Well, most of the yearlings weren't purchased, they were bred on the owners' ranches. But their bloodstock was all first rate. For insurance purposes the combined value of the yearlings is well over $1 million. Of course, that's deceptive. Their real worth is what they would earn at the track and for future stud fees. Maybe millions. Maybe tens of millions. That Five Deuces was supposed to have a lot of promise. Does any of this help you?" he asked.

"I think so. Thank you again—very much."

Rachel then called the Jockey Club and promptly asked the same questions. Not to her great surprise, eight thoroughbreds had been reported missing since spring. None had been found. Rachel wrote down the dates of the disappearances. Were they all yearlings? Affirmative. Considered promising stock? Affirmative again. What was being done? Outside of alerting law enforcement officials and individual race tracks, and owners hiring private investigators, there wasn't much else that could be done.

Rachel hung up. Why hadn't someone put the pieces together? There had to be an organized theft ring, didn't there? She knew that the Jockey Club and AQHA were rivals, but didn't they communicate about thefts? And unlike for missing children or fathers who skipped support payments, Rachel gathered, there was no central clearinghouse for lost horses. But if there were a professional theft ring, why? And why just yearlings? Insurance fraud seemed farfetched. So did some crazy act of revenge. And no one had said anything about receiving a ransom note.

Still, Rachel felt she was getting warmer. If the mystery were a bingo card, she already had half the numbers covered. All she needed now were a few more facts. There was only one place to go.

She waited till almost seven, when the city had gone home for the night, and took a taxi to Warfield, Henson, and Iason. A security guard in the downtown high rise asked her to sign in. "Doris Day" she wrote, smiled brilliantly, and proceeded up the elevator to the penthouse suite. A shuffling janitor eyed her curiously, but Rachel sauntered through the glass doors as if she worked there.

"Don't bother to lock up," she called over her shoulder as she walked past the copying machine and down the plushly carpeted hallway. "I'm going to be a while."

For the first time she began to feel her nerves. Did she really know what she was getting into? But the thrill of breaking the story eclipsed all fear. She wasn't sure to what extent Seth or Calvin were involved in the thefts, but she'd bet the family jewels that Thom Warfield was up to his elbows in it.

Warfield's office was the picture of opulence. It made Austin Mirabeau's look like a caddy shack. The man knew how to live. Expensive handmade Italian tiles gleamed on the floor. The semicircle desk was inlaid with ivory. Designer leather couches and chairs flanked the desk like a central command post. With a nod to high tech, the stereo equipment in the built-in shelves looked like the instrument panels on a 747. Everything was bathed in soft light.

Rachel snooped around till she found panels that concealed several handsome cherry-wood filing cabinets. The drawers were locked tight. It took ten more minutes to find the right keys at the bottom of an antique humidor. She wasn't sure what she was looking for as she dug through myriad files. Maybe a link to Calvin or Seth. She didn't want to believe that Calvin was involved. He was too nice a man; so, probably, was Seth. But she couldn't forget the two phone conversations she'd overheard. File by file Rachel waded through the first cabinet. Nothing. Frustrated, she dropped in a chair. It was almost nine already. For a moment she thought she heard something in the hallway, but when she listened again, there was only the hum of a drinking fountain. She went back to the next cabinet. At the back of the second drawer, bound with a rubber band, was a stack of onionskin papers.

Invoices, Rachel saw as she thumbed through the pile. More specifically, bills of lading. Typed in the box for merchandise was only the word SPECIAL. Every paper was virtually the same. The cargo, whatever it was, had been loaded on an Irish ship docked in New Orleans, which had then sailed for Dublin. The sender was Warfield, Henson, and Iason. Rachel wondered what a law firm was doing in the shipping business. The first bill of lading was dated March 1984. The last one, a mere two days ago, had an actual shipping date for the end of the week.

Jesus, she thought. The bingo card was starting to fill up. Rachel made Xeroxes of all the invoices down the hall. Could Thom Warfield actually be shipping horses to Ireland? It seemed incredible, but maybe there was some logic. What if the AQHA or the Jockey Club didn't notify other countries about domestic thefts? Unless, of course, the horse was famous, but then the whole world would know anyway. *These* missing yearlings were hardly well known. They hadn't even raced yet. Why couldn't new papers be forged and the horses slipped into overseas races? Maybe good, promising horses were in demand in Ireland or Europe. Like the young man had said on the phone, the horses might not be worth much now, but if they proved to be champions, you were talking megabucks. Just the opportunity a man like Thom Warfield couldn't pass up.

Rachel studied the most recent bill of lading. The ship wouldn't leave for another couple days. That had to mean that the last horse was still on terra firma. According to Rachel's notes, Five Deuces was the last reported theft. She began to digest the urgency. But what the hell was she supposed to do, call the police? There were no facts, just her speculation. She had to be absolutely sure before she told anyone. She also wanted her story.

Rachel slumped behind Warfield's immense desk, swallowed in the chair, and thought about the situation. Her glance kept jumping to the photograph of Warfield on the desk, his arm cozily around the governor of Texas. The large man had a grimly set jaw and a sprinkling of moles on his left cheek. He looked tough, Rachel conceded, more so than in the news photos in the library.

Rachel let go of the image, took a breath, and picked up the phone. From correspondence in the file drawers she already knew the name of Warfield's secretary. She dialed information for the number of the 5555 Ranch in Sherman, then rang through. She was relieved that Seth answered. To get Meredith involved now would only mean complications.

"Howdy, this is Carol Lee. From Mr. Warfield's office? Mr. Warfield asked me to work late tonight, because of the upcoming shipment to Ireland? We got ourselves a little problem, Mr. Cartwright. . . ."

Rachel stopped to listen to her heart hammering away.

"What kind of problem?" Seth finally spoke up. His voice was less than steady.

"Mr. Warfield needs you in his office, an' I'm afraid it has to be tonight, Mr. Cartwright."

"I don't understand."

"Well, it seems we got a very delicate situation in New Orleans. The merchandise isn't quite complete."

"What?"

"We're missing part of the equipment," said Rachel. "To be comfortable when she travels, our merchandise requires the right bridle. Mr. Warfield says he needs it tonight if it's gonna be sent on to New Orleans before the ship leaves. . . ."

There was a low moan on the other end, the significance of which Rachel had no idea. Did Seth understand about the bridle, the one Meredith had said her temperamental filly couldn't be without? He seemed lost, confused. Rachel said good-bye, grateful to get off the phone because she was losing her Texas accent. For a moment she felt relieved, but as she paced the room she began to worry.

If Seth checked with Warfield, her little charade was all over. Warfield himself might come down to the office tonight. Or what if Seth Cartwright was totally innocent, what if this little scenario she had pieced together was only fiction . . . if the Irish ship bound for Dublin was carrying not horses but hay? She'd have egg on her face, not to mention a breaking-and-entering on her record.

So get the hell out, she told herself.

But a small, stubborn voice demanded that she see this through. The payoff was too great if her speculation was true. When and if Seth showed up with Five Deuces' bridle, Rachel knew she had her story. It was a good hour drive down from Sherman. Rachel dropped back in the chair and tried to get comfortable.

A noise came from the hallway.

She sat up and listened. It was no drinking fountain this time. Someone had just walked through the unlocked front door.

She flicked off the office lights and hurried into a darkened closet. The door didn't quite close behind her. Sweat beaded down her neck. The lights in the office suddenly went back on. Through the crack Rachel fixed on the stocky, swaggering figure of Thom Warfield. He halted at the threshold of his private, inviolable kingdom, his cold eyes roaming the room in suspicion.

Seth Cartwright hung up the phone and made the lonely walk from his private study to the den. Meredith was behind her desk, lost in a paperback, and Seth quietly took a nearby chair. He tried to ignore the bubble of pain floating in his belly. The traditional two bourbons before dinner had left him in a pleasant daze until now. He waited for Meredith to ask who had called, and was ready to bring a lie to his lips, but the silence only lingered benignly. In the last few days Meredith seemed to have lost hope for Five Deuces. Phone calls no longer represented potential leads or consoling friends, only more disappointment. To his distress, Seth had watched his wife hole up in the house more and more, turning down social engagements and neglecting ranch work. The ranch was hardly falling apart, but Meredith was. He had never seen her so distraught. Twice he had felt like making a full confession, even though it would mean bearing her explosive wrath and a certain divorce. What had held Seth back was the paper-thin hope, and Calvin's insistence, that the whole episode would soon blow over. In another few days the horse would be out of the country, and then there was nothing anyone could do. Time heals all wounds, Calvin had added soothingly. Not to worry, he'd said. Meredith would find another horse to run at Ruidoso.

But Seth did worry. He worried a lot, not just about being exposed as a horse thief, but for his youthful transgressions. The anticipation of public humiliation haunted him, as he knew it must Calvin. But Calvin, unlike Seth, was essentially an optimist. Problems arose to be solved, not to defeat him. At Seth's insistence Calvin had finally leveled about Thom Warfield. Seth was appalled, not to say incredulous. The plan was insane. Even if he accepted that European Mafia money was behind an effort to bring the best horses in the United States back to Europe—what couldn't be bought at sales and auctions might be stolen—

Seth couldn't accept that sooner or later someone wouldn't put the puzzle together. Its very audacity was a cover, of course, but Seth knew Thom Warfield from legal circles, and the man was totally greedy. He gave pigs a bad name. He would keep stealing horses until one day he was finally caught, though surely Warfield's arrogance told him it would never happen. Pride goeth before a fall, and with Thom would go Seth, and with Seth his privileged and happy life.

Seth stirred in his chair, ready to leave for Dallas as soon as he could fashion a good excuse to Meredith. That goddamn bridle. . . . Last month, when they had planned the theft, Seth had explained more than once to Calvin that Five Deuces needed to be handled with kid gloves. She was a baby. Like a favorite toy, her special bridle had been left in the corner of her stall, yet the nitwits who grabbed her had overlooked it. According to Calvin, Five Deuces had been languishing in a New Orleans warehouse for the last two weeks, half sick in spite of medicine from a vet and plenty of food and fresh water. But Seth had been assured she was well enough to travel. Why, then, the call tonight from Warfield's secretary? Maybe the horse was getting sicker, the bridle a desperate, final hope. The last thing Seth wanted was for the poor horse to die. After hanging up with the secretary, he had tried calling Calvin to see if everything was legitimate. No one answered. Seth didn't relish calling Warfield directly. Just thinking about the man gave him a chill.

"Honey, I feel like a movie tonight." Seth smiled, rustling the change in his pocket. "Wanna come?"

She shook her head.

"I'd sure like to get out."

"Please don't go," she said, looking up from her book. "I don't want to be alone."

"I'm restless, angel. I need to step out. I can't sleep. . . ."

For a moment their eyes met. She was looking at him for hope and strength, he realized. Seth couldn't hold the gaze. "Don't wait up for me, hon."

He started toward his jacket but suddenly turned and

reached down to give his wife a heartfelt hug. "I love you," he said.

As he stepped into the chilly night, Seth felt like a clumsy Judas, not sure if or when an act of betrayal was ever over. The new night watchman was away from the stables. Seth picked up the bridle and hurried out. He levered himself behind the wheel of his Eldorado and forced the accelerator down.

To be on the highway, the bridle beside him, was a relief, but after half an hour his hands began to shake. Why had this whole misadventure happened to *him*? he thought for the hundredth time. He felt a vague, futile anger at providence for singling him out. He was a good and honest man, as decent as they came today. He didn't deserve any of this.

On the fringes of Dallas the electric-blue Cadillac swam out of the blackness toward a small neon oasis known as Gordy Lee Howard's Do-Drop-Inn. Seth had made the acquaintance of this particular honky-tonk on previous trips to and from Sherman. The waitresses were friendly, and the night crowd mostly quiet, thoughtful drinkers. It was a decent spot for a nightcap, and tonight his nerves were sufficiently on fire to require the house's best whiskey.

Seth was unaware of the car that had pulled in behind him, the same one that had been following at a discreet distance since he left Sherman and whose lights now softly bathed his Eldorado. The driver watched as Seth disappeared into the bar, but did not immediately venture in after him. First it was time to gather thoughts, make conclusions. The car radio played a duet with Kenny Rogers and Dolly Parton. The thinking was hard and painful.

After a moment Meredith flicked off the radio, guiding her car into the space next to Seth's. She killed the engine and let her fingers drum the steering column. Could Seth be meeting a lover? The possibility had occurred to her only tonight, when Seth had given her the most passionate embrace of their married life. Guilt, she suspected, and on top of the thin, sudden excuse of wanting to see a movie, she had decided to follow him. The idea that he might be taking advantage of her in the wake of Five Deuces induced a silent rage. Still, she hoped she was wrong. Seth had lied about the movie maybe, but couldn't he have private business somewhere? She was just skeptical it would be at the Do-Drop-Inn.

Stepping out, her eyes swam over Seth's car. Something lay in a shadowy heap on the seat. A bridle, she thought, puzzled. She opened the door and picked it up. Her eyes narrowed. What was Seth doing with Five Deuces' bridle?

"Oh, Jesus!" she whispered. Her thoughts raced to the obvious conclusion. She felt sick, couldn't move. Thou shall not steal another man's horse. It was the eleventh commandment. And to be betrayed by her own husband, the man she adored, whom she shared her ranch and life with . . . Meredith's shock was eclipsed by a blinding fury. She tucked her handbag under her arm and stormed toward the Do-Drop-Inn.

Perched comfortably on a barstool, Seth sent the first bourbon down the hatch with an effortless flick of the wrist. He waited for his nerves to take a turn for the better, but when they didn't, he elected for another dose of medicine. The effect this time was immediate. His spirits were bolstered as a benign fog settled in. Once again the world was without danger or malice. He offered a smile to his neighbors and was about to buy them drinks when his eyes lifted to the bar's gold-filigreed mirror. Seth stared uncertainly at the hazy figure of his wife, like a man who had never totally trusted his hold on reality. He turned in slow motion, waiting for the image to vanish. When it persisted, he could only offer a sweet, lame nod.

"Sugar, what a surprise—"

"You son of a bitch—"

"Now hold on a minute, honey."

"Where's my horse?"

"Your horse?" The fog parted for a moment, long enough for Seth to realize that he had been found out, and that some smooth talking was now called for if he wanted to escape. But a silver tongue had never been one of his gifts.

"What horse is that?" was all he could come up with, and a timid smile.

Seth knew instantly he had made a tactical error. He wasn't sure why he had even said it. Jesus, his poor nerves. The indignation and injury that passed over Meredith's face alarmed him. He watched, dismayed, as she thrust her hand in her purse. A silver derringer appeared, the one Meredith always carried when alone at night. But you're not alone, Seth addressed his wife in his thoughts. You're with me, honey. He rose gallantly, to take her in his arms again, but Meredith pulled back and steadied her gun hand. The honky-tonk turned quiet.

"Angel," Seth implored.

The word got lost in a chorus of gasps from his barstool brethren. "Of mercy," someone finally muttered.

Breathing was painful. Short, exaggerated gasps for air. Rachel shifted her weight to get more comfortable, but her legs burned anyway. Hidden behind a half-dozen wool coats, she'd been a prisoner in the closet for almost three hours, and Warfield, comfortably ensconced behind his desk, gave no sign of closing up shop. When he'd first stepped into his inner sanctum, Rachel was sure she was a goner. Warfield had studied his office warily, as if he sensed an intruder, but finally his eyes had grown complacent and he dropped behind the desk and a stack of files. Late night client work, Rachel observed through the crack. It was plain bad luck for her, yet there was nothing to do but wait it out. She just hoped Warfield would take off before Seth arrived. And right now the man was already overdue.

Warfield suddenly rose, giving her hope. But he only drifted to the rows of stereo equipment, flipping toggle switches and pressing buttons until the sweet, bright sound of Mozart filled the room. *The Magic Flute*, no less. Rachel recognized the solo from Papageno. Suddenly a second voice filled the room. Rachel wagged her head in disbelief. The burly, steel-jawed lawyer, who more resembled a bouncer or hit man, was singing along. And not just casually. He was a golden tenor. He had perfect pitch, and every bit the range of the singer on the recording. Finally the phone intruded.

"No, goddammit," Warfield barked. He had listened

patiently for a moment, but then his face crimsoned over. Rachel saw signs of a temper. "The ship's called *Friendly Rose*. No, no, it's Friday night, *Friday* . . ."

Warfield snapped a pencil in two with one hand. "Berth twenty-three. And you don't walk the horse out there, you put him in the truck. I know it's only four blocks to the dock. The captain's name is Meagan. Stupid—"

The receiver was slammed down. Mozart was still playing. Warfield quickly finished at the desk, agitated over the phone call. Then he flicked off the lights and left the office. Rachel waited before crawling out. Her legs still ached from cramps as she picked up the phone. She'd had it with being the Lone Ranger. Let someone else be the hero now. With the copies of the bills of lading and the conversation she'd just heard, she had enough to call the New Orleans police department.

She spoke to a sergeant in stolen property, giving the location of the warehouse as four blocks from Berth 23 and the name of the suspected ship and its captain. Then she called Frank Beardsley. Her hands were trembling and she was out of breath.

"Frank . . ." She dropped into the chair. "I'm sorry, I know it's long after midnight back there, but sit down. . . . You know what I just found out?"

"Rachel?" The voice sounded wide awake, as if Frank had somehow been expecting her. "Where are you?"

"Look, I'm sorry I hung up on you. I just couldn't make myself go to Florida, not with everything happening in Dallas—"

"Oh? Something's happening in Dallas?" He was cold and sarcastic.

"Yes, something's happening in Dallas. I just broke the horse story."

"Really?"

"Why the sarcasm? I've risked life and limb for this, Frank. You ought to give me the Croix de Guerre."

"Now listen," he said sternly. "You just blew it. I've been looking all over for you the last hour."

Rachel couldn't believe the ingratitude. It made her furious. "I didn't blow anything. I know where Five Deuces is. I just called the police in New Orleans. There's a horse theft ring, and the main guy is a prominent Dallas attorney named Thom Warfield—"

"You blew it," Frank repeated.

Rachel gave up. "Just what are you talking about?"

"I'm talking about a shooting in a roadside bar on the outskirts of Dallas."

"And what happened there, oh, fearless editor?"

"Meredith Kingsley just put a bullet through her husband's head."

III
Class

TWELVE

ANYONE WHO HAD OBSERVED MEREDITH KINGSLEY IMME-
diately after the shooting would have described a remarkably calm and composed woman, almost icy in her
detachment from the swift and brutal event, as indeed some
patrons of the Do-Drop-Inn volunteered in their renditions
to the police. Meredith had in fact stood stoically by the
battered oak bar after the deed, looking at her husband as a
paramedic slipped an intravenous needle into one pale arm
and strapped an oxygen mask over the lifeless face. One
patron said Meredith even ordered a drink. Another alleged
that she has asked the ambulance attendant if she might
ride with her husband to the hospital, and when denied,
had exhibited no signs of disappointment. The police, who
arrived shortly after, put her in handcuffs. Meredith gave
her name, freely admitted that the man she had shot was
her husband, and advised a plainclothes lieutenant to look
in her handbag for the derringer. She stood stone-faced as a
police sergeant read her the Miranda card. No one seemed
to know who she was.

The rest of the night she spent in an underheated adult
detention center in downtown Dallas. A jail matron asked if
she wanted to call someone, "like your lawyer or somebody," but Meredith said no, she didn't have an attorney.
The truth was that Seth did all the legal work for the ranch.
There was one S. Roger Rombro, negotiator of her three
divorce settlements, but this was a criminal matter. The

irony was not lost on Meredith that one of the best criminal attorneys in Texas was her husband, but at the moment she had no idea if Seth was even alive. If he was, it was unlikely that the victim of a crime would rush to defend his assailant, even if she were his wife. Meredith suddenly broke down and wept. Nothing the tough but sensitive jail matron tried could stanch the river of tears. The shock that had afflicted Meredith after the shooting—which bar patrons had mistakenly construed as callousness and detachment—had, like an anesthetic, worn off. The natural pain suddenly seeped in.

Another hour passed before Meredith had the presence of mind to call Calvin Garrison, who was alseep in his apartment. In an uncharacteristically halting voice she explained what she had done, that she needed help and he was the only friend she could think of. Calvin promised to call an attorney and check on Seth. He would be down to the detention center as soon as possible.

Meredith was placed in a cell with a sweet-looking but sullen prostitute who kept chewing her nails and talking about her dead mother. Wrapping her arms around her knees, Meredith stared at the walls. The events of the night began to swim into focus. What had she done to poor Seth? She tried to reclaim the indignation and outrage that had compelled the shooting, but it was now lost in the mists of guilt and shame. On the wall above the toilet a perceptive guest had scribbled one of the immutable laws of human behavior: THE MORE IMPULSIVE THE ACT, THE LONGER ITS REPERCUSSIONS. In that one instant of impulse—like a peaceful river suddenly swollen by a storm—Meredith thought—the course of her life had been changed radically, and maybe forever. She had never been in jail, never committed a felony, never stood as a defendant in a trial. With great clarity she perceived the chamber of hell into which she was now descending. Yet part of her insisted it could never happen. This was a mistake. Seth would be all right. He would forgive her. The storm would pass and her life resume.

When Calvin arrived a little after four A.M. he embraced Meredith warmly. The lawyer in tow quickly paid the scheduled bail for attempted murder with a check, foregoing the benefit of a bondsman and instead posting the full amount on assurances from Meredith that she could well afford it. Calvin took Meredith aside and told her that Seth was still in surgery. He was under the care of a top neurosurgeon at Presbyterian Hospital on Walnut Hill. Apparently the bullet had entered the brain just above the left ear but had not penetrated deeply. There was a good chance he would be just fine. Meredith nodded weakly. She tried to feel hope as they walked outside into the dark morning.

"Are you okay?" Calvin said, searching Meredith's face.

"I don't know."

"Can I take you anywhere?"

"I want to go to the hospital."

"Seth won't be out of surgery for another hour. How about some coffee and breakfast? We could talk—"

"You're being very sweet," Meredith said. "And I appreciate all you've done for me. But I think I want to be alone."

"Of course," he said, understanding. "Oh, I almost forgot. I have some news for you—good news."

Meredith looked up skeptically. What could possibly be good after what happened tonight?

"Just after you called, a reporter named Rachel Lang gave me a ring. I know her," he said casually. "She'd been trying to reach you at the ranch, and when there was no answer, she took the chance and called me. She knew you and I were close. It seems she's found Five Deuces—"

"Where?" Meredith jumped.

"In a New Orleans warehouse, of all places. The police there already have the horse."

"Is Five Deuces all right?"

"Run down, apparently, but okay, according to Rachel."

"I have to fly down—"

"Now hold on, Meredith. You can't do that. One of the conditions of your bail is you stay put."

At first Meredith felt a swell of relief, even elation. Then she wondered why the news couldn't have come sooner. She also wondered why she hadn't questioned Seth more closely in the bar instead of giving in to her anger. Why, even, did Seth have to leave the ranch with Five Deuces' birdle? Why did she insist on following? But the more she questioned fate, the more helpless she felt. Answers always came too late.

"I remember Rachel well," Meredith volunteered. "I liked her a lot. We had a little visit the day Five Deuces was taken." She hesitated. "You didn't tell her anything about tonight. . . ."

"No. Nobody knows. But as soon as reporters make their mandatory checks of police records for the night, your name is going to be splashed around."

"What can I do?"

"You'll just have to gut it out. Your big problem is going to come not from the media, but the district attorney," Calvin said bluntly. "A lot depends on Seth, of course. But even if he recovers, attempted murder charges could be brought against you."

"But I wasn't in my right mind tonight. . . ."

Meredith waited to be reassured, but Calvin's uneasy silence indicated that anything was possible. For the first time she was really frightened. A chill broke down her shoulders and settled in her stomach. She wondered how she would cope with what was to come, and if she had the same mettle as her mother. Meredith knew that everyone thought she was tough, even indomitable, but she had doubts.

Calvin flagged a taxi and opened the door for Meredith. "Who took my horse anyway?" she demanded.

Calvin seemed unprepared to answer. "I wish I knew."

"But how was Seth involved?" she persisted.

"I don't know."

"Didn't Rachel say?"

"A bunch of amateurs were trying to ship some horses to Europe. Something really crazy like that. It doesn't matter, as long as you've got your horse, does it?"

But Meredith wanted to know. It was the horse theft that had precipitated tonight's tragedy. She turned to Calvin with another question, but he'd already found a taxi for himself. He waved a hurried good-bye. He was preoccupied about something, Meredith thought. Maybe politics. Only a week away, straw polls indicated an election too close to call. She suddenly realized how little she knew about Calvin, despite years of friendship. He was an able, conscientious senator, but Calvin Garrison was the world's most private person.

At the hospital Meredith talked to several nurses in the Emergency Room, but they could only tell her that the surgery was going as well as possible. The smell of rubbing alcohol made her dizzy. She drank black coffee and called Abel Hanson at the ranch. The trainer was instructed to hitch up a horse trailer and make a beeline for New Orleans. She wanted the vet along too. As soon as a complete physical was done on Five Deuces, Abel was to call her at the ranch. She hesitated, trying to tell him about the night's events, but how could she? She felt so ashamed. Yet in another few hours Abel and the whole world would know. In the end she said nothing and hung up.

She settled in the ER reception area, a war zone of the sick and wounded: a Mexican who'd been stabbed had left a trail of blood from the door to the exam cubicle; a little girl with a broken arm who kept insisting her mother had beaten her; a jealous husband who'd poured lye in his wife's eyes. And Meredith had shot her husband. Sitting among the sinners and victims, the need to repent swept over her. Her first act was to open the handbag the police had returned to her, minus the derringer, and take out her checkbook. For helping her tonight, she wrote Calvin a campaign contribution of $20,000. Then, as promised, she made out the reward check for finding Five Deuces to Rachel Lang for $100,000.

"Ms. Kingsley?" a polite but detached voice called.

She studied the young surgeon whose mask hung limply around his neck and whose gown was spotted with blood. The face was that of a farm boy, deep furrows in the forehead, stubby, cauliflower ears. Meredith rose with an effort as he approached.

"We've finished for now. Your husband's been taken to Intensive Care," the doctor reported. Uncomfortable or just exhausted, he let his foot paw the ground. "I don't know whether we'll have to go back in or not. Depends on any hemorrhaging. The other danger is long range. The damage was to the left hemisphere, which controls speech, linear thinking, logic, some memory—"

"What are you saying?" Meredith interrupted.

The doctor looked surprised at her impatience, as if he'd expected more gratitude, someone to hang on his every word. Annoyed, his tone turned more brusque.

"Your husband's recovery may not be one hundred percent. In fact, it might not be at all. At the moment he's in a coma."

"*Coma?* No one said anything about a coma."

"No one asked," the surgeon replied coolly. He frowned as Meredith marched toward the elevator bank without a thank-you or good-bye, no doubt marveling at her detachment. What he didn't know was that inside the elevator she began to cry again. The idea of Seth in a coma was as painful to Meredith as if she'd killed him outright. To be a prisoner inside your own body was a death in itself.

On the ICU floor she inquired at the nurse's station for Seth's room, only to be told he couldn't have visitors, family included; she might check with the attending physician tomorrow. Meredith promptly headed down the hall to the room anyway, heedless of a wrestler-cum-nurse who lumbered after her. Seth's room was light and airy, but Meredith only felt gloom. Tubes were attached to her husband's arms and face, hooked up to bottles of pale solutions that bubbled silently into the imprisoned body. On a nearby table computerized machines clicked and whirred, needles jumped across graph paper, red and blue lights lit up with scientific certainty. Immobilized, she stood before the deity of technology, wondering if it were a friend or enemy. She was ready to offer a prayer when she felt the nurse's sweaty grip on her shoulder.

An anger rose up, mute and helpless, as Meredith left the hospital. The sky was finally turning red on its edges. The sounds of a city waking up made her cautious. She drifted to a bar that never closed and sat alone to muse a final time on the night. Despite a double shot of scotch, no great revelations came to her. What was past was past. Yet as she watched the sky brighten from the window, she knew that was hardly the whole truth. The past was also prologue; Meredith just didn't know to what.

THIRTEEN

IN THE FIRST WEEKEND IN NOVEMBER RAIN TORTURED the city of Dallas for three straight days and nights. Streets flooded, cars were abandoned in the middle of highways, improvised rafts were dispatched to supermarkets. Most of the city took the autumn storms with good humor, but Rachel felt like a prisoner in her hotel room, watching the sullen skies with a matching temperament.

Six days after she'd nearly suffocated in Thom Warfield's closet, the story of Five Deuces had broken not just locally but in the national media. The *Dallas Morning News* juxtaposed Meredith Kingsley's picture with those of Seth Cartwright and Thom Warfield, reporting in depth the interwoven tales of theft, betrayal, and attempted murder. It was the kind of lurid intrigue among the rich and famous that Texas led the nation in and that Texans loved to read about. Rachel's name was mentioned prominently. The reporter-as-detective was given credit for garnering the evidence that led to Warfield's arrest and exposed his horse-theft ring. Without her wanting it, Rachel's picture and story appeared in a dozen papers and magazines, even in *Image*. Frank Beardsley had done his sackcloth and ashes routine, telling even his publisher he was sorry for questioning Rachel's tenacity and journalist's instincts.

The fling with celebrityhood had taken Rachel by surprise. She'd received letters, telegrams, and flowers from colleagues and admirers she never knew she had. Her hotel room had begun to resemble a funeral parlor, and bellhops were growing weary, even with the tips Rachel unstintingly gave, of bringing up more tokens of esteem. Still, she felt special. It was something that had never happened to her before.

The pleasant air of unreality had been enhanced by receipt of a $100,000 check from Meredith. Rachel had a vague recollection of the reward offer, but receiving the money personally was like winning a lottery. As a poorly paid reporter she had virtually no savings; to suddenly park a six figure check in her account was intoxicating. There was a brief discussion at *Image* whether an employee could accept such largesse, but it was decided that Rachel had uncovered the evidence in the role of private citizen and the money should be hers. She had entertained fantasies of early retirement, preferably on a Caribbean island with a tall, dark stranger. Then an accountant told her about taxes, and that with inflation the money wouldn't go terribly far. In the end she earmarked a portion for a shopping spree at Bloomie's and a car; the rest, she told her mother facetiously, she would save for her dowry.

Everything felt pretty good. Under the veneer of well-being, however, was a growing frustration of not being able to nail down the rest of her story. And Rachel knew there was more. Thom Warfield's confession had been too tight-lipped. He and some European "associates" had arranged to steal two dozen quality yearlings and ship them to Ireland for racing on the Continent, he'd written. Of prime value were the thoroughbreds, since Europeans mainly bred and raced long-distance horses. But the quarter horses were wanted to infuse sprinter blood into the thoroughbred stock and advance new and experimental breeding programs. The same associates had paid Warfield up to $75,000 each for the horses, plus shipping costs. New registration papers had been forged to fool European track stewards, who were not as perspicacious as their American counterparts, or were possibly more susceptible to bribes. An alcoholic plastic surgeon who'd lost his medical license on three separate

occasions had been employed by Warfield to surgically remove any interior-lip identification numbers, but the good
doctor had done less than a perfect job. Five Deuces had
come down with an infection that would have cost her life if
not for the intervention of Meredith's trainer and vet. The
horse was now home on the 5555 Ranch, being nursed back
to health. The other stolen horses were still being tracked
down in Europe.

The only people actually named in Warfield's confession were the plastic surgeon and a couple of petty criminals who'd abducted the horses from various stables and
pastures—hardly anyone of importance or with the knowledge to implicate others. One of the hoods was trying to
sing, insisting he got his orders from a Texas jockey and with
a little more time would find out the name for the district
attorney. Warfield's attorney insisted that wasn't possible.
No one knew any names. All plans about the horses had
been communicated from Europe through nameless cou-
riers. Warfield's attorney called his client basically honest
and decent. He'd fallen in with bad company who'd exploited him. Sure, Rachel thought at the vintage Warfield
defense—and the pope didn't know the names of his car-
dinals. At least Warfield had been pressured to step down
from the Anti-Crime Commission. It was a victory, a moral
one anyway, for the pro-gambling forces of Texas.

Rachel picked up her room phone for the fiftieth time
that day and placed another call to the 5555 Ranch. She had
been trying to get Meredith ever since the shooting, but a
housekeeper inevitably would reply that Ms. Kingsley was
resting and couldn't be disturbed. Rachel hardly blamed
her for staying in seclusion. Meredith had her hands full
with the Dallas district attorney, who seemed bent on nail-
ing both Warfield and Meredith. From what local reporters
had told Rachel, Clarence Bidmore was a short, spiteful
man whose Napoleon complex demanded a humbling of the
rich and powerful. Meredith's trial date had been set for late
February, but her attorneys were trying to push it back in
the hope that Seth would recover from his coma and prove
an ally. Bidmore fought them every step. It was going to be
a hell of a court drama, Rachel knew, and she'd been prom-

ised by Frank that she could cover every scene and act, right down to the curtain calls. No doubt Meredith would be put through the wringer. Still, it was crucial that Rachel talk to her, even if it meant disturbing her at the ranch. Meredith had to have some ideas about Seth's involvement, a motive maybe, a link to Calvin, other business deals with Warfield. Rachel left her number with the housekeeper.

Next she placed a call to Calvin Garrison's campaign headquarters. A secretary with a soprano twang reported that the senator wasn't in, nor was he expected. With only two days before the election there were too many last-minute campaign stops. Rachel went through the motion of leaving her name and number, but wasn't very hopeful. Calvin was too bright not to suspect what she was after. Still, she tried the ruse that her call was purely personal, hoping that their night together had meant something to him. It had meant something to her, she remembered.

After two cups of black coffee she went back to trying to put the puzzle together—but how? Warfield and Calvin weren't talking, Seth couldn't, and while Meredith might, she was hiding. Frustrated, Rachel dug out her raincoat and boots and headed out of the hotel. She trudged twelve blocks in ankle-deep water to the library. Only Dallas's bravest readers and researchers were inside.

Digging up background on Calvin from local magazines and news stories was no more difficult than it had been on Thom Warfield. Calvin's father had been a West Pointer and career officer, won a slew of medals in the Big War and retired a brigadier general. He was now in a nursing home. According to an interview Calvin gave *Texas Monthly*, the old man had been a strict disciplinarian at the expense of giving affection, precipitating several nervous breakdowns in his wife who, when Calvin was sixteen, flew the coop and never was in touch with husband or son again. Under his father's guidance Calvin enrolled at Texas A&M, enduring the dubious distinction of being an Aggie, and four years later entered law school at Rice. Graduating second in his class, he enlisted in the Army, attended Officer Candidate School, and served as a lawyer in the Adjutant General's Corps.

His father was disappointed when he resigned his commission in 1964 and went to work for the prestigious Dallas firm of Jones, Clayton, and Wheeling. Seven years later he was a full partner and *Garrison* had been added to the firm's name. In the interim he'd immersed himself in Democrat grass-roots politics. He made a successful run in 1978 for a two-year house seat in the state legislature, and in 1980 he threw his hat into the senate ring. Calvin emerged victorious by all of thirty-nine votes, one of the closest elections in state history. In the four years since, the liberal Democrat had earned a reputation as bright, personable, and someone who voted his conscience. Almost everyone described him as an indefatigable worker.

Rachel remembered Calvin's excuse for never marrying—just too busy, he said. Maybe it was true. The more Rachel read, the clearer it was that Calvin was well-regarded by his Austin colleagues and the Texas legal community. He was, however, keenly despised by a contingent of conservatives who claimed Calvin's ego was as large as Everest and that the super-legislator had designs on national office. A local tabloid columnist liked to report that Calvin, like a number of his Austin colleagues, was overfond of drink. Otherwise there was remarkably little dirt on the man. To the public, Calvin Garrison had become *the* senator who favored pari-mutuel betting, a stand he hadn't backed off of despite considerable opposition, including from the Anti-Crime Commission and Mr. Warfield. Rachel suddenly wondered if that could be the link between the two men. Had Warfield put pressure on Calvin to soften his stand, and when he didn't, stolen the horse of his good friend, Seth? It seemed farfetched. A couple of links in the chain of logic were missing.

Rachel pored over a final article about the election. Calvin's opponent was a self-appointed altar boy named Orville Clearlake, who like to pose with Jerry Falwell and take the bully pulpit on the evils of gun control, abortion, and gambling. The three vices were responsible for the collapse of Texas civilization as Orville knew and loved it. The rabble-rouser turned Rachel's stomach. Too many political stories written for *Image* had made her a card-carrying cynic.

Yet in Calvin she sensed someone who wasn't cut from the standard cloth.

She was still thinking about him when she returned to her hotel room and found the message that he'd called. Would she be free for a late dinner tonight? Flattered but dubious, she phoned his headquarters. He was supposed to be terribly busy, wasn't he? Calvin wasn't in, but his secretary confirmed the invitation. Rachel suspected a convention affair with truckloads of reporters and campaign staff, a last minute thank-you. But she was told no, the reservations were only for two.

Rachel arrived at The Palm in Dallas's warehouse district a few minutes before ten. She had the impression she was back in New York. The sister restaurant had the same pervading smell of lobster and onion rings, framed caricatures of the famous on the walls, and a simple but elegant decor of wood floors and cane chairs. The only difference was the conversational volume, which was earsplitting, and the good ol' boys at the bar who were dressed in three-piece suits but talked like they were punching cows. Calvin rose graciously from the table, impeccably dressed as always, and as he had before, introduced Rachel to what seemed like half the restaurant. He looked tired, Rachel thought, as well he should, but he still had a presence that she warmed to.

"I never thought I'd see you again," Rachel admitted as they ordered drinks.

"Really?"

"I didn't think we'd be having dinner anyway. Frankly, my last impression was you didn't want me around."

"I never felt that way."

Rachel wanted to believe him, but their icy good-byes in Calvin's apartment were still fresh in her mind. "You thought I was eavesdropping on your phone call, didn't you?"

"Were you?" he asked.

"Reporters can be allies to politicians," she said evasively, "or they can hurt them. I didn't particularly want to do either with you. All I wanted was the real story."

"And you got it," Calvin said. "You put Thom Warfield's

head on a platter. I wanted to thank you for that. That's why we're having dinner. When you exposed Warfield for the fraud he is, you helped my campaign and credibility. . . ."

"Then you wouldn't mind me asking some more questions?" Rachel said, testing the waters. "I don't think the whole story's been told."

"What else is there?"

"Something about you, Seth, your involvement with Warfield . . ."

As a reporter she was used to bluffing and usually found it easy, but for some reason, looking at Calvin, it was difficult.

Calvin was quiet, jiggling the ice cubes in his glass. She tried to read his face, but it was too remote. "Let's set some ground rules, shall we?" he said.

"By all means."

"You can ask me whatever you want, and I'll give you full and honest answers. I promise. But I'll only allow you five questions—no more. Then we can get on to something more pleasant."

"You've got a deal."

"Fire away."

Oh, she would. She would give him both barrels. "Did you have anything to do with the theft of Five Deuces?"

Rachel expected hesitation, at least a facial twitch or a rambling answer, but Calvin was butter smooth. If he was lying, he could have fooled a polygraph machine. "Absolutely not. The whole episode was a total surprise to me. The first thing I knew about it was when Seth was shot. Meredith called me from jail just a little before you did. She told me about following Seth to the bar, finding the bridle. Later she asked me how Seth was involved. I didn't know, and still don't."

"When Seth comes out of his coma, I suspect he'll tell us," Rachel put in. Calvin hardly looked ruffled. "Did you ever have any business deals with Warfield?" she continued.

"Never. I'd say our philosophical differences prevented that."

"Did he ever approach you about doing business?"

"No."

"Did he ever threaten you or your political career in some way?"

Calvin shook his head and ordered another drink.

"How well do you know Seth?"

"We're good friends."

"Business friends? Lawyer friends?"

"Neither. Personal. We've known one another for years."

"Tell me, is what everyone says true—that you want to run for the United States Senate one day?"

Calvin's lips inched up mischievously. "You're out of questions." He raised his glass. "To a victory tomorrow," he toasted.

Rachel clinked glasses. She was disappointed. She felt she had just been getting on track. "I still don't understand," she said, "why we're having dinner tonight. We're practically strangers really, except for one night of hopping in the sack together. And you've got the election on your mind."

"I told you. This is a thank-you. Your story helped me immensely."

"You could just as soon have sent me flowers. Everyone else did."

"You're very pretty."

"That's still not enough."

"And warm and sensitive."

"Why aren't I convinced?"

"You're rich now too, I understand."

Rachel laughed. "Not enough for anyone to be interested in me."

"Then what do you think?" Calvin said.

"I think you want to know how much I know about you, Seth, and Thom Warfield."

"And I just found out," Calvin said. "You don't know anything. Or else you wouldn't have asked me those questions. And since I gave you my answers, all honest and true, I hope you'll stop fishing now."

His tone said the discussion was over. Rachel sighed. What was she doing? He was sweet enough to take her to dinner, and she was giving him flak. Forget the sparring, she thought.

She felt guilty all through dinner. She'd become so cynical about men that she wasn't giving Calvin half a chance. And if it wasn't men, it was this crazy horse story that she'd become obsessed about. She'd judged poor Calvin guilty until proven innocent. Everytime another question about the intrigue came to mind she pushed it aside and tried to relax. Calvin was bright, personable, a perfect gentleman. Suddenly he leaned over and kissed her. It was a gesture that didn't go unnoticed by the waiter and a large number of patrons. Instead of being embarrassed, Rachel liked the attention. It made Calvin's affection more honest.

In his apartment they wasted no time getting undressed. He left the lights on, which usually made Rachel feel shy but now somehow she liked it. Calvin looked even more trim and muscular than the first time. They wrestled playfully, laughing, and she scraped her nails along his back. He responded by pinning her down, taking her with a force that stunned her. Her orgasm came slowly, then with a final rush that made her cry out with pleasure. They rested a moment and began again. She wondered where Calvin got his energy.

"Tell me about yourself," she said in the quiet afterwards.

"You're not being a reporter again, are you?"

"No."

"What do you want to know?"

"Everything."

"Why?" he asked, pushing a wisp of hair from her eyes.

"Because I like you."

"You said you already went to the library."

"I want to hear it from you. I want to know more. Like what your father is like."

"He was from West Point." Calvin made a mock salute. "'Duty, Honor, Country.' The man has a strict sense of right and wrong."

"Like father, like son?"

"People have said that, but no one could really match my father."

"My dad was a real pushover," Rachel volunteered. "He died a few years ago. He taught me to care about the world outside. I adored him."

"I was never that close with mine," said Calvin. "Just his presence in the house meant a lot of pressure."

"That bad?"

"Let me tell you a story." Calvin propped his head on his hand, looking at Rachel. "I had an honorable, hardworking uncle who served on the Oklahoma Highway Commission for over sixteen years. One day an accountant discovered he'd been embezzling from state funds and soliciting bribes. Went to jail for six years. My father was badly embarrassed, maybe worse than my uncle. The incident brought shame on the whole family. He warned me that day that if I went into politics I'd better walk the straight and narrow. So I have. My conscience wouldn't let me breach the public trust."

"My," Rachel teased, "an honest politician."

"With too much pride," Calvin admitted. "I dearly love politics and want to rise as high as I can."

"Ah, the flaw is ambition."

"Afraid so."

"But we all have that. The whole goddamn world is too ambitious. Anyway, who the hell cares?"

"What?"

"It's not important," Rachel declared, wrapping her arms around him.

"Then what is?"

"Whether we're going to see each other again."

Calvin was quiet a moment. "I'd like that very much," he said.

Rachel nestled her head in the hollow of his shoulder. She lay quietly and tried to sleep. For the first time in months she felt at peace. Maybe the secret was finally being with a man she didn't find a pretentious egomaniac. Even if they hardly knew one another, she trusted Calvin. She forgot the overheard phone conversations and her suspicions. Her fantasies carried her away. She would give up the frantic world of *Image*, the worries about competition, of proving herself to the world. She wanted to marry and settle down. Maybe she wanted Calvin. She could have the kids that her friends were already enjoying. All the much-vaunted women's independence had gotten her was frustration. Rachel squirmed closer, listening to his breathing. Calvin was asleep. Married to a United States senator. The fantasy was embarrassingly juvenile, but in the privacy of the night it seemed a delicious one. Then her old fears intruded. Something would come along and screw up this relationship. She would bet on it. Character was fate, wasn't it? When it came to men, why should she suddenly expect to lift her batting average? With an effort Rachel chased away her doubts and draped her arm over Calvin.

She was awakened by Calvin moving around the room. In daylight the apartment had the same immaculate orderliness that she remembered from her first visit. She sat up in bed and tossed her hair back.

"Good luck today," she called.

"I'm nervous," he admitted, straightening his tie.

"You don't look it."

He nodded absently, dialing the phone to his campaign manager. Calvin the whirling dervish had a pre-breakfast meeting with Chamber of Commerce officials, a board meeting at a bank, then it was off to vote. . . .

"Thanks for a terrific evening," she got in.

Slipping on his jacket, he looked incredibly handsome. "When am I going to see you again?" he said.

"I have to fly back to New York for a few days. Loose ends."

"Can't it wait?"

"Why?"

"You could come down to my headquarters tonight."

"For such an important occasion you must have some special lady friend."

"Untrue," he said. "I want to see you tonight."

"You're sure?"

"Win or lose."

"You're going to win," she said happily. "I'll bring champagne."

She wanted to add I love you, but it felt wrong, too soon. Calvin kissed her and was gone. In the silence of the apartment she wandered through the spacious rooms, feeling at home. She wondered what it would be like to live here with Calvin. More fantasy, she thought good humoredly. In the bathroom she found some conditioner and shampoo and took a leisurely shower.

Afterward, toweling the moisture off the mirror, she peeked into the medicine cabinet. There was no good reason for exploring, just plain, irresistible, cat-killing curiosity. The vials of prescribed pills were two rows across. Preludin, Ionamin, Desoxyn, Dextroamphetamine . . . There was one unlabeled vial of green and white capsules that Rachel recognized as West Coast Turn-Arounds, so named by a trucker who, on the strength of one capsule, hauled his rig from New York to California and started back again without a lick of sleep. Too many Hollywood parties had raised Rachel's pill-consciousness to a state of jadedness, but Calvin's private pharmacy was remarkable. No wonder he made love like Valentino and ran his life at three hundred RPMs.

She didn't know what to think. She'd never liked pills or trusted people who used them, but she gave Calvin the benefit of the doubt. The stress of an election campaign probably necessitated temporary relief, she told herself.

Dressed, she sat behind Calvin's desk enjoying the view of Dallas as she called New York. Frank wasn't in. Rachel left the message that she'd be in Texas a few more days for research. Her eyes swam over the desk and the neat pile of papers. It was as if she were in Thom Warfield's office again and had to start prying. But Calvin was not Warfield. He was the man she was falling in love with. The thin line between being a good reporter and invading someone's privacy was not nearly so thin as between being the reporter and the lover.

Jesus Christ, she hated her instincts. She *knew* there was something revealing to be found in that desk. A tie to Warfield or the horse ring. All she had to do was reach in and pull it out. She'd have her whole story. The story of the year.

Rachel sat a long, agonizing moment, thinking about

her choices. Then she picked herself up and left the apartment.

That night at Calvin's campaign headquarters she found herself beside him at the lectern, clapping along with the crowd at his unexpectedly convincing victory. She heard herself praised for having the courage to uncover the true story about Thom Warfield, and in so doing reelecting Calvin to another four years in the Texas state senate. He kissed her in front of the crowd, as politicians kissed their wives. She felt giddy, reckless, emboldened, a new Rachel Lang. And when they finally got back to his apartment and made the kind of love that was not wild or breathless, but warm and intimate, Rachel was thankful she had decided to leave all secrets undiscovered.

FOURTEEN

ADAM JEFFREY DASHED BREATHLESSLY AROUND THE LIVing room couch in pursuit of an imaginary monster named Zoltan, ignoring the sparkling Pacific and Buck's third warning to settle down. Finally Buck had no choice but to seize his son by the arm and with a firm shake send Adam Jeffrey to his room. The little boy burst into tears, hissing at his father, to which Buck responded with a glance of equal sternness. Inside, as usual, he was a marshmallow of guilt. Buck couldn't wait for Christmas vacation to end and Adam Jeffrey to return to his friends at the day care center. The boy was bored and restless, having gone through the toys Buck lavished on him at Christmas in all of three days. Now all he talked about was having a friend to play with. Buck knew virtually none of the parents in the day care center, and in his chic little colony of $1 million-plus homes, there weren't exactly hordes of little children. Over the vacation he had taken his son to Disneyland, Marineland, and Knott's Berry Farm, and while he knew the boy had had a good time, Buck sensed in Adam Jeffrey an abiding loneliness. He did need friends, and a mother too; and Buck's less than ample shoulders could only shrug helplessly.

The phone shrilled from the kitchen. A man with a clipped accent identified himself to Buck as Zallaq Al-Khalifa's personal secretary, and after inquiring about Buck's health and happiness, he politely asked if the actor might be free that afternoon. There was a "coming out" party for Mr. Al-Khalifa's horse, Desert Wind, at Alisal Ranch, forty miles northwest of Santa Barbara. The press had been invited, and the afternoon would hold some drama, the secretary promised mysteriously. It also might be an appropriate time for Buck to see the horse and get started on his public relations work.

"You're sure about the media?" Buck inquired. He was a little annoyed with the short notice, especially after not hearing from Zallaq for a month, but Buck had nothing important planned for that day, and it would be nice to stand in front of a few reporters. It also occurred to him that the outing would be fun for A.J. The boy loved ranches and horses.

In ten minutes, with a six-shooter strapped to Adam Jeffrey's side, they were seat-belted in the Porsche and on their way to Santa Barbara. Buck's spirits picked up on the cool, bright January day. He was anxious to get a peek finally at Desert Wind. He was also eager to get involved with Zallaq.

Despite repeated promises from good old Sidney Pomerantz, no director or casting agent had come knocking on Buck's door in recent months with a hot new series or even a cameo role. Zallaq, on the other hand, had sent him a retainer of $25,000 and the promise of plenty of media attention. How much, Buck was eager to find out.

The more he learned about his Arab benefactor, the

more impressed he was. Afflicted with Hollywood paranoia, Buck had read everything he could find on Zallaq for fear the man might be a sham or out to exploit him. All evidence pointed to the opposite. Besides his incredible wealth, Zallaq had style, intelligence, and ambition. There were pied-à-terres in London, Paris, Rio, New York, Los Angeles, and Acapulco, and according to gossip columnists, a girl in every port. Yet he worked twice as hard as he played. His bioengineering company had gone public two years ago and was considered the best in the field of animal husbandry. Zallaq also had interests in a pharmaceutical company, several banks, New York commercial real estate, and an Atlantic City casino. What he earned, he generously shared; there was no bigger philanthropist from the Arab world. Despite his Western tendencies, Zallaq still adhered to Moslem principles. In Bahrain he had a wife and four children and figured as an important leader in a country that, while liberal compared to the rest of the Arab world, was still dominated by religion. Buck forgave him any hypocrisy. The man led a schizophrenic existence.

There was one footnote to Zallaq's early years that was especially intriguing to Buck. Twenty-some years ago, before he inherited his mantle of wealth, Zallaq had led a basically normal life. After undergraduate work in England, he'd enrolled at the University of Texas as a graduate student in biology, specializing in reproductive physiology. For his doctoral thesis he proposed an experiment called "flushing." He and a veterinarian wanted to inject a genetically superior cow with hormones so it would "super-ovulate," its ovaries releasing ten to twelve eggs instead of just the normal one. The cow would then be inseminated, either artificially or naturally, and its uterus "flushed" with a special solution to remove the impregnated eggs. Each embryo was then to be replanted into the uterus of another, lower quality cow, who would theoretically give birth to superior offspring. Almost every department professor was skeptical of the idea, and over Zallaq's and the vet's dismay and protests, permission was never granted to try the experiment. Angry, Zallaq left the program and never received his doctorate. Today "flushing" was an accepted operation to improve livestock quality. Several biologists had received credit for pioneering the surgery, but Zallaq wasn't one.

The man had been a prophet ahead of his time, Buck conceded. He'd been slighted at the University of Texas, and by Texans. While others might have forgotten and marched on, there was a brooding quality to Zallaq that did not forget. The more Buck read, the clearer it became that his patron was on an odyssey of vindication. What Zallaq had created in Desert Wind was meant to be an altar before which the rest of the world should bow. If he had Zallaq's fortune, would he waste his time getting even with society? Buck wondered. Everyone had pride, but that much? Buck thought he'd rather have a good time twenty-four hours a day. Only life was never that simple. Just as recognition for his acting had become an obsession to him, maybe Zallaq's quest for respect in his field was the magnet in his life. As his Porsche shot through Santa Barbara and made the turn for Alisal Ranch, Buck silently wished the man a lot of luck.

"Think you'll find any bad guys out here?" Buck asked Adam Jeffrey as they approached the 10,000 acres of secluded rolling hills. Dotted with sycamores and giant oaks, the dude ranch had an elemental, pristine beauty. Supposedly Clark Gable had been secretly married here, though to which wife Buck wasn't sure. He also knew a few actors who preferred "retreating" to Alisal than to more conventional spots like Palm Springs. There was more privacy here, but for $400 a day, Buck thought, you were entitled to it. The road led him toward a cluster of sun-washed bungalows, a lake, tennis courts, and a championship golf course. Horses and riders crisscrossed the verdant hills.

"Bang . . . bang . . ." Adam Jeffrey took aim at the nearest rider. "Daddy, have you been here before?"

"First time, A.J."

"How come we're here now?"

"There's a very special horse I want you to see. His name's Desert Wind."

"Can I ride him?"

Buck laughed. "I don't think so, not yet anyway. Just

make sure you don't shoot him. He's too important a horse to get hurt."

As Buck neared the lake he spied a cluster of cars and a crowd of people near two horses. Media, he gathered, but he wondered about the second horse. He parked his car and strolled toward the reporters with an affable smile, shaking hands as he went. Most were sportswriters, but there were a few society columnists. Then Buck spotted Zallaq, shouldering his way through the crowd to stand by his pride and joy.

"Come meet the fastest horse in the world," Zallaq called out to Buck.

Buck felt flattered to be singled out in a crowd that his first glance had informed him contained at least a dozen celebrities. Hoisting Adam Jeffrey on his shoulders, he edged toward the muscular chestnut colt that officially had just turned two. As Adam Jeffrey put a hand out to pet him, the big colt suddenly jigged. Adam Jeffrey squealed in fright. Zallaq quickly stepped between them and calmed the horse while photographers, flashes exploding, captured the human interest shot for tomorrow's papers.

When Buck was sure his son was all right, he turned his attention back to the horse. The conformation was incredible. Desert Wind looked as big and mature as any three-year-old. His croup was sloped, his tail set low. His cannon bones were short and sturdy. The chest and forearms were incredibly muscular. And just by the way the colt looked at you, Buck thought, you could see a presence of mind, an operating intelligence. No question: the horse had class. But there was one thing that struck Buck as strange. Desert Wind's head was small, at least in proportion to his gorgeous body. The distance from the ear to the muzzle looked an inch or two shorter than it should be. But Buck quickly forgave the small slight from Mother Nature. From appearances the horse looked like he could burn up any track in the country.

"Buck," Zallaq called, with a sweeping gesture to the second horse a few yards away, "I want you to meet Bluebeard and his owner." Buck studied the pale but handsome man holding the other horse's reins. He was tall, blond, and had prominent cheekbones. He stood as ramrod straight as a cavalry officer. "This is Warren Garr," Zallaq said.

Buck pumped the man's hand warmly, as if they already knew each other. He wasn't sure whether they really had met or not—maybe at some cocktail party—but he certainly knew of the actor, as did most of the reporters who huddled around now.

"I didn't catch your name. . . ." Warren Garr said.

"Buck Hart."

"That rings a faint bell." For a second the actor's face became a searching frown, then it dissolved into a I-give-up smile.

With great self-control Buck let the insult pass, but he felt embarrassed in front of Zallaq.

"As Bluebeard's proud owner," Zallaq addressed the press, "Mr. Garr wants to challenge my horse in a match race. Here and now on this beautiful ranch. A couple of two-year-olds who never lost a yearling race. What do you think, Buck?"

Buck studied the four-legged adversary, and then its owner. Warren Garr looked smug and complacent, as sure of his horse as he was his Hollywood career. Buck fought off the familiar stirrings of jealousy. Warren had been kissed by the gods of success. His career had taken an upward trajectory and never faltered: a hit ABC sitcom, leading man in some made-for-TV movies, and next fall there was a Broadway play. He was no better looking than Buck and no more talented, but somehow he'd gotten the breaks. Flush with fame and money, he'd bought heavily into quarter horses. And now here he stood: self-righteous and cocky, owning the world, squinting down at Buck as if Buck were a cockroach.

"I'd love to see a race," Buck said to Zallaq. "Some poor fool has got to be Desert Wind's first victim."

"You wouldn't want to put some money on that, would you?" Warren Garr shot back. He stuffed his hands in his jeans, rocking on his heels.

"I think the horses can speak for themselves," Buck offered.

"Really? Well, I think your mouth's a lot bigger than your wallet."

Buck felt his face redden. He wanted to clobber the asshole. Cameras clicked and pencils raced across writing pads. How could he back down now? "How does ten thousand sound?" he answered coolly. Buck suddenly felt Adam Jeffrey at his side, tugging at his jeans like a prod of conscience. The boy was smart enough to be aware of Buck's anxiety over money. Except for re-runs and what Zallaq was paying him now, Buck didn't exactly have barrelfuls of cash coming in.

"I like twenty thousand better," Warren threw back.

"Sure. Twenty thousand it is," Buck said automatically, and shook his rival's hand.

Buck flicked a prayerful glance to Desert Wind. A straightaway had already been roped off for the race, and the horses were quickly saddled and led to the starting line. Two jockeys from Los Alamitos jumped on the respective mounts. With the impromptu bet, Buck judged, the press' appetite had been sufficiently whetted to guarantee Zallaq good coverage. Buck began to wonder if he hadn't been set up. Was this his public relations role—suckering in bets, or maybe being suckered himself? His stomach began to turn.

He led Adam Jeffrey by the hand to the finish line, gazing back the 300 yards as the two horses waited restlessly.

"How come you bet so much money?" Adam Jeffrey suddenly asked.

Buck smiled, feeling even more foolish. "Something to do with pride."

Adam Jeffrey looked up at him, not understanding. "Are we gonna win?"

Buck only turned quiet and circled his arm around his son. The start wouldn't be quite fair without a gate, but even if Desert Wind got off slowly, Buck thought, if he had the speed that Zallaq claimed, he would still win. After a moment Zallaq held up a red flag to the jockeys, let it hover in the still air, and dropped it cleanly.

Desert Wind broke first. The long, lunging strides were almost reckless in their confidence. Buck fixed on the muscular shoulders as the horse charged, the sheer beauty and grace of its motion. Yet it was impossible not to think just as much about the colt's determination and aggressiveness. Desert Wind *wanted* to win. He loved racing. At the halfway point Bluebeard was a hopeless four lengths behind, and by the finish Desert Wind had stretched his lead to seven lengths. Buck raised his fist in the air. He couldn't resist a nod to Warren Garr, whose stern face had turned several shades paler.

"Sorry to take your money, but I did warn you," Buck rubbed it in, loud enough for reporters to hear. He waited as Warren took out his checkbook. Nothing had felt this sweet in a long time. Desert Wind had won, and in the process made Buck a winner too. He winked at Adam Jeffrey, as if to tell him any anxiety had been groundless, that Buck had sensed victory all the time. He decided on the spot to put the money away for Adam Jeffrey's college education.

Afterward several reporters clustered around Buck. One or two remembered him from *Citizen Army*. Riding a new wave of confidence, he was only too happy to expound about his future. He was preparing for a new movie, his agent was exploring some Broadway roles, and being an old and good friend of Zallaq's, he was contemplating buying an interest in Desert Wind. The vagueness of the lies allowed the reporters' imaginations to roam and made Buck's career seem anything but on the wane. This was more publicity than he'd had all year. He thanked everyone for coming when he felt a tap on his shoulder. Zallaq gave him a tight smile and motioned Buck aside.

"I couldn't help overhearing your conversation," the Arab said.

Buck felt embarrassed, especially for his statement about buying part of Desert Wind. "I guess I got carried away," he apologized. "With that bet and everything. I do admire your horse, that's all I really meant."

The Arab was quiet, fixing his gaze on Desert Wind as he was being cooled out by the jockey. "Are you sincere?" Zallaq asked.

"What?"

"Would you really like to own an interest in my horse?"

Buck didn't know how to figure it. Surely Zallaq wasn't getting rid of Desert Wind. The colt was his ticket to fame and respectability. "Sure, and throw in a piece of your Atlantic City casino," Buck deadpanned.

"You know a lot about me, Buck."

"Well, I did some research. . . ."

"Then as much as anyone you know how much this horse means to me," Zallaq said with an intimacy that surprised Buck and made him feel good. "I'm determined that Desert Wind will be the greatest quarter horse since Go-Man-Go or Dash for Cash, maybe the greatest horse ever. But first and foremost I'm a businessman. A year ago I formed a company called Equine Match Exchange. It's a kind of stock market for trading breeding rights shares in stallions. For an annual fee members who join the Exchange can sell the rights to their top stallions at 'asked' prices, or offer to buy rights from other stallion owners at 'bid' prices. The Exchange staff then matches up the offers, making a commission on each transaction. Granted, there was resistance to my idea from some Southern breeding farms, but largely we've caught on now. The horse business today has far-flung international investors who can't always make it to the Keeneland sale every summer. Through the Exchange's computers they can know the bloodlines and racing records of any horse in the world and decide instantly whether they want a share."

"How does Desert Wind come into this?" asked Buck, intrigued.

Zallaq smiled warmly. "By way of a new business that's an offshoot of the Exchange. "There are usually forty shares of ownership in a quarter horse syndication, thirty-three or thirty-six for thoroughbreds. When someone buys a share, he has the right to one or two breedings per year for as long as that stallion lives. A colt like Desert Wind, of course, is too young to be syndicated for any real money. He has to prove his worth at the track for at least two years. And if he's the great horse that we know he is, he'll win all his races.

His syndication value will then become astronomical. Anyone with the foresight to see that, Buck, should have the opportunity to capitalize on it."

Buck couldn't see disagreeing. "Go on."

"My new venture is selling options in syndication shares. Similar to a stock option, the buyer, for a front-end fee, has the right to purchase a syndication share at a future date for a fixed price. In the case of Desert Wind, an option now will cost $50,000, and the syndication share, two years down the road, will be $350,000. Once you purchase an option, it's a negotiable instrument. After a year you can sell it any time you like. When Desert Wind wins the All-American this year, I'd say, conservatively, that an option will be worth $150,000, and an actual share maybe $750,000."

Buck's mind flooded with numbers. At first Zallaq's figures struck him as high, but hadn't a single share in Seattle Slew recently sold for $2.9 million? Thoroughbreds traditionally commanded higher prices than quarter horses, but lately shares in all good horses had gone through the roof. Buck could see eventually where one in Desert Wind would be worth $1 million. And if he ever decided to go into the horse breeding business, like Warren Garr, to actually buy a good mare and mate her with Desert Wind, the profits could be staggering.

"What about a live foal guarantee?" asked Buck. When breeding rights were sold, he knew, a stallion's owners usually didn't guarantee a live birth, and sometimes not even a pregnancy. You could pay a million or two and come up with nothing.

"A live foal on the ground," Zallaq promised, "or the shareholder gets an extra breeding for free."

"Any refund of option money? I guess I keep thinking of King's Ransom. . . ."

"Buck, I can't allow for all contingencies. You can't expect a profit without some risk. Desert Wind could break a leg, get sick, have a heart attack—"

"I understand," Buck cut in, sorry he'd even asked. If he wanted a guarantee, he could always put his money in a savings bank. But in his heart of hearts Buck was a gambler. His whole acting career had been a gamble, lately a disappointing one, but you had to have hope, didn't you? After witnessing Desert Wind's convincing victory over Bluebeard, Buck was filled with enthusiasm . . . and hope. In a matter of seconds he had become a true believer.

"Put me down for four options," Buck said with the same automatic ease that he'd made his bet with Warren Garr. The truth was he could barely afford one, but Desert Wind was a dream, now his dream too. Buck knew their two destinies were inextricably linked.

Before saying good-bye, Zallaq spelled out Buck's public relations duties. Desert Wind was scheduled to race eight times before the All-American at Ruidoso, and Buck was to be at each race a day early for a PR party. He'd be socializing with the media, potential share owners, and prominent members of the public. And that was it? thought Buck. Piece of cake. For a moment he experienced a shudder of his old Hollywood paranoia. When things seemed too good to be true, they usually were. But he couldn't see how or why Zallaq would exploit him. The Arab was richer than sin; he didn't need Buck's $200,000 for the options, they could easily be sold to somene else. He was doing Buck a favor. Trust the man, Buck thought. Ashamed for his doubts, he shook Zallaq's hand warmly.

That evening, walking on the beach with Adam Jeffrey, Buck had never felt better. The late edition of the *Herald-Examiner* showed a photo of Buck and his son on the bottom of the sports page. Desert Wind, high and handsome, was in the background. Buck had cut out the photo and now unfolded it for Adam Jeffrey.

"What do you think?" Buck asked proudly. He expected a *wow* or a *gee*, but all he got was a worried glance.

"What's the matter?" Buck said.

"Nothing."

"I think something's bothering you."

Adam Jeffrey picked up a pebble and tossed it into the waves.

"Well?" Buck coaxed as the water rode up and nibbled at their bare feet.

"It's the horse."

"What about him?"

"I don't know. I don't like him. He scares me."

"What do you mean? When he bucked this afternoon—"

"No," said Adam Jeffrey.

"Then what's the matter? Desert Wind's a beautiful horse. Maybe the fastest you'll ever see."

"Maybe, but he still scares me," the boy said with innocent certainty, and hurled another pebble into the sea.

FIFTEEN

THE FEBRUARY SUN HUNG LAZILY IN THE CLEAR, POWDER-blue sky, arching over Palm Beach's cozy shoreline and the homes of the wealthy and privileged. Swimming pools glistened in the rows of wall-to-wall estates. Wintering East Coast families of old-line wealth mingled on backyard tennis courts and the plush fairways of private golf clubs. High season black-tie charity events that raised hundreds of thousands of dollars in a single night were held with the regularity of afternoon teas. And on Worth Avenue, Bergdorf-Goodman, Gucci, and Sara Fredericks were still doing a Christmas-rush business. The sidewalks on this fine Saturday afternoon were hardly as cluttered as New York's Fifth Avenue, but they were congested enough to annoy Billy Sullivan. He continually had to jerk his head up to navigate. His mood was further darkened by the words of his companion, Sam Cohen, whose scolding had the impact of a chisel on stone, chipping away at Billy's self-esteem.

"Don't look so down," Sam finally ventured. "You're a fortunate man to be out of Argentina."

"Out of the frying pan, into the fire," Billy quipped with no humor.

"Well, don't blame me," Sam pointed out. The small, jaunty man with the deeply furrowed face jingled the change in his pocket. "I'm the guy who saved your ass, remember?"

Billy nodded absently. He was wrong to bitch so much, especially at Sam. And he really was lucky to be back in the States. Argentina had been the biggest nightmare of his life. After airport customs guards had beaten him, he'd been taken to a dark, cramped cell on the city's outskirts. Drug dealers, pimps, and political prisoners were his neighbors. He'd been allowed one call. He chose Olguin. The art dealer not only wouldn't help him, he blasted Billy for being stupid enough to get caught. Customs officials had already been to his gallery and he'd had to deny everything. "It wasn't my fault, I was set up!" Billy yelled into the phone. "And for Chrissake, call someone in the States to help me." Guards hustled him back to his cell, but not before Billy took a clean punch at one asshole of a sergeant. Next to smuggling the paintings, it was the dumbest thing he'd ever done. He was beaten severely, denied food for five days, and became sure he'd die there.

Two weeks later a prissy Army captain made a call. Someone had arranged for Billy's freedom, he said, without looking too pleased about it. The next day Billy was handed his passport and a new airline ticket. He wanted to celebrate, but in Miami he found his troubles weren't over. Sam had had to borrow $30,000 to bribe the Argentines, adding to Billy's debts. Worse, someone in the Argentine police had informed Miami customs of Billy's crime. To his dismay he was arrested again. Because of heat over drug couriers, the Argentines were bending over backward to show the United States how cooperative they could be. Billy was caught in the net. The paintings were shipped up as evidence. Shit, he couldn't believe this, Billy told Sam. There was nothing he could do but hire a lawyer and pray.

"Look, Billy," Sam said as they walked. "I know it seems the world is ganging up on you, but at least by Monday the legal tensions will be over."

Legal tensions. That was a good one. "You think I'll be found guilty?" Billy felt another chill.

The last few months had been like groping through a dark tunnel without knowing where it ended. He'd been arraigned in a federal court in Miami, had pleaded not guilty, and was released on his own recognizance. Then he'd sweated out three months before his case came on the docket. His attorney convinced him to waive his right to a jury trial, entrusting his fate to what the attorney called a "friendly" judge. Some friend, Billy had learned. A swarthy, grim-faced septuagenarian, Judge Memshaw had openly wagged his head when Billy swore he'd been set up. The Argentines, Billy had tried to argue, were a petulant, vindictive bunch who'd been angry at their Palm Beach defeat by Billy's team. In Buenos Aires it was Gallegos who had arranged for the soldiers to wake him in the night, just for harassment. Billy was sure now. But the judge knew nothing about the polo world of spoiled and rich Latins. Final disposition of the case was to be on Monday. The possibility of a jail term made Billy almost physically sick. He couldn't decide which was worse, the loss of freedom or the public humiliation. Just the arrest and trial had already brought him negative publicity, and it bothered him in a way he couldn't describe.

"If you are found guilty," Sam offered gently, "the sentence should be light. You're a first-time offender. You've been a model citizen, your father was eminently respected—"

"Okay, okay," Billy said impatiently.

"The point is, guilty or not, you're in a heap of trouble. How much do you owe your attorney?"

"When it's over, probably $20,000."

"With the $30,000 I dished out to the Argentines, you're way beyond your means. And your ongoing monthly tab is an easy $15,000."

"What are you suggesting?"

"File for bankruptcy."

"My father would have loved that."

"Then you tell me."

"I could sell some horses." He had two dozen ponies

stabled in Palm Beach, but could survive on nine or ten. With the polo season in full gear there were plenty of buyers around.

"How much would you make?" Sam inquired carefully.

Billy could see the human calculator starting to push buttons. "Maybe $100,000."

"That would help. But what we're talking about, Billy, is your life-style. It's too damn expensive."

"You can't ask me to give up polo. It's not a life-style, it's my life."

"I'll make you a deal," Sam said after deliberating. "Keep your polo ponies but sell that race horse you won."

"El Cid?" Billy made a face. "No way."

"You already told me that the colt's going to cost you the Denver mint. You've got to hire a trainer, put the horse in races, haul him around the country, pay the entry fees. . . . If you think polo's expensive, wait till you get into racing."

"You're forgetting one thing. . . ."

"Tell me."

"I'm lucky," Billy said sincerely.

Sam snorted. "Did you tell the judge that?"

"I'll get out of this mess somehow. Anyway, what the hell do you know about horse racing?"

"I've had clients who lost their shirts. Silk ones."

"And nobody who ever won?"

"Never."

"Then maybe I shouldn't be hanging around you," said Billy, tiring of the conversation. He shook Sam's hand and promised to keep in touch. As he wandered down Worth Avenue he felt the full weight of his problems. Thinking of El Cid, he tried to be positive, but all he saw was more trouble. The truth was he didn't know what to do with the horse. What was it that the legendary horse breeder John Madden had decreed? Better to sell and repent than to keep and repent. El Cid was stabled nearby at Wellington, right where Billy had won the horse, eating oats and barely putting on weight. A groom got around to exercising him once a day, but Billy had no trainer, no real regimen. The colt was a long shot, Billy had to face that, and would cost him $35,000 easily between now and the All-American at Ruidoso. If El Cid *got* to the All-American. He had yet to be entered in a single race, much less win one to justify Billy's expectations. Christ, he thought as he headed back to his condo, maybe Sam was right. It was all pie in the sky.

Monday morning he dressed in a conservative suit and made the hour and a half drive to the federal court complex in Miami. The courtroom smelled of furniture polish. Alongside his attorney, Billy stood tentatively before Judge Memshaw, feeling weak in the knees. He still couldn't believe this was happening to him. Even if he was guilty of the deed, Billy thought, he was still a victim of circumstances.

"Mr. Sullivan, approach the bench, please," the judge rumbled. The smallish man seemed lost in his voluminous black robe as he leaned toward Billy and his attorney. "A very curious thing just happened, gentlemen. I was informed by the sterling representative of our federal government that we have an evidentiary gap. Can you imagine that?" The judge swung his stern glance to the glum and contrite prosecutor. "I'm speaking of the evidence against you, Mr. Sullivan. To wit, four Argentine religious paintings. Along with several bags of heroin, the paintings sprouted wings last night and flew out of a locked room to God knows where. I suspect into some deputy's garage or a pawnshop. Which infuriates me and makes me wonder what the hell I'm doing up here." Disgusted, he removed his glasses for a quick buffing on his robe. "Although I don't like it, Mr. Sullivan, I'm duty bound to dismiss all charges against you."

Billy felt the blood leave his cheeks. He couldn't move. When he came to life, he gave his attorney a disbelieving hug and hurried out of the courtroom before someone could tap him on the shoulder and say there was a mistake. His luck had held after all, he thought as he drove giddily back to Palm Beach. Maybe it was okay to believe in miracles. He promised himself never to return to Buenos Aires, never to get involved in anything illegal. He was still crazy about Aymara and wanted to see her, but from now on she'd have to fly to the States.

In the next few days Billy fulfilled his promise to Sam.

He sold half his string of ponies, raising $110,000, and mailed a check to New York. He would not sell El Cid. A Palm Beach realtor offered him $60,000 after only a cursory look, not even asking about bloodlines, but Billy resisted the temptation. Somehow he'd find the money to hire a trainer and enter the two-year-old in a futurity or two.

With his mind finally off the trial, he began to concentrate on polo again. After his arrest, when the winds of gossip had fanned his name through polo's intimate society, Billy had retreated from the game and its social world. Everyone was so proper that he knew he would be judged a disgrace. The self-exile had been painful mostly because of the great matches Billy had missed. But with his acquittal, the pain was behind him. In some ways the timing of his return would be perfect. For the prestigious Cartier Cup this weekend the best players in the world were descending on the Palm Beach Polo and Country Club, including Gallegos and his cohorts. Billy couldn't wait to play them again. He was just as eager for the black-tie ball that would kick everything off. He'd finally have the chance to mix with old friends and talk to the Cartier officers about raising his salary. Nothing would please Sam more, Billy knew, than getting his financial house in order, his life on stream.

He called half a dozen lady friends for the dance, but either they were already going with someone who'd had the courtesy to call more than four days in advance, or were otherwise occupied. The responses were almost all chilly. As many women as Billy knew, he scored a perfect zero, and finally he quit trying.

Saturday evening he arrived alone for the dance, a little self-conscious but hardly feeling lonely. He had looked forward to the night. It felt good to be back at the club, he thought, studying the familiar vista. Rows of condominiums anchored the far side of the polo grounds, and closer in was the polo house with its formal dining area and locker and club rooms. On one of the playing fields an immense enclosed tent had been erected for the evening, and Billy watched as guests streamed toward it under the floodlights, the men in tuxedos and the women bathed in silk and jewels. Inside, potted trees with small, twinkling lights bordered the dance floor. On a raised, revolving platform ten stunning models were perched in dark body stockings, virtually nude except for their Cartier necklaces, brooches, and assorted jewelry. There were enough diamonds on them to pay the federal debt, Billy marveled. An orchestra sat behind the dinner tables, which were covered with fine linen and stunning bouquets of white roses.

A waiter handed Billy a drink, and he began to circulate. He extended his hand to players and tournament officials, but no one seemed overjoyed to see him. When he brought up his acquittal there were few congratulations. Even old teammates greeted him coolly. Slowly he began to understand. Now he knew why getting a date had been so difficult. In the polo world you could do whatever you wanted, breaking every commandment on the tablets—it was okay as long as you didn't get caught. Cocaine was okay, screwing your best friend's wife was okay, shacking up with teenage girls was okay. *Just don't get caught.* Because if you were, you'd always be guilty. Billy's face colored in anger before he spotted a jowly man with long sideburns and thinning hair.

"Harold," Billy called, motioning the Cartier vice-president aside. The two were old and good friends. At Yale Harold had taught the one business course that Billy had floundered through as an undergraduate. A year later, tired of his meager salary, the professor had left academia to take a public relations job with Cartier. When the international jewelry company decided to lend its imprimatur to the professional polo circuit, it was Harold who had signed Billy to his first contract. Billy knew he'd drawn from the well of their friendship more than he'd given back, but now he had to draw again.

"Billy boy," Harold said warmly, draping an arm over his shoulder. "Enjoying the party?"

"Of course. It's great to be here," he said diplomatically. "Harold, I was wondering if we could talk. This may not seem the right moment, but something's on my mind."

"Speak up, man."

"It's money, frankly. Playing this sport isn't getting any

cheaper, and you know how well I've been playing lately."

"Before you were arrested," Harold allowed, discreetly dropping his voice.

Billy nodded uncomfortably. "What do you think?"

Harold shrugged and focused on his drink.

"We can talk tomorrow, before my match starts," Billy said. "I'm not playing till three."

An embarrassed sigh rose from Harold's lips.

"What is it?" asked Billy.

"Shit, you really don't know?"

"Know what?"

"I thought someone had already told you." Harold looked pained. "We've talked this over at Cartier. It was decided you shouldn't play in our tournaments. Not for a while anyway."

Billy stared at him.

"I think you understand, Billy."

"Don't give me that, not from you, Harold—"

"I'm sorry. We're friends. But in the interest of the game's image, we all thought it wouldn't be right for some-one who's had the unfavorable publicity you've had—"

"I was found not guilty," Billy interrupted. "Everybody here knows that. If they came down from their goddamn pedestals for a moment they'd all admit they've been in worse trouble."

"There's more to it than that, Billy," Harold offered del-icately. "Some of the players have spoken to me. Frankly, they're not sure they want you on their teams."

"Other players?" he repeated in cold astonishment. "They wouldn't be Argentines, would they?"

Harold nodded reluctantly.

"Jesus Christ—"

"Billy, face the economic facts. The Argentines may be prima donnas, but they happen to play the best polo in the world. They draw the fans, they make us money. Players like you don't. I think very highly of you, Billy, you're im-proving your game all the time, but you can be replaced. Gallegos can't."

All Billy could feel was an impotent rage. It was a con-spiracy. He was caught in the middle of a trap someone else had designed, and no one was going to throw him a lifeline. He weaved in a daze through the mushrooming crowd until he spotted a bevy of lean, tousle-haired Latins. Billy focused on Gallegos, who gestured like a showman to the clique around him.

The dam of temper that was close to bursting in Billy suddenly receded. His glance jumped to the tall, striking woman who'd been partially obscured by Gallegos until she moved forward. Billy was stunned. The woman smiled smugly at Billy, as if knowing the surprise gave her an advantage.

"What are you doing here?" he managed, walking over. "Why didn't you tell me you were coming?"

Aymara's soft eyes turned diamond hard, and her mouth was fixed with uncharacteristic severity. "Because I never want to see you again."

"What are you talking about?"

Gallegos and his clique were watching, he saw, enjoying his public humiliation. Billy wasn't sure whether to take a swing at the Argentine or keep talking to Aymara. "You owe me an explanation," he said, and took Aymara by the wrist.

"No I don't. It's all very simple. We're through." Aymara broke away and slipped an arm through Gallegos's. "I don't want you anymore, Billy."

"Because of what happened to me?" Billy was incredulous. He'd put his career and freedom in jeopardy partly to help Aymara's father, so in turn he could continue to spoil his daughter. And now she was telling him it was over, that his rival had taken his place? "Who put you up to this?"

"You," she said coolly.

Billy shook his head.

"You! Don't you remember?"

He saw a tear now. He began to recall their parting in Buenos Aires, the fit Aymara had thrown when he rejected the idea of marriage. Hell hath no fury . . .

"I'm sorry about that night," he said.

"I never wanted to marry you anyway," she spat out, her voice swelling in anger.

Barely in control, Billy turned away. Only his pride in being a gentleman kept him composed.

Aymara's taunting voice called him back. "There's something else you should know." The sensual lips drifted up in cold, hateful delight. "It wasn't Gallegos who called customs at the airport."

Billy felt his body lurch forward, as if someone had given him a soft push, and his hand swung out to strike Aymara. He watched as Gallegos flew toward him. Billy was shoved back and toppled to the floor. He rose defiantly, levered a fist into Gallegos's stomach, and stormed toward Aymara.

The Argentines closed ranks and knocked him down again. The orchestra stopped playing. Silence descended like a spotlight on Billy as he struggled up. Security guards rushed over. For the first time in the history of the Cartier Ball a guest was forcibly removed from the festivities without the excuse of being drunk. Billy was dragged past the bejeweled models, startled guests, and disapproving tournament officials and unceremoniously shoved outside. Alone, he wiped the blood from his nose and tried to find his dignity. It wasn't easy. Broke, friendless, humiliated, he'd been drummed out of the corps.

SIXTEEN

TO CRITICS, THE DALLAS RESIDENTIAL ENCLAVE OF HIGHland Park was known as the Bubble. As safe and sanitized as any urban cocoon in the country, Highland Park boasted as many Mercedes and Cadillacs per square block as Beverly

Hills or Palm Beach. What made the Bubble different was ethnic distinction. It was not a place where Jews felt welcomed with open arms. This was the province of White Anglo-Saxon Protestants, Texas variety, who sequestered themselves in modest homes that started at $700,000 and marched up to something really comfortable at two or three million. Anything under $500,000, if it could be found, was a tear down. Outsiders complained that the only time blacks were seen in the neighborhoods was when the cleaning ladies arrived, and once every October 31, when the Highland Park Police Department charitably tolerated hordes of dilapidated station wagons packed twelve deep with children looking for a candy score. The police otherwise ran a tight ship; any intruder venturing through the town's idyllic parks or quiet streets after ten P.M. did so at his own peril. Outsiders might scoff at the storm trooper mentality, but to the residents, their well-defended kingdom was the only place in Dallas to live. Security and WASP clannishness were merely self-protection. The rest of the world was going to hell in a hand basket, but here civilization was honored and maintained. A young woman could walk the streets without fear of being mugged. Neighbors were friendly and respectful. Trust and security were not hollow words.

When David Sanders parked his beat-up 100,000-mile Chevy on one of Highland Park's fine streets and timidly took the brick path to the mansion of Robert Huss, he too was an intruder. His religion and skin color were eminently acceptable, but the jockey was hardly famous, wealthy, or the progeny of a proper family. The diminutive young man, dressed in his full jockey silks tonight, was overwhelmed by the 10,000-square-foot neo-Grecian home that boasted on its seven acres an indoor tennis court, outside and indoor swimming pools, and a small lake. It made Bunker Hunt's homestead, several doors down, look poverty-stricken.

The Husses, as Austin had told David, were one of the first families to settle in Highland Park, sixty years ago establishing the tone for the community to come. Huss owed the house and his fortune primarily to his father, Richard, whose story was a Horatio Alger paradigm.

In 1884 Richard emigrated with his parents from Czechoslovakia, settled in Chicago, and by the age of ten had fled an oppressive home. Somewhere along the way he learned to box and ride horses, and in his early twenties became a sports reporter for the *Chicago Tribune*. Hooked on the equine world, on weekends he became a jockey's valet and exercised mounts for the thrill and love of it. But there was more to the man than horses. Intuitive, adept with numbers, and opportunistic, Richard soon started a taxi company in Chicago, painted the cars yellow, and watched his Yellow Cab fleet grow to become the largest in the country. Yellow became synonymous with taxis everywhere, and eventually Huss used it as the racing color for his horses. He went on to start a rental car company which, like his cab endeavor, so dwarfed the competition that one rival, Avis, adopted the defensive slogan, "We try harder."

All the while Richard Huss was building his horse kingdom. In 1921 he purchased an interest in a racing stable and bought an English mare for breeding named La Dauphine. She became the dam of Anita Peabody, Huss's first successful runner, and when *her* racing career was over, Anita Peabody was the foundation mare for Huss's stud farm. The foundation sire was Reigh Count, a feisty two-year-old when Huss bought him for only $12,500. The colt was known to bite opponents on the neck, but he won the 1928 Kentucky Derby in a field of twenty-two horses, the largest ever assembled for the Run for the Roses. Eventually retired to stud, in 1940 he sired the most spectacular of his progeny, Count Fleet. *That* horse became only the sixth to win the coveted Triple Crown, and in the process cemented Richard Huss's reputation as one of the top breeders in the country.

In the 1960's Robert Huss inherited his father's mantle of success and the considerable fortune that ran with it. David knew he'd expanded the horse empire and now raced more thoroughbreds than anyone in the country. All of which did nothing to diminish the young jockey's anxiety on this breezy Saturday evening. What he was about to go through would be as unpleasant as it was necessary, he thought. After repeated requests for an interview, Mr. Huss had finally met with David, then called him a week later with the good news: he could ride some Huss thoroughbreds in California. All that was left was the formality of signing a contract—and tonight's little test. It had been a P.S. from Mr. Huss. Would David mind helping out for his daughter's debutante party, by way of breaking in a $40,000 colt that had been one of her parents' many gifts? Stephanie would be pleased. The jockey's job would be to ride the horse around the immense grounds, getting him settled, then let Stephanie mount the animal. David had gathered a quick impression of the sixteen-year-old at his interview. Pretty, sweet—and wild. She had given the jockey a friendly wave before streaking off in her spanking new Mercedes 450 SL, on her way to Neiman-Marcus for a full-day shopping spree.

The debutante week, David was informed, had begun with a cotillion ball; followed by a little jaunt on a chartered 727—mariachi band on board—with fifty of Stephanie's closest friends to Puerto Vallarta for a weekend; and finally a trip to Houston, where Mr. Huss had rented the Astrodome for a private rock concert. Tonight's party was the official end of the festivities, of a week of unabashed, orgiastic spending. If it had cost Mr. Huss a penny, David decided, it had cost him a million. The figure made him feel all the more like a pawn, yet he warned himself not to feel resentful. Mr. Huss was the kind of man who didn't grant a favor without asking one in return. That was the way the game was played.

From his pocket David gingerly removed a tissue that contained several yellow pills, dry-swallowing the first Valium, which was really his second. He'd already taken one before leaving his apartment. He couldn't help it if his nerves were on fire and his back in hopeless, perpetual pain. Two days ago he'd taken a spill while breezing Austin's latest acquisition and hope for the All-American. David had never mounted a horse quite like Miss Muffet. Stubborn and moody weren't encompassing enough as adjectives, yet the filly, when she felt like it, could turn on her afterburners. If not for her speed, David would have recommended selling the temperamental horse with her crazy earmuffs and blinkers. Taking more falls was not something he relished.

A maid with a white lace apron over her black uniform opened the front door. David stared past the entry hall to the cavernous living room, where tall, loping figures danced to the blasting music. The kids were all good-looking. His first thought was that *his* teenage parties had never been like this, just a couple of six-packs and a radio. Here caterers swung in and out of the room, an eight-piece band played in one corner, platters of food were everywhere. As composed as David considered himself to be, he suddenly wished he were elsewhere. Quietly he asked the maid where he could find Stephanie, and as he was led to a parlor room with sumptuous Victorian furniture, he felt the stares. His silks might as well have been a clown suit. He found Stephanie surrounded by five or six girls, whispering and giggling until David intruded. They turned their glances on him in unison.

"You're David," Stephanie declared in a delighted voice. She was a tall, lanky blonde with budding breasts and slim hips. Her face had delicate, even features, a slightly pixieish look, and mischievous eyes. Behind the adolescent awkwardness and beauty yet to flower, David saw charm and spunkiness. "I've been waiting all night for you. Do you think I can ride like this?" She fanned out the billowy party dress as if doing a curtsy, and would have landed on the carpet if a girlfriend hadn't caught her. The giggles erupted around a stone-faced David. Drunk, he thought uneasily.

"Your father asked me to break him in first," David said diplomatically.

"But that might take forever. He's a gentle horse. I've already seen him."

"It's still a good idea if I saddle and ride him around. It won't take very long."

"How long is not very long?"

David shrugged. "I'm just doing what your father wants," he tried, laying the blame somewhere else. Stephanie looked at him crossly, letting him know her displeasure and strong will. After all, she was saying, whose party was it?

"I guess I can saddle him up pretty quickly."

"Terrific!" she gushed, clapping. "Can I come with you?"

The idea was greeted with enthusiasm by all the girls, who clamored to tag along. David cleared his throat. "I don't know. The horse could spook with a lot of people."

"All right, then just me," Stephanie decided with her imperial powers. To the disappointment of the others, she walked with David through a kitchen door to the mammoth backyard, which resembled a golf course. Acres of perfectly manicured grass loomed under the soft floodlights. Giant elms and sycamores interrupted the vista like shadowy guests.

"What's it like being a jockey?" she asked as they approached the stables.

"A lot of work. Some fun. Challenging," he told her.

"What's the challenge?"

"Winning. Seeing if you can make your horse respond to you. Every horse is different. You try to bring out the best in each one."

"I'd like to try that—I love horses—but I'm too tall for a jockey," she announced, thrusting up to David to show she was a hopeless two inches taller. The gesture startled him, but he liked the sudden warmth of her body.

"I don't think you'd be happy being a jockey," he ventured. "Someone from your background—" He cut himself off, afraid of being too forward. But the Valium was having its effect. Suddenly he felt looser, his inhibitions gone. As his eyes paraded over Stephanie, he thought how pretty she was.

"Oh, isn't he gorgeous?" Stephanie exclaimed as they edged toward the birthday horse that had been tied to a tree. A red ribbon was around his neck. "His name's Paradise Lost. Daddy and I picked him out together." David hoisted up the saddle and bridle lying on the grass nearby and slowly approached the handsome colt, extending an open hand. The dark, brooding eyes instantly registered suspicion.

"Wait," Stephanie called, and opened a canvas bag she'd brought along. David took in the bottle of champagne warily. "See—two glasses," she said, smiling, and handed him the bottle.

"Maybe we should wait."

"Why should we? My maiden ride on Paradise Lost calls for a toast."

She was too drunk and iron-willed to reason with, David concluded. Reluctantly he accepted the champagne bottle, took a distance away in order not to scare the horse, and popped the cork. They downed two glasses each before Stephanie would let him saddle the horse.

"Easy, boy . . . easy . . ." David coaxed as he adjusted the bridle and stirrups.

"Can I get my friends now?" asked Stephanie.

"In a minute." He glided his foot in the stirrup and hoisted himself onto the Western saddle. The horse jigged, but David flicked the reins and led him out into the cooling night.

"Help me up," Stephanie called, trailing behind.

"I want to ride him first."

"Help me up," she insisted.

He wasn't strong enough to pull her up like in a John Wayne western, so he dismounted, kept the horse calm, and gingerly wrapped his hands around her waist. He gave her a gentle push.

"Aren't you going to join me?" she asked from on top.

"It might be a tight fit."

"I'll ride behind you. I can hold onto you, can't I?" she asked.

She was flirting, he realized, amazed, as he boosted himself up next to her. Without warning her arms clinched possessively around his middle.

"Giddy-up!" Stephanie called playfully.

"Where to?"

"The house. I want everyone to see us."

As the horse maneuvered through the night shadows, Stephanie leaned closer until her cheek brushed David's. Her soft breathing aroused him. Was she really flirting, or was this just a flight of his imagination? Valium was good for self-delusion, he knew, as was his sorry, girl-starved life. It dawned on him suddenly where he was—romping around in the middle of the night on a $10 million estate as if he owned it, with the princess of the party no less. He couldn't help dreaming. One hand dropped on top of Stephanie's. She didn't pull away. Emboldened, David dug his heels into the colt's flanks. In his dazed euphoria he wasn't sure whether he was trying to impress Stephanie or simply playing out his own fantasy. It felt as if he suddenly owned the world, that nothing could go awry.

Something glistened in front of them.

Jesus, he thought. It was the swimming pool. Reflexively David jerked the reins. As Paradise Lost reared up on two legs, Stephanie let out a low whoop of surprise. "Whoa . . . hey, no, no, easy . . ." David called soothingly, settling the colt. A moment later he reared again. David's instincts were too slow this time. He reached back to grab for Stephanie but she was already on the ground, face down and motionless. His foot slipped out of the stirrup as he twisted back to control the horse. Paradise Lost shot out from under him. His fall was like a graceful dive, arms extended and legs locked together. The cold ground swam up and slammed into his side. The pain bolted through his ribs.

Raising himself, he watched the spooked horse streak toward and then around the pool, toppling lounge chairs in his wake. As if pursued by a private demon, the colt abruptly leaped over a low hedge and toward a four-foot cyclone fence bathed in shadows. The horse would stop in time, David thought. Despite size and weight, horses were miraculously nimble when it came to dodging obstacles. If a jockey fell in a race, pursuing horses would do almost anything to jump over the rider. Or facing a fence, a horse could turn on a dime. If he could just see it clearly. . . .

But if Paradise Lost did see the obstacle, it was too late. He slammed into the fence at twenty miles an hour. His neck caught on the jagged edges and was torn open. For a second the horse stepped back, as if nothing were wrong, then toppled on the grass. His coat was shiny with blood.

Sickened, David turned away and groped toward Stephanie. As he helped her up he saw she was only dazed.

Much too drunk and relaxed to break any bones. His relief vanished when he glanced toward the house again. Kids were swarming around the dead horse and staring back at David.

It was the goddamn pills, David thought hours later as he drove aimlessly around the city. His shame and embarrassment had been so acute that he could barely apologize to Stephanie or hang around and wait for her father to return from another party, though it was the proper thing to do. In the end David and some of the stronger boys had moved the bloodied horse away from the house, and then he'd left quietly, promising to call Mr. Huss tomorrow. But the deed was done. Besides the horse, the casualties of the night included his reputation, his future as a thoroughbred jock, and not the least, his self-respect. How could he have let a sixteen-year-old girl browbeat him, or possibly believe there was some romantic interest between them? He was a working jock and always would be till he rode to fame and fortune, which at the moment seemed terribly unlikely. Stephanie's millions were sugar plums dancing in the head of a fool.

He thought at that moment he never wanted to get on a horse again.

The ritual of self-flagellation entailed another hour of random, sulking driving, vows of reform, and a swear-to-God that he would never swallow another pill, even an aspirin. Ironically, he was now in as much physical pain as ever. His side felt like a trampled football field. How could he survive without some crutch?

It was after three A.M. when he pulled into his apartment complex in a neighborhood on Dallas's south side. The sorry little enclave was called Rustic Views, but in fact the only views were of a line of telephone poles, and there was nothing remotely rustic about the frame-stucco units. The rent for a one-bedroom, however, was only $345 a month, so David didn't mind the nearly one-hour commute to Mr. Mirabeau's ranch in Frisco.

As he lumbered up the stairs he spotted a figure in the shadows, short and slim, arms akimbo. He approached warily, not out of fear—because the figure belonged to a woman—but the last thing he wanted after a night of too many surprises was one more. There were moments when he believed his life was passing into the Twilight Zone.

"Who is it?" he called.

"Trixie," a voice answered brightly. "Trixie McKinney."

He struggled with the name, and gradually, focusing on the young, cute girl, remembered the apprentice jockey who'd wanted to ride for Mr. Mirabeau. David only had two questions. What the hell was she doing up in the middle of the night? And why in front of his apartment?

"Hi," she said, sidling up to him with an intimacy that contradicted the circumstances.

"This is a surprise."

"I hope you don't mind. I've been here for half the night."

"No, good to see you," he lied, fumbling for his keys.

"I wanted to share my good news with somebody. I don't have a lot of friends in Texas, and I remember how nice you were to me at Mr. Mirabeau's ranch. . . ."

"What news?" He was too damn tired to much care about anything.

"I got a riding contract at Ruidoso Downs!"

"Great. That's really nice." He smiled, but all he could think of was his own fiasco tonight. Trixie followed him in as he flicked on the lights. The room's sparse and cheap furniture embarrassed him. "Coffee?" he asked, though he really didn't want her to stay. It amazed him how he was always polite, so timid about speaking his mind. That was what had gotten him into trouble with Stephanie.

"Sure. Let me make it." Trixie was in the kitchen before he could protest. Just as well, he thought, dropping exhaustedly to the lumpy sofa. After a moment she stopped moving and looked over at him. "Are you sure it's okay for me to stay?" she asked.

"It's okay. It's just me. I had a bad night."

"What happened?"

"You don't want to know."

"Yes, I do. Tell me."

He had not planned on telling anyone, especially a near stranger, but the poison suddenly welled up inside him and he had to get it out, the full confession. He found it easy talking to Trixie. She seemed sympathetic.

When he finished the tale, she said, "I don't think that's so bad."

"Really? What could be worse?" He put his finger to the side of his head and pulled the trigger.

"What you learned tonight is that you're going to be a quarter horse jockey. You can forget about thoroughbreds."

"You've got a crystal ball?"

"It's just facing up to the obvious. Your disaster was a message, as clear as if someone had written it down."

David was hardly cheered.

"That's the way life is," Trixie continued, speaking as if she were more mature than her years. "It's a series of choices. Sometimes you consciously make them. Other times, like tonight, they're made for you. Your bad luck could ultimately turn out to be good—you might become one of the greatest quarter horse jocks ever."

"You're an optimist," David observed, suddenly wishing he were too. If anything, he admired Trixie for her tenacity, but he couldn't help feeling a little envious of her success. She was on a high with her first riding contract. David felt as if he'd just been shoved off a ladder. She brought in two cups of coffee and and sat beside him. In the soft light her olive skin had a translucent quality. He thought again how pretty she was, the innocent, cherubic face made unforgettable by her staunch determination.

"Any girl who wants to be a jockey has to be optimistic," Trixie said finally. "Perseverance doesn't hurt either. In some ways I'm fortunate. My father always insisted I stand up for myself. I was the only girl in a family of seven, and the youngest to boot. I played a lot of sports in high school in Florida, but when I fell in love with horses, I knew I wanted to be a jockey. As soon as I graduated I came to Texas. Some trainers told me that was the best place for a jockey to get a break, even though there're no race tracks."

"You're tough," David half joked, "but you're sweet too." He slipped his fingers through strands of her hair and gently pulled her closer.

The kiss felt more than natural to David. It was a necessity. He needed some passion in the bleak, everlasting desert of his all-work, no-play existence. Tonight's bruises on his ego made him all the hungrier. They made love eagerly in his unmade bed. Trixie didn't seem to mind the less-than-violins-and-candlelight ambience. The two young lovers rolled and sweated and laughed as their lovemaking ended with a satisfying climax.

"Do you still feel awful?" she asked him afterward.

"I think you made me forget." She nestled against him. "I hope this is more than just tonight, Trixie. I'd like to see you again."

"You will," she promised. "Hey, can I ask you something?" She sat up with an embarrassed smile. "And be honest."

He raised his hand solemnly. "Shoot."

"Do you think I'll ever make a good jockey? Right now I know I'm just learning, but if I stick with it, do I have the potential? You saw me ride—"

"You have the talent," David said sincerely. "All you need is an extra dose of perseverance, being a woman in this crazy field. But you have that. I think you'll do fine."

"Honestly?" She gave him a hug, her breasts flattening teasingly against his chest. "I never worry about being great. Just good. I want to prove to myself I can succeed at this."

"What about me?" he asked casually. As much as David hated to admit it, he had a stubborn core of insecurity. He wanted assurances about the future, wanted Trixie to tell him what he needed to hear.

"Why? Are you doubting yourself?"

"First King's Ransom falls in the All-American. Next I'm having trouble with Mr. Mirabeau's latest hope, Miss Muffet. And tonight—"

"You used up all your bad luck. The future *has* to be better."

"Promise?"

"You're great, David. And you're going to be even greater."

David drifted toward sleep, at peace now, wounds dressed, hopes salvaged. With an arm draped gratefully over Trixie, he knew then that he didn't want to let her out of his life.

SEVENTEEN

FOR MEREDITH THE THREE MONTHS THAT ELAPSED BE-tween her arrest and the first day of her trial at the Dallas County courthouse had been a stubborn nightmare that wasn't close to ending. Seth remained in his coma, despite strong vital signs and assurances from the city's top neurosurgeons that his recovery might be imminent. At first Meredith had made daily pilgrimages to his bedside, slipping in back doors when the press began to ambush her; when reporters found the back entrances she tried disguises until they were recognized too. For the last month, beaten down by the publicity, she'd given up and stayed at the ranch.

As surely as a rooster recognizes dawn, it was de rigueur for Texans to stage a society trial of epic proportions, and Meredith knew she was this year's victim. HORSE MATRON SHOOTS FOURTH HUSBAND IN ACT OF REVENGE had screamed the front page of the normally restrained *Dallas Morning News*, and that was only the beginning. Meredith had been forced to watch as every nook and cranny of her life was exposed. There were sidebars on her colorful mother, the splashy All-American Futurity parties, her previous up-and-down marriages and the spectacular divorce fights. The press pretended to probe for the truth with the dedication of a fine surgeon, but there was hardly the skill or finesse.

This was crass commercialism and nothing else, Meredith told her close friends, who sympathized but could hardly stop the flow of events which had taken on a life and momentum of their own. Led by the type of thrill-seekers who had gravitated to Austin Mirabeau's burial of King's Ransom, a devoted core of readers bored with their own lives fed on this piece of lurid drama. Meredith began not to recognize the woman the press implied was a cold-hearted villainess. What about all the money she gave to charities, the work she had done on behalf of the American Quarter Horse Association? What about her daughter, Alexis, who could drive her crazy but whom she still loved and doted on? So she was feisty and spoke her mind—why did the press focus only on that? As frustrated as Meredith was, her attorney cautioned her to say nothing to reporters. She had a habit of shooting from the hip, she was told bluntly, and a stray admission could inflame an already sensitive situation. So Meredith stayed home, drank to kill the anxiety, and with a masochism she couldn't stop, read the daily newspapers along with the rest of Texas.

The media wasn't her only enemy, she understood as she dressed in her bedroom on an overcast, damp March morning before getting into Abel Hanson's car. Her trainer gave her a comforting hug and then began the silent drive to Dallas and the courtroom.

Calvin Garrison had again warned her about the district attorney. Clarence Bidmore was a pretentious orator who was fond of quoting Yeats and Shelley, a man who loved to hear himself talk. Bidmore had soft, pink, well-scrubbed skin, his blond hair never lay straight and all his suits came from Sears. In the pretrial flurry Meredith's attorney had asked the judge for a motion to suppress testimonial evidence because Meredith had volunteered a confession before the police had read her the Miranda card. Bidmore confidently retorted that the police didn't have time; Ms. Kingsley's confession had been too spontaneous. The judge concurred. A second motion, to suppress physical evidence, was promptly entered on the rationale that the police had searched the Do-Drop-Inn without a warrant. Bidmore seemed nonplussed. Under the "plain view" doctrine, no warrant was required, he replied arrogantly. A patrolman stopping a motorist for a traffic violation and perceiving a body on the backseat did not need a warrant to arrest the man on suspicion of murder. Similarly, the bloodstains were in plain view at the Do-Drop-Inn. Once more the district attorney's argument prevailed. Hopes scuttled, the defense's final gambit was to try to change venues because of pretrial publicity. It was Meredith who objected. She believed in and trusted the people of Dallas and east Texas, and she would take her chances.

Everyone was resigned to a long and difficult trial. The defense's plea of temporary insanity was not burdened with imagination, yet Meredith knew it was true enough. Under stress because of the horsenapping, she had not been herself when she shot Seth, who she had genuine reason to believe helped in the theft. Her attorney warned that the bridle in Seth's car would raise more questions than it answered and possibly expose Seth to criminal charges. Thom Warfield, playing a clam, so far had implicated nobody, so there was little point in their mentioning Seth. The defense would try to find other means to prove that Meredith had been pushed beyond the limits of rational thought and control.

Meredith entered the mahogany-paneled courtroom too unsettled to focus on the jury box or the gallery of spectators. The whispering built to a crescendo as she sat at her attorney's table, only to be abruptly silenced when the paunchy judge stalked self-righteously toward his bench like a swaggering king. Meredith pulled herself to her feet but resented the act of respect. And when her eyes finally noticed the jury of eight men and four women, she resented them too. They didn't know anything about her and Seth. What right did they have to pass judgment?

The morning unfolded less than pleasantly. More than once Meredith wanted to assault Clarence Bidmore. On behalf of the people of the great state of Texas, he told the jury in his opening statement, he would prove beyond any reasonable doubt that Meredith Kingsley had deliberately and callously shot her husband because she openly despised the man.

"Where the hell did he get *that*?" she whispered to her attorney.

Randall Sedgefield was a thin wisp of a man whose bifocals and high, wide forehead made him look more scholarly than he was. Yet he'd impressed Meredith as being extremely thorough, and Calvin had recommended him as a crackerjack courtroom strategist. "Patience," he answered back, telling Meredith this was only the first round; the war promised to be a long one.

Fine, she thought, let there be a war. But when was her side going to start fighting? Sedgefield's opening statement turned out to be as tepid as day-old tea.

In the days that followed, Meredith began to sense total disaster. The parade of state's witnesses were all damning. Three separate bar flies from the Do-Drop-Inn described a remarkably controlled woman who had pulled the trigger, and then, as if glad the deed was over, calmly helped herself to a drink. The surgeon who'd operated on Seth and met with Meredith afterward was similarly blunt with his impressions. Nurses on Seth's floor testified that Meredith hadn't visited her husband in over a month. With each witness Meredith turned to her attorney with an explanation, which Sedgefield duly scribbled down, yet when he cross-examined, he scarcely raised the points, or if he did, they somehow seemed inconsequential.

At the end of each day she battled wearily through the crowd of reporters, physically and spiritually leaning on Abel as he ran interference on the way to her car. Usually she stayed in a hotel in the city, but sometimes she'd ask Abel to drive her back to the ranch, where inevitably she tried to drink herself to sleep. Well-wishers and admirers sometimes called to boost her fragile morale, but the next day in court any hope would be deflated and she'd feel the tide resume its inexorable rush against her.

On the eighth day the district attorney began to drive the nails into her coffin in earnest. All three of her ex-husbands took the witness stand, where, from that untouchable Olympian height, they looked down on her with undisguised hostility. Meredith couldn't believe the ingratitude. She had supported their sorry asses for every second of the marriages. The most damage was inflicted by her first husband, a former of U. of T. halfback and now Pontiac salesman named Bob Woodie Munson, whose rock-like physique had softened to Jell-O under El Paso's sunny skies.

Bidmore: "Sir, could you briefly describe your marriage with Ms. Kingsley?"

Munson: "Certainly. We tied the knot in the spring of 1962. We had one child, a daughter, Alexis. Shortly after she was born, Meredith and I separated. The divorce was finalized three years later."

Bidmore: "And how would you describe your marriage to Ms. Kingsley?"

Munson: "One with very little communication and affection."

Bidmore: "Could you be more specific?"

Munson: "Meredith was incredibly difficult to live with. She was whimsical, stubborn, autocratic. Her will always had to prevail. She liked to humiliate me."

Bidmore: "And how did she do that?"

Munson: "At parties she liked to tell stories about me, about our sexual habits, for example, in front of my friends."

Bidmore: "Why did she do that?"

Munson: "She never offered an explanation. I think she had a mean streak. I think she didn't like men."

Bidmore smiling: "But outside of verbal abuse, she never physically threatened you?"

Munson: "She did, sir. After an argument one night she picked up a carving knife and came at me. I ran upstairs and called the police. Another time she threatened to run me over with a pickup. It was more than intimidation. She meant it. That's why I finally asked for a divorce."

With the last statement Sedgefield promptly shouted "Objection!" It was already on the record, he pointed out, that Meredith had requested the divorce from each of her husbands, not the other way around. The prosecutor was trying to imply that Ms. Kingsley was physically dangerous and a threat to her husbands' safety—a point that had hardly been substantiated by other witnesses. The judge sustained the objection and told the jury to disregard. But

Meredith knew that damage had been done. Even Sedgefield was agitated.

"Is that true?" he whispered to Meredith at their table. "Did you go after him with a knife? Why didn't you tell me?"

"What difference does it make?"

"A lot. It makes you into a man-hater. It makes shooting Seth seem anything but a spontaneous act."

"Maybe my mistake was in not stabbing the bastard," Meredith said bluntly, glaring at the man she had once trusted. "Look, I do have a temper. I'm insecure. I do things I shouldn't do. But I wouldn't hurt anybody, not if I was thinking clearly. That's the truth. . . ."

As she listened to her attorney cross-examine, Meredith wondered what the truth had to do with anything. Bob Woodie, as if he were still running the football for his alma mater, dodged Sedgefield's questions like tacklers on the way to the end zone. By late afternoon the prosecution rested after its last witness. Meredith was hardly relieved. The ship was sinking and there was no way to jump off. That night in his office Sedgefield bared his ego and delivered his don't-worry-I'm-in-charge pep talk to Meredith. Tomorrow was *his* turn. He would start by asking the judge for an acquittal becase the district attorney had hardly proved beyond a reasonable doubt that Meredth wanted to kill her husband. If that failed, he would introduce the defense witnesses. Rest assured, he said, the tide was about to turn.

Meredith ate dinner alone and took a cab to Presbyterian Hospital. She was shocked at seeing Seth. He looked paler and thinner than ever, closer to death than recovery. For half an hour she raised hell with nurses and doctors, then pushed everyone out of the room to be alone with her husband. She took his powerless hand into hers and held it tenderly. If Seth did recover in time, she knew how he would testify at the trial. He would forgive her. She would be vindicated. Everyone would know that the nature of their relationship was warm and caring.

That night, waking in her hotel room, Meredith was certain she was suffocating. She sat rigidly on her bed and tried to breathe. After a shower she picked up the phone and placed a long distance call. A testy operator at Bennington College informed her that it was well after one in the morning and that unless this was an emergency, it was not school policy to rouse students from their beds. It *was* an emergency, Meredith swore, waiting impatiently while the operator rang Alexis's room. No one picked up. So where was her daughter? Out with some boy? Alexis didn't really date much. Maybe she was studying in the library. Meredith didn't know whether to blame the school for laxness in watching over its students, or Alexis for being too independent. For over a week she'd been trying to reach her daughter, only to be told Alexis wasn't around. Resigned now, Meredith left another message for Alexis to call back. What she really wanted was for her daughter to come home, just for a visit. Meredith needed somebody in her corner. Alexis had called once, when Seth was in the hospital, expressing her sympathy, but then she'd drifted back into her private world.

As painful as it was for Meredith to admit, the two had just never learned to communicate. Meredith had been a conscientious mother, but from the start there had been conflicting chemistries. No mother and daughter had ever been less alike. As a little girl Alexis had preferred trips to the Sherman public library to riding horses, which frightened her, or solitary play in the basement to having friends over. She grew up a distant, self-motivated child, not particularly warm, who always brought home straight A's and whose favorite subjects were math, Latin, and music appreciation. Those were as familiar to Meredith as playing ice hockey on Mars. Meredith had finally accepted their differences, yet she had never given up hope that one day mother and daughter would grow closer. At the moment that hope seemed as likely as Meredith's acquittal. She dropped her head back on the pillow and tried to sleep.

In the courtroom the next morning a chipper Randall Sedgefield informed Meredith that the judge had denied his motion for acquittal, but the attorney was hardly discouraged. As they took their seats, he produced his list of character witnesses, starting with Calvin Garrison. Meredith listened, pleased for once, as Calvin told the jury he'd known the defendant for a decade and regarded her as an intelligent, sensitive human being, and further, her relationship with Seth—his old and good friend—was one of the happier marriages he knew of. The district attorney rose solemnly, sweeping his unruly hair into place, and tried to pick Calvin's testimony apart. Had not the state senator heard Seth complain of the tyranny of his marriage? Absolutely not, said Calvin. To the contrary, Seth had never been happier. Really? exclaimed Bidmore, cocking his head to the jury in surprise. Well, had the senator ever attended one of Ms. Kingsley's famous parties? Calvin said he had, many in fact.

"Then, Mr. Garrison, what did you observe to be the relationship of Seth and the defendant at these parties?" Calvin remained quiet. "Were they a close couple, having a good time together?" the district attorney prodded.

"No, they were seldom together," Calvin admitted.

Before he could explain Seth's reclusive nature, Bidmore flashed his presumptuous smile and said "No more questions."

"Asshole," growled Sedgefield at his table, and thundered back toward the witness stand for his redirect. He allowed Calvin to say what he wanted, then flicked his adversary a menacing glance, as if daring him to re-cross. Bidmore politely declined. One for our side, thought a grateful Meredith, and for the first time she had the courage to look squarely at the jury.

The next witness was Abel Hanson, who did nicely under Sedgefield's tutelage, but Bidmore made him admit to overhearing conversations where Seth was the butt of Meredith's jokes. That Seth hardly minded was an opinion that Abel was not able to express, cut short by the district attorney's imperious wave. But on redirect, Sedgefield undid most if not all the damage.

Meredith took a cautious breath as Rachel Lang was called and sworn in. She spoke of the defendant as a woman of rare strength, courage, and integrity, though she admitted knowing nothing of Meredith's relationship with her husband. She testified too, that the defendant had been visibly agitated over her stolen horse, to the point of seeming temporarily unstable. The defendant, after all, had leveled a shotgun at her, a total stranger. Bidmore fired off a quick objection: the witness was making a conclusion, and in a field in which she had no expertise. The objection sustained, Sedgefield asked Rachel if she were in any way partial to the defendant. No, she said. If anything her experience as a journalist had made her leery of people she met only casually.

"But, Ms. Lang"—Bidmore jumped up—"were you not given a financial reward for recovering the defendant's horse?" Rachel sighed, nodding. "Could you tell us how much that reward was, Ms. Lang?" The figure of $100,000 tripped off Rachel's tongue, and more than one juror frowned openly.

"Objection!" Sedgefield shouted. "The point is irrelevant and immaterial. Ms. Lang already established that her impressions of the defendant came well before she received the reward."

"Sustained."

Meredith squirmed back in relief.

The defense counselor rose to call Austin Mirabeau to the stand. "Don't worry," Sedgefield whispered to Meredith. "I know you two butted heads recently, but Austin's going to help your case."

When the witness was sworn in, Sedgefield walked him through a maze of questions, establishing that Meredith had an exemplary reputation of winning races. Her filly had captured last year's All-American, at the expense of Austin's fine colt no less, and her heart had been set on winning this year with Five Deuces. When the horse had been stolen, Austin testified clearly, Meredith had been beside herself to the point of giving up her usual life of ranch work and evening parties. Austin said he understood her reaction. When King's Ransom had died he was tempted to forsake racing altogether.

"Then you're saying, Mr. Mirabeau," Sedgefield told the jury, "that when Five Deuces was taken, it broke Ms. Kingsley's heart. She was a changed woman, not in control of her emotions or faculties—"

"Objection!" Bidmore popped up like a jack-in-the-box. "Leading the witness, your honor."

The judge frowned at the district attorney's theatricality. "Sustained, Mr. Bidmore. But I'm going to let the witness answer in his own words. As long as the jury knows this is an opinion, and not the words of a trained psychologist." He turned toward Austin. "Mr. Mirabeau, how would you characterize the psychological state of the defendant at that time?"

"I spoke to her on the phone immediately after the theft. She was extremely distraught and agitated."

"I have no more questions, your honor," Sedgefield announced in quiet triumph. "The district attorney may cross-examine, if he wishes." Meredith gave her attorney a pat on the arm, and from the bottom of her heart she thanked Austin for rescuing her.

The district attorney paced the floor a moment, as if gathering his thoughts. For the first time, thought Meredith, the cockiness of the man was missing. Maybe they finally had him on the run.

"Mr. Mirabeau, does the defendant consider you a good and close friend?"

"I think she does."

"And how do you feel about the defendant?"

Austin paused. "I have mixed emotions."

"Really?" said Bidmore, surprised by the answer.

Meredith thrust an elbow into her attorney. "Objection, your honor," he bellowed. "The witness's personal feelings toward the defendant are irrelevant. It's common knowledge in Dallas that the defendant filed a libel suit against Mr. Mirabeau, which undoubtedly has colored his feelings but has absolutely nothing to do with this trial."

Austin spoke up: "That's not what I mean when I say I have mixed emotions."

"Then undoubtedly," Sedgefield continued, his voice still heated, "you were upset by Ms. Kingsley's comments about King's Ramsom—that he died because he was pushed too hard by your trainer. All of which was only opinion and conjecture upon Ms. Kingsley's part—"

"That rankled me," Austin admitted calmly, "but that's also not what I mean."

Sedgefield, troubled, dropped back in his chair. The courtroom grew still. Bidmore drifted back to the witness, his old arrogance returning. "Then what *do* you mean, Mr. Mirabeau? Why do you have mixed emotions about the defendant?"

Austin adjusted his posture and slung his arms over his chest. He seemed to enjoy the question. "I know a side of her that most people haven't seen."

"Could you please elaborate on that?" Bidmore asked.

"Certainly."

Meredith felt the darkness closing in. The district attorney was on a fishing expedition, yet he knew he was going to catch something. She wished she knew what it was.

"What I'm talking about happened twenty-three years ago," Austin said, his eyes marching briefly to Meredith. "I'd just dropped out of college and was looking for work. I had to. I didn't have two nickels to rub together. An old roommate told me about the 5555 Ranch near Sherman. I thought, what the heck, I've always liked horses, and ranch work might be a nice change. I went up to Sherman, spoke to Katie Kingsley, and got hired—room, board, thirty dollars a week."

"Objection!" roared Sedgefield. "Irrelevant and immaterial."

"Overruled."

The district attorney thanked the judge and turned back to Austin. "And what did you do on the ranch, working for the defendant's mother?"

"Mucked out stalls, exercised horses, put up fences, helped build a barn . . ."

"At any time during your employ did you meet the defendant?"

"Sure did. Meredith helped run the ranch with her mother. She was always around." Austin smiled. "She was one very attractive lady."

"What did Ms. Kingsley think of you?"

"I strongly doubt she even remembers me. There were

ten or twelve ranch hands at any one time, and they came and went like tumbleweed."

"But you remember Ms. Kingsley?"

"Hard to forget. I sort of liked her. When I finished work every day I'd hang around the house, just to talk."

"And how did she respond to you? Was she perhaps smitten, as Shelley once said, by the 'spirit of beauty that does consecrate with thine own hues all thou dost shine upon of human thought or form'?"

"No, sir. She was about as warm as a pair of Eskimo's thighs."

A peal of laughter rose from the courtroom and didn't subside until the judge thumped his gavel down. "Did that discourage you?" the district attorney asked.

"I'm not easily discouraged, Mr. Bidmore. Whenever I encounter resistance, my reaction is to try harder. The next evening I took the liberty of kissing Ms. Kingsley."

"And?"

"She slapped me across the face."

More laughter. Sedgefield leaped up and objected. The meandering questions about such an ancient series of events were pointless. But before the judge could rule, Bidmore begged the court's indulgence. He believed the witness was going to establish something crucial about the defendant's character. Hesitantly the judge let Austin continue.

Randall Sedgefield turned uneasily to Meredith. "What happened between you two?" he demanded. Meredith could only shrug. The truth was she didn't remember.

Like a blind man Bidmore continued to grope along, yet he seemed to know he was getting closer to home. "Was that the end of your relationship with Ms. Kingsley?"

"No, sir. A few days later she came over to the bunkhouse."

"And what happened there?"

"It was the middle of the afternoon. I was alone because I had a couple hours off. I think she knew that. She came over to me—I was reading—and said she'd really liked my kissing her the other night. I was surprised, but pleased. Then she started flirting—"

"What kind of flirting, Mr. Mirabeau?"

"Flirting flirting. Playing with my hair, holding my hand, doing a lot of giggling. Suddenly, without my asking, she took off her blouse and lay next to me—"

Sedgefield exploded in a volcanic rage. If he shouted the word *objection* once, he made it a litany that drowned out the rush of voices from every corner of the room. The judge hammered his gavel down and threatened to throw everyone out on the street. When quiet finally resumed, he told the district attorney to continue.

"And what did you do about these overtures of affection, unsolicited by you, sir?"

"Being the naturally friendly type," Austin said, lightly touching his mustache and focusing his coffee-colored eyes again on Meredith, "I reciprocated. I began kissing her. Just when things were progressing nicely she smiled mischievously and pulled away . . . slipped into her clothes and walked out of the bunkhouse. Didn't say a damn word."

Bidmore coughed into his pink fist. "And you had no idea why? What did you think?"

"Honest to God, I didn't get it. Until later that afternoon . . ."

"Yes?"

"Katie Kingsley called all the ranch hands together. Anyone could see she was pissed off. The lady was really smoking. Meredith stood beside her, all quivery and pouty, like she'd been crying. Katie looked us all up and down and said that someone had tried to rape her daughter. There was this pause. Christ, I couldn't believe it. Meredith came right up and pointed at me."

Silence descended over the courtroom. Meredith closed her eyes, finally remembering. Had Austin really been the young man? She'd only told on him because her mother had caught her coming out of the bunkhouse buttoning her blouse. Afraid of a whipping, she let her mother's fury fall on Austin. That was her only excuse. She'd been a spoiled, petulant girl. She was sorry. She'd been sorry at the time, but she'd never told Austin. Sedgefield sighed and sunk lower in his chair.

"You were accused of rape?" Bidmore said almost cheerfully to Austin. "How did you react?"

"How did I react?" exclaimed Austin. "How do you think I reacted? Here was this young lady, this tease—and it was her word against mine. What chance did I have? Everyone thought I'd really done it. Katie Kingsley kicked me off the ranch, but only after taking my back pay and calling the sheriff. It was only then that Meredith backed off and wouldn't perfer charges."

"I see. How terrible," the district attorney offered, almost bowing to the witness in gratitude. "Then you're saying she humiliated you. She delighted in that act. For no good reason she was punishing you. . . ."

Judas, thought Meredith, fixing her angry gaze on Austin. This was her friend and racing colleague? This was the man who always came to her parties and ate at her table?

Sedgefield leaped up like a man possessed. The district attorney was trafficking in innuendo and hearsay, he charged, and in the process slandering the defendant. The judge didn't agree. Clearly ruffled, Sedgefield tried to rehabilitate his witness, but Austin wouldn't change one line of his story. Tiring of the ordeal, the judge declared a three-day recess until Tuesday.

A stunned Meredith lingered in the empty courtroom. Rachel Lang approached her momentarily, but Sedgefield forbade any conversation with the media. With Abel leading the way, Meredith moved through the phalanx of reporters and photographers waiting outside. On the way to the ranch her anger at Austin returned. Why did he have to go back and resurrect a past Meredith hardly remembered? Maybe he'd always held a grudge against her. Jesus, the hypocrite, she thought bitterly.

At the ranch she guided herself through the dark and lonely house, settling in the den where she and Seth usually spent their evenings. She flicked on a light and was edging toward the liquor cabinet when the outline of a figure caught her eye. Meredith turned with a start.

"Hello, Mother," the voice called softly.

Alexis rose from behind the desk and walked over to kiss her on the cheek.

"Let me see you," Meredith said, pulling back happily. Alexis was turning into a woman. Her figure was decidedly shapely, the once curly red hair now straight and long, the face serene and confident. Didn't look a damn thing like her daddy, Meredith crowed silently, thank God. Meredith embraced her. "I wasn't expecting you," was all she could say. "I kept calling—"

"I caught a plane yesterday afternoon," Alexis explained. "I'm sorry I didn't answer your calls."

"How long can you stay?"

"Not very long. Just a few days."

"Not longer?" Meredith was hurt as she offered Alexis a drink. "I thought we could spend some time together."

"You've got your trial and—"

"You could always come down to Dallas. You might improve my luck."

Alexis took the drink, but after a sip put it aside. "Since when did you need luck?" she asked a little coolly. "I always thought you were such a strong woman. You always seemed that way to me."

"I thought I was too. Only now I'm beginning to wonder." She studied Alexis, thinking how in some ways she hadn't changed. She was still so distant and judgmental. "Don't you have any sympathy for what I'm going through?" Meredith asked.

"I don't know. It's hard to believe you need sympathy, especially from me. If anything, I've always been intimidated by you. Daddy was so sweet and caring, and you were the tough one."

"I think you should know your sweet and caring father testified against me in court."

"What did he say?"

The same thing as you, thought Meredith, frustrated again. It felt as if she were battling the whole world. Maybe she really was the one at fault.

"I'm sorry you had a hard day," Alexis finally murmured in the silence.

"You know what I'm sorry for," Meredith spoke up. "I'm just sorry that you didn't tell me any of this a long time ago."

She waited for Alexis to relax, to be more accepting, but there seemed something forever guarded about the girl. "Are you happy at school this year?" Meredith asked, hoping to find neutral ground.

"Very," she said, and suddenly Alexis looked at ease. "That's really what I came home to tell you. It's why I have to get right back. . . ."

Meredith finished her drink and poured another.

"Mother, why do you drink so much?"

"Because I have to. If you were on trial you would too. What did you want to tell me?"

"I don't know if you'll really be interested. You've got your mind on your problems. I think it was always that way, wasn't it? You were too busy for me—"

"Tell me, Alexis. Please."

She stood, thrusting her hands into her jean pockets as she stared out the dark window. "I'm in love. I used to think that wasn't possible for me. To really feel for someone, I mean. But I've never been happier. It's like nothing else matters in the world. . . ."

"You're in love?" Meredith was stunned. She couldn't believe it. Alexis's history with the opposite sex could be written on the back of a penny. She was so reserved and private, it seemed none of the boys she knew wanted to date her. But beneath her shock Meredith felt nothing but happiness for Alexis. Maybe a boy was what she had always needed. It picked up Meredith's spirits too. Just when you thought nothing was ever going to go your way again . . . She walked over and hugged Alexis. "Is he tall, dark, and handsome?"

"Actually, Tim's very blond, medium height, and muscular."

"Why didn't you bring him home with you?"

Alexis shrugged, smiling. "I didn't think it was time yet."

"What's Tim like?"

"He's from Princeton. He wants to be the next Hemingway. Lots of ambition."

"A writer. That's wonderful," Meredith said, though she couldn't get over how different the boy sounded from

Alexis. She didn't think her daughter had ever had ambition or been attracted to it. But Meredith knew better than to sound off now.

She stayed up with Alexis for another three hours, just talking. Neither had been so relaxed or enjoyed the other's company like this in all their lives together. It was as if the stalemates and confrontations of the past were finally behind them. Falling in love, Alexis had become more independent and was forging a new relationship with her mother. Life sure took funny turns, Meredith thought, unutterably pleased. It was long after midnight when they exchanged good-night kisses and slipped off to bed.

But sleep was impossible for Meredith. The nightmare of the trial, seeing Austin on the stand, had driven her up a wall. When would it ever end? But when she calmed down and took stock of her world, life didn't seem so threatening. Somehow she would survive, make peace with Seth when he recovered, and pick up the pieces. Her enemies were the vocal ones now, but she had her friends and supporters too. The press was wrong. She was *not* a monster. She might wear a plate of armor and do crazy things sometimes, but underneath there was a good heart.

She put on her robe and wandered into Alexis's room. A window was open a crack to let in the night air. On the shiny plaster walls the moon silhouetted the flickering branches of the oak outside. Alexis was curled up in a corner of the bed under just the sheets. For a minute while her daughter slept, Meredith sat on the bed, just as she had when Alexis was little, keeping vigil against the night's invisible enemies. Alexis was no longer little, Meredith reminded herself, she had found that out tonight. But mothers' habits were hard to change. They were always around to fight off ghosts and dragons, and the reward was in no one ever knowing.

EIGHTEEN

WHEN AUSTIN MIRABEAU STEPPED DOWN FROM THE WITness stand, half the reporters in the press gallery darted out of the courtroom to the nearest bank of phones. Rachel, spared the deadline pressure of a daily, focused on a helpless and deserted Meredith. The woman was in definite trouble. Austin's testimony had been as damning as it was shocking, and a press that was acting like pigs at a pastry cart would make the most of it. The hatchet job the poor woman was receiving had to be balanced, she'd told Frank, and since she was now on her editor's good side, he'd spared her copy anything but a few punctuation changes. The trial story that Rachel had scripted for the latest issue of *Image* had included a sidebar explaining that she was a character witness for the accused, and therefore her report might be somewhat biased—but she'd aimed for impartiality.

Rachel waited while the judge declared a three-day recess before she approached Meredith and her attorney, ensconced at the defense table like two forlorn statues.

"Things will be better after the recess," Rachel offered, dropping a sympathetic hand on Meredith's shoulder. The two hadn't spoken since the shooting, though Rachel had tried to get through to the ranch a dozen times.

"Thanks for everything you said on the witness stand," Meredith said, half smiling in an effort to break the gloom.

"I'd like to ask a favor," Rachel said. "If I could just speak to you in private for a minute . . ."

Randall Sedgefield, staring down his glasses at Rachel as if were looking through the cross-hairs of a sight, shook his head. Rachel was sympathetic and discreet, he admitted, but he feared any stray admissions his client might make. Besides, if he let Meredith talk to one member of the press, then the rest of the Fourth Estate would be clamoring for their turn.

"I'll only take a minute or two," Rachel pleaded. "What I want to ask has nothing to do with the shooting or anything raised in the trial. And I won't print a word of what she tells me—it's all off the record."

"Then what the hell is so urgent?"

"I can't tell you."

"Fine. You don't get an interview."

Meredith started to object, but Sedgefield, still stunned by Austin's testimony, was in no mood for tolerance. With a sympathetic but frustrated glance from Meredith, Rachel went back to her hotel. Away from the courtroom excitement she felt restless and lonely. Calvin was partly to blame, she thought. When he wasn't at the state legislature she stayed with him in his apartment. But that wasn't often enough for her. Calvin the workaholic had a hard time liberating himself. He'd offered Rachel his place anytime she wanted, even giving her the key, but out of her old sense of caution or independence, she'd declined. The posturing was absurd, she knew. She was obsessed with the man and missed him constantly. Every day after the trial she would call and they'd declare their mutual loneliness. Calvin always asked about the trial, and Rachel faithfully gave him the blow-by-blow. She knew he'd be shocked about Austin.

Back in her room she eagerly picked up the phone. The court recess would give her a chance to fly to Calvin if he couldn't make it home. A secretary answered his office phone. The senator was in a closed-door meeting, trying to win allies for his horse-betting bill, the woman explained. Rachel hung up in disappointment.

She ordered a light dinner and a bottle of wine sent to her room, and made a few notes for her trial update. She might have gone downstairs for dinner, as she'd done last week, being accommodated as star reporter, but she knew the glow of recognition would be greatly dimmed. Her fame for breaking the horse-theft story had faded almost as spontaneously as it had ignited. It was a little painful, she had to admit, to have it all taken away. She began to feel more for people like Buck Hart. Her one consolation was that she had a lover she adored—if only Calvin were around more, she could show him.

But her self-pity vanished after a glass of wine. Her thoughts returned to Meredith and the trial. Despite the fact of the bridle found in Seth's car, it was clear now that the defense wasn't going to introduce the evidence, out of deference to Seth Cartwright. And since Warfield wouldn't implicate anyone else in the theft ring—no doubt because it would add blackmail and extortion to the list of charges against him—the jury was left to believe that Meredith had little grounds for the shooting.

The hoary old defenses of temporary insanity or diminished capacity had been so misused in courts that they'd been leached of their credibility. If Meredith was going to escape prison, Rachel decided, Seth's name had to be brought up, as painful as it would be. In most states convicted felons were barred from racing so Meredith's future was at stake, not to mention her freedom. The truth was at stake too. Without jumping on her white horse, Rachel was still determined to unravel to its ends the story that had started in Warfield's office. She just needed a little assistance from Meredith. Despite Seth's reputation as a recluse, his wife had to know something about his habits, friends, maybe a motive for his getting involved with Thom Warfield.

Rachel tried twice more to reach Calvin at his legislative office, but now no one even picked up. It wasn't like him, she thought. If he didn't hear from her then Calvin always tried to call Dallas. But it was Friday, she realized; maybe he was on his way home. She was at his doorstep in Turtle Creek within half an hour. The key he'd entrusted to her slipped into the lock and the door swung open to the usually immaculate apartment—not a dish in the sink or a pillow out of place. Rachel turned on the stereo and settled back on the couch. But by ten there was still no sign of Calvin. She called his Austin office again. Nothing. Maybe he wasn't coming home after all. She tried futilely to remember the name and number of the Austin hotel where he stayed. Calvin had to keep it around his apartment somewhere.

In the top drawer of his desk, behind some stationary, she found a snub-nosed silver revolver. She was startled at first, yet she knew that next to a horse there was probably nothing held dearer by a Texan than his right to bear arms. Under the gun was a leather-bound black blook. Rachel hesitated. She was only after a phone number, wasn't she? That's what you found in little black books. She wasn't being nosy or tampering with fate.

When she opened the cover she found numbers all right, but they had nothing to do with the phone company. In one column were dates, starting in the fall of 1980, and in the other were notations of amounts of money. In the four or so years recorded, there had been exactly thirteen payments—one every three months, like clockwork—each for a couple thousand dollars. Money received or money spent, Rachel couldn't decide. There were no names of banks, other institutions, or individuals. The fall of 1980 was when Calvin had been elected to his first term. . . . Payments under the table? she wondered.

"What are you doing?"

Rachel's head shot up. Calvin looked pale and drawn as he stood in the doorway. He dropped his overnight bag by his feet and loosened his tie.

"You're back. . . ." she managed.

Calvin just stared at her standing behind the desk.

She dropped the book back into the drawer and went over to kiss him. He held her for a moment, but she felt a distance. "I was going to surprise you," she explained. "I've been calling you all night. I got frustrated. . . ."

"So you started looking in my desk?"

"Only for the phone number of your hotel." She saw

that Calvin wasn't appeased. "Look, I'm very sorry. I don't want to be having this kind of conversation. I've missed you."

Calvin dropped on the sofa. "What did you find in that book?"

"Just some meaningless numbers."

"Really?" He was sarcastic.

"I guess it was money—"

"Don't you want to know what the money means? If you're going to spy on people, you might as well go all the way."

"Calvin, please." She wished he'd stop.

"They're payments I make for my father. For his nursing home care. He was admitted almost the same time I won my first election. It's a financial drain, but I have no choice."

"I understand," she said. She meant it. She still felt mortified that he had caught her at his desk. She fixed two scotch and sodas as Calvin built a fire, then they slipped off their shoes.

"Miss me?" Rachel asked, giving him a kiss as they sat on the couch.

"You know I did. I always miss you."

"You look tired."

She'd never seen him so exhausted, she thought, and blamed his legislative workload. She asked how his pari-mutuel bill was progressing. He was optimistic, but from experience he knew about the ephemeral nature of political alliances. Pouring them each a second drink, Rachel told him about the bombshell Austin had dropped in court.

"Meredith seemed as surprised as anyone," Rachel added. "I felt sorry for her. Why did Austin do that?"

"You have to understand his pride. Once someone's hurt him, as apparently Meredith did, the man doesn't forget. In some ways you can't blame him. Growing up poor, Austin's always seen himself battling the whole world."

"But aren't you concerned for Meredith? I think she's doomed. Unless Seth recovers and testifies, what chance does she have?"

"Sedgefield's a clever attorney. He'll get her off without bringing Seth into this."

"But how?"

"What I can't control I don't worry about," Calvin answered impatiently.

"Why are you so on edge?"

"Because I'm tired."

"Then let's relax." She began to unbutton his shirt.

"What are you doing?"

"Dummy, isn't it clear?"

"I don't know. . . ."

"I'm going to energize you." She kissed him. "Please . . ."

"Wait a minute."

She watched him trail into the bathroom and close the door. She heard the squeak of the medicine cabinet hinges. The pills were how Calvin got by, she knew now, and not just through an election. If they were really in love, she could convince him to slow down, take a breath, begin to cut down on them. She would be enough for him. Calvin needed someone. To the public he seemed composed and self-contained, but she knew a man who was all alone in the world.

Rachel slid under the sheets and sat gazing at the fire. When Calvin joined her after his shower, any traces of fatigue had vanished. His mood was lighter, playful. She brought him to erection amid a barrage of his Aggie jokes that were to Texas what Jewish American Princess jokes were to New York. There were any number of moods for making love, and tonight they both were giddy, shutting out the world and its problems.

In the morning, as usual, Calvin was off and running. Rachel knew better than to protest. His public life came first. If they ever started living together, she would have to accept that. She wasn't unhappy. When Calvin had left, she found herself on the phone to the 5555 Ranch. After Calvin, what else did she have but her work? Meredith answered on the second ring.

"I hope you don't mind my bothering you at home,"

Rachel began. "And if you don't want to talk, I'll understand, but I at least have to ask. I want to get to the bottom of the horse-theft ring. There're a lot of unturned stones."

"What do you mean?"

Rachel took a breath. "I'd like to ask you some questions about Seth."

"You're not thinking he was behind all this?" Meredith said defensively.

"No," Rachel calmed her, "my instinct is that he was a victim somehow. But I need to find out more. If I could establish the facts of how Seth was entrapped, then I could help you at the trial."

Rachel waited out the silence, afraid that Meredith would hang up. "What do you want to know?" she finally said. "Mr. Sedgefield would crap little gold nuggets if he knew we were talking, but who cares? I'm tired of having my life run by an attorney."

"Let's start with a motive," Rachel said, her pen poised over a writing pad.

"For Seth? I don't know any."

"Did he act strange or different in the days before the theft? Did anyone visit him? Any long distance phone calls?"

"No. Nothing terribly unusual. But I did overhear him talking on the phone to Calvin several times."

"What did he say?"

"I can't remember. He wasn't his usual self, though. He acted upset. You don't think Calvin's involved in this—"

"No," Rachel said quickly. Lord, she hoped not, anyway. But all she could think of suddenly were the calls *she'd* overheard.

"Usually Seth and Calvin are very relaxed together. They've been friends since law school."

"They went to school together? Calvin never told me."

"They were roommates at Rice. Rachel, don't expect Calvin to tell you much. Even if you two are as close as I think you are, the man's natural inclination is to reticence. That's what he and Seth have in common."

Rachel sat back, trying to think. "Is there anyone else from law school that Seth was friendly with?"

"Oh, there are several. At least, Seth still does some business with them. Let's see. There's an attorney in Houston name of Peter Rennard."

Rachel wrote the name down. "Thank you. Very much. And I'll see you at the trial on Tuesday."

Her call to Rennard's Houston law firm was taken by a friendly junior partner who volunteered that he hated working on Saturdays and wondered if Rachel were free for lunch. Unfortunately, she answered, she was calling from Dallas, and she just wanted his boss's home number. "What the hell," the young man said, and gave out the unlisted phone. A moody teenager answered at the Rennard residence, taking forever to summon her father. But Peter Rennard was friendly and not unwilling to talk. Rachel apologized for the intrusion and explained that she was covering the Meredith Kingsley trial for *Image* and wanted some background on Seth Cartwright. "On Calvin Garrison too," she added.

"Poor Seth," the lawyer muttered. "But I'm afraid I can't tell you much. I knew both men in law school, sure, but just as acquaintances. Nice guys—both on the quiet side."

"Who else might have known them?"

"If my memory serves, they belonged to a study group together. I think a guy named Henry Boylan was part of it. I sure don't know what happened to him."

"No address at all?"

"Corpus Christi, last I heard. Henry got into a little trouble with the law and got himself disbarred. He's not the type to answer alumni-inquiry letters."

"I'll see if I can find him," Rachel said. She wasn't sure what she could learn from Boylan, but right now she had no other leads.

There was no phone for a Henry Boylan in Corpus Christi, either listed or unlisted. There were two in Dallas and three in Houston, but when she called each number, nobody there admitted to being a lawyer. Amarillo, Austin, Galveston, and San Antonio were dead ends. When she finally tried Sweetwater she was given the number of an H. L. Boylan and took her chances.

"This is Henry Boylan," a man answered in a carefree, singsong voice, as if he'd been drinking.

"My name is Rachel Lang. I work for *Image* magazine. I'm trying to find the Henry Boylan who went to law school with Seth Cartwright and Calvin Garrison."

"Big Cal? The state senator?" the voice rang out derisively. "Yeah, I went to school with the man. Seth too."

Jackpot, thought Rachel, though she wondered about his tone. "What can you tell me about them?" she asked. "What kind of friends did they have? You were all part of a study group—"

"Until the jackasses kicked me out."

"What?"

"Lady, you don't want to know."

"Yes, I do."

"You're just like whatsisname. . . ."

"What do you mean?"

"*Whatsisname* . . ."

"Who?" she demanded.

"Mr. Holier-than-thou. The anticrime guy . . . the one who just got busted. He called me once. Hey, you were the reporter—"

"You mean Thom Warfield? What did he want from you?"

"This was a long time ago, lady. Five, six years maybe. I was down and out. The Texas bar gave me the boot for writing one bad check. Now if that wasn't chickenshit . . . Said I might have been prosecuted if I wasn't a lawyer. Some break. I end up teaching junior high in a town like Sweetwater—how's that for a law school alum?"

"What did Thom Warfield want?" she asked again.

"Info on Calvin. Mr. Dudley Do-Right himself."

"What did you tell him?"

"I told him the goddamn truth—the reason they kicked me out of the study group."

Rachel bit her fingernail. "Why was that?"

"I knew they were a couple of queers."

She started to hang up, but Boylan beat her to it with a vindictive slam.

Jesus, thought Rachel. She helped herself to a glass of

wine. The pain welled up in her stomach and she closed her eyes. When she was able, she called every nursing home in Dallas until she found a patient named Winthrop Richard Garrison, U.S. Army, retired. A reedy-voiced woman in the accounting department informed Rachel that Mr. Garrison had been a resident of the home only since 1981. His bills were either paid by the U.S. Government or by a private insurance company. His son had not written the nursing home a single check.

Rachel wondered how deep Calvin's lies ran, gnarled and stubborn like the roots of an old tree. Should she feel sorry for him, or angry? All she wanted was to get drunk. When Calvin breezed through the door just before noon, Rachel looked at him sullenly.

"Cheer up," he called, touching her on the chin. "You look like the canary who ate the cat."

"Could we sit for a second?" she asked.

"We've got a lunch reservation—"

"Please. I want to ask you something."

"You wearing your reporter's hat again?"

She shook her head, fighting back a tear. "Calvin, why have you been lying to me? And don't tell me you haven't. I spoke to Henry Boylan. I spoke to your father's nursing home. . . ."

For a moment Calvin was motionless. Then he dropped onto the couch, running a hand wearily through his hair. She thought he looked more scared than surprised.

"What did Boylan tell you?" he asked, slowly.

"That you're a homosexual, or you were. That Warfield knew it. Was that why you gave him the horse?"

Calvin was quiet.

"Are you going to tell me or not?" she demanded.

"Why did you do all this anyway?" he said, his voice suddenly cracking. "Why couldn't you leave everything alone? Things were all right, weren't they?"

"Not if you've been lying to me. You're just like everyone else in my life."

"You shouldn't have pried."

"I'm a reporter. It's my nature. That's the way I am. Just as you're the way you are."

"You mean gay?" he said sarcastically.

"Well, are you or aren't you?"

"All right, since you asked—yes, I am. The reason I was late in coming to Dallas last night was because of a lover."

Rachel felt her stomach cave in again. "I don't think I want to hear anymore."

"I'm going to tell you anyway. You're so eager to snoop? Well, here, have it all. I've always been gay. I've just learned to cover it up well. Whenever I go to a party, to a posh restaurant, whenever I've got an appearance to make, I'm careful to have an attractive woman on my arm. I'm careful to make love to her afterward too. People talk in this state. Any single male beyond the age of thirty is suspect. There've been rumors about me, I can tell you. Warfield started them before he came to me, just to show the trouble he could make. The payments in the black book are all to him.

"I've been lying a long time, Rachel. To everyone. Don't feel singled out. I even lied to Seth, my closest friend, when I told him that I'd never been bothered by Warfield until Five Deuces came up."

Rachel felt sick. She wanted to leave, to run. Calvin could assure her this wasn't personal, but clearly he'd been using her, just as he'd used every other woman in his life. Just as she'd been used by other men. The pain wouldn't go away.

But she didn't leave. She didn't run. She wondered if it was because she really loved him. "I don't know if I can believe you anymore," she whispered in frustration.

"You have to."

"Why?" She looked at him, demanding he tell the truth.

"Because I'm being honest now. I've told you everything."

"Have you? How do you really feel about me? You're gay—"

"I love you, Rachel. More than I do anyone else. My male lovers are hardly deep relationships. You're the only woman I've ever really felt for. I've never gone as long with anyone as I have with you. And I don't want it to end."

Rachel shook her head in doubt.

"I need you to believe me," he said. "You don't know how tough my life is. Everything is pretend. I don't have anything real except you and my career—"

"Which is more important?" she asked.

"Christ, stop it—"

"Tell me."

"You!"

"Why aren't I convinced? Why do I keep thinking you're just trying to make me feel better?"

"Rachel, I really need you." He held her by the shoulders, making her look at him.

"So I won't tell anyone your secret?"

"No, because you mean something to me."

"Why? We don't have any kind of future. I'm not into pretending for the rest of my life, like you are."

"I want to change," he said, sitting back.

"You mean stop being gay? Just like that?"

"Yes."

"You're just pretending again." She thought of all the men in Hollywood she knew who had made the same wish, been willing to offer any god any sacrifice, but all the good intentions in the world couldn't save them.

"You're wrong," Calvin said. "Why don't you give me a chance?"

She wanted to believe him. Hadn't she told herself she felt responsible for Calvin, that she could get him off the pills? Why not this too? But too much was happening too fast. "Okay," she said. "Prove it. Go talk to the district attorney and tell him the truth."

"That's crazy—"

"You really want to change? You have to start by undoing all the lies. You have to tell how Warfield blackmailed you. You and Seth were forced to take the horse—"

"So Meredith will be acquitted?"

"Yes."

"And what happens to me? I'll be indicted along with Warfield. . . ." He paced the room, looking bewildered.

"Maybe they'll grant you immunity. You can get a good lawyer."

"Even if they did, what about my career as a senator? What about the future? Can't you see the headlines? It's all over. You know about my father, the values he upholds. This would kill him."

"I know it'll take courage."

"Bravely spoken."

"I thought you were sincere about changing," she countered.

"You're making this sound like an ultimatum. You're asking too much of me."

"I don't think so," Rachel said, standing. Too upset to keep arguing, she left the apartment.

For the next twenty-four hours she locked herself in her hotel room and went through the cleansing ritual of self-pity. Why was her track record with men so dismal? Why did she keep falling for victims or losers? Was it just bad luck or something in her character? It was always the same questions and the same lack of answers. All she could think of was being at a permanent dead end.

Calvin's calls kept interrupting. She told him she wanted to be alone to think. He sounded miserable. She began to understand how hard this had to be on him. For someone who had tried to live his life as honorably and perfectly as possible, the homosexuality had to be seen as a mistake. One he hadn't been able to make right. He was haunted by the failure, and she felt sorry for him. He kept telling her that he needed her, that only she could save him, but Rachel wondered if she could save anybody. She didn't have that kind of confidence in herself. She had thought all along that Calvin would be the one to save her.

She ate alone in the hotel that night, though she was starting to miss Calvin terribly. What was keeping her from going back to him? She was in love, she told herself, so what was she afraid of? Believing in him again and then being disappointed? Maybe he really was sincere about changing, but she knew he'd stop short of going to the district attorney. Calvin was right—she was asking too much of him. But what was she supposed to do? Just accept him and his weaknesses and forgive him? What about the others who were involved? She owed something to Meredith, something to herself, maybe even something to Frank by finishing the story. . . .

Monday morning she called Calvin's apartment, but no one picked up. When she took a taxi to Turtle Creek she was startled. The apartment looked like a disaster area. Bed unmade, dirty dishes on the table, clothes piled in a corner. There was no sign of Calvin. Maybe he'd flown back to the legislature. She sat down and wrote him a lengthy note. Legally and morally, Rachel wrote, she had an obligation to tell Sedgefield and the district attorney everything. But that was impossible. She wasn't able to betray the man she loved. Still, it was best she didn't see Calvin anymore, and she told him in detail of her thoughts over the weekend. She wasn't deserting him. It was necessary he understood that, and that this was painful to her because she was in love with him. But for her own survival she had to learn to be independent again. It wouldn't be the end of the world for him, she added at the bottom of note. He was strong and resourceful. He'd rebound from this crisis without her. And she would always love him.

Rachel wiped away tears and left the apartment for good.

NINETEEN

MONDAY MORNING CALVIN DID NOT TAKE HIS USUAL 7:45 flight from Love Field to join his legislative colleagues in Austin. Instead he bought a dozen freshly cut mums and made a solitary pilgrimage to Presbyterian Hospital. Official visiting hours were not until late morning, but the brunette with pillowy breasts at the nurse's station was charmed by Calvin's smile and allowed him into Seth's room. He placed the flowers on a bedside table and sat motionless on the room's only chair. Wanting to avoid the press, he had not visited the hospital since the start of the trial, but this morning, stirred by guilt, he had come to see his old friend. Seth looked surprisingly fresh, like someone enjoying a comfortable nap, as if the crisscrossing tubes that imprisoned him were only a prop. Calvin walked over and gently touched his friend on the arm, almost certain that he would wake.

In one way, Calvin thought, Seth was fortunate. The man had missed the nightmare of the trial and all its publicity, which would have hurt and embarrassed him, particularly the revelations that were still to come if someone found out what Rachel had. By the time Seth did recover, the whole incident might be buried and forgotten. Seth could pick up the pieces and go on. It was Calvin's fate to live through the ordeal and maybe never recover. He probably deserved it. He had had no right to involve Seth, and all the covering up had only done more damage. The thicket of lies that had been his life had finally entrapped him.

He should have been more leery of Rachel, he thought. She was too sharp, too tenacious, but he'd fallen in love with her, and had ignored the danger signs. Falling in love had taken him by surprise. Rachel was perfect for him, intelligent and sympathetic, but it surprised him that he had been right for her. She admired him for his hard work and sense of responsibility; they had that in common. He was grateful for her affection. When he had said she meant more to him than any other lover, it was true. His life resembled a frenetic juggling act, and she had given him an interlude of peace and stability.

Now it was over. He had tried to convince her he was sincere about wanting to change. The optimism came from a belief in his own will and discipline. If he had Rachel's support, he told himself, he could do anything. But she'd ignored his calls to the hotel, which had only made him more anxious. There was little to do now except fight off a sense of doom and hope for mercy. Or did he not deserve it?

He had tried to do his best with his life, helping people all he could, but he'd begun to realize that the people he loved and cared for the most were the ones he had most hurt and disappointed.

Calvin gave Seth's hand a final squeeze of affection and took a cab back to his apartment. Somehow he hoped Rachel would be there. At the lobby newsstand he glanced at the early edition of the afternoon paper. He looked again. Henry Boylan's name was in the headline. With a choking feeling Calvin read the first few paragraphs. It couldn't be, he thought. He knew in his heart Rachel hadn't done this. It didn't matter whether Boylan, who'd always been an S.O.B., had just come forward to tell his story, or the district attorney had learned about Boylan and applied pressure. Calvin couldn't even think. His sense of doom eclipsed everything. Yet he'd always known that this might explode in his face. It had just been a matter of time. He also knew what would happen next. There would be a subpoena for Calvin from Bidmore. He would have to testify. The charade was over. He thought of the headlines. The good readers of Dallas would have another scandal to wake up to.

Upstairs Calvin dropped onto the couch, dazed. It was another minute before he found Rachel's note. He was stunned. How could she leave him now? She really didn't think that he could change, that was the bottom line. Or maybe with Boylan in the picture it just didn't matter. Nothing mattered. Except for one thing, Calvin thought. He was not as selfish as Rachel painted him to be. He was not a total coward.

He put on a jacket and tie and stepped outside to flag a taxi. Above the Dallas skyline the clouds were marbled with light. He was at the painted brick building of the Riverdale Nursing Home a little after lunch. An aide led him down a sun-splashed linoleum corridor to the recreation room. Several worn card tables were being used for checkers and chess. Heads swung up to greet Calvin. His father rose uncertainly, as if not sure it was really Calvin, since his son's visits usually came on Saturdays. Like the general he would always be, Winthrop Richard Garrison's posture was ramrod straight, the eyes strong and clear, his mane of white hair full and proud. What didn't show was a heart weakened by four coronaries, and severe arthritis that made every step an act of courage. But the old man had plenty of that, Calvin knew.

"Dad, how are you feeling?" he said and gave the old man a firm embrace.

"What are you doing here?" came the question for a question. The hawklike face squinched up quizzically.

"I came to say hello."

The old general looked doubtful. "You came to collect on that bet, didn't you? You were damn lucky the Lakers won. Here . . ." His hand reached in a pocket and pulled out a five-dollar bill that was as soft as cloth.

"Are you feeling okay?" asked Calvin, helping him sit.

"You want to know how I'm feeling? The same as always. I'm in bad health and waiting to die. How are you?"

Calvin smiled.

"Why aren't you in Austin?"

"Took the day off."

"Doesn't sound like you. . . ." The old man looked suspicious.

"Everyone's entitled to a day off."

"So that's what you came to tell me? I thought you'd been given another civic award or something. . . ." The old man's smile was a proud one.

Calvin only nodded. Go on, he thought, tell him. Tell him everything. That's why he'd come here. His father would forgive him. The old man's honor and high standards aside, there was love and understanding too. The good in Calvin's life far outweighed the bad. He didn't have to apologize. But as he stared into his father's unyielding eyes, the words locked in his throat.

"I love you, Dad," he whispered, and gave the old man a good-bye hug.

Back at his apartment he tried to reach Rachel, but was almost grateful there was no answer at her hotel. He didn't know what he would have told her anyway. For a moment he thought about his failure of nerve with his father, whether that might not represent his whole life. He couldn't seem to escape his own judgment. He sat at his desk and slowly removed the .38 snub-nosed revolver. He rested the cold muzzle against his temple and looked out at the city. With a last, calm breath, he finally found his courage.

IV
Winners and Losers

TWENTY

THE FUNERAL OF CALVIN GARRISON WAS HELD ON A COOL, windswept afternoon in late April. An overnight storm had washed the city clean, readying it for a spring that had yet to arrive. Over a thousand mourners formed a cortege that snaked from the Highland Park United Methodist Church to Restland Cemetery, and included in its cast of elite and powerful every last member of the state legislature, Calvin's political allies and enemies alike. The governor himself read a short eulogy at the gravesite, not far from where Austin Mirabeau had buried King's Ransom. There were more flowers laid at the foot of the plain oak casket, estimated one *Dallas Morning News* reporter, than at any public funeral since Lyndon Johnson's. Austin was there, along with Meredith, though hardly standing together, as was half the Texas horse community out of respect and appreciation. In a wheelchair, Calvin's father observed the ceremony with a proud, unflinching face, giving no hint of the turmoil and hurt inside. On the fringe of the crowd, hidden behind her black veil, Rachel went unnoticed by reporters and acquaintances, and drifted away before the service was over.

What went discreetly unmentioned at the funeral was brazenly announced by newspaper headlines almost every day. Calvin's homosexual past and link to the theft of Five Deuces exploded in the public's face like a volcano, its ashes scattering far and wide and eclipsing the scandals that had preceded it. No one was more shaken by the fallout than

Meredith. The revelations about her husband's sexuality shocked and hurt her. At first she didn't believe the media, but when Boylan testified in court, her face paled. She wasn't angry or disappointed in Seth—youthful transgressions were something Meredith had suddenly been forced to remember—but in herself. What kind of relationship had she had with her husband if he'd felt he could never confide in her? Didn't he think she was loving and forgiving enough? All she felt was more guilt.

The morning after the funeral, prepared to go back into the courtroom, Meredith began weeping spontaneously in the hallway. A startled Sedgefield tried to comfort his client and shield her from the reporters and trial-watchers who stopped to gawk. But Meredith's shoulders shook uncontrollably. She couldn't speak. She felt buried by circumstances and bad luck, that there was no way out. Yet she had to pull through, pull herself through, she thought as she finally straightened and took a handkerchief from her purse. No one else would help her. Boylan's testimony hadn't exactly hurt the defense, but she sensed that the jurors were still undecided. As she marched toward the defense table, Sedgefield turned to her for the umpteenth time and said, "Are you sure you want me to call you to testify?"

"Yes," she said firmly.

"You know that Bidmore is going to cut you in little pieces."

"Let him try."

"Meredith, as your attorney I really have to recommend against—"

"You know what the difference is between you and me?" she said, looking Sedgefield in the eye. "You're a chickenshit and I'm not."

When Meredith was sworn in at the witness stand, she faced the jury box, and unsolicited by Sedgefield, gave everyone her life story. Bidmore objected repeatedly to the rambling and irrelevant testimony, but the judge seemed fascinated, and shut up the district attorney on every count. When she had finished describing her courtship and relationship with Seth, Meredith felt she had the confidence of the eight men and four women. Then she talked about the trauma of waking up one morning and finding her horse stolen. Not just any horse, but her hope for the All-American, the most important and prestigious quarter horse race in the world. To Meredith it was tantamount to losing a child. There were nods of sympathy from the women.

On cross-examination Bidmore hammered away at Meredith just as Sedgefield had predicted. The defendant, he said, was more enamoured of horses than people, and had as much compassion for the human race as a dog had for its fleas. That wasn't true, Meredith answered calmly. All her current employees would swear to her generosity, and she reckoned she gave more money to charity than any horse breeder in Texas. Normally smoother than a ten-year-old scotch, the district attorney grew shrill and defensive. Instead of quoting Shelley or Yeats to the jury, he harangued them for daring to take the word of a woman who had given her husband a good-night kiss a few hours before shooting him. Meredith didn't respond. It was the judge who grew irascible and warned the district attorney to cool his inflammatory tone.

Closing arguments followed for each side. Bidmore took, in legal parlance, the last bite of the cherry. Despite the judge's warning, he continued to thunder and rail at Meredith as a conniving woman with a documented history of oppressing men. The jurors seemed less than convinced. Meredith hoped as much anyway. The judge, looking exhausted from the endless weeks of melodrama, gave his final instructions to the jury of twelve: unanimous decision was needed either to convict or acquit. Anything in between might necessitate a new trial—a thought, he added, that was most alarming to him, and would cost the taxpayers of Texas another million dollars.

The courtroom emptied amid nervous whispers and guarded hopes. Those who remained in the corridors, hoping for an early verdict, weren't disappointed. Led by a portly bailiff, the jury returned to the courtroom only three and a half hours after it had left. The foreman, quiet and poker-faced, rose as the judge sipped from his water glass and focused on the jury.

"Have you reached a verdict?" he asked.

"Yes, sir." The foreman's voice echoed with relief and satisfaction. "The people of the state of Texas find the defendant, Meredith Kingsley, not guilty by reason of temporary insanity. . . ."

Applause broke out and built to a crescendo. It was interspersed by a chorus of "yaaaaa-hooo!" as if the spectators were enjoying a rodeo. Meredith dropped her head into her hands. It was over, finally. Sedgefield wrapped his arms around her in joy and relief, and shot his archenemy, Bidmore, a glance of triumph. Friends and admirers flocked around Meredith outside the courtroom. Where had they all been hiding? she wondered. With a smile she waved to everyone before Abel guided her into the car. "Take me home, please," she said.

The next day, resting at her ranch, Meredith learned that while the trial might have been over, the surprises weren't. As if to find some glory after his dark defeat, the district attorney announced a breakthrough in the horse-napping crime. One of the petty criminals who'd stolen most of the horses, including Five Deuces, was able to identify the man who'd hired them. His name was Sal Forester. The jockey and ranch hand of Austin Mirabeau was promptly arrested, and upon a full confession, that included his association with Thom Warfield, indicted for grand larceny. Sal's only comment to the press was that he had done it for the money and he was sorry if he caused his employer any embarrassment. Austin was quoted in the papers too. He denied any knowledge of or involvement in the thefts. He had thought Mr. Forester was honest and law-abiding. Unfortunately, he said, he had been wrong. The police had questioned Austin and formally cleared him. Meredith shook with anger as she picked up the phone and dialed.

"You son of a bitch," she shouted into the receiver before Austin could even say hello. "You're more crooked than an eight-foot snake."

"Just hold on," Austin answered. "I didn't have anything to do with the thefts. Sal knows it, the police know it, you know it—"

"I don't believe you. I'll never believe you. You must

really want to punish me. That grudge you've carried must have eaten you alive. When I was acquitted, did you start dreaming up another scheme? In a few more months I'll give you a real reason to carry a grudge—"

"You wouldn't mean at the All-American, would you? I'd really like to see you try, Meredith. I want you to be good and ready come Labor Day. Because then I can shut you up for good."

Meredith hung up. In fifteen minutes she was dressed and out with Abel in the pastures. It felt like years since she'd been with her horses. All she could think about was Labor Day and the All-American. Just you wait, Austin Mirabeau, she thought, just you wait.

When the verdict was announced, Rachel went back to her hotel room and wrote nonstop. Since Calvin's suicide her concentration had deserted her and she'd been tempted more than once to drop everything. A sense of pride kept her writing, and by late that night after the trial ended, she'd finished her story. Then she drafted her letter of resignation to Frank. She had decided to leave *Image* as soon as she'd heard about Calvin. Instead of going on a destructive odyssey of cutting off her hair or driving the freeways at ninety, she had kept her guilt and sorrow to herself. His death had stunned her. How could she have so badly misjudged Calvin? How could she have been so sure of her own judgment? By leaving him, maybe she'd helped destroy him. She had only been trying to protect herself, but in the process forgotten about the vulnerability of others.

As Rachel expected, Frank phoned as soon as he received her letter. She told him not to take the resignation personally. She was giving up journalism for good. She'd written her big story and it hadn't brought her much satisfaction. A career with the Fourth Estate seemed to be no more in the cards for her than a successful relationship with a man. Frank tried to bribe her with a salary hike and more reportorial freedom, but Rachel knew nothing would change her mind. "What are you going to do with your life?" Frank demanded like a caring father. "You can't just drop out. You've got too many gifts to throw everything away."

Rachel thanked him for everything and promised to be in touch, though she doubted she ever would. Cutting ties to her past was one way, maybe the best way, to forget Calvin.

The place she chose for her exile was New Mexico. There was no logic in the move except that friends had told her of the charms of the high desert country around Santa Fe, and though the rents were pricey, she found a condominium on the city's north side more easily than she could have found anything in Manhattan. From the living room window she had restful views of the snow capped Sangre de Cristo mountains, and the kitchen looked out on rolling hills of piñon pine and spruce. What she liked most about her new home was the solitude. She knew nobody and nobody knew her. The money that Meredith had given her would enable her to hold out for a while. She had no plans, no ambitions. Mornings she slept late, then walked the town's quaint, winding streets, dropping into art galleries and museums and gifts shops. People were friendly, and it was easy to talk to strangers. In restaurants she tried sitting alone but was inevitably approached by some gentleman who insisted on buying her a meal. Sometimes she accepted, but she always declined offers for a date. At night she stayed home with a book. A piñon pine fire would crackle in the fireplace, its fragrance scenting the cool mountain night.

The regimen worked in the beginning. Putting a geographical distance between her and the memories of Calvin helped her find an emotional distance. She might have gotten over him even sooner if not for a letter in her mailbox one afternoon. The handwriting on the envelope was small and crabbed. There was a Dallas postmark, but no return address.

May 10, 1985

Dear Miss Lang:

We have never met, and you may know little or nothing about me, so I hope you'll excuse my being presumptuous in writing to you. I have no other recourse, you see. Someone told me you were very close to my son in the months preceding his suicide, closer than anyone else perhaps, certainly closer than me. I was appalled by his death and I don't understand why he did it. I thought I knew Calvin. My son and I may not have been as intimate as some fathers and sons, but we did have an understanding of, and respect for, one another. Would you be kind enough to share anything Calvin might have said about me in those last months? I am afraid that I can't think of much else these days. I do miss Calvin more than I can articulate. He was a fine son and I loved him.

> Yours sincerely,
> Winthrop Richard Garrison

She did remember the father, of course. The stark, lonely figure at the funeral had only made her feel more guilty. She felt she had hurt the old man almost as much as she had Calvin. Survivors suffered too, maybe more than the victim. Rachel didn't know how to answer. Calvin had scarcely breathed a word to her about his father, and nothing that indicated affection. If anything he resented the old man for his strict, unforgiving values. The next day she rolled a sheet of stationery into her typewriter.

Dear Mr. Garrison:

Thank you for your letter. I do know of you, and I'm sorry I didn't visit you at the nursing home before I left Dallas. I'm afraid that I was as upset and distraught as you were. I can assure you that Calvin may not have expressed to you in person how he felt—he was a guarded man in many ways—but he spoke often of how much he loved you. He cared for you in ways you probably didn't realize. There was strong affection. You're right, he was a fine man, and a loving son.

> All best,
> Rachel Lang

She hoped that would be the end of it. Her letter would bring some peace and comfort to a man who deserved solace. But while making the father feel better, Rachel only felt troubled. Her lie bothered her, as well-intentioned as it was. There had already been so much deceit and fabrication. It had been the basis of Calvin's relationship with everyone, including with his father and her.

For the next few days she tried to lose herself in a new novel, forgetting Calvin altogether. She took long afternoon walks along the ski basin road, sometimes dropping off into the national forest and trekking into the hills. The clear, dry air had a healing quality. She wanted to stay in Santa Fe forever, she thought. When she returned home one evening she found another letter from Mr. Garrison.

May 19, 1985

Dear Rachel:

You were kind and thoughtful to answer my letter. I had always hoped that Calvin felt for me more than he let on, as I certainly felt for him more than I communicated. I realize now that he had deep and serious problems, but at least there was a real if unspoken bond between us. Perhaps you could tell me some of the specific things he said about me. I'm sorry to impose, but at my point in life I have little left but memories.

Very gratefully yours,
Winthrop

She resisted writing back. She rationalized that the old general would be fine if he never heard from her again, yet her conscience made her at least call the nursing home and make discreet inquiries. Calvin's father was still shaken by the suicide, Rachel was told, but her letter had cheered him immensely. Rachel knew she had no choice. She invented dates and places for Calvin to speak warmly of his father. She made it sound as if he had worshiped Winthrop, owed him for every success that Calvin came to enjoy.

When the letter was mailed she felt another surge of anger at herself. Why was she lying to him? She didn't have to answer his letter; she was just feeling sorry for him. Or was she being too hard on herself, as she'd been too hard on Calvin? Everybody lied to some extent. Society existed on lies—well, at least a lot of half-truths. People like Calvin and his father won your confidence out of love or pity, and when you finally understood about the web of lies, you were too stuck to get out. And as painstaking a reporter as Rachel tried to be, gathering only facts, magazines like *Image* twisted them conveniently because they owed their circulation to gossip and hearsay.

On the last Sunday in May Rachel celebrated her thirtieth birthday alone. Her mother called to wish her well, but the message was laced with self-pity for being neglected by her daughter. Rachel only offered more lies. She was sorry for not calling, she'd been so busy having a wonderful time in Santa Fe. For the rest of the day she didn't go out or answer the phone, which rang continually. She suspected Frank and a few friends, but there was no one she wanted to talk to.

The weather in Santa Fe began to turn even more breathtaking, coaxing in the normal flood of summer tourists. Instead of venturing out, Rachel elected to stay at home. She abandoned even her mountain walks. The only time she went to town was for groceries and an occasional newspaper. What went on in the rest of the world no longer concerned her. At home she mostly slept. The house went uncleaned, laundry left piled high, shopping lists made but ignored. Another letter finally came from Winthrop. She was beginning to dislike him. He was an intruder, just like everyone else.

In a moment of weakness she opened the letter anyway. There were more profuse thanks and a hunger to know more. Surely there was something else she could tell him about his son. Some small anecdote that she might have forgotten?

This would be endless, she realized. He would never stop asking. She was keeping him alive so he could keep writing her. She would have to end it sooner or later. The next morning she pushed a sheet into the typewriter.

Rachel's spirits improved in the next few days. She returned to her solitary walks into the foothills of the Sangre de Cristos. The snow was beginning to vanish from their tops, revealing a belt of budding aspens. In town she made friends with a woman who had lived on Rachel's block in Manhattan; now she owned a jewelry shop on Canyon Road, catering to tourists and keeping leisurely hours. It was the way life was meant to be lived, she told Rachel.

In the first week of June another letter arrived from Dallas. The logo of the nursing home was embossed in gold leaf in one corner. The note from the administrative director informed Rachel that Mr. Garrison had died of cardiac failure a few days ago. His last days were peaceful and happy, the noted added. Ms. Lang's letters had been a deep and abiding consolation to him.

In the kitchen Rachel studied her last letter to Winthrop. She had never mailed it. She wondered if she'd done the right thing not to, or maybe it just didn't matter.

Dear Winthrop:

This will be my last letter to you because I don't want to keep on lying. What I have told you about Calvin was mostly fabricated. The fact was that I felt sorry for you and myself as well. Your son was a very warm and caring man, I can tell you that, and that I miss him, but I honestly can't say how much he loved you. Some things in life no one can be certain of.

With all best wishes,
Rachel Lang

TWENTY-ONE

To Sparky Maligan there was no place like Hollywood. Paradise! In his musty double-breasted suit he stepped off the Trailways bus near Gower Street and let the sun wash over his pale face. Every winter, chasing the racing circuit, he drifted either to Florida or California, but he preferred the West Coast. In southern California alone there were five thoroughbred and quarter horse tracks, while Florida was as concerned about jai alai and greyhounds as horses. And in Florida there were five pigs running for every decent horse; track owners only wanted to fill out their fields so they could entice naive bettors with an alphabet soup of wagering combinations. Sparky ordered a nine-piece box of Chicken McNuggets at the nearest McDonald's, ignoring the usual collection of Hollywood weirdos, prostitutes, and panhandlers, then took a leisurely stroll down Hollywood Boulevard to gaze at the star-shaped plaques in the sidewalk. After horses and race tracks, his abiding passion was movies; there wasn't a name on the sidewalk he didn't know. At Mann's Chinese theater he shouldered his way through the tourists to ogle once more the foot and hand prints embedded for posterity. The movie playing there was *The Killing Fields*, but Sparky had already seen it twice. Not far away he found a bank that would cash his Social Security check, bought the *Daily Racing Form* from a vendor, and was on a bus to Hollywood Park before one.

For a while he dozed. The three-day milk-stop run from San Antonio had left him feeling a little wobbly. His clothes weren't exactly fresh either, but with the track beckoning, the laundromat would have to wait. He felt lucky today. He was well aware that every year millions of bettors patronized tracks around the country, and that probably each and every one considered himself lucky, but Sparky had one quality that most lacked—perseverance. Handicapping horses was his whole life. Nothing else mattered as he roamed the country. In a small weathered leather suitcase he kept a change of clothing, toilet supplies, a calculator, handicap notes that were updated every month, a Bible, a faded photo of his dead wife, and pictures of a beautiful redwood cabin high in the Big Bear mountains outside Los Angeles—snapshots taken on his last trip west, of the cabin he would buy as soon as he hit paydirt with the ponies. Maybe he'd even retire there. Who wanted to be a nomad forever?

Sometimes it seemed to Sparky that there'd never been a moment when he hadn't been on the road. The only child of a divorced Army staff sergeant, he had moved from city to city until, at eighteen, he joined the Navy and fought the Japanese in the South Pacific. Within a year after his honorable discharge, he married a shy, pretty Mexican girl he met while working in Arizona. His bride of nine months was driving east toward New Mexico when her car was swept away in a flash flood. Sparky was devastated. He had survived a whole war, and his wife had been struck down by a freak act of nature? There was no trusting fate. Like a lost soul he drifted from jobs as shoe salesman to hard hat to bus driver as he aimlessly crisscrossed the country. Somewhere along the way he started playing the ponies. He worked at a job only long enough to support his trips to the betting window. It was more than the money that lured him—it was the horses. Man's abiding friend in war and peace, there was something gallant, almost immortal, about the four-legged beast which produced in Sparky an endless sense of wonder.

At Hollywood Park he bought a three-dollar general

admission seat and planted himself near the paddock area. Beyond, the lush grass centerfield held a manmade lake. As Sparky's gaze darted over the first field of horses, he recognized all but one from previous races. Four-year-olds and up, they had to run eight furlongs. Today's was also an allowance race, which meant that the weight carried by each horse was decided by its past performances. In Sparky's opinion the favorite, Thief-By-Night, with 123 pounds, was carrying far too much. If history held true, the stallion would shoot out of his gate like a tornado, tire at the first turn, be buried in the pack at the half mile, and probably finish dead last. Another horse, Sweet But Sassy, was a great mudder—mud-runner—but track conditions today were fast. Two of the others were five-year-old maidens, which made them long shots and to be avoided like the plague, and another, Lucky Raven, though assigned the rail position and a great finisher, was generally too temperamental to be trusted. The horse Sparky liked was Tobacco Red. The five-year-old bay gelding had won three of his previous six starts, all a mile or longer, and his jock was a fiery little Mex who had had considerable success at Hollywood Park, and particularly on Tobacco Red. Sparky also was satisfied of the 5:2 odds. When he wanted to be technical and thorough, he handicapped a race by a strict and complicated point system, giving value even to track soil composition and a horse's biological birthday, but the first race today didn't require it. Common sense and a little knowledge were enough.

He produced a crisp fifty-dollar bill from his tattered billfold and smiled confidently at the betting window clerk. Back at the rail he ignored the wafting smell of beer and cigarettes and the milling crowd, his gaze trained on the starting gate. As he anticipated, Thief-By-Night charged out first, sprinting to a lead, but was quickly overtaken by the pack. Tobacco Red ran on the outside, taking long, confident strides, hanging back to conserve strength. At six furlongs the jockey made his move, bringing down his whip and leaning forward in the saddle. Tobacco Red breezed past one of the maidens, then swept around Sweet But

Sassy and Lucky Raven and roared across the finish with a three-length victory. Sparky gave a little whoop of glee. Back at the window he collected his winnings.

The second race he sat out, leery of the field because there were too many long shots. Sparky estimated that out of every ten races run in the country one was fixed; slipping in a long shot who proved to be a ringer was one of the easier ways. For the third race he got ambitious and bet on a four-horse trifecta box. Everything went smoothly. His twenty-dollar bet brought in $240. In the fourth he liked a horse named Cotton Ball and promptly pocketed another eighty. Sparky, old boy, you're on a roll, he thought giddily. By the seventh race he'd made a total of $1100, and decided to risk it all on another trifecta. He pushed a pencil for a few minutes, worked some numbers on his calculator, then ran to the window with the certain knowledge he had the top three finishers. One minute thirty-six seconds later he was $3846 richer.

He had almost $5000 in his pockets now. The familiar dilemma of whether to pack it in or try to continue the streak bothered him only for a moment. When you're hot, you're hot, he thought. He sat out the next two contests to concentrate on the final race. Sparky liked a small three-year-old filly named Dancer's Hat: respectable previous times, a tenacious front-runner who never looked back, and she faced a weak field today. Just to be sure, Sparky opted for various combinations on the same horse. With a good luck kiss to his money, he handed $4500 to the cashier. Back at the rail he tapped his foot nervously. Dancer's Hat shot out quickly, but around the first turn she began to lag. The worried jockey threw a glance behind him. When he turned back it was too late. A leaderless Dancer's Hat plowed smack into the chestnut filly in front of her. Christ, thought Sparky, turning away with a shudder. It didn't matter that his horse finished in the money. The track stewards were unanimous in disqualifying her.

It wasn't his day after all, thought Sparky. Everything had gone right down the toilet. Over the years he'd learned to take his losses philosophically, yet he felt distressed now as he peered into his wallet and saw what remained. He

took a bus back to Hollywood and registered at a hole-in-
the-wall where the empty pool had been scarred by graffiti
and almost every door looked as if it had been kicked in at
least once. He drifted to sleep and dreamed of barbecuing
hamburgers on the deck of his mountain chalet.

The next morning he leafed through the *Daily Racing
Form* and scrutinized the Los Alamitos card. He'd always
loved the Orange County track just north of Long Beach,
with its sweeping mountain vistas and the best hot dogs of
any track in the country. And quarter horses, he thought,
might bring him better luck than thoroughbreds. David
Sanders would be riding a couple of mounts for Austin
Mirabeau, though Sparky had never heard of a filly named
Miss Muffet. Still, he liked the young jockey and often bet
on him. Killing time until Los Alamitos opened, Sparky
meandered down Sunset Boulevard to the blocks of television studios. He knew most of the game shows by heart.
Three or four times he'd sat in the audiences, and when he
saw the zigzag line of hopeful contestants in front of *Stump
the Celebrity*, he joined the queue.

Inside the studio he was given a lengthy questionnaire
that required putting on his glasses. Contestants were to be
chosen on the basis of interesting jobs or unusual pasts; the
rest of the dummies had to sit in the audience. What was so
unusual or interesting about him? wondered Sparky. Absolutely nothing. On a lark he described himself as a Hollywood character actor, listing *Rear Window*, *Judgment at
Nuremberg*, and *Iwo Jima* as credits. Who was going to
know any differently? Anyway, the whole thing was only for
fun.

An hour later, as cameras rolled, his name was called.
As he'd seen countless others do, an incredulous Sparky
rushed on stage amid thunderous clapping. Was this really
happening to him? he wondered as the host read from
Sparky's questionnaire. More applause. When the day's celebrity was introduced, Sparky studied the lean, impeccably dressed actor with jet-black hair. The name Buck Hart
wasn't a familiar one until the host spoke of a horse that
Buck owned, Desert Wind. In recent months the quarter
horse had earned the nickname Wondercolt; not just for his

laboratory origins, but his stunning successes at the track. The two-year-old had run five times and hadn't come close to being challenged. Jesus, Sparky suddenly remembered from the *Racing Form*, the colt was entered against Miss Muffet this afternoon. Now that might be some race. Track mavens were already calling Desert Wind the fastest quarter horse ever.

Sparky nodded along with Buck when asked if he knew the game show rules. The guest contestant picked a category, from which the celebrity was asked a question; if he didn't know the answer, the guest was given a shot. Points were awarded for each correct response, and if either celebrity or guest answered everything, he walked away with $5000.

Sparky chose the category of sports over motion pictures. A dial on a giant wheel spun around, cliking past football, basketball, tennis—and died on horses. Sparky beamed. He was on a roll.

Host: "First question to you, Mr. Hart. To a horse player, what does the term *stragglers* mean?"

Buck (knitting his brow): "I wish I knew. Someone who's always late getting to the track?"

Host: "Our celebrity is stumped. How about our character actor hailing from New York?"

Sparky (rubbing his chin): "Stragglers are valid tickets not cashed before the next race."

Host: "One hundred points for Sparky! Next question to our celebrity again. Mr. Hart, if someone told you he was training a standardbred, what would he be referring to?"

Buck: "That would be a breed of horse, as opposed to a thoroughbred or a quarter horse."

Host: "I need a little bit more than that. Sparky. . . ?"

Sparky: "A standardbred is a horse registered by the U.S. Trotting Associations and restricted to harness racing."

Host: "Correct again! Sparky, you're rolling up the points. Another question for Mr. Hart. Please tell the audience what a claiming race is."

Buck (smiling confidently): "That's a race where a horse is entered with the understanding to actually sell the horse to any other owner or trainer for a price listed before the race."

Host: "Give one to our celebrity! Questions now go to our guest. If he can answer three in a row without missing, he earns five hundred points. At ten dollars a point, that means $5000. Or he can elect to answer questions from our bonus pool and earn $10,000. But I have to warn you, Sparky, those questions are tougher than horsemeat. Which will it be?"

Sparky squinted through the harsh camera lights toward the audience, emboldened by their cheering. He was on a high. "I'll try the bonus pool, please," Sparky said calmly.

"You're a brave man. Okay, for all the marbles, here we go. The American Mule Association was formed in 1977 in Fresno, California, for the purpose of promoting mule racing in this country. Whom did the association select as its top racing mule in 1979?"

"That would be Miss Hazard County," Sparky answered automatically. "She won a little over $15,000."

"You must read the almanac every night, Sparky. Either that or you're the smartest man since Einstein. Question number two: What is the distinction between an outrider and a pony rider?"

In game shows there were always meddlers from the audience who shouted out an answer, wanting simply to help the contestant or prove their own cleverness, but at the moment Sparky encountered only befuddled silence. He didn't mind. It was all shooting fish in a barrel anyway. "An outrider," he said in a clear voice, "is one who leads an entry from the paddock area to the starting gate. A pony rider helps a jockey with his horse after the race during the parade to the post."

"Chalk another one up for the human encyclopedia," said the amazed host. "Okay, Sparky, here's your last question. It's for the whole $10,000. Please listen carefully: Who was the trainer of War Admiral when he won the 1938 Triple Crown?"

"War Admiral's trainer?" Sparky echoed, searching his

memory. "That was George Conway. War Admiral's breeder was Samuel D. Riddle. And his jockey was Charley Kurtsinger. But War Admiral didn't win the Triple Crown in 1938. He won it in 1937."

The host and Buck shook their heads in awe. The number $10,000 flashed above Sparky's head as the audience exploded in cheering. Sparky received his check from a skimpily clad brunette who also gave him a peck on the cheek, then held up one of his arms triumphantly. He walked off stage, trailed by more applause, and suddenly felt a hand brush his trousers. The small blond boy cocked his head up sadly. A rubber spider was sticking out of one pocket.

"Who are you?" Sparky asked as he crouched down.

"Adam Jeffrey Hart."

"Pleased to meet you. I'm Sparky. Is something the matter?"

The boy shook his head unconvincingly.

"Are you looking for your dad? He should be back here any second—"

"No."

"Then what is it?"

Adam Jeffrey looked Sparky over carefully, sizing him up as someone he could trust. "I dunno. I guess I miss my friends," he said.

"Where are they?"

"Back in school."

"Why aren't you there?"

"Because I'm always traveling with my dad. Today we're going to another race track."

"To see Desert Wind?"

He nodded.

"Everyone says he's a great horse. Maybe the greatest ever."

But Sparky saw that the boy was less than excited. The horse was keeping him from his friends. Buck suddenly strolled up and pumped Sparky's hand, congratulating him on his victory and the $10,000.

"What are you going to do with the money?" Buck said.

"Actually, I was going out to Los Alamitos."

"Really?" Buck said, pleased. "Then why don't you join us? We've got a front-row box in the Jockey Club. I can even tell you what horse to bet on," Buck said with a wink.

Sparky said he'd be pleased to go. There'd probably be a free lunch, something more substantial than fast food. Buck promised to send a limo to Sparky's home.

"That won't be necessary," said Sparky.

"I insist. An old actor like you is probably squirreled away somewhere in Hollywood Hills, right?"

"Right," Sparky said quickly, "but I have my own driver."

He was relieved to say good-bye, wondering what Buck and his son thought of his dowdy clothes, but in Hollywood you could get away with almost anything. Courtesy of a bettors' shuttle, he was at the Los Alamitos track as the bugle sounded for the first race. A VIP page whisked him upstairs to the Jockey Club. Sparky felt self-conscious as he gave Buck and Adam Jeffrey a friendly wave. Everyone looked so stylish, even downright rich. Buck talked nonstop about Wondercolt and his Arab owner while Sparky devoured a Waldorf salad. Adam Jeffrey played with his rubber spider, then began running around the club like a wild man, to Buck's discomfort. Desert Wind and Miss Muffet wouldn't meet until the seventh race, so Sparky only bet lightly as he waited, and just after the sixth he wandered down to the paddock area.

"Hey, David!" he yelled across the dividing rail.

When there was no response, Sparky prevailed upon a security guard to let him cross the track. A preoccupied David finally glanced up and gave Sparky a warm smile. "I came to bring you a little luck," Sparky said.

"Can always use a little of that. How are you, Sparky?"

"Kicking and breathing. Here," he said, reaching for his wallet, "that money I owe you."

"You don't have to," David said.

"You don't have to worry about me. I just hit the jackpot on a quiz show."

"Really?" David looked happy for him.

"Listen, what kind of horse is Miss Muffet?"

"Not the easiest to ride, but she's damn fast, I can tell

you that. I know all about Desert Wind, but I'm not about to write off Miss Muffet."

Sparky got out of the way just as Austin Mirabeau approached to give his jockey final instructions. Sparky turned to the small filly who might have been mistaken for a circus pony. The bright yellow earmuffs and polka-dot blinkers had already drawn stares and not a few hoots from the peanut gallery. Sparky knew virtually nothing about the filly, except that she had to have something to recommend her because Austin Mirabeau was determined to have a winner for this year's All-American.

Sparky scrutinized the competition as the horses left the paddock. He had never seen a two-year-old like Desert Wind. The bruiser of a horse was all muscle, the eyes determined and intelligent, the chestnut coat shiny as polished mahogany. He dwarfed the petite Miss Muffet by a good two hands as the two horses were led side by side toward the starting gate. The tote board showed Desert Wind a prohibitive favorite. Miss Muffet was at 9:2. Sparky liked to stay clear of underdogs, but he knew Austin and David, and in Miss Muffet's previous two races she'd finished third and second. There was also something about Desert Wind that bothered him. You couldn't ask for a more impressive conformation, but this whole science business, making a horse partially in a laboratory, fooling with Mother Nature—it was tampering with the natural order. Sparky didn't like it. He didn't like the horse's principal owner either. From what Buck had said, Zallaq sounded like some rich Arab who thought he could buy his way to respectability. After waiting in line at the nearest window, Sparky plunked down $2000 on Miss Muffett to win.

He rejoined his host in the Jockey Club as the horses jigged nervously in the gate below. Buck looked even more anxious than Desert Wind. His face had paled and the binoculars in his hands trembled slightly. The gates sprung open. Like an unstoppable fullback breaking through an invisible line, Wondercolt strode into the lead. Sparky focused on the disproportionately small head that bored straight ahead, as if eyeing the finish. Around the 220-yard mark Miss Muffet made her move. On the outside she had kept pace with the pack; now she shot out like a cannon ball. Sparky hadn't seen anything quite like it. The filly wasn't an experienced racer, but she was a speed freak. One hundred yards from the finish Miss Muffet was a neck ahead. Buck looked in pain. Sparky felt real hope. Maybe the great Wondercolt, who'd been so impressive in earlier races, hadn't really been challenged.

In general admissions the crowd was on its feet. The ugly duckling of a horse had won some hearts and minds. Sparky couldn't help yelling too. Two lengths from the wire, as if responding to the adulation, Miss Muffet swung her head to the crowd. In that fraction of a second, Desert Wind galloped ahead. The chestnut colt won by a neck. The great crescendo of approval turned to dismayed silence.

"What did I tell you, Sparky," Buck enthused, recapturing his poise. "That was some race." He peered at the stopwatch around his neck. "Twenty-one point three. That's the fastest time any quarter horse has run in a couple years. That little filly really pushed my colt."

That little filly, with a little more savvy and experience, thought Sparky, might have won. He thanked Buck for his hospitality and gave Adam Jeffrey a rub on the head. Maybe he'd been wrong to bet against such an overwhelming favorite, Sparky considered as he boarded the bus. But what the hell, if life wasn't for taking chances, what was it? He still didn't care for Wondercolt, and doubted if he ever would. The horse was a damn machine. Still, there was no arguing with speed—or success—and Sparky honestly wondered if any horse could beat him.

Buck carried his sleeping son out of the Jockey Club, battling the foot traffic until he reached his Porsche. He wondered why he wasn't in better spirits. His horse had just won another race, even if it'd been closer than expected; Zallaq was pleased with his public relations work and paid him generously; good old Sidney, with the publicity Buck was getting from Desert Wind, was receiving television offers again. The game plan was actually working. Yet Buck was nervous. He had invested his last penny, including taking out a new mortgage on his home, to buy shares in Desert Wind. Every time the horse ran, Buck held his breath. What if the colt fractured a leg? What if he got sick? What if he just lost his instinct for winning? Horses were a lot like bananas, someone had once said—good today, bad tomorrow.

The racing game was not only chancy, Buck thought, it was selfish. He felt the familiar waves of guilt as he thought about dragging poor A.J. halfway around the country. Buck had tried to explain what public relations was, why it was necessary for him to be on the road, that he was getting paid to do this job. Adam Jeffrey wasn't appeased. Buck had thought of leaving him at home with a housekeeper, but the fact was, he couldn't afford it. On the road, at least, Zallaq picked up all expenses.

His Porsche shot onto the freeway for the long drive home. He felt as tired as his son. Just as soon as Desert Wind ran in the All-American, Buck thought with relief, this would all be over. That was Zallaq's crusade—a victory at Ruidoso. The more races Desert Wind won, the quicker the Arab was to climb on his pulpit to berate a world that had ignored his scientific genius. Zallaq wasn't just out to prove something, he was conducting his own holy war. There were still skeptics in the racing world waiting for Zallaq to fall on his face. Not only did the Arab intend to disappoint them, he was going to make his enemies bow at his feet.

Buck didn't much care about revenge. All he wanted was money to live comfortably and a chance to work in television again. And some peace, and time with Adam Jeffrey. He owed the kid and wanted to make it up to him. He pulled A.J. closer as he drove, thinking that Labor Day and the All-American couldn't come soon enough.

TWENTY-TWO

FROM NEAR THE RAIL BILLY SULLIVAN WATCHED AS AN outrider led El Cid from the paddock area to the starting gate and coaxed the skittish colt in. Seven other horses joined him in their respective gates, dancing uneasily as their jockeys settled in the irons and the crowd paused in expectation. The bleachers at Santa Fe Downs were hardly full for the afternoon's first race, and few if any of the locals had heard of El Cid, reflecting the colt's long odds. But Billy didn't care. For El Cid's maiden race of 350 yards, all that counted was how well he performed under pressure. Billy knew that if he had any fantasies about entering the All-American, much less winning it, his horse had to show some mettle here and now.

Billy's confidence in himself was also something to be tested. After the debacle at the Cartier Ball, he had holed up in his Palm Beach condominium for two days on a royal drunk; with the sobering process came the realization that the good times, the adoring women, the cozy niche on the international polo circuit, were all a thing of the past. And he didn't need another nudge from Sam Cohen to know that his debts had reached unmanageable proportions. Creditors were calling him directly. Within the week he swallowed his pride and sold his condominium, the rest of his polo ponies, all his art work, his stock market holdings, and his car—virtually everything except the horse he'd won from Gallegos. As painful as the divestiture was, he felt a great burden lift from his shoulders. The ride on his father's coattails was over. If he was to succeed now with El Cid, it would strictly be a test of his own abilities.

Putting the horse in a trailer, Billy drove from Palm Beach to New Mexico on advice from friends that if he were serious about the All-American he might as well get his horse acclimated at Ruidoso. The high altitude would help in conditioning, and with the All-American only four months away, Billy had to enter some good stakes races to prepare his horse properly. But Ruidoso Downs proved the wrong place. Track officials had only a few May and June openings, entry fees were high, and stable rents even higher. Ruidoso struck him as a playground for rich Texans. Billy had walked El Cid back into his trailer and driven four hours to Santa Fe. The altitude was virtually the same. He rented a one-bedroom, dilapidated adobe near Santa Fe Downs, stabled his horse nearby, and counted his money. If he lived frugally, he had enough to enter five or six races, hire a trainer, groom, and jockey, and keep El Cid and himself in groceries.

At the track one afternoon he met a garrulous, stubborn horseman named O'Connel who struck an immediate rapport with El Cid. The burly Irishman had been around tracks for two decades, bullshitted with the best of them, and while hardly one of the country's most renowned quarter horse trainers—having been bounced from one breeding farm to another because he argued with his bosses too much—he still had trained several good horses, one of which, a gelding named Rogue's Delight, had taken second in the 1980 All-American and was later syndicated for $350,000 a share.

O'Connel was impressed with El Cid's conformation, but was only too happy to inform Billy that looks weren't everything, that his horse was basically lazy and needed a rigorous regimen, such as running through the high desert country and taking daily swims. Billy knew there were basically two schools of thought on training a horse: either you bought one with proven bloodlines and merely helped him realize his potential, or you took an unproven commodity and worked and worked him until you made him a champion. So many great horses in both categories were never heard of because they were pushed too hard too young and broke down, but Billy knew he had to take a chance. He hired O'Connel on the spot, and for the past two weeks the gruff Irishman had gotten El Cid used to the starting gate, the track, and being handled by stable boys. He'd also put him through a few iron-man workouts and hired a jockey on a per diem. Now it was time to see if the colt would hold up under fire.

Billy raised his eyes to the starting gate.

The eight horses broke out of the gate as if it meant life or death. Plumes of dust spiraled up from their heels and hung lazily in the still afternoon. Billy's gaze fixed on the sixth horse as he moved into the front, built on his lead, and by the 220-yard mark was three lengths ahead. El Cid was not a graceful runner—his stride was too awkward—but what he lacked in fluidity he compensated for with outright speed. He blew past the finish with a two-length lead. Billy shot a fist in the air in relief and joy. Then his eye strayed to the winner's circle. El Cid was jigging uncomfortably, and O'Connel was already rushing over.

"What is it?" asked Billy, right behind his trainer. El Cid's breathing was labored, worse than any polo pony Billy had ridden.

"I'm not sure," the Irishman offered. "Colic would be a good bet. Or broken wind."

"What the hell is that?"

"Some air vessels in the lungs collapse, causing premature fatigue. Maybe it's the 7000-foot altitude, maybe your horse has just got weak lungs. . . ."

Billy stroked El Cid's neck. He was soaked with perspiration. "What do we do?"

"Right now, cool him out. Then rest him a couple days, then start working him again. If this happens a second time, we see a good vet. Hey," the Irishman said with a smile, when Billy looked disconsolate, "that sure was a pretty race."

A stable hand cleaned the horse's coat with a scraper and covered him with a blanket, then walked El Cid around the paddock area. Billy told himself not to worry. While often fragile, horses were also capable of shaking off their share of infirmities. By evening El Cid seemed rested. He gamboled near his stables like a restless yearling. Billy personally gave him dinner—a mixture of oats, barley, wheat bran, a little salt, legume hay, and a supplemental "cocktail" of carotene and other vitamins. Then he wearily headed home. At two in the morning he was awakened by a call from the stable watchman. El Cid was running a fever and couldn't stay on his feet. Billy called O'Connel and hurried over.

In the stables he cradled the horse's feverish head. El Cid's stomach was bloated as well. Horses had small stomachs, Billy knew, and no ability to vomit, so if they overate or the food didn't digest, there could be intestinal damage. O'Connel showed up with a vet, and the two huddled like doting parents over the animal, taking his temperature and examining his mouth and throat, his nose and ears. The diagnosis was uncertain—maybe something the horse had eaten, maybe something more serious. Tests would have to be done. Billy stayed with El Cid the rest of the night. It was as if Gallegos had put some curse on him or the horse, he thought. He brushed aside his frustration and hoped for the best.

El Cid spent the next three days in an equine hospital. With studhorses like Seattle Slew worth as much as $100 million, veterinary care had become as sophisticated and technology oriented as human medicine. Yet when the tests on El Cid were completed, the doctor had little to say. Blood, albumen, and cholesterol counts were normal; bone and muscle tissues were firm; heart size and artery flow were fine; lungs on the small side, but completely healthy. Maybe, the vet concluded almost apologetically, El Cid was just experiencing growing pains. It happened a lot with two-year-olds. Billy hardly felt comforted. He thought of horses like Swale, who had dropped dead without warning, and even an autopsy couldn't confirm the specific cause of death. The vet gave Billy a sympathetic pat on the shoulder and a bill for $4000.

"Where the hell am I going to get all this money?" Billy

complained to O'Connel the next day. "If we're going to enter the All-American, I've got till next month to pay the late nomination fee. I don't even know if I've got a horse that's going to live."

"Oh, he'll be fine," O'Connel predicted. "My gut tells me." He patted his sizable belly with affection.

"So we should nominate him?"

"My friend, what else are you going to do? You've seen El Cid's speed. The vet couldn't turn up anything. This morning the horse couldn't have been more frisky. We've got as good a chance as anybody, Billy. I say let's get on with the training, say our prayers, and stop worrying about what hasn't happened."

When Billy gave his approval, O'Connel wasted no time living up to his word. El Cid was galloped a mile every morning, and following a rest, breezed for intervals between a quarter and half a mile. Billy monitored the workouts closely. El Cid showed no signs of another breakdown; if anything, his stamina improved. To build up the colt's muscles, O'Connel began running him through flat, sandy stretches of nearby Indian pueblo land, then making him swim in a not too cold lake. By early June the trainer pronounced him ready to race again, and while Billy was pleased, he continued to worry about money. Because he virtually had no assets, banks wouldn't lend to him. He had talked to Sam twice but gotten nowhere. Now he was trying everyone in his address book. Most friends were sympathetic and happy to hear of El Cid's first victory, but one win did not a champion make, came the refrain. Others were more direct: "What, invest in a race horse?" Billy felt he was practically giving away El Cid by offering a half interest for $25,000, yet he couldn't get a single taker.

The next weekend at Santa Fe Downs he watched El Cid come from behind and win his second straight race. The colt showed confidence, stamina, and concentration. That night Billy bought his trainer dinner at an in-town establishment called the Bull Ring, a hangout for politicos, track people, and free-spirited cowboys, and celebrated till midnight. The purses at the Downs weren't enough to open a Swiss bank account, but every penny helped with expenses. And if El Cid just stayed healthy, Billy was starting to hope, he had a real shot at the All-American.

Saying good night to O'Connel, Billy's eyes strayed to an attractive blonde who occupied a corner table. She'd dined alone, late, and now sat pensively over a cup of coffee. In the last few months, preoccupied with his horse, he hadn't had the time or inclination to date, and had virtually forgotten about women. Whenever he thought of Aymara, it was with disgust, but the blonde looked familiar, and not unfriendly. Billy strolled over.

"Excuse me," he said. "I just wanted to satisfy my curiosity. I'm sure I've seen you. . . ."

The woman glanced up, searching Billy's face, as if she might know him as well. "I don't think so," she finally said, pleasantly enough.

"I'm Billy Sullivan," he said anyway.

"Rachel Lang."

Billy cocked his head, and finally tapped the right memory bank. "You're the reporter, aren't you? The one who covered Meredith Kingsley's trial. Your photo was in the papers—"

"Ex-reporter," Rachel corrected.

Billy remembered the difficult, and in some ways tragic trial. The suicide of a Texas state senator had won national headlines, and Meredith's husband still hadn't recovered from his coma. But Meredith had been acquitted, and the feisty woman had promised the world that she would nurse her kidnapped horse, Five Deuces, back to health in time for the All-American. Billy hadn't paid too much attention to his competition, but Meredith and her horse were such celebrities that it was impossible not to be aware of Five Deuces' record times. In four starts the horse had overwhelmed competition at Los Alamitos and Sunland Park, never coming close to losing, and as she'd done at her ranch party last year, Meredith was predicting another victory at the All-American.

"What are you doing in Santa Fe?" Billy asked.

"I'm semiretired," Rachel offered. "And you?"

"Trying to race a horse."

"That's something I know a little about. I've met a lot of your kind this year."

"I'm afraid I'm a novice. My horse's only raced twice."

"What's his name?"

Billy told her, and about the two victories, then extended Rachel an invitation to come to the Downs next weekend when El Cid would run again. She seemed surprised by the offer, but after some coaxing she promised to meet him at the Jockey Club at two o'clock. Driving home, Billy wondered why Rachel hadn't asked him to sit and have coffee. Romance was the last thing he needed in his life at the moment, yet companionship wouldn't be so bad. He looked forward to next Saturday. His thoughts flew to El Cid as he negotiated the dark and winding dirt road home, his gaze taking in the thick vault of stars that at that moment seemed rich with promise.

Rachel took her time finishing her coffee. Talking with Billy Sullivan had been a nice diversion, and getting back in touch with the horse world might be fun, but in the last two weeks she'd begun to admit to growing restless doing nothing. With some hard lessons learned, she'd put the past behind her at last. She needed to get on with her life. Returning to *Image* or a newspaper job wasn't really tempting. With the windfall money from Meredith, she'd toyed with the idea of starting a gallery in Santa Fe, but there were already so many, and anyway, what did she know about art? What she wanted and needed was some excitement in her life again. But from what source? she wondered.

On Saturday she drove to Santa Fe Downs and found Billy at the entrance to the Jockey Club. He was even more pleasant and gracious than at the restaurant, until the seventh race approached. He suddenly turned stonily quiet as he fixed his gaze on El Cid.

"He's a beautiful horse," Rachel volunteered. "Don't be so nervous. I think he's going to win."

"This horse always makes me nervous."

"I guess that's better than being overconfident."

"I hope you have all your fingers and toes crossed," Billy said as he glanced over at her.

"Don't need to. El Cid'll win. You have my solemn word."

Rachel watched as the horses were led to the starting gate and locked in. Billy sat absolutely still, as if afraid to breathe. The gates opened with a clang and the eight horses charged out in a perfect line. El Cid moved in front by a head, increased his lead almost with each stride, and by the finish was a comfortable winner. Billy gave Rachel a grateful smile. She drifted over to the nearest window and came back with three crisp twenties in her hand.

"You didn't tell me you bet on my horse," Billy said, visibly surprised.

"Of course I bet on him. I told you he was going to win."

"What about his next race?"

"Is there any doubt?"

"You're really something," Billy said. "I want to borrow your crystal ball."

They had dinner at The Ore House overlooking Santa Fe's historic plaza, sipping margaritas as Billy told her about his hopes for the All-American. Rachel related her own anecdotes about Meredith, including their first meeting over a shotgun, but Billy already knew the lady would be a tough adversary. An even bigger enemy, he confided to Rachel, was money. His nomination fee for the All-American was due, and there were so many other expenses. His current hopes were pinned on a meeting the next day with a venture capitalist.

"How much do you need?" Rachel inquired.

"I'm selling a half interest for $25,000."

"And he's won all his races? You should get that."

"I'm new at this game, as unproven a commodity as my horse. And I don't know all that much about the quarter horse world. It's sure different from polo—but a helluvalot more straightforward."

"I can give you a quick history." Rachel said. "I got a crash course during last year's excitement. The All-American wasn't always one of the richest horse races in the world. It got started in 1953 when two chip-on-the-shoulder Texans sat in an Albuquerque hotel bar arguing over who owned the fastest horse. Whiskey wasn't enough to solve it, so a winner-take-all race was proposed. Up till then quarter horse racing had been largely confined to the bush track circuit of Texas, but in New Mexico wagering on horses was legal, and Ruidoso had a small track and a couple of grandstands. The purse was a mighty $15,000. Half the town came out for it. I don't know who won, but the important thing was that it started a tradition. Over the years the purses got bigger, and so did the fields and the controversy."

"Like what?" said Billy.

"An early promoter named Hensley enlarged the Ruidoso track and stands and thought up the long-range nominating payments known as the futurity system. It was a big success. But the quick and easy profits were too tempting for Hensley. He went to jail for doing a two-step with the books. He was forced to sell to the San Diego National Bank, which was fine until the bank collapsed in 1971 and the track's financial records were found tampered with again. Out of the ashes a father and son named Alessio took over the reins. Within three years they were charged with running a Mexican bookmaking operation that laundered millions for Vegas casino owners. The father went to prison, and so did the loyal son when he was caught bribing guards to make life easier for Papa." Rachel sipped her drink. "Shall I go on?"

Billy laughed. "I'm not intimidated."

"I know, you already told me you were an optimist."

"When you've got nothing to lose, it makes it easier." They both smiled at the truth of that.

He drove Rachel back to her condominium and stayed for a nightcap. The conversation shifted from horses to baseball and presidential politics. Rachel idly thought how much she was enjoying Billy's company. He was sincere and bright and not at all pushy. When he told her good night, he didn't even try to kiss her.

She tossed restlessly all night long. The temptation was strong. She was going on instinct again, but everything felt right. She had the money, she was eager for something to do—so why not? Then a red flag of caution shot up. Wasn't she being a fool to trust someone she hardly knew? Was risking money all that different from risking emotions? You were still putting yourself on the line. And what if she had just given Billy the quirky history of Ruidoso? What the hell did she really know about horses anyway? The debate went on until her mind turned off from exhaustion and she slept.

But in the morning Rachel was sure. She called Billy and told him she had good news.

"What's up?" he asked.

"Forget your venture capitalist. I'm going to buy that half interest in your horse."

In the solemn pink granite building that was the state capitol of Texas, Austin and Fern sat impatiently in the legislature visitors' gallery. They were squeezed among straitlaced Baptists who were peering down on their elected officials with the threat of righteous revenge in their eyes. If the vote this morning went contrary to the laws and wishes of God, who frowned on horse wagering as surely as He did adultery, stealing, and worshiping graven images, someone was going to *pay*. Austin couldn't even look these folks in the eye. A similar bunch had raised angry fists and waved placards at the burial of King's Ransom. Even with Thom Warfield ready to do time at Huntsville, his hypocrisy exposed, they wouldn't change their position. A gavel pounded down and the din abruptly subsided on the legislature floor. After two hours of eulogies to Calvin Garrison and heartfelt pleas to remember what their colleague had worked so diligently for, the horse bill proponents waited for the roll call to begin.

Austin kept silent count of each yea and nay. Some Baptists *wrote down* every vote. After years of endless argument, untold political donations, broken promises, and more committee meetings than angels could stand on a pin's head, Austin felt the day of reckoning was at hand. History would be served. Texas would finally join the enlightened majority of other states. But as the nays began to pepper the air, Austin looked at Fern in distress. There were four votes left to be cast, and all of them were needed to pass the referendum.

It got only two.

The Baptist gallery broke into loud applause.

"Goddammit," Austin swore, taking Fern by the hand and leaving in disgust. Other betting advocates joined the exodus. Without Calvin leading the charge, Austin began to wonder if the Lone Star state would ever escape the Middle Ages. The defeat rankled him almost as much as losing last year's All-American. Lord, he was tired of losing.

He was still smarting from the scandal about Sal. He'd been badly jolted to learn that one of his most trusted employees was associated with a vulture like Warfield. Fern consoled him, saying he was fortunate Sal hadn't arranged for the theft of Mirabeau Ranch bloodstock, but that wasn't much of a silver lining. The press had judged Austin guilty by association, despite the district attorney's official absolution. Thanks to Meredith's vindictive charge, Austin felt that his reputation had been unfairly tarnished. Come the All-American, he had a lot to prove.

With a kiss, Austin put Fern on a plane to Dallas and boarded his Learjet for Ruidoso. He tried to rally his spirits by thinking of Miss Muffet and her race tomorrow. After the filly's one narrow defeat at Los Alamitos, she'd won her last three starts, though not always handily. The eccentric horse had a hard time keeping her mind on business. She would have beaten Desert Wind if she hadn't decided, thirty feet from the finish, to take a leisurely gander at the general admission section. David Sanders did his best, but the filly, sweet and aiming to please half the time, could turn moody and rebellious without warning. Austin was betting that with more races under her belt she'd learn some discipline. She'd better. Time was running out.

Austin parked his plane on the tarmac, and when David rolled up in a Jeep, they took off straight for the track. "How's our little filly?" Austin asked eagerly.

"I've been breezing her every day, Mr. Mirabeau. Then I run her out of the gate. I've tried different invisible aids. I think she responds best if I don't push her too much—she likes to run her own race, just like King's Ransom."

"Is she ready for tomorrow?"

"I think so." David's stomach experienced a not uncustomary bubble of queasiness. He understood all too well his boss's obsession with the All-American, and in his eagerness, Mr. Mirabeau often tried to pin David down, as if predictions could become prophecy. The fact was that David had seldom ridden a more temperamental horse. While he believed in Miss Muffet's potential to win everything in sight, how could he account for her mental vagaries? At the track stables David waited as Austin inspected his filly, chatting with her about tomorrow's competition and the need to show the world that just because she wore blinkers and earmuffs didn't mean she shouldn't be treated with respect. Miss Muffet responded with an understanding nod of the head.

David quietly excused himself. He had another mount this afternoon, one of Austin's secondary hopes for the All-American. The bay gelding named Spend-Some-Money was big and strong and reasonably fast, though not the sprinter that Miss Muffet was. But David knew he should easily outclass the afternoon's competition. The jockey meandered over to the paddock area and for the moment dropped on the grass, relaxing as he angled his face to the sun.

"Lazy bones," a voice called playfully.

David reached up for Trixie's hand and pulled her to the grass. "Where have you been?" he asked.

"Talking to some of the jocks."

"What about lunch?"

"I don't think I'm hungry."

He gave her a wink.

"It's not nerves, wise guy," she said, "just because I'm racing against you. I just want some time by myself."

"Okay," he said, and gave her a quick kiss.

As she trailed away he thought again how much he liked Trixie. How much he owed her too. David would never forget the horrendous evening at the debutante party. In an act of mercy, Mr. Huss hadn't made him pay for the dead horse; his only punishment had been to dash David's hopes for a thoroughbred riding contract. But a supportive Trixie had already prepared him for that. With equally calm logic and artful persuasion she'd helped him give up his pills. He'd had difficulty admitting he might be addicted, but Trixie pressed him not to feel any shame. He had to apply himself to quarter horses as if nothing else mattered, she said. Which wasn't quite true. Trixie mattered just as much. He was crazy about her. Whenever David came to Ruidoso to race, he shared her apartment.

Off hours, of which there were too few, David had been helping Trixie perfect her riding skills. Her contract was with a moody, pipe-smoking Southern gentleman named Quantrell, and while not exactly burning up the track, she had finished in the money four times. She was a quick study and a natural athlete. In her Fort Lauderdale high school days she'd played baseball and run track, but as she'd told David, horses were her obsession.

David loved teaching her, but sometimes, watching her mix with other jocks and trainers and grooms, he felt a twinge of jealousy. Trixie was always so friendly. She treated others almost the same as she treated him. Didn't she feel anything special for the guy she lived with? But whenever David acted possessive, Trixie was surprised.

"Of course you're special," she would say. "You've been there for me when everyone else in my life said I didn't have a chance. You're a great teacher, a great rider too."

Still, he noticed she didn't say anything about love.

Midafternoon, as the horses and jockeys were announced for the fourth race, David settled in the irons of Spend-Some-Money and gave Trixie a wink. The horses were led one by one to the starting gate and locked in. Two holes over, Trixie was the picture of concentration on Quantrell's chestnut colt, refusing to glance at David. He called out "good luck" anyway and bore his eyes toward the finish.

As the gates clanged open, his powerful gelding thundered to a quick lead. David crouched low, and with his strong, oversized hands, held the reins snugly, resting his stirrups close to the horse's flanks. As the rest of the field began to catch up, he brought his stick down repeatedly until the gelding broke in front again. Perfect, he thought. Spend-Some-Money was no Miss Muffet; he needed and wanted to be controlled every stride. Nearing the stretch

David felt another horse closing in. Again he brought his whip down, and the gelding surged. It wasn't enough. From the corner of his eye he watched another horse streak across the finish.

It was only when David looked up that he realized Trixie had won. He smiled at her in congratulation, but he was stunned. How could Trixie have beaten him? Maybe she just had a better horse. But he knew it wasn't true. Spend-Some-Money was the class of the field. So what had gone wrong? He knew he'd ridden his race. Had Trixie ridden a better one?

He watched as she sat proudly on her mount in the winner's circle while her name was announced. For her first victory the rookie turned and raised a triumphant fist to the crowd. Applause broke out, then the jocks and grooms came up to offer congratulations. Everyone's darling, thought David, wondering why he didn't go up and give her a kiss. He hung back sullenly, realizing he was waiting for her to come over and thank him for being a great teacher.

That night he fixed her a victory dinner in her apartment.

"What's the matter, you're not eating," she said after they sat down.

"I can't stand my own cooking," he joked.

"Be honest. Something's wrong. . . ."

"No," he said. "Eat up."

"Please tell me. I want you to be happy. It was a great victory for us today."

"Us? You were the winner."

"But I couldn't have done it without you."

"Sure you could."

"David, will you please stop it?"

"Stop what? Listen, you rode a great race. That's all there is to it."

He heard his peevish tone, wondering why he couldn't admit to Trixie his jealousy and insecurity. He'd been supportive of her when she didn't threaten him, but now, head to head in competition, everything was different. Old Sal was now in jail, but his comments about woman jocks came back to haunt David. For the rest of the evening David kept to himself, which hardly helped his relationship with Trixie. They didn't make love, even though David sensed they both wanted to, and he slept poorly. In the morning he told himself he'd blown everything out of proportion. He apologized to Trixie and felt better. Why should he feel threatened? She'd only beaten him in one race; that hardly meant his career was in eclipse. He was still the rising star—Trixie herself said so.

Yet waiting with Miss Muffet in the paddock that afternoon, David had difficulty concentrating on the upcoming race. He kept thinking he had something to prove. David only interpreted Mr. Mirabeau's pre-race pep talk as more pressure. He looked for Trixie in the stands as an outrider led Miss Muffet to her gate. Nowhere. Jesus, he couldn't believe it. Where was Trixie? She knew how important a race this was.

In the gate David gave Miss Muffet a pat of confidence and waited. His heart hammered in his throat. Concentrate, he thought. As the horses shot out in unison, David's foot was jarred out of the stirrup. By the time he recovered, Miss Muffet was a half length behind. David could feel Austin's disappointed stare. Panicking, he brought his whip down hard. The horse gained a little ground but not enough. David whipped her again and the temperamental filly reared.

Dumb, oh so dumb, he thought, as he half jumped, half fell to the track. He rolled over and over like a berserk pinwheel, clutching his hands around his head as another horse thundered toward him. Only when the earth trembled and the dark, muscular legs passed over his head did David stagger up, shaking. Pain eddied through his back and he dropped to the dirt again. It was his fault, all his fault, he thought. Stable hands helped him off the track. He saw that Miss Muffet was all right, but that wasn't comfort enough. An ambulance ferried him to the hospital. X rays showed nothing broken, but his muscle spasms were real enough. A doctor prescribed codeine and released him.

Back at the track, when Mr. Mirabeau visited him in

the jockey room, David had a hard time looking at his boss.

"What the hell happened out there, son?" Austin asked.

David could see disappointment in his eyes. "I don't know, sir."

"Why did you whip her so hard?"

"I was behind."

"Miss Muffet knew she had to move her ass. She would have come along on her own. That's her style. You know that too."

"Yes, sir." He studied Mr. Mirabeau uneasily. He was going to get canned; David could feel it.

"I want you to know one thing," Austin said sternly. "You made a mistake today. That's not like you. But I want you to know you're still my jockey. You're riding Miss Muffet in the All-American. You've got my faith and confidence."

"Thank you, sir," he breathed.

Thank God he had a second chance, David thought. Yet that evening, crawling into bed at Trixie's, he grew nervous again. What Austin was saying between the lines was don't screw up again—or else. David tried to sleep, but his back pain flared up. Trixie brought him ice packs. He asked her to leave him alone. He didn't want her sympathy. She called him proud and stubborn, but he didn't care. He'd blown it with Mr. Hess and now he'd let down Mr. Mirabeau. What could happen next?

The codeine tablets were on his bedside table. David stared at the pills with trancelike devotion. Take some, he thought, chase the pain away. A couple pills didn't mean he was a junkie.

After a long moment he slipped out of bed. Trixie was right, he thought—he did have a lot of pride. But not the kind she was thinking of. Slowly, determined to fight his pain cold turkey, David marched into the bathroom and dumped the pills down the toilet.

TWENTY-THREE

EVERY SUMMER RUIDOSO DOWNS CHARMED TENS OF thousands of visitors with its rustic cabins tucked behind rolling hills; its quaint, winding hiking trails; the clean air scented by towering ponderosas; and a mañana life-style that was a tonic for stressed-out city dwellers. In these respects it was no different from Aspen or Mendocino or Coeur d'Alene or a dozen resort towns that peppered the West, their economic wheels greased by the tourist dollar. What did set Ruidoso apart was its famous race track, and on this late June weekend, an influx of Mercedes and private jets that for the time being took the place of the usual Winnebagos and suitcase-laden station wagons.

The occasion was the running of the 350-yard Kansas Futurity, the first leg of the quarter horse Triple Crown and an acid test for anyone hoping to win $1 million on Labor Day. But even locals accustomed to wealthy Texans and Oklahomans were not prepared on that sunny afternoon for a caravan of thirty tinted-glass limos and their seventy-some occupants, who had arrived via a chartered Boeing 737 at Alamagordo Airport.

The host for this extravagant visit was Zallaq Al-Khalifa who, in the company of several stunning blondes, waved to local reporters like an arriving head of state as the limos first stopped at the race track. A splashy press conference followed, the air filled by Zallaq with predictions of a runaway victory for Desert Wind in the Kansas Futurity.

As the limos proceeded on to the cabins scattered through the hills, Buck and Adam Jeffrey sat quietly in a rear car, their thoughts on anything but tomorrow's race. For Buck the continual traveling in promoting Desert Wind had become almost as monotonous as it had for his son. A.J., in fact, no longer complained of missing his friends or his favorite toys; like the prisoner of fate he was, he had finally accepted that this nomadic existence would continue until the All-American. Buck couldn't wait to get back to a regular life. Drinking gallons of booze and pumping flesh was all right once in a while, but as Desert Wind had kept winning, and Zallaq stepped up his publicity campaign, the parties came with dizzying frequency. For the Kansas Futurity the Arab had flown in sportswriters, bioengineers, and horse breeders from around the world, prepared to wine and dine them all weekend. Give the man credit, Buck thought, he didn't know how to think small.

"Where are we going now?" Adam Jeffrey asked, gazing out the window at the thickly wooded mountains.

"Zallaq asked me to stop at his cabin for a few minutes. Then we'll have our own little place to unwind. Do you like it up here?"

"I like the ocean more."

"We can take hikes, see some animals maybe. It'll be an adventure."

The boy nodded automatically, as if there were no point in arguing.

When the limo stopped at the end of a private road, a mammoth redwood cabin rose up behind towering pines. On a planked sun deck three blondes were stretched out in the skimpiest of bikinis. "This way," Buck called to Adam Jeffrey, carefully leading him away from the girls. He tried to shake off the familiar stirring of guilt for forcing his son into an adult world, even if Adam Jeffrey didn't understand very much of it. Inside the cabin he found Zallaq in sport clothes, sipping a martini, newspaper in hand.

"Sit down," he said to Buck without looking up. His tone was less than cordial. "Have you seen this?"

As Adam Jeffrey and Buck dropped on a sofa, the Arab held up the sports section from *The New York Times*. Buck wagged his head. He hadn't looked at a paper in several days. Just too tired. "It's a piece on Desert Wind," Zallaq spoke up. "An uncomplimentary piece. Both on me and my horse. The reporter quotes you."

Buck frowned, trying to remember. There had been so many parties for sportswriters, so much talking.

"You told the reporter that I was a man on a mission—a mission of revenge against the world. And Desert Wind was my weapon."

"No," Buck said automatically.

"*The New York Times* doesn't often misquote."

Buck finally remembered. "What I said was that when you were at the University of Texas, you got kicked out of your doctoral program. And that Texas wasn't your favorite place—"

"That's none of your business—or the rest of the world's."

"The man just wanted background," Buck said defensively.

"My past is irrelevant. What's important is my bio-engineering company and the horse I created. That's all anyone has to know about. When I hired you I told you exactly what had to be said. It's all very simple. I'm paying you well. I don't expect you to screw up again."

Buck was too surprised by the sharp rebuke to counter effectively. Yet he had seen the Arab's increasing moodiness over the past weeks, eclipsing his usual graciousness. The more victories Desert Wind enjoyed, the more outspoken Zallaq had become, as if success gave him license to thumb his nose at the world. God only knew how he'd act when he took the All-American.

For a moment Buck was indignant. He didn't have to take this tongue-lashing, especially in front of his son. Hadn't he thrown in over $300,000 of his *own* money on Wondercolt? He was more than a hired hand, he was an investor.

"At the track tomorrow," Zallaq announced coolly, "I'm hosting a luncheon for all the horse owners in the Kansas. I expect you to be there, Buck. On time. And I don't want you boozing it up again—"

"Wait a minute," Buck stopped him in cold astonishment. "Are you saying I drink too much?"

"You've taken this job for granted. I've done a lot to help your career, and it's time you reciprocated."

"I have been reciprocating," Buck shot back. "I've lived up to our agreement—"

He stopped himself from telling Zallaq to shove it. In the back of his mind he knew that real rebellion was futile. Zallaq effectively had him blackmailed. Buck's financial and acting future was mortgaged to the damn horse, and it was the Arab who controlled Desert Wind. Buck marveled at his own stupidity. He'd been so circumspect before agreeing to work for Zallaq, trying to avoid a trap, but in the end he'd fallen for the Arab's flattery. Had he thought that only Hollywood had a monopoly on phonies? Buck took Adam Jeffrey by the hand and left the cabin.

"Why is he so mean, Daddy?" Adam Jeffrey asked as they ducked back into their limo. "Why did he talk to you like that?"

"It's just business." Buck bit his tongue.

"What's 'business'?"

"That's where one man pays another to do something for him."

"Like when I do chores for you and you give me money?" said Adam Jeffrey. "You're my boss?"

"Something like that," Buck said, sitting back wearily. He felt a bruiser of a headache coming on.

"Daddy?"

"Hmmm?"

"Are you afraid of that man?"

"Why do you think that?"

"Because you let him be mean to you. At school there's a kid—"

"I'm not afraid of him," Buck interrupted, abruptly closing the subject.

When Meredith received the Arab's invitation for lunch at the Jockey Club, she had thought it was to be just her and Zallaq. But entering the private room on the overcast morning, she faced a large table of familiar and not altogether friendly faces. Her first instinct was to turn around and walk out. She wouldn't even look at Austin. Shaking Zallaq's hand, she then nodded curtly to the other horse owners, not one of whom had supported her during the trial or offered congratulations afterward. As drinks were served, Zallaq rose with a toast to the race ahead and the canons of good sportsmanship. That sounded to Meredith as sincere as a fox wishing pleasant dreams to a hen house. Then he lectured his captive audience on the magnificent horse he had bred, and predicted that this afternoon Desert Wind would run the fastest time in the history of the Kansas Futurity. Meredith shook her head in awe. When it came to ego size, the man wore a 14-DD. Whoever said Texans had a corner on that market?

"With all due respect," Austin spoke up when Zallaq paused, "I think you just got lucky in your laboratory. Your horse has run some good races, but my filly should have taken him last time out, and Lord knows she surely will today. . . ."

"One hundred thousand dollars," the Arab said, his voice turning eager, "says she won't."

Meredith watched the indecisiveness flicker over Austin's face. His pride on the line, he had to back it up with money. Meredith almost felt sorry for him. As wealthy as Austin was, he could be tight with the buck, and he didn't have nearly the resources of a Zallaq, who could have bought the race track and every horse on it with a week's oil revenue.

"No need for me to take your money," Austin tossed back cheerfully. "I don't like to pick on the ignorant."

What a chicken, thought Meredith. After finishing a bourbon and water she promptly told Austin so.

"*You're* calling *me* chicken?" he said in front of everyone. "You're the hit-and-run artist of east Texas."

"A chicken—just like at my trial. Afraid to tell me to my face what you told the whole world." She rose, letting her gaze sweep over the table. "Everyone at this table was a goddamn chicken."

"Your trial," Austin shot back in the stunned silence, "was the biggest miscarriage of justice since the Mexicans won at the Alamo."

"I think your not being indicted along with Sal deserves that prize."

"My, you're never going to give up trying to tar and feather me. You're a desperate woman."

"Not as desperate as you'll be when your horse falls on its ass again today."

"She won't, not if your horse doesn't bump her," Austin said calmly, and went back to his lunch.

Burning, Meredith stormed out of the luncheon and marched to the stables. The stands were beginning to swell with horse-loving humanity. She couldn't wait until the tenth race and the chance to put Austin and Zallaq in their place.

As the sun peeked out from behind silvered clouds, Five Deuces stood like a gleaming statue, her copper coat almost radiant with a promise of things to come. That Abel Hanson had nursed the poor horse back from death's door in a New Orleans warehouse had given the filly a mystique in racing circles, and the fact that she'd won every race she'd entered only added to the myth. In many ways she was an even stronger runner than Four Aces, who was currently burning up the derby circuit. Meredith gave her jockey final instructions—out of the last hole, Five Deuces had only to hold the end position, which she loved, and also keep an eye on Desert Wind and Miss Muffet. Unlike a lot of fillies, Five Deuces had no problem with attention span or motivation. She was as tough as any colt. The jockey nodded agreeably, as if he understood everything, though Meredith could never be sure. The wiry little Cuban spoke little English.

To pass the hour Meredith calmed her nerves with another bourbon and water. With the tenth race approaching, she watched Austin venture down to his customary position at the rail while the other owners mingled in the Jockey Club. Isolated in a corner, Meredith kept her own company. She missed Seth. He had always accompanied her to the big races, and now she felt very much alone. Five

Deuces was locked into her gate, followed by the other horses. In another second they were out like a shot.

Meredith had watched her horses run a thousand times, but the thrill was always the same. Her eyes narrowed in concentration and her heart galloped in her throat. Five Deuces, Miss Muffet, and Desert Wind traded the lead with almost every stride, until at the three-quarters mark Meredith watched her horse slip behind. The filly was running her heart out, but down the stretch she didn't have the kick of her rivals. And Desert Wind had the strongest kick of all. Fifty yards from the finish he accelerated past Miss Muffet and won by a full length.

Meredith couldn't describe her stronger emotion—disappointment in Five Deuces' finish or sheer disbelief at Desert Wind. Zallaq had proved prophet enough. His colt's time wasn't the fastest ever at the Kansas, but it was the best in a decade. She watched the sycophants flock around Zallaq by the Jockey Club bar. The Arab looked sure and complacent, Meredith thought, as if nothing could stop him now. But the All-American was still two months away. Abel would have to work Five Deuces harder, much harder, she knew, because the horse was still far from reaching her potential. And her jockey would have to put in more time too. The party wasn't over yet. Anyone who'd overcome the obstacles Meredith had this year wasn't about to give up so quickly, particularly to an overconfident Arab who made horses in laboratories.

Meredith turned, ready to leave, when she saw Zallaq approach Buck Hart. She hardly knew the actor, but he seemed affable enough, and his child was adorable. Except for hair color, Adam Jeffrey struck her as a younger mirror image of Alexis.

"Buck," the Arab ordered, "go down to the winner's circle and pose for some pictures."

The actor looked unsure. "I promised A.J. I'd buy him an ice cream."

"That can wait."

"It'll only take a minute. The ice cream's right downstairs."

"Buck, I think you heard me. . . ."

There was quiet defiance in the actor's eyes as he picked up his son in his arms. "What do you think, Adam Jeffrey? Should I buy you an ice cream or go down and see the horse?"

The little boy was nervous as his glance studied Zallaq. "I want an ice cream."

"Then an ice cream you'll have," Buck said to everyone, ignoring Zallaq's reddening face and heading off.

Meredith departed right behind him, admiring Buck for his stand. The Arab really knew how to take the bully pulpit. He'd even intimidated Austin, which was no mean feat. Meredith swore then and there that he'd never intimidate her.

Late afternoon, still brooding about her defeat, Meredith and Abel boarded a small jet to Dallas's Love Field. There her trainer took the pickup back to the 5555 Ranch, but Meredith flagged a taxi to the Presbyterian Hospital for another lonely vigil. Seth's pale, calm visage behind the overlay of tubes and wires was unchanged. Still, she pulled up a chair and proceeded to tell him about the day's race, that Five Deuces had run well but not well enough. A cocky Arab who was a mad scientist in disguise, she added, was trying to change the face of quarter horse breeding as if he were God Almighty—and she would be damned if she put up with *that*.

She looked at Seth again.

Her heart jumped.

"Sweetie?" she whispered.

But it was no illusion. His chin pushed out again and an eye fluttered open.

Meredith rang for the duty nurse.

TWENTY-FOUR

"OUR JOCKEY *WHAT*?" RACHEL DEMANDED.

"Quit."

"Billy, he can't just quit."

"He did. Took two saddles and a bridle with him too."

"Jesus, the stinking thief," she said in frustration. "I can't believe this. The trials start in three days. We finally get El Cid healthy and our jockey takes a powder. Why aren't you pulling your hair out like I am?"

As they sat outside the Ruidoso stables, Billy looked like he always did—serene, contemplative, unfazed by disaster. Rachel was nonplussed by his composure. Did he have advance knowledge that they'd weather this crisis as they had the others, or was he finally to the point of not caring? Since they'd joined forces two months ago, Rachel hadn't lacked for the adventure and excitement she thought she wanted. Billy's horse had given her more sleepless nights than any overdue magazine article. One minute the colt was hale and hardy, winning races, then disaster would strike as whimsically as a summer storm. Three weeks ago El Cid had developed ring bone—a bony enlargement at the top of the hoof—because the farrier hadn't changed the colt's shoes often enough. Before that he had knee spavin, a growth on the back of the knee caused by too much strain, and the week before, a bad case of thrush. O'Connel did his best with his patented Irish cures, but often the horse ended up at the vet hospital and Billy and Rachel with another whopper of a bill. Rachel's initial investment had been all but eaten up. She'd written her mother that she'd finally found something more expensive than living in Manhattan.

Almost everyone thought she'd taken a plunge off the deep end. Her mother begged her to bail out. Friends told her there were better percentages for success in getting married. Frank Beardsley predicted that any reporter investing in a race horse would wind up a reporter again. But Rachel saw it differently. A horse was a lot like a child, someone to nurse along, comfort, play with, and grow up with too. Sometimes, when you least expected it, your efforts were rewarded.

When El Cid ran and ran well, Rachel didn't think another horse could touch him. In his last race he'd run a 21.52, but in other races, bothered by one ailment or another, the colt had struggled. Handicappers' enthusiasm had waxed and waned with El Cid's health. The biggest blow came when Billy had been forced to scratch from the Kansas and Rainbow Futurities, both of which were won by Desert Wind, whom the media were touting as the greatest horse ever. Thoroughbred owners took umbrage, of course, but Rachel felt only awe and fear.

If it weren't for Billy and his inexplicable confidence, she might have given up. He'd offered to buy back her interest more than once, but she knew it wasn't right. Billy was more broke than it was decent to admit. The man also spent every waking hour with El Cid—coddling, encouraging, fretting over him. He even helped O'Connel with the day-to-day training which was as strenuous and intensive as any human athlete went through. That left him no time to handle racing dates, jockeys or entry fees, so Rachel was only too happy to fill the breach. To her surprise, she enjoyed the business side.

"We won't scratch from the All-American trials," Billy promised, "if I have to call every jock in the country."

It was an impossible situation, Rachel thought. There were thirty-six separate heats of ten horses each for the early qualifying. The top three finishers by position in each heat then raced against one another in a second and last round of heats. From those, the top ten finishers by time made it to the All-American final. For now, every good jockey was already spoken for. That afternoon Rachel called half a dozen jockey agents, but the few leads she got didn't pan out. Local owners were even less helpful. From her reporting days she knew of the envy and resentment in the horse world, but now she tasted it first hand. One yahoo put it bluntly: "Hell, you want me to *help* you? Lady, you're a competitor." Desperate, Rachel finally rang the 5555 Ranch. Meredith had played the good fairy once before; maybe she could help again.

Meredith answered the phone herself. The suspicious voice sounded like a loaded gun.

"It's Rachel Lang," she spoke up in the icy silence, wondering if she'd done anything wrong.

"Rachel? Really? Where are you?" The suspicion melted and a warmth flooded over the phone.

"Ruidoso," Rachel spoke up. "I guess you haven't heard. It's my fault for being out of touch. I own a half interest in a quarter horse."

There was dismayed silence. "You own a quarter horse? You're racing him?"

"Trying to. It's a long story. We have to have lunch or a drink soon."

"I'd invite you to my All-American party, but I decided to cancel it. Seth's home—"

"Seth? That's wonderful!" Rachel said. "Is he better?"

"He came out of his coma, and physically he's fine. His memory is faulty at times, though, and he's moody. He doesn't want to see anybody. I've told him all about you, how you helped at my trial." Meredith gave a contemplative sigh at how much had happened. "And now you own a horse. . . ."

"His name's El Cid. The other owner is Billy Sullivan. I think you know each other—"

"Sure do. Billy came to my party last year. His father and I were good friends. What's a polo player doing with a quarter horse?"

"Won him in a polo match."

"Is he any good?"

"God knows we've trained him. Almost every day for two months. El Cid's in fighting shape for the All-American." She hesitated. "Meredith, I need a favor. I know you don't owe me, you've been generous enough—"

"Just ask."

"We're looking for a jockey," Rachel said. "I know it's the eleventh hour, but we're desperate."

Meredith turned quiet, thinking. "Let me call you back."

Rachel was dubious that anyone could really help, but a few hours later Meredith rang back with three names. The first was a young man from California with international experience, but he'd broken his leg in a spring race and still hadn't recovered. An old salt who had once been a peer of Cordero and Pincay turned out, upon checking, to be an alcoholic. The third was an apprentice named Trixie McKinney. On the phone the girl sounded cheerful and eager, and the man she was under contract to wasn't using her in the All-American. She was sure she could get permission to ride El Cid. Rachel set up a meeting for the morning.

"You look tired," Rachel said to Billy over a late dinner, "but still the handsome prince." She hoped he wouldn't misconstrue the compliment. While Billy was the quintessential gentleman, and under other circumstances she might have fallen for him, their relationship had been strictly platonic. In their cabin sublet they each had their own bedroom and no one had taken advantage. The equal footing and mutual respect that came with a business partnership was all Rachel wanted.

"Here's to Trixie, whomever she is," Billy said with a cautious smile, and raised his glass of wine.

"If she works out, we owe it all to Meredith. It's hard for me to feel we're competing against her. She's a friend."

"May the best horse win," Billy said.

"You know, you're too good a sport. Most everyone else we meet around here is a jackal."

"My father brought me up to be a gentleman."

"Was polo that way too?"

Billy fought off a laugh. "Polo is worse than quarter horse racing. I could tell you stories. . . ."

"So tell me," she said, interested.

"They're not important."

"But I want to know." They had never discussed anything personal beyond simple likes and dislikes. There had never seemed to be time, and Rachel didn't exactly want to dredge up *her* past in a tit for tat. But she needed to know more about Billy. He was as much an enigma as El Cid. She listened, shocked, as he told her how he'd run stolen art up from South America, only to be betrayed by his Latin girlfriend, and later booted out of the polo world in disgrace. Life, he said, had been absurdly difficult for him. Everything should have been a cakewalk for a Yale grad with a rich and famous father, but somehow there were always debts, the frustrations of living up to an image, worries about fitting in.

"Your turn," Billy said.

"You already know everything. I was a burned-out reporter who needed a change of pace."

"There must be more than that."

"There is. When El Cid wins the All-American," she promised, "I'll bare my soul."

"I'll remember that."

At the track the next day O'Connel joined them as they watched Trixie pace El Cid around the oval.

"What do you think?" Billy asked his trainer.

"She's a little hesitant when she breaks from the gate, but after that she rides with authority. You can tell she's an athlete. As smooth in the saddle as any jock I've seen."

"And she's got a real rapport with El Cid," Rachel seconded.

Billy rocked on his heels, his hands pushed in his jean pockets, still deciding. When Trixie came up, slightly out of breath, she announced that the horse had been a pleasure to ride, faster than any mount Quantrell had given her. She glanced up expectantly.

Billy turned to Rachel and back to Trixie. "Okay," he said. "It's all a gamble anyway. Excluding O'Connel, we'll be as inexperienced a triumvirate as you could ask for. El Cid's all yours. I'll pay you a per diem plus ten percent of winnings."

"You got yourself a deal," Trixie bubbled, extending her hand.

Days later, looking back, Rachel would tell herself that she should have known that the worst wasn't behind them. In a fight between you and the world, Frank Beardsley had once said, bet on the world. They had a jockey, sure, a good one despite her youth and inexperience, but just when the equation got balanced, another unknown cropped up.

The night after they'd hired Trixie, O'Connel called Billy. El Cid was running a fever and acting sluggish again. Rachel and Billy spent the night in the stables. In the morning El Cid was improved, but he fought Trixie in even a light workout. The vet did a throat culture, which was diagnosed as positive, and the horse was put on antibiotics. The colt would be weak for several days, the vet opined, and without being asked, advised against running him in the trials.

Rachel didn't even have to discuss the matter with Billy. She knew he would enter El Cid if at all possible. Billy stayed with the horse day and night until the morning of his heat, instructing Trixie not to go all out, just enough to place in the top three, so the colt could qualify for his next and last qualifying heat. Rachel stayed away from the track altogether. Her nerves were shot, and at this point she believed her presence wouldn't help. Everything that could be done had been.

Billy called her around noon, a quaver of excitement in his voice. El Cid had won his heat easily, without being pushed, and the colt showed no signs of fatigue or strain. In the upcoming days, as the trials continued, Rachel kept busy and left Billy to the railside hand-wringing. The formula seemed to work. The news was always good. As the field was whittled from 360 horses to 108, El Cid had posted one of the top dozen times and seemed to be growing stronger with every race.

"How are *you* holding up?" Rachel asked Billy that night in their sublet. They sat on the living room floor before a crackling summer fire. She knelt behind him and began rubbing his shoulders. "You look like you haven't slept too well."

"Just two more days and we'll know if we're in."

"Part of me can't wait till this is over. Are you sure you're all right?"

"I'll survive. I'm used to tension."

"So am I. But that doesn't mean I like it."

"It goes with competition."

Rachel smiled knowingly. "Tell me about it."

"It goes with winning too. I want to win."

She leaned over and kissed him on the cheek.

"What was that for?" he asked.

"Luck. And if I can do anything else . . ."

He reached back and playfully pulled her down beside him. Her head dropped on his lap. "Yes, you can," he said. "You can gaze into your crystal ball again."

"I don't like doing that very often," she admitted. She knew Billy only meant the All-American, but all she could think of was her and Calvin. "I don't like looking ahead and raising hopes. It only gets me into trouble."

"Why?" he asked, stroking her hair from her eyes.

"I'm just the cautious type," she said evasively. "Why is winning so important to you anyway?"

He gave her a smile. "Besides the fact I'm broke and if we don't finish in the money I'll be waiting tables at a local restaurant?"

"Yeah, besides the small stuff."

"I feel the race is my last chance."

"At what?"

"Proving something to myself."

"Which is?"

"That I can be a winner."

She took Billy's hand and held it to her cheek. "You're so serious. Why are men always like that? Life or death. Just because of what happened to you with your father, and the polo. . . . I mean you're still so young. Your whole life's ahead of you."

"Is that how you feel about your life?" Billy said, looking at her carefully.

She was quiet a moment. How much did Billy know about her? She hadn't told him anything about her losing battle with finding a man, her bleak view of the future. Was she that transparent or was Billy just perceptive? "What I feel," Rachel answered, "is that I'm definitely not out to prove anything. Not to myself, and certainly not to the world."

"Nothing burning inside you? No goals, no hopes?"

"No," she lied. "I just want to be happy."

"Nobody in your life?"

Rachel shook her head.

"That's too bad," Billy said.

"You have to understand. After journalism, where everyone was always looking over my shoulder, all I want is peace and isolation."

Billy leaned down and kissed her gently. "I don't believe you."

Rachel felt foolish. Why was she lying to him? Billy was being straight with her. "Okay. I want something. Something very reasonable. Or I used to think it was reasonable. I want to fall in love with a man who's honest and thoughtful and caring—and who's in love with me."

Rachel couldn't believe she'd said it. She hadn't even had a drink. Billy didn't move his gaze from her. "And then you'd be happy?" he asked.

"Yes. I think so."

"Would I make you happy?" he asked.

She was startled. Billy was so smooth, and he seemed sincere. But a man with his looks and poise had to have had lots of women. "I don't know," she admitted.

"Should I try? You haven't shown much interest in me."

"We're business partners."

"It could be more."

She hesitated. "Do you really care about me?" she asked, a bit uneasy, but hopeful, too, in a way that surprised her.

"Very much. I'm sorry I didn't tell you sooner."

"You can tell me now," she said softly, then let him lead her into his bedroom.

Billy undressed her and they slipped under the sheets. He was a skillful and tender lover, better than she'd expected. Under his heated embraces she was quickly aroused and felt herself surrender totally to him. His body was firm and perfect, his every move sure and sensually astonishing. As pure sex went, she couldn't remember a more satisfying time, even with Calvin. But afterward, as Billy dozed in her arms, she began to examine her feelings. She liked Billy very much, she admitted, but was it love? Between her natural caution and worrying about the All-American, she hadn't allowed herself to think of Billy as anything but a business partner. Yet he had clearly seen more in her. She suddenly calmed: everything was out of her control. Meeting Billy, buying into a race horse, having a shot at winning $1 million—it was all a crazy dream, and dreams had their own crazy logic. She was on a wild ride and no one could predict how it would end. She had to live it one day at a time. But as she drifted off to sleep, Rachel kept waking and looking over at Billy. As dreams went, she thought, this was certainly promising.

At the Jockey Club the next day Rachel had lunch with Meredith, who'd flown in early for the heats and to watch over her horse as if the precious filly were in danger of being kidnapped again. The All-American meant a lot to Meredith, Rachel knew, but the two talked easily, without once mentioning the possibility of competing with each other. Meredith's words mostly focused on Zallaq and Desert Wind. The Arab had replaced Austin as the enemy.

"I just think the son of a bitch is fundamentally dishonest," Meredith said about Zallaq.

"What do you mean?"

"This whole business about making a horse in a laboratory—it's an unfair advantage, and I don't think the AQHA should have allowed Desert Wind to race. That A-rab isn't playing by the same rules as the rest of us. It's like a bunch of Boy Scouts competing to see who can start a fire by rubbing two sticks together, and suddenly some smartass sneaks out a book of matches. . . ."

"Are you saying you don't think Desert Wind can be beaten?" Rachel asked, surprised. Meredith wasn't a quitter.

"If someone spiked Wondercolt's breakfast, maybe the rest of us would have a decent shot."

The politicking and fueding would make colorful copy if she were still a reporter, Rachel considered, but now they were only a distraction. El Cid was facing his last heat tomorrow, and with all the marbles on the line she had to focus on the race.

"This has really been fun, Meredith, but I guess I better get back to Billy," Rachel said at last.

"How is Billy doing?"

"Just fine. Holding up better than I am. My nerves aren't as strong as the rest of yours."

"But you two are getting along? I always had a hard time with partners. One wants one thing, the other something else—"

"No, no trouble at all. Things are just fine," Rachel said quickly, but didn't elaborate. Meredith looked at her as if she sensed what was happening, and gave Rachel a pleased cat-ate-the-canary smile.

That afternoon Rachel and Billy watched as Trixie put El Cid through a light workout. The horse responded as if he'd been racing for years. Rachel was thrilled. "Are you coming to the track tomorrow?" Billy asked.

"I shouldn't, you know. It might bring bad luck."

"We'll take that risk."

"I stayed away for the other heats. Why fix what already works?"

"Because it's the final heat. And I'd like you here with me," Billy sad. "We're partners, aren't we?" Then he paused. "I also happen to be falling in love with you."

She wrapped her arms around Billy and just held him. She thought she was falling in love too, but was afraid to say it. "Okay," she promised, "I'll be there."

Hovering at the rail the next day, Rachel knew she should never have come. She could barely stand, let alone breathe. She waved encouragingly to Trixie as the horses were led to the starting gate. The jockey stared straight ahead in fierce concentration. Miss Muffet and Five Deuces would be racing in a later heat, but Desert Wind was just one gate away. As the metal doors sprung open, Rachel grabbed for Billy's hand.

Her stomach dropped almost immediately. Trixie was too slow coming out of the gate. As the pack charged ahead, she was at most a half second behind, but in a twenty-two second race that meant a hole big enough to run a Mack truck through. "Come on, come on," Rachel whispered as Trixie began to close the gap. There was no way on God's earth for her to catch Desert Wind, but Rachel hoped at least for a fast heat. El Cid crossed the wire at 21.69, in third. Rachel gave Billy a tentative hug, her hands still shaking.

"Do you think that's good enough?" she asked.

"I hope so," he said uncertainly.

"But what do you think?" She wanted a definite answer.

Billy only shrugged, finally showing the strain that Rachel had been feeling all along.

They waited by the bar in the Jockey Club, turning to the television monitor for the other heats. Five horses, including Five Deuces and Miss Muffet, finished in under 21.5. That left El Cid with the eighth best time, Rachel calculated, crossing her fingers for the last heat. She stared in a trance at the monitor, somehow hoping the horses would all stumble, or a headwind would come up, or lightning would strike. It didn't happen. A gelding named Fly By-Night streaked across in 21.22, followed by Angel's Victory with 21.35. The third horse, a black beauty of a colt named Home-At-Last, squeezed out third with a 21.69. Jesus, Rachel realized, the same time as El Cid.

She and Billy had anticipated several scenarios for this do-or-die day, but a tie for the tenth and last spot in the finals wasn't one. A track steward appeared and summoned them to an executive office along with the owner of Home-At-Last. "What's going to happen?" Rachel asked.

"We have to have a shake," Billy said, trying to stay composed.

"A what?"

"Two pieces of paper are put in a cup. One—the winner—is shaken out."

"I'd rather face a firing squad." Rachel watched as the steward, surrounded by every important track official in Ruidoso, placed the two slips of paper in a plain ceramic cup. Rachel closed her eyes. After an interminable moment, murmurs of surprise and relief filled the room. Rachel felt Billy's arms wrap consolingly around her shoulders. She felt sick. All she wanted was to go home.

"Open your eyes," he told her.

She looked up, puzzled by the broad smile.

"Let's go get a drink," Billy said with his old confidence. "We just won a spot in the All-American."

They made love again that night. Sex was the perfect therapy for her case of nerves, Rachel had thought. But afterward, when they lay before a fire with bodies entwined, her thoughts were about Billy, not their horse. She knew how much winning meant to him, but Rachel realized that whatever happened, it wouldn't be the end of her world. It was Billy who meant something to her, and in a way she was almost sorry the All-American would be over so soon. She wanted to believe in what she was feeling, but just didn't trust the end of the dream.

TWENTY-FIVE

THE DAY BEFORE THE ALL-AMERICAN A DEPRESSED BUCK roamed downtown Ruidoso like a sleepwalker, oblivious to the swelling crowds and fever-pitch excitement. Adam Jeffrey was back at the motel, playing with his G.I. Joe convoy under the watchful eye of the motel owner's doting wife. Buck had excused himself to make a long distance call, and waiting his turn at a public phone now, he suddenly fixed on a striking blonde in jeans and a Ralph Lauren polo shirt who definitely looked familiar. It took him a moment to make the connection.

"Hi, there," Buck said in his friendliest voice as he approached the woman. Her return gaze was a little distant. "You're Rachel Lang, aren't you?"

"Yes?"

"I'm Buck Hart. You remember—the interview a year ago . . . ? You know I've been working with Zallaq and Desert Wind?"

"Oh, yes. Of course." She suddenly responded with warmth. "How have you been?"

Buck wished her luck in the All-American, and Rachel graciously allowed how Desert Wind was the most remarkable of horses. Buck said no more, captivated by Rachel's loveliness. In the silence he began to edge closer, and was about to circle his arm around her when his eye strayed to the man approaching. Buck was introduced to Billy Sullivan, and as he watched the handsome couple disappear down the street, the actor could barely hide his disappointment.

When he finally got his turn at the phone, Buck's ego took still another beating. Sidney Pomerantz was so incensed he hardly stopped to breathe. How could Buck have let himself be canned by Zallaq, especially before the All-American? Buck had flouted one of the richest and most powerful men in the world *just to buy his son an ice cream*? Sidney was beside himself. He didn't care what Buck thought of the Arab. He could be the biggest son of a bitch since Samuel Goldwyn, he could carry a chip on his shoulder the size of a two-by-four, he could beat up old ladies, he could wear a dress—it didn't matter. What counted was that while the attention and publicity Buck had won on the coattails of Desert Wind had been just peachy so far, nothing was really going to jell for the actor until Desert Wind won the All-American. But now the damn horse was going to win it and Buck wouldn't be anywhere near the photographers and parties and talk-show producers. A single act of selfishness had put him right in no man's land. Sidney begged his client to go on hands and knees and ask Zallaq to take him back. Buck had to think about *that* suggestion for only a moment. If Zallaq were his last hope in this world, Buck swore to Sidney, he'd just have to find another planet to live on.

But as he meandered through town, he realized that total extrication wouldn't come so easily. As much as he disliked Zallaq, there was the matter of his financial future. The shares he'd purchased in the horse meant that he was still tied to Zallaq. Unless . . . What if he asked the Arab to buy back his shares, right now, just for what he had paid for them, no profit at all? Buck might have offered them on the open market but the complex syndication rules forbade a shareholder to sell his interest until after a year. Buck wanted out *now*. Other investors could be found with no more than a phone call—everyone was dying for a piece of Wondercolt—so why shouldn't Zallaq buy him out?

Buck called Zallaq's publicist, who told him the Arab was at the track. Buck hurried down. In a custom-tailored suit and Gucci loafers, Zallaq looked out of place in the paddock area, though he hardly acted uncomfortable. His jockey and trainer paraded Desert Wind in front of ogling cameras while sound men scrambled to hook up mikes. That could have been me with the horse, Buck thought for an instant, but any regret vanished quickly. He waited impatiently as Zallaq waxed eloquent for the media.

Interviewer: "Looking ahead to tomorrow, Mr. Al-Khalifa, what are your thoughts?"

Zallaq: "I'd like to see Desert Wind break the United States quarter-mile record of 21.02. Nothing would please me more. I've told everyone all along that he's the fastest horse ever, and I want to show any lingering doubters what he can do."

Interviewer: "What doubters?"

Zallaq: "There are people in the scientific community who've called my research incomplete, my experiments a fluke. They've always doubted my capabilities, starting when I was in graduate school. Just because I'm from a third world country and have great personal wealth . . . I ask you, does that contaminate my research?"

Interviewer: "Some owners would be happy just to have their horse win. They wouldn't care what the rest of the world thought."

Zallaq: "Life is more of a challenge for me than that. I've already proved that Desert Wind can beat any horse around. Now I'm after the record—and the respect that comes with it."

Interviewer: "You've been attacked sometimes for being arrogant. . . ."

Zallaq (with an amused smile): "The arrogant ones are my competitors. I see myself as an outsider, a spoiler. Before I came along, Mr. Mirabeau and Ms. Kingsley fought between themselves for the bragging rights to east Texas. I plan to end that hegemony. There's something about Texans always being cocksure that offends me. They're so inclined to braggadocio that ranches are measured in Rhode Islands, horses by godlike speed, wealth by analogies to the United States mint. Texas has always been overly impressed with its size, history, heritage, resources. It wants to perpetuate the myth that everything it has is bigger, better, or stronger. I am prepared, when it comes to horses, to debunk that myth."

Interviewer: "No one's rolled over dead yet. I've spoken to a few who think your horse, as impressive as he's been, can be beaten tomorrow."

Zallaq: "What you're hearing is simple jealousy. I've tweaked some noses and people are mad. They're disgruntled. I've already received threats on Desert Wind's life. That's why I've put the horse under tight security—"

Interviewer: "Could you elaborate on that, please?"

Zallaq: "There's been talk . . . rumors . . . innuendoes. . . ."

Interviewer: "From whom exactly? Are you suspicious of someone?"

Zallaq (raising his eyes): "That man over there is capable of most anything—"

It took Buck a moment to realize that Zallaq was actually staring at him. The cameras spun around too. Jesus, he couldn't believe it. Buck hadn't said boo to Zallaq since getting fired a week ago. The man's paranoia had grown as out of control as a brush fire. He had the world by the balls and he still didn't trust his power. At the risk of appearing guilty, Buck spun around and retreated from the track. There was no point in approaching Zallaq about buying back his shares. For punishment alone the Arab would say no, or accuse Buck of some sinister plot. His anger welled up as he made his way to the motel and Adam Jeffrey. He had half a mind to fly back to Los Angeles today. But he knew he had to stick it out for the race.

As was customary for the day before important races, Austin watched David lead his horse through a light workout. Then the owner took Miss Muffet aside for a heart-to-heart. His other entries in the trials had all been eliminated, making the filly his lone chance for victory and redemption. "Seventh time's the charm," Austin said to the horse, who nodded obligingly. "We're going to win this, old girl. I'm counting on it. I know the competition's tough, but you're tougher. You almost beat that son of a bitch Desert Wind before, and you can do it tomorrow." Austin wrapped his arms around Miss Muffet and gave her a heartfelt hug. He suddenly realized how much he'd come to admire and love the filly. After David's spill earlier in the summer, Miss Muffet had settled down and run her heart and lungs out in every race. Tomorrow would be the acid test. And something told Austin he wasn't going to be disappointed, no siree. Desert Wind was due for an upset. No horse could keep winning forever. All it took was a slow start from the gate, a jockey to get careless, or something. . . .

An hour later, waiting for Fern and the kids to return from shopping, Austin enjoyed a solitary beer at the Inn of the Mountain Gods. Complementing the resort hotel's postcard views were a sprawling golf course, a lake stocked with trout, an indoor tennis court, and an Olympic-size pool. Owned and operated by the Apaches—arguably the most disciplined and business-oriented of the Indian nations, who at least had had the foresight never to sign a peace treaty with the United States—the resort was mobbed for the All-American weekend. Yet Austin had found a private corner and had induced himself into a trancelike state of well-being. When Miss Muffet won tomorrow she'd vindicate him—for all the terrible things Meredith had said, for his years of frustration at the track, for what had happened with Sal. Good things were finally in store for Austin Mirabeau. The Texas legislature, when it met again, was going to legalize horse betting. And in celebration Austin was going to start his own horse museum. That had been another dream, almost as important as winning the All-American. Texas was the most museum-crazy state in the union. It had the Audie Murphy Gun Museum, the Cowgirl Hall of Fame, the Texas Rangers Hall of Fame . . . hell, the town of Marshall alone had ninety-five museums and historical markers. Austin wanted to add his own. He'd have a quarter horse exhibit with all the great colts and fillies and geldings immortalized in life-size wax statues, just like they did with the movie stars in Hollywood.

The television over the bar suddenly revealed the flickering image of Zallaq and his horse. The Arab was prattling on about victory and destiny and an end to Texas hegemony in the quarter horse world. "Jesus, what the hell is *hegemony*?" Austin wondered out loud. Who did this sonovabitch pretentious Arab think he was? Joined by other bar flies, Austin hurled several well-chosen epithets at the Arab, and would have gladly found something more substantial to throw if the bartender hadn't wisely changed the channel.

A late afternoon breeze stirred the towering spruces and ponderosas that flanked a cabin high and secluded in the Sacramento Mountains. Hurrying back from the race track, Meredith parked her car in the gravel drive and looked for Seth on the sun deck, where she'd left him after breakfast. "Hon?" she called when she couldn't find him. She didn't like leaving Seth for long periods, because he grew moody and disoriented. He had always been a private man, but after recovering from the coma and learning about Calvin and the dirt they'd all been dragged through, he'd become even more reclusive and sensitive. But she couldn't be with Seth all the time. Five Deuces demanded her attention too. She'd made Abel, against his wishes, work the filly particularly hard the last two months, and Meredith liked to hang around just to watch over her pride and joy. The horse had to be in peak condition—how else could she have a shot at winning?

"Seth, hon?" she called inside the cabin.

"Here," a faint voice answered.

She found him in the kitchen sipping a cup of cold coffee. He gave her a distant, preoccupied nod as she straightened the counter.

"Everything okay?" she asked. "Sorry I was gone so long."

"Some calls for you," he said.

"How about some fresh coffee?" Meredith suggested, not caring about the messages. Seth was more important.

When he didn't answer, Meredith began to worry again. Seth looked like he was back in dreamland. That was where he'd spent most of his time since coming home. She had no idea what he was thinking. Filled with guilt, Meredith had done everything she could for Seth. She'd given up her parties, stayed home to keep him company, begged his forgiveness a hundred times for what she'd done, but he'd never directly said he did. Despite the many outrageous acts she'd committed in her life, she wasn't a woman used to feeling guilt. Guilt drove her up the wall. Was Seth acting like this to punish her? Sometimes she thought he still wasn't right in the head. The doctors had warned her that full recovery might take some time.

"Let's take a walk," she said after she'd made fresh coffee. "It's a real nice afternoon."

"I took a walk."

"What's the law that says you can't take another?"

"I'm tired."

"Is something wrong?" she asked directly.

He shook his head and picked up the newspaper.

"Hon, you've got to *talk* to me. Else I'm going to go crazy. We're husband and wife. We're living together. There has to be some *point* in that. . . ."

As he turned to Meredith his face hardened. "All right. We can talk. I was planning to sooner or later."

"What do you want?" she said, uneasy.

Seth hesitated, as if gathering his courage. "I want a legal separation."

Meredith fell into a chair. "Jesus Christ—"

"It's what I want, Meredith."

"It was you who said you couldn't tell me about your past because you were afraid *I'd* divorce *you*—"

"Things change."

Meredith didn't know whether she was more hurt or angry. She couldn't think. Christ, she hated surprises. This was like being back on trial. "You're confused, Seth," she said gently.

He denied it.

"Give me a reason."

"I want to live alone for a while. I've got things to think about."

"Like what?"

"Private things."

"Why won't you share them with me?" she said stubbornly.

"No."

"Seth, I won't give you a separation. I want you. I need you. I know you've been hurt by what happened, but so was I. We'll work things out. . . ."

Seth waved his hand intolerantly and slipped out of the kitchen. He didn't doubt the genuineness of her sympathy, but she was incapable of understanding how he felt. Nobody could, he thought. Coming out of his coma had been like waking to a nightmare. His best friend had killed himself, but not before his ties to Seth had been splashed across the front pages of every paper in east Texas. Even if he deserved all of this punishment, it was too heavy a cross for him to bear. Meredith had told him that it didn't matter to her, that the world was full of snakes and jackals who were hardly worth a glance. All that counted was how they felt. But inside, Seth's embarrassment and humiliation burned brightly. He felt naked before his law colleagues. He couldn't stop feeling their eyes on him and hearing their whispers. Only a month after returning to his firm he had taken an indefinite leave of absence. He wanted time alone, he told a distressed Meredith. She had hinted he should consider therapy, but Seth refused. The spotlight on him was already painfully bright. He only wanted to escape. He tried distracting himself with books, but he couldn't stop thinking about the shooting. He was always restless now, and he worried about things, things he couldn't pinpoint but that seemed so real. There was no peace at all. Maybe if he left Meredith for a while he would find it.

He hadn't wanted to come to Ruidoso at all, but Meredith had begged him. She told him she planned to win this All-American for him, but he was hardly flattered. He'd told her he didn't want anything to do with the race. Just looking at Five Deuces reminded him of his inglorious theft and the horror story he'd set in motion. Lord, he was starting to hate the horsey set. He had once accepted the competition and the hoopla and the chase for glory because it was the world of the woman he'd married, and because it added color to his gray life. Now all he could see was the hollowness of it, the conniving of prideful souls.

Without a good-bye to Meredith, Seth headed outside and got into the Cadillac. The car purred to a start, an intrusive sound amid the wind's quiet whispers, and off he drove to the very track he'd come to despise.

"Leave the horse and let's go," David begged again. He flicked Trixie an annoyed glance. "For a race like the All-American you don't have to be taping his ankles—that's a groom's job."

"I want to take care of my horse, that's all." She rose and gave El Cid a friendly pat. "He's a beaut, isn't he?"

"What, are you falling in love?"

"Stop being such a wiseass, David."

She slipped her arm through his as they wandered outside. The champagne-colored sky was starting to darken. Virtually all the horses had finished their workouts and were now in the stables. David had tried to put a distance between himself and the race tomorrow, wanting to unwind, but Trixie was the opposite. She needed to live and breathe it. He couldn't help bristling at her brassy enthusiasm. She had lucked out to get a mount for the All-American, just walked into it, and she didn't even understand her good fortune. A lot of jocks who'd been racing for twenty years would kill to have her spot. And because El Cid was a long shot, Trixie felt little pressure. How lucky could you get?

David had pressure coming out his ears, and not just from Austin. The thought of going against Desert Wind for the fourth time was more than a bit daunting. The fullback of a colt had started to get under David's skin with his almost automatic victories. And the memory of last year's debacle was etched permanently in his memory. But he was determined to vindicate himself. He was off the pills, he was riding better than ever, he was *hungry*.

"You don't think I'm really ready for tomorrow, do you?" Trixie said. "You don't think I deserve this chance so soon in my career."

"You got a break. That's terrific."

"But you're unhappy about riding against me, I can tell."

"Look, I don't want to talk about it—"

"You shouldn't be jealous of me, that's all," she said firmly. "So I beat you one time. Lightning's not going to strike twice. You've got a real shot at winning. I don't."

David shook his head in exasperation. Trixie was driving him up a wall. "Look," he suddenly exploded, "you can stop stroking me, okay? I'll be fine. I just don't want to discuss the race."

"What's bothering you?"

"The way you float around on a cloud like you own the world. The way you're so friendly with everyone. The way you treat me—do I mean any more than those other guys?"

Trixie looked stung. "You know you do!"

"I do? How do you really feel about me, Trixie? Am I a boyfriend or just a competitor?"

"What's that supposed to mean?"

"I don't think you can make up your mind. You don't really feel comfortable with me. That's why you're always talking about what a great jock I am. It's just covering up for your nerves. In the back of your mind you're always wondering how you're going to ride against me."

"I don't see myself riding against you. I'm riding for

myself, David. I told you, I really hope you win the All-American—"

"Bull," he said. "You mean you don't want to win?"

"Stop putting me on the spot."

"Do you want to win—yes or no?" David insisted.

"I always try to win. So do you."

"So how can you root for me? Don't be a hypocrite, all right? You and I can't have a real relationship. It's convenient for you right now, but once you win some more races and begin to feel more independent, you won't need me anymore. Isn't that right?"

"No! We do have a relationship! For reasons I don't understand, you're trying to destroy it."

David threw his hands up and strode away. Trixie called after him but he ignored her. How could he have been so blind about her, he wondered as he drove to a nearby honky-tonk. If he hadn't been half in love, and in need of her emotional support . . . She *had* helped him, he couldn't deny that, and he'd helped her. But the good times were over. Trixie was wrong, he wasn't jealous of her. He just resented that everything had been handed to her on a silver platter while he'd had to struggle.

At the bar David nursed a beer and tried to forget Trixie. The honky-tonk was home to the most dedicated track patrons and self-described handicapping geniuses. In a dimly lit corner, bent over reams of paper and a calculator, a wizened old man in a baggy suit looked up at David.

"I should have known you'd be here," the jockey said with a smile as he walked over.

"Sit down, sonny! Take a load off. You must be proud of yourself. You've done pretty well on Miss Muffet. I've been following you. Fame and fortune, right?"

"Everything would be easier if Desert Wind weren't around," he acknowledged. "Sometimes I wish that colt would just go away."

"No horse is unbeatable," Sparky said with a twist of a smile. "Don't even think about the competition. Just concentrate on Miss Muffet."

"That's what I aim to do. I guess we'll know the truth tomorrow."

"Right as rain," Sparky agreed.

"Who are you betting on?" David couldn't help asking. His eyes dropped to the papers concealed under Sparky's arm.

"I can tell you this—you've got a real chance, kiddo."

"But where are you putting your money?" David pressed.

"I honestly can't say yet. Still doing my homework." He glanced down at his beer. "Say, David, I was wondering . . . ."

"How much do you need?"

"I want to explain first—"

"Hey, it's okay. You paid me back last time."

"No, what I mean is, I was hoping to borrow a little more than usual. I'll pay you back *double*. On my dear wife's grave. Because I'm going to win tomorrow, David, I'm going to win big. . . ."

Sparky's eyes dilated in excitement. David had seen such confidence in him before, only to watch it eclipsed by the sour look of defeat. "How much do you want?"

"I'm asking fifty people to loan me a hundred each. And I'm throwing in two thousand of my own."

"You're betting $7000 on one race?"

"Sonny, it's the All-American. I'm going for all the marbles. I've been down on my luck the last couple of weeks, but that's because I've been paying attention to the All-American. I know the field better than anyone. . . ."

"Okay, you got it," David said, happy to help out, and fished two fifties from his wallet.

"Thanks, sonny. You won't be sorry. Good luck tomorrow!"

Sparky watched David drift to his solitary spot at the bar. He wondered where his girlfriend was. Trixie Elizabeth McKinney, Sparky knew from his diligent research, was from a middle-class Florida family, had attended public schools, was inclined to rebellion, knew what she wanted in life and went after it. She was a better jock than track pundits gave her credit for. Quantrell, the sorry bastard, had given her mostly pigs to ride, but with El Cid, she could show her potential.

Sparky knew almost as much about the ten jocks racing tomorrow as they knew about themselves. Meredith Kingsley's Cuban jockey was superstitious about the color red, which the owner was making him wear for the All-American, but the young man lacked the nerve—and sufficient English—to tell Meredith. Angel's Victory's rider, after too much partying, had come down yesterday with a cold. Fly-By-Night had a jockey who tended to choke in major races. In the irons on Desert Wind was a basically sweet, intelligent kid; but like his owner, he had become more arrogant with each victory and was now overconfident.

Sparky let his eyes sweep over his notes again, wondering if he had left anything out. Of the ten horses, he knew how many races each had run in its life, its order of finishes, its times, the class of races it had run in, and its preference for different tracks; he knew each horse's vet bills, how often a farrier changed its shoes, the vitamins it was given, the time it woke in the morning, the workouts it was put through, the time it went to bed; he knew not only its jockey but the habits and inclinations of its trainer and grooms; he knew plenty about the owners, that some were so rich they didn't care what they spent or won on their horses, while others were dirt-poor cowboys who had gone into hock and defied the odds to get into this race of races; he knew the weight each horse would carry tomorrow, how fresh or tired it was from its last race, its record of injuries; knew that while the race tomorrow was 440 yards, quarter horses also ran distances from 200 to 870 yards, and some performed better at shorter distances and others longer; knew that some of the horses liked the rail while others preferred the outside, but with lots being drawn for post position some would be happy and some wouldn't; knew that the weather forecast was for a clear, bright, sunny day, which would help most horses but leave a few at a disadvantage.

Everything had to be factored in. And still there was always the unknown, the unfigurable, the slim elements of chance that every handicapper both hated and respected.

Of all the variables in handicapping, Sparky knew that one of the most crucial but least understood was track surface. On most tracks the top nine inches of soil consisted of six inches of sandy loam, screened to remove any large pebbles, two inches of loose sand, and usually one inch of wood chips to give the mixture more bounce and resiliency. A track in Illinois had once used dried mushrooms purchased from the Campbell Soup Company instead of wood chips, but the results had been just fine. There were no regulations from either the Jockey Club or the AQHA about track composition. Usually the top two of the nine inches were left loose and aerated, while the bottom seven were compacted to give the horses' hooves something to grab. The difference between a proper thoroughbred and a quarter horse track was the bottom seven inches. For thoroughbreds it was never as compresed, denying them the chance for speed in the name of stamina and distance. For quarter horses the harder the better. And for tomorrow's race, Sparky knew from comparing past performances at different tracks, there was one horse who would especially benefit from tight compaction. The fact that Ruidoso had one of the most compacted tracks in the country was his secret weapon.

It was dinnertime when Sparky left a virtually empty bar and headed back to his flea-bag hotel. Munching on crackers and cheese, he slumped on his bed and closed his eyes, intending to get up momentarily and finish his handicapping. Instead he lay in an exhausted state until midnight. Face it, old boy, he thought when he finally arose, you're not getting any younger. The years of traveling and living off the ponies had worn him down to the same fine edge as the soles on his shoes. His dream of retiring to a California mountain cabin had begun to seem like chasing a rainbow. Tomorrow, he promised himself, would be his last fling with the ponies. All or nothing. He would wait to study the morning line, of course, but using the odds effectively to maximize his leverage, $7000 could bring in the mother lode. He could retire and never board another Greyhound bus in his life. Dropping into a rickety chair, Sparky pushed aside the Gideon Bible, and under a dim ceiling light let his fingers dance over his pocket calculator for the hundredth time.

It was almost light outside when a smile finally appeared on his lips. After two weeks of checking and rechecking and checking again, the facts and figures had come into focus. Handicapping was an inexact science at best, but with a trembling hand Sparky wrote the names of the first, second, and third place finishers on a scrap of paper and tucked it in his wallet. Exhaustion finally claimed him. With his precious tote bag containing the $7000 under his pillow, he slept.

The phone woke him after what seemed only moments later. "Who is it?" he wheezed, trying to brush away the veil of sleep. A local bookie was supposed to call him with the morning line, but the voice on the other end was youthful and frenzied.

"David. David Sanders . . ."

"What's the matter?" Sparky asked, waiting for the jockey to calm down.

"I was just over at the stables. I couldn't believe it. I thought you should know. I mean, it's my money you're betting with—"

"Know what?" Sparky demanded.

"Desert Wind," he said in a peculiar out-of-breath voice.

"What about him?"

"He's been poisoned."

TWENTY-SIX

SPARKY THOUGHT HE'D SEEN IT ALL. JOCKEYS WHO'D thrown races to pay their mother's hospital bill. Horse owners who'd set fire to their own stables to collect insurance money. Stolen horses shipped to Ireland to raise the racing and breeding level in Europe. Yet on Labor Day morning, 1985, the old-time handicapper got a fresh jolt. The poisoning of what was first thought to be Desert Wind turned out to be that of the colt's stablemate, Goldmine, a similar bruiser of a horse but with slightly different markings. With obvious logic the police suspected that the perpetrator, while clever enough to penetrate Zallaq's security guards and enter the Arab's stables, didn't know Desert Wind with any intimacy. Sparky could get no closer to the scene of the crime than the track grandstands, and along with other spectators he watched as plain clothesmen drifted in and out of Desert Wind's stall. The poison, rumor had it, was a strychnine compound common in rat poisons and sold by commercial exterminators. Clear and odorless, it had been mixed in with the horse's oats and barley. Sparky was happy to learn that Goldmine had had his stomach pumped and was recovering. The veteran handicapper watched as a hostile-looking Zallaq, surrounded by a phalanx of guards, walked his horse around the paddock area in full view of television cameras and reporters who had come out of the woodwork and represented more than their newspaper's sports sections, as if to prove to everyone that the champion colt was just fine. This was big news, important news. It made Desert Wind more famous than ever, Sparky realized. Excitement over the race, already as high as the American flag that fluttered nearby, ratcheted up another notch.

Outside of Rachel and Billy, Meredith had decided not to socialize with anyone until after the All-American. All she could focus on was the race. But it wasn't easy to be left alone. Like a swarm of killer bees, reporters had besieged her all morning about the poisoning of Zallaq's horse. At first she thought the questions were a joke, and she had joked back—if she'd wanted to poison Desert Wind, she would have known not to feed the wrong horse. No one saw the humor. Hadn't Ms. Kingsley spoken disparagingly of her rival in public? one reporter pressed. Hadn't she

walked out of a luncheon at the Jockey Club hosted by
Zallaq? Less than subtle allusions were made to her history
of erratic behavior. Vultures, she thought bitterly. Meredith
denied everything, and Rachel and Billy, surrounded by the
same reporters, had backed her up. Meredith remembered
clearly her uncharitable remarks about the Arab, but she'd
only been sounding off like she always did. Why was it people never understood her? In one short year she'd gone
from heroine and favorite to bad guy and underdog.

Frustrated, Meredith bulled her way through the reporters and found sanctuary in the Jockey Club. She settled
down next to Seth in an isolated corner with a clear view of
the track. The first race had just been run, and the grandstands, already full, were still being squeezed. Maybe attention would finally be focused on the horses, she hoped.
She wove her arm through Seth's as they looked on. After
the All-American things would be different for them. All
this talk about a separation was crazy. Seth would see that
when things quieted down. He kept denying that he was
interested in the race, but Meredith knew that he really did
care. She wanted a victory more than anything. Not just to
beat Zallaq, or prove to everyone she wasn't defeated after
her trial, but to pull Seth out of his tailspin. Oh, God, she
could taste the victory!

Austin had done everything possible. He'd given his horse a
final pep talk, instructions to David; duckbill hats to friends
inscribed with SEVENTH TIME'S THE CHARM, and money to
Fern to do his betting for him. His grandfather's railroad
watch was in his pocket and his favorite lizard skin boots on
his feet. He was such a goddamn creature of habit it was
disgusting, he thought, but he was what he was. The Jockey
Club had filled with tall Texans in white Stetsons, blue
jeans, and Bill Blass blazers. As he stood by the bar Austin's
glance flew down to Zallaq and Wondercolt, both proud as
peacocks as they paraded near the track. The poisoning incident hadn't overly surprised Austin. No one liked the
sonovabitch Arab. Austin just wondered why someone
hadn't had the sense to poison Zallaq instead. But it really

didn't matter. In less than an hour, he thought, he was going to whip the sheik's ass for good.

All but Austin's oldest and youngest children were at a video arcade in town, as interested in the race today as mowing the lawn. His oldest boy was just like him, though, flint tough and ambitious, which pleased Austin and filled him with the hope that one day there'd be someone to take over Mirabeau Ranch and keep running their horses in the All-American. He studied his little girl, cute as a ladybug, as she sat on Fern's lap. He remembered how she couldn't even walk when they had come to Ruidoso last year. Everything about last September suddenly seemed fresh, especially the agonizing moment when King's Ransom fell. . . .

Austin gave Fern and his daughter pecks on the cheek and then he and his son wandered downstairs to join the railbirds. The All-American was only a few minutes away.

"Don't look at El Cid too closely," Rachel quipped to Billy with a nervous smile, "he'll catch a cold." They stood quietly in the paddock area as Trixie finally climbed in the irons and an outrider led her onto the track. The nine other horses paraded out behind her. An announcer called everyone's attention to a pre-race ceremony, where the governor of New Mexico was mugging it up with track officials. Billy was only interested in El Cid. He kept thinking that something still had to be done, that after months of busting his tail chasing this rainbow the struggle couldn't possibly be over. He thanked God that El Cid had stayed healthy the last week, eating and sleeping well, and seemed as spirited and confident as ever. In a draw for post position, his horse had been given the rail, which might have pleased some owners but troubled Billy. El Cid had all of his best times running in the middle.

A chorus of ooohs and aahs trickled down the grandstands as Desert Wind was led into his gate. Zallaq, incredibly, took a bow from where he stood—not unintentionally, Billy felt—near the winner's circle. It was a cheap psychout, worthy of his old enemy Gallegos. "If that man just had humility," Rachel observed, "he'd be perfect."

Billy slipped his arm around her waist and pulled her to him for a kiss.

"What was that for?" she asked. "Luck?"

"Oh . . . appreciation. You've been a great partner, Rachel. I wouldn't have had anyone else."

"Will you feel that way even if we lose?"

"Even then. Forever."

"That sounds amorous," Rachel said lightly, scarcely believing the love she saw reflected in Billy's eyes.

"It's supposed to," he said, tightening his hold on her.

"Oh, God, I can't think of anything but the race." Crossing her fingers, Rachel dropped her head on Billy's shoulder.

Buck and Adam Jeffrey had spent their morning at the Ruidoso police station, answering questions about their whereabouts during the night. Buck was incensed that Zallaq had given his name to the police as someone who might have poisoned Desert Wind, and embarrassed to be interrogated in front of his son. But Buck had finally calmed himself and given the facts. He and Adam Jeffrey had had dinner at McDonald's, seen a Disney movie, and gone to bed around nine. The motel night clerk confirmed that Buck's rental car had not left the lot after that. It wasn't until noon that he was allowed to leave the police station, and when he arrived at the track, his anger still burned with a white-hot intensity. He bought Adam Jeffrey a hot dog and they settled into general admission seats.

"I can't wait," Buck announced, stroking the hair out of his son's eyes, "for this thing to be over with."

"Are we really going home then?" A.J. asked.

"I promise on a gallon of chocolate ice cream."

Adam Jeffrey looked hopeful. "Really?"

"I've never meant anything more. A.J., I'm real sorry we ever got into this mess."

"Are you still mad at your boss?"

"Yes," he said, seeing no point in denying it.

"But not the horse. The horse didn't do anything wrong."

"I guess not," Buck muttered.

"I like Desert Wind."

"What?"

The little boy smiled. "I didn't used to like him, but now I do. Is that okay? I'm going to cheer for him."

Buck didn't say a word.

Sparky waited till the last moment before rushing to the betting window that read $50 AND UP. He threw a final glance at the tote board. Desert Wind was listed at 1:2. Miss Muffet, to Sparky's surprise, wasn't far behind at 3:5. Five Deuces was 4:5, and El Cid, whom no one seemed excited about, was a distant 24:1. Another horse, Sweet 'n Sour, was an even longer shot at 30:1. The rest of the field fell in between.

In her years of working at the track, the matronly woman behind the betting window had seen all varieties of humanity, high and low rollers alike, but the wiry little man in the oversized suit, his pockets stuffed with cash, made her look twice.

"Count it, and quick, please," Sparky said. The track announcer was already calling the horses as they were led into their gates. "I want the trifecta pool," he added, and gave her the names of the horses. First, second, and third, in the exact order of finish. Guts ball all the way, he thought, with only a touch of nervousness.

"You're betting $7000 on a trifecta?" the woman echoed, handing over his tickets, as if Sparky was in need of a fast psychiatric consultation. He would have been happy to tell her that he was anything but crazy, that he was about to become a very rich man, but there wasn't time.

"Come on, Miss Muffet," David called gently as the filly jigged in her post, "hold on, sweetheart. Hold on . . ." Even with her earmuffs David was convinced the horse understood. She settled down, leaving him the only one with a bad case of nerves. His glance swung to Desert Wind, who uncharacteristically was putting up resistance as two handlers coaxed him into his gate. Then David looked at Trixie on top of El Cid. She shot him a quick look that was hardly warm or friendly. David was surprised, but relieved too. Maybe she'd never really cared for him. He suddenly wanted to beat Trixie, beat her convincingly enough to shut her up forever.

"Okay, here we go, baby," David said as he crouched forward, waiting. For a moment he thought about Trixie, then Desert Wind, then Mr. Mirabeau's dreams, and his own hanging-in-the-balance career. But when the gates flew open his fears vanished. The adrenaline surged. He got out cleanly and streaked to a half-length lead. When Desert Wind began to pick up speed and pulled even, David resisted bringing down his whip. Mr. Mirabeau had said no, unless it was really needed. Miss Muffet would do it on her own.

At 200 yards the horses were still even. The filly was physically dwarfed by Wondercolt, yet Miss Muffet had speed that was undeniable, that came from within. Dust swirls eddied up without warning and forced David's eyes shut. When he looked up again, checking the field, he was stunned. El Cid was in front of both his horse and Desert Wind. Trixie was pouring it on in the ride of her life. David brought his whip down. He had to win the race. The handle slipped in his sweaty hand. It caught the horse's earmuffs and knocked them loose.

The startled filly swung her head around. The yelling from the stands was the same as lighting a firecracker under Miss Muffet. She veered toward Sweet 'n Sour, yet never quite bumped the long-shot colt. Frightened, Sweet 'n Sour swerved inexorably to his right and broadsided Five Deuces. David heard Meredith's jockey swear in Spanish just as the horse staggered. The Cuban jumped off cleanly, but the filly stumbled and fell.

The chaos of a few seconds was digestd by David without fazing him. The Russians could have droped the bomb and it wouldn't have mattered. Only winning counted. He knew he still had a chance. Desert Wind was a half length ahead, but Miss Muffet, despite the loss of concentration, wasn't yielding any more ground. If anything she was gaining it back. Jesus, they could do it, they could win, David thought. Usually he was calm and collected in a race, even close ones, but now he was rigid and out of breath. For a

moment he thought he might black out. The finish seemed
so far away. They were riding through molasses. At 400
yards David took a final glance at El Cid. He couldn't be
sure. The colt seemed to be a stride in front, but Miss
Muffet was still gaining. Desert Wind was right there too.

David brought his whip down again. Come on, Miss
Muffet, come on, he prayed.

Sparky watched almost calmly as Desert Wind, El Cid, and
Miss Muffet blurred across the finish in a dead heat. The
roar of excitement, the further suspense, didn't trouble
him. The track announcer gave the standard speech about a
photo finish, that results wouldn't be known for a few minutes, but Sparky was already on his way to the cashier's
window. He knew who'd won. It was a crying shame about
Five Deuces, he thought, but the fact was, Meredith had
overtrained her filly. The two-year-old was tired, her muscles sore, her reflexes hardly pin sharp, all of which made
her susceptible to an accident. Meredith would probably
claim that Austin's horse had caused the fall, but the stewards wouldn't uphold it. Unless it was the stewards themselves who made a claim, a horse owner was usually out of
luck. Just like last year when Austin had claimed Meredith's
horse had done the bumping. History had a way of playing
tricks, evening old scores.

The announcement finally came, only seconds before
El Cid's name was flashed ahead of Desert Wind's and Miss
Muffet's on the tote board. The crowd exploded with cheers
and shouts of disbelief. A 24:1 long shot had gone all the
way, and won the big one. Sparky's only surprise was the
winning time. El Cid had burned up the track in 21.01 seconds, breaking the old record set four decades ago. Used to
running on the hard ground of his native pampas, the Ar-
gentine-trained colt had been favored by the tight compaction of the track. But there was something else too.
Wondercolt had a weakness, and it had cost him the race. It
wasn't a question of spirit or will, or training or discipline; it
was something neither the colt nor Zallaq could control.
Mother Nature had dealt the final hand. The fabulous colt's
head, from ear to muzzle, was a good inch shorter than it

should have been. Necks outstretched toward the finish, noses pointed ahead, El Cid's head had reached an inch farther than Desert Wind's. It was as simple as anatomy.

As for Miss Muffet, Sparky knew, the earmuffs and her sensitivity had come back to haunt David and Austin.

Parking himself in front of the cashier's window, Sparky's mouth began turning dry as his heart pounded in anticipation. He thought of the mountain cabin he'd buy, the peace and tranquility that had eluded him so long. Maybe there really were such things as happy endings. He didn't know Rachel Lang and Billy Sullivan personally, but he was sure they'd be celebrating tonight. As for Zallaq and his laboratory-bred horse, even bad guys had bad days. But it had been one helluva race, Sparky thought. In the future any one of the three horses might shatter the formidable barrier of twenty-one seconds. If it happened, Sparky knew he would read about it in the papers. He was finished with horse racing. People had told him that he was addicted and would never quit, but they were the same ones who'd said he'd never find his pot of gold.

The cashier ran Sparky's tickets through the computer, looked at the figure again, and shaking her head in awe, directed him down a passageway to the ticket-room manager. Sparky didn't need the totalizator machine to tell him how much he'd won. The odds against picking the trifecta, thanks to a long shot winning, were indecent. On $7000 the payout was a cool $665,000. Not unlike when someone hit a large slot machine jackpot, Sparky's tickets were carefully inspected before being judged authentic. He was then asked to fill out some papers for the Internal Revenue Service, and a portion of the money was withheld for taxes. Sparky didn't mind. There was plenty left over, and his life was just beginning.

For the whole afternoon Rachel and Billy were besieged by reporters and photographers. Their horse had made history by beating the unbeatable super colt and set a record in the process. Instant celebrity was theirs. Rachel had been down the road before, and she treated the whole phenomenon as the transitory tease it was. Billy, she was happy to see, kept his head too. Whenever a long shot won anything, people summoned up the word luck, but anyone who said that didn't know what Billy had gone through with this horse. The harder you worked, Rachel thought, the luckier you got.

In a sport famous for its participants throwing large and lavish parties, Rachel and Billy broke with tradition that night and celebrated alone. They chose an out-of-the-way restaurant and sat, still a little stunned, over a bottle of Dom Pérignon.

"Cheers," Billy toasted.

"To a great team with a great horse," Rachel said.

"It makes it all worthwhile, doesn't it? When I think back to Gallegos, the Buenos Aires jail, and all the grief my polo 'friends' gave me—winning is sweet revenge."

"Not to mention one million." Rachel smiled. "Thanks for making me a half partner, partner."

"Smartest thing I ever did."

"Well, you hired Trixie. That didn't turn out to be exactly dumb."

"We really owe Meredith for that. She was an awfully good sport," Billy said. "I'm sorry Five Deuces turned up lame."

"I called to tell Meredith we were sorry. She's upset, but she'll bounce back. The woman knows how to do that. I'm not so sure about Zallaq. Did you hear? There was a witness to the poisoning, a stable boy—"

"Tell me!"

"At first he pointed the finger at Seth Cartwright. His car was parked near the stables, and Seth was seen wandering around the area. But when the police interviewed him, they decided he wasn't playing with a full deck. Meredith confirmed he still had lapses. He said he was looking for Five Deuces' bridle. . . ."

"Then who—" Billy said.

"It was Zallaq."

Billy squinted in disbelief.

"The stable boy saw him mix Goldmine's food. . . ."

"Come on—"

"It makes sense. Look at all the publicity it got him.

That's what the man's after. He's such an egotist. We all knew that. Anyway, the police can't do anything because basically he was tampering with his own horse, and he's not about to bring charges against himself."

"Let's talk about something more pleasant. What are you going to do with your share of the money?"

"I haven't the foggiest. What about you?"

"Well, we're still partners. We've got a horse we can syndicate and race next year in the derbies. There's no limit to what we can do. If you want to stick together . . ."

Rachel hadn't really thought much about the future. She'd been too afraid. For months everything had pointed to one race, and now it was behind them. The opportunities and the money it had brought would take some getting used to.

"Are you telling me this is the beginning, not the end?" she asked softly, uncertain what answer she wanted to hear.

"I'm in love with you, Rachel."

"Say it again, please? In case I'm dreaming?"

"I don't want to lose you. I love you."

"Are you really sure you want me?" she asked. "I'm not the most lucky person when it comes to love."

"You're afraid your bad luck will rub off on my good?"

"It might."

"I think it'll be the other way around. Anyway, I'll take the chance."

"That's what I love about you. You're such an optimist."

"You'll be one too, as soon as you begin to believe in yourself again."

"Maybe," Rachel said. "I've been confused lately. This is all still unreal to me. All I can think about is you . . . us. I do love you, Billy. I don't know if that's right or wrong for me, but—"

"I can answer that."

"I don't think so. I have to do it myself."

An interior voice warned her to go slowly, to sit on the sidelines until she was sure. But there were always chances to take, Rachel thought. The horse world had taught her that. Taking chances was how you learned to believe in yourself, how you found your happiness.

She looked at Billy a long moment before raising her champagne glass. "To loyal partners and fast horses," she said. Then she leaned over and kissed him. "And to dreams that don't end."

EPILOGUE
DECEMBER 1987

AFTER SUFFERING HIS ONLY DEFEAT IN THE 1985 ALL-American, Desert Wind won eleven consecutive races as a three-year-old. A single ownership share in the colt rocketed to $750,000, and hopeful brood-mare owners stood in line in anticipation. But after several matings there were no pregnancies. Laboratory tests confirmed that Desert Wind was infertile, and the culprit was suspected of being the hormones injected into the embryonic horse. Overnight the syndication shares and options that Zallaq had sold became worthless. Not a few angered investors sued the Arab and his genetic engineering company for failure to disclose possible breeding dangers. Zallaq ignored the lawsuits by departing for his native Bahrain, where he tended to his knitting in the oil patch. In his absence a press secretary informed reporters that Mr. Al-Khalifa had permanently abandoned his interest in raising and breeding quarter horses.

After the mandatory year of waiting, Buck Hart had sold his options in Desert Wind for a substantial profit—several months before the infertility was diagnosed. He'd returned to his Malibu home, paid off the mortgage, and concentrated on his career. Despite his agent's fears, the rebuff from Zallaq before the All-American did little damage in light of the colt's defeat. Buck made several guest appearances on *Real People*, *Saturday Night Live*, and *Simon and Simon.* In the spring of 1987 he was cast as the lead in a new adventure series, *Bound for Glory.* Shortly after, he married a studio secretary named Angela Whitney, a warm, loving woman who'd had enough of Hollywood machinations and celebrities. She fell immediately for Adam Jeffrey and set about making a good home for both her men.

In the 1986 Futurity Austin Mirabeau once again tried for his elusive victory, only to fail for the first time to make the finals. But the following September, after he'd purchased a colt named Regal Commander from a newspaper publisher in Ohio for only $25,000, his horse came from behind to win the elusive race in a photo finish.

Meredith Kingsley, despite money, desire, and good horses, finished out of the money in both the 1986 and 1987 All-Americans. Instead of fretting about the dynasty that wasn't, she told herself she was lucky to have a loving husband and daughter, and that horses had to come second in her life. She did not, however, abandon her wild parties or curb her tongue. With her mother's blessing, Alexis married her first love and began teaching with her husband in a New England prep school. After extensive therapy with a prominent Dallas psychiatrist, Seth went back to his law practice, and renewed his love for Meredith and their ranch.

David Sanders broke up with Trixie shortly after her victory in the All-American. Depressed, he endured a year-long slump and would have left racing altogether if not for Austin, who maintained his faith in his jockey. When he finally won on Regal Commander, David was thrust into the limelight and his old confidence returned. A winter riding contract in California was signed and, while it was not exactly the fame and fortune he'd imagined, he won a comfortable salary and the respect of his peers. He also fell in love with a girl who cared nothing for riding or the horse world.

Trixie McKinney became the media's darling after her All-American Futurity victory, landing on the cover of *Sports*

Illustrated. After leaving David, she lived briefly with a wealthy Oklahoma horse breeder who, in alcoholic binges, beat Trixie as he would a stubborn horse. She was rescued by a dapper young Broadway actor who convinced the jockey to give up riding and live in New York with him. She abandoned horses, but also, eventually, the actor. With the same pluck and single-mindedness that helped her triumph in the male kingdom of jockeys, she took up hot-air ballooning, and in the summer of 1987 became the first woman to cross the Atlantic in a solo flight.

As he knew he always would, Sparky bought his mountain cabin near Big Bear Lake and took up fishing. Despite his promises to reform, he sojourned occasionally into Los Angeles to sample its many tracks and visit old friends, all of whom he repaid for their generous loans. But Sparky's betting was always light, and any win paled in memory of what he'd accomplished at the All-American.

Billy and Rachel were married in the spring of 1986, on the eve of El Cid's maiden run as a three-year-old. The colt won handily and went on to have the second best season of the year, after Desert Wind. Rachel was approached by Frank Beardsley to write an article—from an insider's point of view—on the All-American, focusing on Zallaq poisoning his own horse, but she refused. Billy toyed briefly with the idea of returning to the polo world, but Rachel convinced him to leave the ghosts of the past undisturbed. With El Cid's winnings and syndication fees, they started their own breeding ranch in San Diego County. Rachel reveled in her new domestic life, delighted to tell her mother and friends that she and Billy had conceived. Annie Cid Lang-Sullivan was born, appropriately, on Labor Day.

The great state of Texas, despite heartfelt and well-funded efforts from Austin, Meredith, and other betting advocates, is still without pari-mutuel race tracks, and the Baptists have promised it will always be that way.

ABOUT THE AUTHOR

A native of Los Angeles, MICHAEL FRENCH attended public schools in that city and was graduated with a degree in English from Stanford University in 1966. He later received a graduate degree in journalism from Northwestern University. After two years in the Army where he was editor-in-chief of a stateside post newspaper, he married and moved to New York City. There he worked as a corporate executive and began writing fiction in his spare time. He currently resides in Santa Fe, New Mexico, with his wife, Patricia, a real estate developer, and two children, Timothy and Alison. Michael is the author of ten published works of fiction, including *Abingdon's, Rhythms*, and five novels for young adults. He also has written book and film reviews for numerous publications, and taught creative writing at the college level. Time permitting, he is a serious mountain trekker who favors remote destinations, among them New Guinea, the Amazon Basin, Java, and Rwanda.